Replacements

The kids knew we were headed into combat. But "combat" was just a word to them. They had no idea of the bullet hails and razored shrapnel that would slash at them. And they knew the Wehrmacht was tough. But, again, they just had no idea of the steely-eyed, pitiless, battle-hardened killers who would assail them.

I was scared for them.

I was scared for me.

Brought To Battle

BROUGHT TO BATTLE

----- A Novel of World War II -----

By J. Scott Payne

ARGON PRESS

Published in the United States of America
by Argon Press

Cover design by H. William Ruback,
InColor Digital Design

Cover Photo courtesy of Shutterstock.com
Copyright Real Deal Photo

ISBN: 978-0990883111

Library of Congress Control Number
2016909152

Other books by the Author –

A Corporal No More
A Novel of the Civil War

One, Two, Three Strikes You're Dead
A Brad Powers Mystery

When called heroes, old combat veterans often look stricken. With broken tones and misty eyes, they're prone to say, "No, the heroes are the boys who didn't come home."

Well, those who made it home had to be heroic, too.

What's more heroic than pushing into the jaws after witnessing what the jaws had done to those who would never go home?

Author's Note

In 1944 and 1945, the Eighth Infantry Regiment of the U.S. Army's 4th Infantry Division had a First Battalion and that battalion had a heavy weapons company, D Company, called Dog for its initial's name in the military's phonetic alphabet.

Dog Company used 81 MM mortars and machine guns to support the riflemen of Able, Baker, Charlie and Headquarters Companies.

But though this story faithfully depicts 4th Division's Normandy assault and its horrific travails in France and Germany, the Dog Company and its mortar platoon and their members in the following pages are fiction.

Something else.

Combat imposes unbelievable mental and physical stress. In trying to prepare its warriors for combat, therefore, the military makes training highly stressful. And whether training or fighting, the troops' chief means of dealing with that stress is foul language. Recent U-Tube videos from Afghanistan and Iraq show that in combat, 21st century American soldiers cuss differently from those of the last.

But only slightly.

And three words remain in perpetual and predominant use. Two refer to fecal matter, the third to the reproductive act.

Infantrymen used those basic Anglo-Saxon terms during the battles of Waterloo and Gettysburg and, I bet, Hastings. I also suspect the Israelites spoke the Hebrew equivalents at Jericho. At any rate, those words appear in the dialogues that follow. The text does not, however, employ them with anything like the frequency that fighting men do (and fighting women, presumably). Otherwise, this novel would far surpass the size of *War and Peace*.

Scott Payne
Allendale, Michigan, 2016

To Jan and Johanna VanderHeijden
Of Waalwijk

With gratitude for explaining so much
of what happened from the civilian perspective

Chapter 1
March 8, 1943 -- El Guettar, Tunisia

I'm Allan Dudley, Regular Army. My story about a bunch of college brat soldiers starts when I was a 22-year-old infantry corporal in North Africa where something hit my noggin.

Well, it really starts when the ear-splitting crack of a nearby cannon jarred me back to consciousness.

Yeah, and pain.

It was a throbbing that felt like someone was rapping my skull with a size 39 mallet. As I elbowed myself up out of the foxhole, M1 in hand, the pounding doubled. Then a layer of desert sand and dust showered from my helmet and uniform, making me sneeze. That *really* hurt.

"Oh, my God," I groaned.

Somebody else said, *"Mein Gott!"*

Twisting around, I saw a German soldier five feet away staring wide-eyed. He was kneeling to bandage the leg of another kraut who also looked spooked. Maybe they figured me for a GI corpse rising from the grave. Anyhow, when I saw the Red Cross arm bands on his Afrika Korps uniform, I relaxed and put the rifle down. I was so cross-eyed and dizzy that I couldn't have aimed anyway.

I pulled at my helmet which came off with a kind of peeling rip. Blood started trickling down my nose and into my left eye.

The medic scrambled to me across the stony ground and gave me a broad grin. *"Sie sind ja ganz glüklich!"*

Having picked up quite a bit of German in Milwaukee before the war, I understood him. "Why am I so lucky?" As the medic eyed my forehead, I reached to touch it.

With a big sun-browned hand he grabbed my wrist. *"Nein!"* He fished the field dressing from my first aid pouch and placed it against my forehead. He had me hold it there so he could knot the ties behind my head. Squatting back in front of me, he picked up my helmet and showed me a finger-length hole in its steel, bright edges curled inward.

Still grinning, he said, *"Die Kugel traf hier, und . . ."* he whistled, zipping his finger around inside the helmet. Bullet or shrapnel, it jammed fragments of the fiberglass helmet liner into the skin above my left eyebrow. *"Nur fleischwunde,"* he said, and slapped my shoulder, raising a cloud of dust and making me wince. "Okay! *Verstehen sie?*" He pointed at me. "You, Ami! Okay."

I nodded . . . very gingerly.

"Aber vielleicht . . ." He leaned closer, using his hand to shade my left eye, then the right. He asked, *"Verstehen sie 'Gehimerschuetterung'?"*

I said, "Look, Fritz, I understood 'flesh wound' and 'but perhaps'. But not that long word, 'Gehim . . .' whatever. Are you saying maybe I've got a concussion, Herr Doktor? Concussion?"

He shrugged and returned to his buddy with the leg wound.

Another blast made me wince and jump. I turned to see a Kraut gunner, a big bruiser, about 100 feet away. He shoved a 4-foot shell into the shoulder-high breech of the big artillery piece beneath a tent of camouflage netting. The set-up confirmed the sinking feeling that I was a POW. But I was curious, too. "Hey, Doc! Is that gun an 88?"

The medic shrugged again. So I tried German. *"Bitte, ist das ein Acht-und-Achtzig?"*

The injured German raised up and shook his head. *"Nein. Nein. Man sagt 'Acht-Acht'."*

"Oh, you call it 'eight-eight,' not 'eighty-eight'." Just then, the gun captain yanked the lanyard and, barrel almost level, the cannon blasted again toward some First Division target. Desert wind blew the smoke and dust cloud across us. I almost forgot my headache watching the piece recoil and kick out the empty shell casing. *Damn! It's semiautomatic. Ejects just like one of our rifles.*

The medic stood to meet a stocky Wehrmacht corporal who walked over to us. He looked like a real hard-ass -- lips compressed, cold blue eyes. He pulled a Luger from his holster. I raised my hands, but the 88 fired again and I said "Oh, shit!" and dropped my mitts to nurse my aching skull. I really didn't give a rat's ass if he shot me or not.

He didn't.

He picked up my M1 and scowled. *"Schmutzig!"*

I pointed into the foxhole. "Of course it's dirty! It was half-buried in there with me."

Sticking the pistol back in its holster, he gave me a non-com's that's-no-excuse look.

As the medic and wounded Kraut watched, he examined the M1. Whacking the muzzle against the sole of his boot, he glanced to see that the bore was clear. Corporal Kraut then took a snowy handkerchief from his back pocket and wiped sand and dust from the action. The guy took firearms seriously.

Finally, he sighted the M1 on the far side of the wadi south of our knoll. He pulled the trigger. When it didn't fire, he frowned. *"Was gibts?"*

"What gives, Herr Corporal *Dummkopf*, is that the safety is on." He stiffened and glared, but I waved him over to me. Still leaning on the rim of the fox hole, I reached up inside the trigger guard to click the oblong safety tab forward.

The corporal nodded. *"Ja. So."* He raised the rifle, aimed and fired.

He fired three more times and the empty clip pinged out over his right shoulder. After glancing down into the open action, he spotted a bandoleer beside Sgt. Warner's body. Pulling the last 8-round clip from it, he blew the dust from the bullets and, after a pause, shoved the clip down into the rifle's open action. Nothing happened.

I beckoned again. He leaned down and I reached to pull back the operating rod handle. When I released it, the bolt slammed forward, closing and loading the action. "Now! *Jezt! Feuer!* It'll give you an idea of what you're going up against."

The corporal nodded, raised the rifle and fired three shots slowly, aiming carefully. He fired the last five shots very quickly. When the clip ejected, he lowered the rifle looked at his comrades and said, *"Ausgezeit!"*

"Damn right excellent!" I said. "Just speaking corporal to corporal," I added, touching my own chevrons, "it beats hell out of your bolt-action Mauser." The word "Mauser," conveyed my meaning and he glowered at me.

I didn't feel like it, but I gave him a big nasty grin.

He pawed around Warner's body for more ammo, but found none. Warner and I had just about run dry when the Kraut battle team, aided by mortars, overran our squad at dawn. I peered around trying to spot other Americans. The foxholes we'd labored over appeared to have corpses in or beside them, German and American. I apparently was the survivor and felt as crappy about being alone as about being a POW.

Someone at the 88 shouted orders and its crew started getting ready to pull out. The corporal trotted over to join them. He and the bruiser tilted the weapon's out-riggers up from the ground and jacked up the front of the gun platform, rolling a set of truck-sized wheels under it.

Two other men commenced the same procedure in the rear as a truck backed to the gun.

Suddenly, the air roared.

I rolled down into the foxhole and the medic piled atop me as all hell broke loose. Artillery shells whopped in, crashing on the knoll, big shards of shrapnel snapping and slicing overhead.

With each explosion, the medic shuddered and jerked.

Me too. The blasts didn't help my headache one bit.

The shelling – I think it was 105s – felt like it went on for an hour, but was probably only five minutes. When it stopped, the medic and I slowly raised up to peek from the foxhole like frightened mice.

He hissed and went pale because the 88 now was a wreck draped in torn camouflage netting. The gun's top recoil cylinder also was split and burning and the muzzle was tilted about 30 degrees upward. Along with dust from the barrage, the wind carried acrid black smoke to us from the blazing truck – plus all the other battle stink: dust, gunpowder, burning oil, frying rubber and roasting meat. Dust and sand covered the splinter-torn corpses of the German corporal and the rest of the gun crew. Nasty sight, but one I was used to by now. Shrapnel also had chopped up the medic's patient.

Too bad. I wanted them to spread the word about how our M1 outguns their rifles.

A machine gun clattered beyond the knoll, way too slow to be German but faster than the American .30 caliber. The medic and I crouched back into the foxhole. A minute later he groaned and I gave a little cheer as a British Bren carrier ground its way down the wadi and turned up onto our knoll. I started climbing out of the hole but then saw the soldier in back aiming the vehicle's machine gun at us.

I lifted my hands. "Yo! Don't fire. I'm American."

The vehicle stopped. "Advance and be recognized!" I climbed out of the hole and wobbled toward the vehicle, hands in the air.

"Who's the chap with you?"

"German medic. Seems like an okay guy."

"And what might you be doing here, Yank?"

"I'm all that's left of our squad." I nearly lost balance as I turned and pointed to the holes and corpses on the knoll's perimeter. "We set up an OP here last night. I speak some German and was supposed to question any Krauts we caught. But before first light the bastards overran us."

The man stood up from the carrier and donned a dishpan helmet. The three chevrons on his sleeve pointed down.

"Sergeant, are you British?"

He gave a broad smile. "Christ no, mate. We're Aussies."

I chuckled and resumed walking toward the vehicle, but vertigo made me sit down suddenly. "Sorry. I got a clout on the head."

"No worries, Corp. We'd better get you to the MO. And I'm sure your captive would rather lend a hand there for a bit than go direct to a prisoner cage."

# # #

It was there at El Guettar that the First Division, now recovered from Kasserine, began shoving the Afrika Korps around. Pushed by Patton, the Big Red One battered Rommel's forces, crushed their counterattacks and forced them north and east toward the Mediterranean and the British Eighth Army which was in touch on our south flank.

But they did it without me.

The Aussies drove me and the German medic to a British Army field hospital, all of us trying to sing *Lili Marlene*, but sounding horribly out of tune.

The MO, an exhausted British surgeon, diagnosed me as having severe concussion. He put me in the hospital, saying I needed rest. They soon trucked me to a U.S. Army field hospital where they diagnosed me as having severe concussion, saying I needed rest. They then transferred me to a Limey hospital ship – the U.S. had none in 1943 – which took me to the States where I could rest.

For weeks, I felt like singing a different song -- *Mood Indigo*. I was in a mental rut. See, when the Krauts invaded Poland in September 1939, I stood in line right behind Ray Warner waiting for the Milwaukee recruiting office to open. We both figured that war was coming and wanted to be ready for it.

Well, that's only half-true. We both had been working in the Civilian Conservation Corps and wanted out of it. Yeah, dumb move.

Anyway, we went in and stripped, coughed right and left for the docs, gave blood, got shots, dressed, and then stood in the front row together taking the oath. We spent the next 26 months training, hiking, chasing girls, traveling – everything but guzzling booze because I don't do that. We became NCOs and were all in the same platoon wading ashore in Algeria with First Division.

Now he and our buddies were dead. I was glad to be alive, but still in the dumps about losing my friends. Sometimes, I still whistled or hummed *Lili Marlene* to myself, the ballad about the girl waiting under the street light for her soldier – or maybe any soldier. But no one in the States knew the ballad or understood how much it meant to every damned soldier in Africa . . . Krauts, Limies, Aussies, Indians and Americans.

Sometime during the two months of rest – plus some leave with Mom and Sis -- I shook off the blues. Nightmares still bugged me as they had off and on since I was 18 when I killed my hero.

But I kept all that to myself.

The Army gave me a third stripe along with the Purple Heart and the North Africa Campaign Ribbon. They also assigned me to start all over again. Limited duty this time. No more combat – fine with me.

I was to be one of the cadre for the Army's Specialist Training Program. I'd be nurse-maiding brainy draftees at some college.

Chapter 2
August 17, 1943 -- Lawrence, Kansas

I first saw Pfc. Michael Oliver Forster when he and 40 other basic training graduates clambered down the cast iron steps of an Atcheson, Topeka and Santa Fe passenger car.

It was at the riverside depot in a hot, dusty little burg that looked like it still hadn't recovered from Quantrill's raid. Oh, hell, I don't know . . . maybe it was the Depression.

Anyway, all the kids' brand-new khakis were wrinkled, sweaty from the heat and grimy from steam locomotive soot. And even after the conditioning of basic training, most of them still struggled to carry a full duffle bag.

Except Forster.

He was a hard, gangly 6-3, wide in the shoulders, long in the arms and showing a big beak of a nose. He wore the only stripe in the group. In 1943, finishing basic as a private first class was something – especially for an egghead.

And they all were eggheads, most of them wise guys thinking they knew everything.

I ordered them to load their duffel bags into our deuce-and-a-half. As if was filled with feathers, Forster tossed his duffle bag into the truck. Then he helped his shorter comrades who had a hard time even lifting the weight over the tailgate.

"You a farm boy?"

He gave me an aw-shucks grin. "Yeah, Sarge. Been tossing hay bales most of my life."

"Hey, Sergeant," one of the others asked me. "Any chance we can stretch our legs around town? We been cooped up on that train since two this morning."

I almost laughed. "Young trooper, I'm glad you asked. Matter of fact, we're just about to take a nice walk. We'll stretch your legs real good."

"Oh-oh!"

Forster grinned. "Be careful what you ask for, Halls."

I liked the grin. It showed he felt he could tackle anything that came his way. I ordered them into a column of twos, placing Forster at the rear to see how well he'd ride herd on stragglers . . . because by the time we got up atop The Hill, some would straggle.

I set a hot pace on New Jersey behind the little business district, then cut over to the main drag -- Massachusetts Avenue – heading for the ridge-top campus. We marched 11 blocks due south with the noon sun blazing in our faces through the sidewalk elms. Then we turned west onto Fourteenth Street and marched 13 more blocks.

Don't ever let anybody tell you Kansas is flat. Fourteenth was all uphill. The last seven blocks mounting to the campus were steeper than any slope they ever hiked at the Pearl of the Ozarks, Camp Leonard Wood.

By the time we crested the ridge, the boys were running with sweat and most of them had a good case of cottonmouth. Some acted like their skinny little 201 Personnel File folders were too much to carry. They never would have made it toting duffle bags. Forster lagged a bit because he was chivvying along six fat-assed mommas' boys whose cheeks ranged in color from pale green to raspberry.

I hear the word "Kansas" is Indian for "land of the south wind." For sure the wind atop the campus was strong. And though it seemed to come out of a kiln, it perked everybody up -- maybe because it molded coeds' skirts against their thighs.

The campus occupies a horseshoe ridge, open end facing the river valley to the north. Though it was hazy, you still could see for miles through the gaps between the university's stately old buildings.

The boys gawked until I ordered them into a column of fours. "Now, for God's sake, try to look like soldiers instead of a bunch of rag dolls!" I marched them down Jayhawk Boulevard calling cadence to keep them in step.

We halted in front of Lindley Hall at the southwest corner of the campus. It was a brand-new 3-story science and technical building doing wartime business as barracks, mess hall and training center. Already populating the ground floor and half the second floor were 400 swabbies – brand new Navy recruits training as machinists' mates.

The army filled up the rest of the second floor and most of the third. My gang was one of the last GI batches arriving for the opening semester of the Army Specialist Training Program.

After they pulled their duffel bags off the truck and processed in, I took them in groups of 12 to classrooms serving as squad bays. Most of the kids were anxious and unsettled. Any soldier, even a recruit just out of basic, feels like a fish out of water when reporting to a new duty station. Where's home -- your bunk and locker? Everything is a question mark and Momma and Daddy ain't there to give the answers. Us NCOs have all the answers, of course, but we give them to everybody all at once, in very large doses . . . and at the right time.

Forster's group lucked out, getting a third-floor room with windows on north and west, guaranteeing at least some cross-ventilation on 100-degree afternoons and 80-degree nights. The kids all were sweat-soaked and gamey. Me too. They were whipped, too, but not me. I'd hiked that hill so many times now it was just a walk in the park. My concussion vertigo from North Africa was long gone.

"Get your gear stowed," I ordered as I left for a quick shower. Forster already was opening his duffle bag.

When I got back, everybody but Forster had simply stripped to their skivvies, rolled out their mattresses and collapsed onto their bunks. Forster had followed orders, stowed his gear in the foot locker at the end of his bunk and one of the wall lockers that partitioned the bunks in pairs.

"All right, you men!" I shouted. "Get your dead asses off those racks! NOW!"

As they wearily got up, Forster gave me a grin. "Some of them seem a bit tuckered from their constitutional."

"No shit!" I paced up and down the room barking out my litany. "All right, listen up! Get showered. Get into clean fatigues. Stow your gear in your lockers per regulation and make your bunks real nice and tight. Then police up this place. Inspection at 1700 hours, so you don't have much time." A subdued chorus of groans followed.

"Knock it off!" I yelled. "Now, if everything is in order and you pass inspection – and that's a real big 'If' -- you men will get chow. If it ain't, you'll work here until you pass . . . even if it takes all night. Clear? And make Goddamn sure there's no cigarette butts on my nice clean floor or in the ashtrays. And don't be throwing them out the window onto Capt. Maxwell's lawn. Otherwise, I'll take all of you for a hike down to the railway depot and back. Got that?"

One of the kids, Halls again, held up a hand.

"What?"

"Well, what if somebody on one of the other floors throws a cigarette butt out there. It wouldn't be our fault . . ."

"We'll hike anyway," I said, trying to imitate my old man's sarcastic grin. "See, son, I really *like* hiking and I'll take any excuse I can get. So . . . no butts! Got it?"

"But that isn't fair!"

"If you don't learn nothing else, Boy, let this lesson sink in right now. Forget fair! Fair don't exist! Not here, not nowhere! Especially not during war."

Some of them nodded, others looked sullen.

"Okay. Now . . . just to show you how well organized we are here at the University of Kansas, you men comprise Squad Six because this fine, brand new barrack room is Bay No. Six. Questions? No? Okay. Pfc. Forster?"

"Yes, sir!"

I grimaced. "Forster, I am not a sir." I glanced around the room. "You men! You're out of basic, now, so you call me 'Sergeant.' The name's Dudley. My friends call me Dud . . . but you ain't my friends.

"Now you people listen up! Forster has the highest rank, so he's the NCOIC of Bay Six and the squad leader of Squad Six. For you young troopers, NCOIC stands for 'Noncommissioned Officer In Charge.' Hear those words 'In Charge?' You, there! Halls! What does 'In Charge' mean?"

"Sergeant! It means Pfc. Forster is in charge."

"Very good, Halls. I can tell you'll go far in the Army. Now, if any of you has a problem, tell Forster. He'll see me about it. But if you give him a problem and I'll land on you like a ton of bricks.

"Forster, get your men moving."

"Yes, sir . . . er, sergeant. Will you be inspecting?"

I grinned. "No such luck, Forster. Me, I'm a real softie. The inspecting officer today is 1st Lt. Albert Meier. He's a German refugee and an instructor in German and Russian and he is a stickler! Fair warning, he'll probably ask you to recite your General Orders."

As I left, Forster took a deep breath and said, "Okay, guys. I'm Mike Forster, a hick farm boy from Belle Plaine, near the Oklahoma line . . ."

# # #

Promptly at 1700, Lt. Meier and I entered the bay and Forster called the squad to attention. He saluted and reported the bay ready for inspection.

The lieutenant was a cold-eyed whipcord thin little guy. He never smiled. Rumor was that his relatives might be in a Nazi concentration camp. He took his time going man to man, checking the open foot and wall lockers. Forster and I paced in his wake, Forster noting down the lieutenant's comments.

Lt. Meier awarded two gigs for an unbuttoned shirt pocket and one man, George Evans, too flustered to recite his Third General Order. He ordered each to do 25 push-ups and let it go at that.

He raised his eyebrows when the white glove treatment revealed no dust on the tables and chairs. That impressed me.

Forster had made the kids turn to.

# # #

Lights-out was 2200, but when I stopped in earlier to talk to Forster, I had to roust him out of his rack. He had turned in because he wanted to be alert for tomorrow's orientation.

As he and I went over the next day's schedule, we heard a women's chorus singing outside. Smoking and looking out the double window above his bunk, Halls said, "Well, now, ain't that sweet? There's a sorority right across the street – Chi Omega -- and it sounds like they're practicing their songs."

"Well," Forster said. "It sure beats basic training's night music."

"Music? What music?"

"Don't you remember? Machine guns on the night infiltration course."

"Oh, yeah." Evans said. "Well, this ASTP thing is the way to fight the war. Might be nice to meet some of those girls."

I said, "You boys ain't gonna have much social time."

"Yeah," Halls leered, "but don't you think some of those girls might feel it their patriotic duty to neck with a soldier-boy going off to war?"

Forster said, "I bet they think their duty is to protect their virtue."

The kid sitting on the next bunk snorted. "Broads in Kansas are probably just like broads in Brooklyn -- some are like ice and some are hot to trot."

"Yeah, Torrelli? Well, let us know how you make out."

Chapter 3
August 18, 1943 -- Lawrence, Kansas

My own yell awakened me before dawn. I sat up, soaking with sweat.

My roommate, Sgt. Rosloniec, pulled his pillow over his head and did some muffled cussing. He didn't bitch at me, though. He wasn't a combat vet and I guess he figured I was having a combat nightmare.

Nightmare, yes, but not about North Africa. No, my mom's kitchen in West Virginia.

I sat there in my rack trying to stop my shudders. Seeing the smashing, back and forth, back and forth, and blood spurting onto the white porcelain oven door.

With no chance of getting back to sleep, I got up and shaved and hit the shower

# # #

After chow, I marched all the new arrivals to a lecture theater and called them to attention when Capt. Maxwell came on stage. He was in full dress with three rows of ribbons beside his empty sleeve with its Big Red One patch. He introduced himself as commandant of the ASTP program at the university.

Without a trace of warmth in his grating voice, he welcomed them as being among about 150,000 GIs whose intelligence was in the top one percent of the army's draftees. Those ASTP draftees were reporting in at colleges and universities all over the country.

"You troops may be special," he said, "but I warn you, you're not here to have fun . . . not when your brother soldiers are in combat. You're here under U.S. Army discipline."

I felt a quiet stir of resentment.

"You will dress in Class A uniforms and march in squads to and from classes," the captain said. "You will not wear civilian clothes. At nights you may wear fatigues and you will remain in your barracks or libraries or classrooms. Your NCOs will require you to keep your gear and personal areas ready for inspection at all times. Reveille will be at 0500."

Amid stifled groans and murmured curses, Forster chuckled. For a farm boy, 5 a.m. is a sleep-in. The captain saw the smile and returned a frosty grin.

Then he paused and swept his eyes across his audience. "Yes, I know," he said, "some of you think this is just a lot of chickenshit. Well, like the song says, you're in the Army now. You will have formation and then, on alternate mornings, do a mile run and the Daily Dozen. You will have close-order drill three times a week and go to the rifle range every two weeks.

"I sense that this prospect displeases some of you. Well, while you're running the mile or doing push-ups, you have it easy compared to fighting soldiers who are under mortar barrages in Sicily or plucking leeches off their asses and ducking Jap snipers in New Guinea."

The captain gave a brief smile. "The two military things you won't do here at KU is peel spuds or have KP. That would take from study time. Oh, and don't be surprised if you hear someone yell a command like *'Stillgestanden!'* to a drill group. Foreign language students will learn and practice foreign army commands."

We all returned the obligatory chuckle.

Serious again, the captain told the men they'd be free both Saturday afternoons and Sundays. "If your marks are top drawer, you can get a pass to go to town, not that there's much to do there. But I warn you, as of Monday, you'll take very tough, accelerated courses. I give you good counsel to hit the books the minute you get back to your bay and to put every spare minute you have – weekends included – to good use.

"I want to stress that Gentleman C grades won't cut it here. Army testing says you men all have far above average intelligence. So if your exam marks are merely average, you're gone!"

A long pause.

"I want this to be clear! Your duty here is to *master* your material, just like it's a rifleman's duty to go on night patrols or a cannon-cocker's duty is to ram shells into a howitzer's breach.

"If you don't excel, you'll be sent to one of the infantry divisions or replacement battalions forming on the east and west coasts – and they'll put you on the first troop ship to the European or Pacific Theater of Operations. And instead of interrogating captives in a nice neat tent or using a slide rule in an office, you'll sleep in the mud with an M1."

After another a pause for effect he added, "As an incentive to study and master your material, never forget that the infantry's job is to suffer, to fight and, perhaps, to die."

A four-eyed Pfc. clerk tiptoed across the stage from a side door to hand the captain a note. He read it, arched his eyebrows and looked up at us.

"Well, men, good news on the radio. Patton's troops have captured Messina. The Americans and the British have driven the last German troops from Sicily." Someone started clapping and the applause and whistles erupted among the men. After a moment, the captain held up his hand. "Next stop -- mainland Europe!"

The cheering stopped when the captain stepped back from his podium and held up his hand again.

"A final word," he said. "We are guests of this university. At all times you will conduct yourselves as gentlemen.

"That is all."

I shouted: "TENN-hut!" The captain did an about-face and departed.

# # #

The men in Forster's bay clustered along the tables, smoking and leafing through texts and lesson plans. Four of them got out a deck of cards and, for Christ's sake, starting playing bridge! These were soldiers?

I joined Forster and the bay's six other GIs who were taking German. He had persuaded them to trade bunks and lockers so they could live side-by-side speaking the language together as often as possible. I was ahead of them in conversational Deutsch, but I wanted to learn the language properly. I might not be going back into combat, but I figured that if I qualified as a German linguist I could interrogate POWs.

Vincenti Torrelli was one of our other German students and didn't like it. "Ugly fucking language," he said. "I've spoken Italian since I was a kid. It's beautiful and musical, but German – ugh! And it looks like the grammar is a bitch."

"Oh, it ain't so ugly," I said. "Of course, Marlene Dietrich can sing it better than me, but listen to *Lili Marlene*. All of us in Africa loved it – friends and enemies. I led off with the first stanza.

Vor der Kaserne
Vor dem grossen Tor
Stand eine Laterne
Und steht sie noch davor

"Well, you're right." Torrelli said.

"Yeah, sarge," Timmer jumped in. "Marlene Dietrich does have a much better voice."

"But the words are still ugly," Torrelli said.

"That doesn't matter," I snapped. "You heard the captain. German is your duty. Master it and you'll come in damned handy when we end up fighting the Krauts."

"Yeah," Forster said, "and you're right about the grammar – it's real tough." He had a year of high school German under his belt. "You've got to buckle down -- sheer brute memorization -- on conjugations and declensions and the cases that the prepositions take. Right now. Otherwise, you never catch up."

I noticed the others paid him close attention. This kid was serious. He might have what we called OLQ – officer-like qualities.

"Hey, guys," Halls called from an adjoining table, "It took Patton and Montgomery about a month to capture Sicily. Now by the map here, Sicily looks about five per cent the size of France and Germany so I figure it's going to take about four years to beat the Nazis."

Evans, another German student, raised his head. "Stuff it in your barracks bag. We don't need a drop in morale."

Halls, who was built like a fullback, jumped up, raising and clenching his fists. As he bounced on the balls of his feet, he snarled, "I'll fix your morale, buddy."

I sobered him. "Halls! Anybody fighting will ship out immediately to a replacement battalion. Clear? They'll see that you get to fight all the time." He backed down with a sour look. I quickly changed the subject.

"Now listen up, men! I forgot to pass the word to you that I gave to the other squads -- a couple of important things about going into town on pass. First off, there are no bars in Lawrence, or anywhere else in Kansas."

Torrelli, the New Yorker, looked stricken. "Sarge. Are you kidding?"

"You heard me. It's a left-over from Prohibition."

"Oh, my God!"

Bull, a Mormon from Denver laughed at Torrelli. "I count that no great privation."

"Don't interrupt," I said. "Now, Torrelli, they *do* have liquor stores where you can buy whiskey and wine and they have taverns here in Lawrence where you can get beer on tap."

Torrelli looked relieved.

"But," I added, "first off, it's only 3.2 beer. Second, you got to be 21 to buy it or drink it."

The whole bay laughed aloud as Torrelli said, "Sergeant, do you mean 21 years old?"

"Yep."

Torrelli bunched his fingers and jerked his hand up and down, exclaiming *"figlio de puttana!"* Something like that.

"We have a couple of MPs downtown," I added. "They ain't real bright, but we told them that if you were born after 1922, you ain't legal."

Torrelli broke the silence. "What a dump! Why couldn't they have sent me to NYU?"

Forster just said, *"Bitte, sprechen sie Deutch."*

Chapter 4
September 12, 1943 -- Lawrence, Kansas

It was almost dusk when I had to get outside for a walk.

Bay Six was foggy with cigarette smoke after Forster and I and the other Krauts drilled for three solid hours on German vocabulary and the prepositional declensions. Then – very tough for midwesterners -- we tried some high-speed pronunciation of some of those run-on German words. My favorite stumbler was *Kriegsstärkenachweisungen* . . . meaning 'table of organization'

I gave up and took a break. Besides, my nerves already were jangling. Everybody was keyed up. Earlier in the day room we listened to the shortwave radio reports of the Salerno landing.

The broadcast from a ship called *Ancon* wavered and whined, but through the interference you could hear loud thumps and a spastic background drumming. Capt. Maxwell, who dropped in to listen with us, said it sounded to him like 40 mm antiaircraft fire. The broadcaster repeatedly spoke of Nazi and Italian aircraft using some new weapon called the guided bomb.

I set a hard pace along North Campus Drive and was mentally drilling *". . . an diese technichen angelegenheiten . . ."* but my study discipline broke down as I noticed groups of formally-dressed co-eds headed the opposite direction. I had to keep stepping off the sidewalk to give them room. Not that I minded. They were a real treat to the eyes. Their dresses' shoulder pads and hairdos poofed out at neck level gave them a delicate tapering shape. I made a mental note to ask Lt. Meier about whether Germans have an equivalent of va-va-voom.

When I made way for a trio of girls, one of them – a blue-eyed brunette – smiled at me and said, "Good evening, sergeant!"

"Evenin' Ma'am," I said, touching the bill of my cap and started to walk on.

She stopped and turned. "Oh, please," she said. "I'm a miss! We all are. None of us is a ma'am."

"At least not yet," her blond companion said.

Now I'm a combat veteran and I'm pretty good with my fists, but I clutch and get tongue-tied around girls. Yet the brunette's smile invited me on. "Well, you may be a miss," I said, "but you're sure a hit with me."

The remark produced more giggles than it really deserved, so I asked, "Whereabouts all you ladies headed?"

"Oh, sergeant, there's a wonderful string quartet performing tonight at Hoch Auditorium. It's back that way," she pointed the direction I had come. "It's only a couple of blocks from Lindley. Why don't you come with us? It's free for students."

"Well, thank you so much, but, Ma'am . . . Ooops, sorry! . . . Miss, but being in my fatigues and wearing Army clodhoppers, I'm sure not dressed for any concert. Besides," I pointed to my temple, "I'm drilling in here on German grammar and vocabulary."

She half-closed her eyes and nodded. *"Oh, mon chevalier,"* she said, showing me a pouty lower lip, *"Quelle damage."*

"I'm sorry. What?"

"That's French for, 'Oh, my knight, what a pity.' I'm doing the exactly the same thing in French."

"Well, you and I better stick to English or we'll never understand each other."

"I'd like that," she said, fixing her eyes on mine.

"Betty!" the blonde giggled, sounding slightly shocked. The third co-ed smiled.

Aww, what the heck? I extended my hand, "Well, Betty, I'm Allan Dudley. I'm just a hillbilly from down south and a working man in the army so I sure don't know much about high-class music."

She gave my hand a gentle pressure. "Well, Sergeant, Alice and Amy and I are all from Alpha Delta Phi – our house is three blocks from here. And you don't need to *know* about music. You just listen and enjoy it. So maybe we could get you to come along to the next concert."

"That would be nice, Betty, 'cause we sure don't have a lot of time for entertainment."

She nodded sympathetically. "I'll find the concert schedule and I'll call. And now we've got to run or we'll miss the curtain."

"Good bye, all," I said. "And thanks. Oh, and Betty, please, what is your last name?"

"It's Edwards . . . Betty Louise Edwards."

"Enjoy the concert, Betty Louise."

"Please, just Betty."

"Got it, Betty. G'night."

On the rest of my walk, I hummed *Lili Marlene.*

#

When I got back Torrelli was razzing Forster who said he met a coed, too. "Eleanor!" Torrelli said. "Eleanor? That's all? You didn't get her last name? Mike, you're damned near as backward as Kansas."

Forster bit back. "Ease up, Vince. I know you think we're just hayseeds out here, but it ain't a SNAFU yet. She said she'd call and tell me about a concert."

"Okay," Torrelli said, "so if she does and she invites you to a concert, what are you going to do?"

Timmer chimed in. "Ask if she has a sister."

"Shut up, Marty," Torrelli said. "This is serious. Mike, have you thought about asking her to the hop that USO is setting up for us?"

"No." Forster frowned. "I don't know this jitterbug stuff. Back in Belle Plaine, we just waltzed."

"Waltzed?"

"Yeah, you know, *The Tennessee Waltz?*"

Torrelli rolled his eyes. "Forster, you're hopeless. Look, Sgt. Dudley, why don't you see if you can promote a radio for us? Tell the quartermaster it would help us study if we could have some relaxing music here at night. If there's a decent station out here in this wasteland, we maybe can find some Benny Goodman or Jimmy Dorsey so we can teach Mike to jitterbug."

Next day I hiked downtown and bought us a little table radio.

# # #

When Eleanor called, Forster had to speak with her on the orderly room phone. I shooed the CQ clerk out to give him some privacy. As I walked away to get out of earshot, I heard him say, "Hello, Eleanor. Thanks for calling and before you say another word, please tell me your last name."

It turned out that she also was an Alpha Delta Phi and, of course, knew Betty. It also turned out no concert was scheduled before mid-November. In the end, Betty and Eleanor invited me and Forster to the sorority's dress dinner Sunday afternoon, the 19th. Yes it was formal, and, yes, it would be keen if we wore our Class A uniforms.

Keen! Ye gods, who says things like that?

With so many men away in the military, only a dozen other guys attended the dinner. Five were students, three of them needing coke bottle glasses and one being an artiste type more lady-like than the girls. The fifth was an Air Corps crash victim still on his crutches. The others obviously were dads.

Betty tried to put me at ease, but found it an uphill battle. My uniform made me feel as if I stood out like a sore thumb. Besides, I'm no prize -- built like a fireplug with a face blunt as a bulldog's. The scar on my forehead doesn't help.

For a farm boy, though, Forster was smooth. The ladies liked his looks because, hey, the kid was tall and handsome, even if his nose was too big. Girl after girl repeatedly asked about the black steel Maltese cross and wreath pinned above his left breast pocket – his Expert Rifleman badge.

Betty was the only one to ask me about *my* Expert badge (rifle, pistol *and* machine gun) or my campaign ribbons or Purple Heart. Betty, by the way, was an attractive girl with a great smile. But Eleanor was a raving beauty running a real close second to Rita Haworth.

By taking Torrelli's strident advice to splurge three bucks apiece for a long-stemmed red rose, we both made a hit with our dates. They seemed almost overwhelmed -- from which I gathered that roses were damn near as rare at KU as men. Each found a little vase and put the rose right on the table between her place and ours. I whispered to Betty I was new to formal dining and didn't know which fork to use. (Mom showed me the few times we had big family dinners, but I forgot it all.) Betty whispered back. "Just follow my lead." It worked pretty well, but at first was as nerve-wracking as planning a patrol.

After dinner, I proposed taking a walk. Betty put on a light sweater and we followed the stone pathways across the sloping quarter-mile swale between the two north-south arms of the campus ridge. Our hands brushed together and soon we held hands.

Betty told me she was studying to become a surgical nurse. She wanted to follow her mom's footsteps in World War I. "When I get my RN," she said with a twinkle, "the Army will commission me a first lieutenant and then I'll outrank you."

"You already outrank me," I laughed.

She told me her mom, a native of Ireland, met her father when he was wounded in France. They now lived in his hometown, Topeka, where he owned a jewelry store and she worked as a nurse at Stormont Hospital. Betty's brother was a Navy ensign in the Pacific.

I didn't want to tell her about my old man, the worshipped father who turned out to be a wife-beating sadist.

Betty had a way of drawing me out, however, and I ended up spilling some of the sad tale -- how I beat him to a pulp, stole his car and fled with Mom and Sis from West Virginia to Ohio and then Michigan. We caught the last ferry of the season across the lake to Milwaukee where the rattletrap died and we settled, learning to live with Yankees.

My voice got to trembling a bit. But even seven years later, I still couldn't tell – or face -- the whole story.

She hugged me in the dark and whispered, "Do you drink?"

"Never have, Betty. Never will. Don't want to wind up like my old man. I stick to coffee, water and root beer."

"Does your church prohibit drinking?"

"Nope. I don't really have a church. And if others drink, it don't make me no never mind, but I fear what might be inside me."

As we turned back, damned if Forster and Eleanor weren't walking hand-in-hand and about to cross our path. The four of us headed toward the sorority together, they a few paces in the lead. Forster asked if Eleanor liked dancing. "Oh, yes," she said, almost dancing right there on the sidewalk.

"Well, do you jitterbug?"

She bounced on her toes and clasped her hands under her chin. "Oh, yes! Yes! Do you?"

"No." Her face fell. "I'm real clumsy with these gunboat feet of mine."

Eleanor smiled and held a finger to his lips. "Don't worry, Mike. I'll teach you. Now are you asking me to the USO hop?"

"You know about it?"

"Everybody does. All the girls want to go to it."

"Well, I guess I'm asking you. I just hope I don't spoil it for you."

I took Betty by the hand and led her past them. A few paces further, I looked at her. "How about going with me to the hop? I'm not too bad on the dance floor. Back in '36 I won $5 in a dance marathon."

"Wow," she smiled and hugged my arm. "Mon chevalier, it's a date." Betty mounted the single step to the front porch and turned so her face was level with mine. Her eyebrows knitted in concern. I just stood there like a dope.

Then she grinned.

"Sgt. Allan Dudley, if you don't kiss me I'll never speak to you again." I leaned to kiss her and the bill of my cap struck her forehead. I whipped off the hat and encircled her waist with the hat at her back and pulled her to me.

After the kiss we hugged and caught our breath. "Betty?" I blurted out. "I do thank you for asking me to the dinner. It was real, uh, nice and the walk made the night perfect. And, uh, Betty -- this wasn't my first kiss, but it was the best ever."

She beamed. "I'm glad," she said. "And thank you for the rose, Allan." She hugged me, gave me peck on the cheek and danced up the steps to the front door.

I marched toward Lindley mulling over that dance marathon. Winning $5 nowadays would be nice – enough to buy movie tickets and a steak dinner for two, but in '36 it meant a week's groceries for Mom, Sis and me.

Forster came trotting up behind me and got into step with me.

"Hey, Sarge?"

"What?"

"Do you know you're out of uniform?"

I still had the damned cap in my hand.

#

The nightmare woke me after only an hour. It seemed more real than ever. It was all because of the kitten some yahoo snuck into the barracks.

I've got nothing against cats or kitties. But mewing gives me nightmare shakes.

Chapter 5
November 18, 1943 -- Lawrence, Kansas

Betty and I were going steady but dating was hard. Neither of us owned a car, making it almost impossible to be together alone.

We could hold hands watching a movie at the Jayhawk or the Granada Theaters downtown or a concert at Hoch Auditorium. But we could hardly chat at either place, let alone kiss. Walks on campus became rare because of autumn rain and cold wind. You've heard the old saw about being colder than a well-digger's ass on the prairie? Well, let me tell you it's based in pure fact, and even worse on a hill jutting above the prairie.

The only way we could be alone at length was riding Lawrence's city bus circuit after circuit. The rickety vehicle was cold and drafty, but we kept fairly warm with my arm over Betty's shoulder. We'd stop to warm up with cocoa at the drug store, and then catch the last bus back to campus before the coeds' closing hours.

"I'm worried," Betty told me one Saturday night as she snuggled against me. When I glanced at her, eyebrows up, she said she was afraid I'd be sent away soon.

I pooh-poohed her concern. "I'm part of the permanent party here. And even if they did take us away, I'm near 100 per cent on my German exams. Lt. Meier says I probably would qualify as a second-echelon interrogator. That means I'd be behind the lines."

Betty wasn't the weepy sort, but a tear coursed down her cheek. She said she was afraid anyway. In the past two weeks, the army had shipped out several other girls' soldier friends.

"Yeah, well, Betty, I think the only thing you have to worry about is that I find some way to get you alone somewhere. You'd really have a struggle to avoid the fate worse than death."

"Ohhhh, Dud," she said, looking me in the eyes, "I'm not a roundheel, but I don't think I'd struggle too much. I'm really nuts about you."

We kissed . . . passionately . . . right there in public in the back of the bus. Then she fanned her hand at her face. "Maybe it's best we can't be alone more than five minutes."

# # #

As we cuddled during another marathon ride, I asked Betty for a promise.

"Anything," she said.

I told her I had a buddy in North Africa who received a Dear John Letter. "It killed him," I said.

"He let me read it and what she wrote was so Gawdawful mean and cold. She wrote that she had gotten engaged to some other guy and didn't want to see him again. 'So don't write again. Or try to call . . .' He gave up, moped around and just quit caring. Didn't pay attention. So the Krauts nailed him."

"How awful for . . ."

"Wait," I interrupted. "Betty, I can understand if you end up having second thoughts about me or that you find someone smarter. And anybody would be better-looking . . ."

"Dud, I don't like this . . ."

"Please, Betty, just let me wrap this up. I think about you in class. I dream about you. I have imaginary conversations with you in German. Your face will be in my mind if the Army sends me away . . . or when it sends you away. But if you've got to send me a Dear John, please try to let me down easy."

Tears welled in her eyes. "I promise," she said. "I promise when you come back, I'll be there . . . at the train station or the bus depot or wherever it is . . . my arms open for you. There, Allan Dudley. That's my promise."

We held a kiss until the bus driver began noisily clearing his throat. I looked up and told him, "Just keep your eyes on the road, Jack!"

That's when I first saw that sign. On the back of the driver's seat, somebody had chalked "Kilroy Was Here."

# # #

On Sunday the following week, Forster entered the bay complaining about the winter wind. "Boy, it just knifes right through a fella's coat . . ." He stopped in surprise. I was overseeing three very glum soldiers emptying their lockers and packing their duffle bags.

"What the hell's going on?"

"Come out here a minute," I said. Once in the hallway, I told him the three men were on deployment to the infantry.

"For Christ's sake why, Sarge? I been keeping tabs. Their grades are pretty solid – all three of them."

"Forster, can you keep your mouth shut?"

"Sure, Sarge."

"It looks like solid grades don't cut it now. I think ASTP is starting to drop anybody without near-perfect grades. Cap'n Maxwell says casualties in Italy have been very heavy and neither us nor the British are gaining ground. The Army needs replacements and I think everybody should be prepared to be pulled."

"But, this program was supposed to be . . ."

"Look, Mike, you enlisted for the artillery, right?"

"Right."

"Do you remember when you signed up, that they said there were no guarantees -- that the army would use you where it needed you?"

"Oh . . . right. Yeah. I remember."

"People have been shipped out from several other bays. These are the first men from yours. For all I know, they may just ship the rest of us out any day."

"Well, God help us if they do, Sarge. None of us knows the first thing about combat except aiming and pulling the trigger."

I told him couple of us old hands already talked with the captain about that. "We're going to try to work something up. Meanwhile, I recommend you eat all you can to put on some weight. If you wind up in Europe this time of year, you'll need the insulation."

# # #

I jerked awake, sitting up with a loud "Ufff!"

Sweat soaked my T-shirt and shorts. I swung my legs over the side of the rack and held my forehead in my hands, trying to clear the vision of swinging a marble bludgeon side-to-side, the impact in my right hand, shouting with each swing and strike.

It took two hours to get back to sleep.

Chapter 6
November 21, 1943 -- Lawrence, Kansas

"Aww, this is bullshit!" The men in Bay Six were reading the captain's order I had just posted. Free time was down to Sunday afternoons. Maxwell was adding lectures and squad-level infantry tactic exercises somewhere south of town.

"No," Timmer said, "it's not bullshit. It's chickenshit. Last thing I need is another damned lecture or to go out and play shoot-'em-up. I've got enough trouble memorizing irregular verbs."

"Chickenshit is right," Halls said. "We're supposed to be going into intelligence or staff work. Not into the infantry."

I was about to blow my top, but Forster beat me to it. He slammed his big German-English dictionary onto the table. "Dammit!" he yelled. I stepped out into the hallway.

"Three of us already are gone to the infantry," he bellowed. "You or I might go tomorrow and the idea of facing German veterans with four years of war behind them gives me the willies.

"The Nazis have kicked the shit out of the Poles, the French, the Dutch, the Limeys, the Greeks and the Russians. If I end up in a rifle company I won't know what to do. Neither will you. We'd be like mice in a lion's cage.

"And I'll tell you something else. You know we saw that training film we saw about the German MG-42? They said its bark is worse than its bite? Well, Dud says that's bullshit. And he's been there! It fires three times as fast as our machine guns. And they've got those 88s that go through our tanks like a hot knife through butter. So I think we'd be smart to learn any lessons they share with us."

Just then, Capt. Maxwell startled me by tapping my shoulder. He was eavesdropping, too. He signaled with his head and I followed him to his office. "Sounds like Forster might make a decent corporal," he said. "What do you think?"

"He's green, sir, but he sure catches on quick. I wouldn't mind having him in my squad. That little pep talk was pretty good."

"It was just about what I was going to drop in and say," the Captain said. "But did you really tell him the MG-42 training film was bullshit?"

"No, sir. I ain't seen that film . . . but it must be bullshit if it says that gun's bark is worse than its bite."

The captain snorted. "Well, I'm not authorized to promote anybody, but I can sure put a hot recommendation in Forster's 201 file."

# # #

Trying to teach seminar-style along with the captain and me was Frank Bowyer, a scrawny sergeant first class with a voice like a bullfrog. He was old enough to have seen action late in World War I and later in the banana republics. He had a depressed white scar where they stitched together what remained of his left cheek – his Kasserine souvenir. The Afrika Korps had taught the three of us some lessons and we wanted to pass them on the kids.

First, we drew a sharp contrast between the U.S. Army's fire-and-movement tactics and Wehrmacht assaults.

"You maybe got a little bit of this in basic," Bowyer said. "You're part of a squad -- the tip of the spear -- 12 men, if you're lucky. You're gonna be in the scout group, the rifle group or the gun group: four each.

"Using cover and concealment, the scout group checks things out and reports back. The gun group uses its BAR or its light machine gun to set up a base of fire -- keeping the enemy's head down, know what I mean? Meanwhile, the rifle group assaults by flanking the enemy."

"The difference between us and them," the captain said, "is that the Wehrmacht uses a 9-man squad built around the MG-42. That weapon is light-weight and easy to move. And the whole squad carries ammo cans for it. It shoots a cartridge about like our .30-06, but it puts out so much firepower – 1,200 to 1,500 rounds a minute – that it almost has a ripping sound. When you hear it – and you can't miss it -- stay low or get shredded.

The captain continued the theme. "The Krauts think of the MG-42 as kind of a battering ram. The gunner uses it to pound the enemy position and then he picks up the gun and advances. As he does, the rest of the squad advances with him, their main job being to protect him and the gun with rifles and submachine guns."

"Sir," Torrelli asked, "what happens when one of our squads tries to flank one of their squads as it advances?"

"Accuracy beats firepower," the captain said.

My heart sank a little bit. *Yeah, and vice versa.*

"Training and using your head wins, too," Bowyer added.

Sarge! Who's better trained than Wehrmacht veterans?

"You got to stay low," Bowyer stressed. "And when you move, move low and move fast. And you only fire aimed shots."

"That's right," I agreed. "You don't shoot 'til you have a target. And here's where the M1 is so good. You can shoot eight rounds in the time it takes a kraut to fire two shots from his Mauser. And he needs to break aim every time he cranks that bolt. With your M1 you can keep aim 'til you need to shove in a new clip."

"So, you see," the captain said, "you've got firepower, too, and with accuracy . . . if you keep your head." *Oh, boy, that's the old rah-rah*

"And something else," I added. "The MG-42 is a great weapon, but it has one little disadvantage. Where we shoot three to five-round bursts with our 1919 light .30s, they're shooting 10 to 15-round bursts.

"Now, we can shoot the .30 like that for almost a half hour before we have to change barrels. And if it's a water-cooled .30, we can shoot it all day without a barrel change. But it doesn't take more than five or six minutes of steady firing before the MG-42 barrel gets white hot. Then they gotta change it. Takes maybe five seconds and that's our chance to assault with grenades and M1s and wipe them out."

"The main thing," the captain said, "it to keep your yap shut and pay close attention to your squad leaders. The squad is a team, just like in football. You've got to know where you fit in. But if you goof up, you don't get a 15-yard penalty -- you get killed. Worse, you get buddies killed!"

By the time each little seminar wrapped up, the boys were no longer grousing. Some had that this-could-happen-to-me look.

I spotted Forster hanging around as the rest of the troops left one of the programs. "What do you want, Forster?"

"Well, I just got to thinking and maybe this is a stupid question, but I got to wondering where mortars figure in all this."

"Ah, yes," the captain said. "Mortars." He exchanged grim looks with Bowyer. "I'm impressed that you're thinking ahead, Forster. What made you ask that?"

"Well, my dad was with the artillery in France and he said the Germans were awfully good with mortars back then."

"For now I'll tell you this much -- the Germans are very adept with that form of artillery." He glanced down at his empty sleeve. "Very adept. But so are we . . . with all our artillery, not just mortars. In fact, we have a lot more medium and heavy artillery than they do and we're very, very good with it. We'll get into that in detail in one of the next sessions."

As I left, I was glum. The lectures and a couple of field exercises out in the corn stubble wouldn't hurt. But I couldn't see it getting these soft-boiled eggheads ready for Wehrmacht.

# # #

"Hey, Sarge," Forster asked that evening, "I've got an idea how to really get the guys toughened up. What if Bay Six started running the mile by itself every morning and included the Fourteenth Street hill in our run?"

"Holy shit, Mike, do you think they could do it?"

"Yeah, I think so. They'll bitch about it like crazy at first."

"Well it's not going to improve our popularity," I said. "But I doubt if they'll bitch a lot."

"Why, Sarge?"

"They won't have the breath."

Chapter 7
January 31, 1944 -- Lawrence, Kansas

"Sir, the news from Anzio worries me," Sgt. Bowyer said. "The Fifth Army was supposed to take Rome in a week, but then they run up against this Monte Cassino place."

It was Monday night and snow was swirling against the window of Capt. Maxwell's office. He and Sgt. Bowyer and I were talking as they shared some the captain's Four Roses. I was sipping a Dad's root beer.

"You're right Frank," the captain said. "It sounds like a damned stalemate and I bet they'll draw on us for replacements . . . maybe all of them."

"Cap'n," I said, "I'm afraid you're right. I think Gen. Marshall is just beginning to see how costly it is, going toe-to-toe with the Jerries. The Wehrmacht is the first team . . . lots of veteran NCOs and company grade officers." I was thinking back to the Afrika Korps corporal with my M1. "They're tougher than shoe leather and very efficient."

Bowyer interjected. "You've heard the old British Army saying."

"What's that?"

"You don't know war until you've fought Germans."

"Umm." Capt. Maxwell and I nodded.

"Well, I've got an idea," Bowyer said. "Sir, I think we ought to place a couple of calls and see that if it's going to happen, that maybe we can get these kids shipped at least in squads.

"Look," he said. "Half of 'em is gonna wind up being casualties. But if they all get sent to some damned repple-depple and get stuck as odd man out with some broken-down bunch, they'll *all* get killed. No kidding, sir! It takes time to work into a squad. And if they're single replacements in some squad that don't know or give a good God damn about them, they won't last five minutes."

Capt. Maxwell sighed. "Right again, Frank, but I wouldn't know who the hell to call. I'm only a reservist. After I recovered, they let me stay on only because I got my congressman to pester them constantly."

Bowyer took an incautious swallow of Four Roses and coughed. "Waaow . . . that's smoothhhh!" Then he grinned, tilting his glass and rattling the ice cubes. "Sir, I been in this man's Army going on 26 years and I kept my ear to the ground. I've got a lot of fat, old time-serving buddies in Washington who push personnel papers. Now I heard that Gen. Bradley . . ."

"Who? Omar Bradley?"

"The same, sir. I heard he's taking over First Army and that he's moving its HQ to England sometime this spring. So we can figure on him heading a cross-channel invasion come summer maybe. And some of my old NCO friends might could help us out – maybe ship these kids as groups rather than individuals."

"Frank, if you can wire something like that, have at it."

"Sir," Sgt. Bowyer said, "I would ask a favor."

"Yeah, I know. You want to go with them."

"Me and Dud here together, sir. He earned his stripes in North Africa. We're both fully recuperated. We can nursemaid at least some of these kids part of the way. Besides, we owe the Krauts."

"Well, what the hell am I going to do without you guys?"

I chimed in. "Sir, you've got plenty of four-eyed clerk-typists that can take care of pay and travel orders and all that crap. But I think that once the Army closes with the Krauts in France, Washington will pull the chain and ASTP will empty out like a flushed crapper.

"Frank says he hears they've already cut way back on flight schools. Guys that signed up to fly now have a choice of rifle, machine gun or mortar. I think it might make sense to make our boys available now if they could move in groups."

"It's gonna get lonely around here," the captain mused, sipping and glancing up at the ceiling. "Frank," he said, at length. "Go ahead tomorrow and make your calls. And do a favor for me if you can."

"Yessir," Bowyer said. "I'll see if they've got a slot for you, too. I think the Pentagon's going to need lots of veteran officers."

# # #

"It's beginning to sound like you were right, Betty." I was walking her to the house from the bus stop. "We might ship out."

"Oh, God," she said. After a pause, "Well, it had to happen someday. Have they said when?"

"No, but probably pretty soon."

"Do you know where?"

"Not yet."

"Well, I take my RN board exams late next month. I don't think I'll be too far behind you."

# # #

It was about 0230 when I burst out of my room in a boiling rage. Switching on the squad bay lights I bellowed, "Alright, goddammit! Who's got the cat? That goddamned meowing is driving me crazy. I can't sleep."

They all sat up in their sacks looking puzzled and disgruntled at the same time.

"I'm not kidding," I yelled. "Who the hell has a cat in here?"

Torrelli said, "I do, Sarge. It's only a stray. I was just . . . "

"I don't care. It's against regulations. Get rid of it or I'll wring its little neck for you. Clear?"

"Okay, Sarge! Okay! Jeeze!" He got up, carrying the little fur ball, and headed down the hallway still in his skivvies.

I switched off the lights and headed back to my rack. But I couldn't sleep.

If I did, I'd be right back in my old bedroom when the insistent mewing awakened me.

And the same old story, knuckling my eyes as I sat up in bed. *A stray? Sounds like the little devil's starving.* All the same, it didn't sound quite like a kitten. Just as I threw off the sheet, a muffled thud puzzled me. Then another mew.

Tiptoeing to the top of stairs, I was surprised – it was 3 a.m. but light from the kitchen shown on the living room floor. Another thud. More mewing. *What the hell?* Louder now. *Hey, that's not a cat!*

Squinting, I turned into the lit kitchen and forgot all about saucer and milk.

Mom was mewing.

Because of my hero.

His huge thick fingers were biting into her cheeks, left palm stifling her cries.

He pinned her head against his left chest as his steepled right fist slammed her. Thud! Thud! Thud! Her split eyebrow bled freely down her face onto his hand. Her eyes widened as she glimpsed me. He turned his head toward me.

Too late, Dad.

Chapter 8
February 12, 1944 -- Lawrence, Kansas

Sleet pinged on our helmets as we stood in long files, waiting to board the train. Queued there with the rest was Sixth Squad: Forster, Bob Bull, Evans, Torrelli, Stanley Jacobs, Robbie Frost, Billy Halls, Charlie Whitehorse – our genuine half-wild Indian – plus Timmer, Stanislaus Manthei and me.

We wore brown calf-length greatcoats cinched by cartridge belts. Each of us had a full canteen and a full musette bag on his shoulders. Everybody was subdued – except Torrelli. The Italian fizzed like a bottle of hot soda pop because we were under orders issued by the New York Embarkation Authority. "See those words. 'New York'? I'm going to show you boys some great night spots, and get this! In New York, you don't have to be 21 to drink."

"Yeah?" Manthei said. "Five bucks says we go right aboard some rust bucket without a chance to see anything."

As they wrangled about whether we'd get passes, I spotted two women walking along the tattered snow fence that separated us from the public. I tapped Forster and jerked my thumb over my shoulder. "Eleanor's here, Mike. Mrs. Maxwell brought her. You got maybe two minutes."

"Thanks, Sarge." Forster broke ranks and leaned over the fence, pulling Eleanor's face to his. Weeping, she clung to him.

"I'm sorry to be such a crybaby . . ."

"God, your cheeks are freezing," he said. He pulled the gloves off his big paws to warm her face.

"It's okay, Dear," she sobbed, tightening her arms around him and burying her face in his chest again. "I'll warm up back at the house."

The squad started to climb into the Pullman and I tapped his shoulder again. "Sorry Mike. Sorry Eleanor. We got to go. Hey, Eleanor, please give my love to Betty."

"I will Dud."

"I'm sorry, Sweetheart," Forster said. "I'll write as often as I can."

Handkerchief to her eyes, she nodded violently. "I'll write every day. Try to be safe."

"I will. I'm looking out for Number One, which is both you and me." I was about to say love doesn't stop shrapnel or 8 MM rifle slugs, but bit it off,

Mike returned to line beside me. He glanced back and saw them walk toward Capt. Maxwell's old green Lafayette, Eleanor's head on Mrs. Maxwell's shoulder. Their torture made me damned glad Betty and I got it over with last night.

Forster slumped into a seat beside. Forster put his helmet on the table and laid the OD stocking cap over his desolate face. "You okay, buddy?" Torrelli whispered.

Forster snapped, "Leave me be."

We were lucky. Ours was an 80-seat lounging car, seats in groups of four facing across tables so we could play cards or put our legs on the tables in order to stretch out and snooze. God knows we had nothing else to do.

We couldn't watch the scenery because the Pullman's windows were coated thick with gray paint. Naturally, the boy geniuses started arguing whether the army was trying to keep the countryside secret from us or trying to keep all the Nazi spies – presumably an espionage cell at every crossing – from seeing that GIs were aboard this train.

Timmer said neither – that it just was a typical stupid policy of That Man in the White House. Timmer hated President Roosevelt with a passion and didn't care who knew it. "Remember that one speech he gave? He told us, 'To one generation, much is given. To another generation, much is taken. This generation of Americans has a rendezvous with destiny.'

"Now what the hell is that supposed to mean? Really? I think it means this train load of GIs has a bloody rendezvous with the Wehrmacht."

Torrelli jumped to the administration's defense and, within 30 seconds, we had a shouting match on our hands. It took about five minutes to get the pair to pipe down.

As the train finally jerked to a start, Bull said that even the stupidest Nazi probably already figured American soldiers were being shipped by rail to the east coast, so the paint was there to keep us from seeing the countryside and getting homesick.

Manthei, who usually was pretty quiet, said they were all wrong. "I bet they use these trains to take German and Italian POWs out to Arizona and Nevada. I hear that's where they're keeping them."

Whitehorse – who sometimes claimed to be Apache and sometimes Navajo – said Manthei was right. "The goddamn *chagnash* is driving Injuns off our reservations again."

"The what?

Whitehorse looked up with a snide grin. "*Chagnash*. It means 'long knives,'" white man. You know. Custer?"

Forster snapped at them to shut up so I punched him in the shoulder, hard. "Snap out of it, Mike. You think you're the only guy here that left a girl behind? Get busy right now. Write your first letter to Eleanor. Keep it cheerful. Make it funny.

"Meanwhile, we got about two hours before we get to Union Station in Kansas City and a whole new load of troops gets on. So let's get these guys together – get the best seats, maybe some sleeping space rotation. It's gonna be a long, long ride before we get to the east coast."

"Well, hell, won't we get off for . . ."

"Not this trip, Mike. The word is we'll just keep rolling, picking up troops as we go – Jefferson City, Missouri, St. Louis . . ."

"Where's that?" Timmer asked.

"Jeff City? It's halfway across Missouri. That's where we'll pick up kids from Colombia -- the University of Missouri -- and then after St. Louis, on through Illinois, Indiana and Ohio, Pennsylvania and New York. Lot different from my first trip."

I told them that early in 1942, I was with the First Infantry Division when it shipped by rail from Florida to Pennsylvania. "It was a long haul," I said. "But there wasn't so much rush back then. On coal stop sidings, our battalion got out, stripped to T-shirts and shorts and did the Daily Dozen."

"God, I'll bet the train smelled like a pig pen," Forster said.

"Oh, it wasn't too bad. We could open the windows then. And then each time out of the train, we got a quick water tower shower. Only about 30 seconds in groups of 10, but it helped. Now, though, we're staying aboard at coal stops. Besides, it's too damned cold for outdoor showers."

"Hey, Sarge?" It was Evans.

"What?"

"Who's this Kilroy joker?"

"What are you talking about?"

He pointed to the ceiling of the car where someone had written 'Kilroy was here'.

"Beats the hell out of me. Last I saw, he left a sign on the back of the bus driver's seat in Lawrence."

"I'll get busy," Forster groaned. He stood up, "Hey, guys! We got a long trip so let's get organized." I grinned and sat back. It was nice having somebody do my work for me.

After Kansas City, half the men slept, oblivious to a noisy crap game on the floor. Halls tried to start group singing but after the third round of *I've Got Sixpence* Evans threatened to bust him in the mouth.

Meanwhile, I shook my head because a bridge foursome was arguing heatedly about bidding.

"I can't believe this shit," I whispered to Forster. "Dogfaces playing bridge? The army's just gone to hell."

Forster grinned, "It sounds like a lot different crowd from you boys that landed in Algeria and Morocco."

"Damned right, and it scares the crap out of me. I don't know if these kids can deal with Germans. A lot of our guys were tough. They'd been scrabbling for a living for years, hooking rides in boxcars, dodging railroad bulls, working outdoors with the CCC. They paid attention to orders. But these damn college kids, first off, are soft and, second, every time you give an order, they got to know why."

"Well, maybe our boys aren't so soft after spending a month running the Fourteenth Street hill."

"Yeah, but Mike that's nothing compared to combat," I said. "Just nothing." I paused, thinking back to Tunisia.

"Being a farm boy, Mike, you'll probably be okay. You're tough -- used to hard work and bad weather. But some of these kids – well, we'll see what happens the first time they have to take cover behind a manure pile or in a sewage drain."

"Sarge," Forster interrupted, "just what do we really have to look out for when we go into combat."

I reached into my musette bag and pulled out the infantryman's bible, FM 7-10. "I'm gonna give you this, Mike. It tells you what the infantry does -- a hell of a lot of good info. Still, it doesn't tell you what combat's really like, because it can't explain what the other side does in response.

"The thing about combat, Mike, is you got to keep very alert – even when you're exhausted, which you mostly are. You go into a town, you got to look out for snipers back inside the windows. You got to look out for booby traps everywhere you step -- kick open a door and you could get your foot blown off. You walk on paths or through fields, you got to look constantly for mines. Headed for a tree line? Don't! People with rifles and machine guns are waiting to open fire on you."

"Jesus," Forster said.

"Yep, you *better* pray to Jesus 'cause in the infantry you need all the help you can get."

"You heard me play down the Mauser rifle," I added, "but it's a good weapon and the 8 mm – actually it's 7.92 mm, but they call it 8 -- is every bit as good as our 30-06, which is 7.62 mm.

"You've heard about the MG-42, of course. I hear tell the Krauts got a new thing, the Screaming Meemie – some kind of rockets or something.

"But, Mike, you already asked about the worst things -- mortars. They're one of the nastiest weapons around and the Krauts are real Sgt. Yorks with them. You might be close enough to hear them fire, but you usually can't hear the shells coming down on you the way you can hear bigger artillery."

"So what do you do about them, Sarge?"

"Use that million-dollar brain. Look, the Krauts love to suck the enemy into a kill zone and then blast hell out of them from all sides.

"So put yourself in Jerry's shoes. Figure where he wants you to advance and pick another route. You examine the ground as you move."

"What do you mean?"

By now, Timmer and Halls were listening.

I pointed at the floor, "I'm talking about the dirt right there in front of you. If you're headed for a wall to take cover, or want to duck behind some logs, keep your eye peeled for a crater or two – just a hole in the dirt about the size of a soup bowl. If you see them, steer clear.

"See, a mortar shell just leaves a little bitty crater, but it sprays about 500 pieces of razor-sharp steel in all directions. They can rip the meat from your legs – right down to the bone. That's how Cap'n Maxwell lost his arm. So look for some little craters where they fired for registration."

"Registration?"

"Jesus, don't you punks know anything? When a mortar crew sets up, they fire a round or two to make sure they're on target. That's registering. So registration craters are your clue to take another route.

"Look, Mike, here's the best advice I can give. It's straight from Sgt. Bowyer: Don't ever take the easy way . . . because Jerry either mines it or registers it for a mortar barrage."

I poked him in the chest.

"Or both!"

Chapter 9
February 18, 1944 – On The Road

As we pulled out of St. Louis, our car was near full. Sixth Squad clustered in the right center of the car to get the benefit of what little sun got through the painted south windows.

Forster had his nose buried in FM 7-10.

A monster of a soldier with a slightly smaller buddy came into the car – both still wearing their packs. He looked around casually, and then demanded that Halls and Timmer give up their seats. Halls, seated next to the window, started to get up, but Timmer put a hand on his chest and pushed him back. "Go find your own seat, Buddy," he said, "just like the rest of us did." The man grabbed Timmer's arm and hauled him into the aisle.

"Hey!" Forster yelled, getting up to intervene, but Timmer held up a hand to forestall him.

Timmer turned back and looked up at the interloper's face. "Are you in earnest?" he asked quietly.

"Oh, oh. Look out," Forster said.

The soldier looked down at Timmer, snorted, and said, "Hell yes, I'm in earnest."

"Just checking," Timmer said.

He screwed up his eyes and tilted his head as if searching for a word. Suddenly he grabbed the man's cartridge belt, yanking it toward him, while slamming the heel of the other hand up against the intruder's jaw.

The soldier wheeled his arms to keep balance but fell straight back, landing on his butt and pack. His helmet rolled against his companion's feet. The companion started to move toward Timmer. But Halls, now standing, balled his fists and warned, "I wouldn't."

The rest of Sixth Squad – including the bridge foursome – was on its feet, ready to 'splain things to the newcomers.

Instead of fighting, the man on the floor propped himself up on his elbows. He rubbed his jaw and looked at Timmer with a mystified grin. "Damn, that was good. How the hell did you do it?"

Through the laughter that followed, Timmer pointed at me. "Sarge taught me."

"Yeah," Torrelli taunted. "He taught us lots of other stuff, too."

The man got up, grinned and held out his hand to shake with Timmer. "I'm Charley Wilson. This here is Karl Nau. Suppose we could stay with you guys on this car? I'd like to learn some of this."

"I'm Marty Timmer. It's a free country. If you can find a place, you're welcome."

Seeing the whole squad jump up like that, ready to defend a buddy, eased my concern a bit. It was the first time I'd seen them act like soldiers. Maybe there was hope for them. It occurred to me that if they had an enemy to hate, they would unite and start pulling together.

An hour later, God provided.

God's gift to Squad Six was Richard B. Schiltz, an Army Reserve captain and a USDA-certified Grade A prick.

Picture an idiot who seemed to think it was his job to treat enlisted people like dirt. I don't know why. Maybe he was paying back some guy who kicked sand in his face at the beach. Maybe his mom caught him beating off.

Or maybe girls wouldn't go out with him.

Easy to see why. He looked vaguely like a vulture, carrying his head lowered and thrust forward, peering suspiciously with glittering, hooded eyes. He also had paper-thin lips and a squawky voice – sort of like a file chafing corrugated iron. And he was jittery, reminding me of one of those yappy little dogs that barks at the doorbell, the mailman, kids on tricycles, anything.

He had no sense of humor. In fact, I'd say he had no sense at all. He supposedly was an accountant by training.

In my book, he was a bureaucratic sadist who used rules to balloon his own ego. How the jerk got a commission, let alone in the infantry, is beyond me. But the U.S. Army was expanding a thousand-fold in two years, so a certain number of foul balls who never should have made Pfc. wound up with bars on their shoulders. And we got stuck with this one.

I think it was about five seconds after our first encounter that Timmer stuck the captain with his nickname: The Dick.

Anyhow, Capt. Schiltz marched into our railway car minutes after Wilson and Timmer had their set-to. He lit into the first man he saw, a kid near the door, dozing with his feet up on a table. "Call this car to attention!"

The kid jerked awake. "What?"

"Private, you call me SIR!"

The kid jumped up and braced to attention, hardly awake. "Sorry, sir. Sir, what is it you want?"

The Dick acted as if he were in a rage. "Damn it, I ordered you to call this car to attention! Now!"

By then I stood up and bellowed, "Tenn-HUT!"

Everybody came to their feet, but that wasn't enough. He kept all of us standing while he chewed the poor kid a new one. Then he demanded to know who was in charge of the car.

"I am, sir! Sgt. Allan Dudley."

"What unit?"

He knew the answer as well as I did, but he wanted to show he was boss, so I rapped it off for him. "First and Second platoons, Able Company, 58th Replacement Battalion, sir!"

Unfortunately, that's just when one of the craps players bent over to snatch his winnings off the floor. The Dick's squawk went an octave higher into a grating squeal. "Soldier, you are supposed to remain at the position of attention. What's that in your hand? Money? You were gambling!"

"No sir," the gambler lied. "I was just counting my back pay."

"You're lying! By God, I know you're lying! Gambling is a court-martial offense. I'm going to punish this whole car. At the next stop, both platoons in this car will do a five-mile run."

"Cap'n!" I yelled in my loudest parade-ground bellow, "We are not permitted to disembark until this train reaches its destination." That made him blow his stack, bleating about the lack of respect for superiors in this miserable excuse for an army. He ordered me to accompany him to the command car for a dressing down by the major.

Look, military life means doing a hell of lot of things nobody wants to do. Most officers I've met recognize this and, when they can, they leave the troops alone. But this other kind of officer, The Dick type, seems intent on making life hell for enlisted people for the same reason a dog licks his balls -- just because he can.

And, in The Dick's case, I think it also was because he could not competently carry out orders from his own superiors. So when one of his superiors chewed him, he just kept rolling it right on downhill. If he was to suffer, why not kick the dog by making life a living hell for everyone of lower rank?

At any rate, the train's troop commander, Maj. Kelly, turned out to be a decent National Guardsman, probably an insurance salesman in his civilian career. He looked irked as he listened to The Dick. He asked me why I was allowing the men to gamble. "I don't permit it, sir," I lied. "We had two bridge foursomes going, but I never heard betting or saw money changing hands."

The major perked up. "Bridge, eh? Do any of your boys have masters' points?" I sensed an enthusiast.

"Sir, I wouldn't know. Not my game. But I sure can check."

He smiled. "Please do, sergeant, and report back. Maybe we can get a tournament going. Pass the time. Meanwhile, tell the men to exercise more discretion."

"I will, sir."

The Dick started to protest, "Discretion, sir? But gambling is a court-mar. . ."

"That's enough, Richard," the major said. "The men are bored. We all are. So just let it go. The issue is closed. Sgt. Dudley, you are dismissed. And don't forget to ask about master's points."

"I will, sir, and thank you." I saluted and did a smart about face, and left . . . not before I saw fury in The Dick's eyes.

We had our enemy.

To show what a prince he was, The Dick started arriving at odd hours, demanding that we come to attention and recite things like General Orders or the nomenclature of the M1 or the carbine.

On our last night before reaching the coast, The Dick showed up with a set of aircraft silhouette cards and put us through recognition drill . . . as if Nazi Dorniers might be about to take out the Pittsburg rail yard.

As he went through the cards a second time, Timmer yanked his chain by deliberately misidentifying a Stuka as a B-17. The Dick gave the only grin I ever saw on his face. "Wrong, Private! Drop and give me 30."

By then, 30 push-ups was nothing to any of the guys. The game caught on. Whitehat proceeded to tag a B-24 as a Kondor bomber and, later, Halls said a Kondor was a Spitfire.

At first The Dick thought the errors were genuine, but Torrelli went too far, identifying an ME-109 as a Piper Cub. The car exploded in laughter. The men doing push-ups laughed so hard they collapsed to the floor.

After The Dick quelled the pandemonium, he yelled "For that, you're all going to do 50 push-ups in relays right here in the aisle."

The car went quiet. Then somebody near the back of the car with a deep voice – it could have been Bull -- said, "Cap'n, get your scrawny ass out of this car or we'll throw you right off this fucking train."

Except for the high-speed rattle of wheels over the joints in the rails, the car stayed dead silent. Eighty pairs of eyes fixed on The Dick.

The Dick turned pale. He looked right and left and spotted me. "Sergeant," he quavered, "get that man's name." He darted out the door.

He wasn't done with us . . . or me, but at least The Dick's pure spite was uniting the guys.

# # #

"Hey, Sarge, mind if I ask you a question?"

"Naw, Torrelli. Shoot."

"What do you have against cats?"

"Nothing. I've just got a real personal problem with the sounds kittens make."

"What's the problem?"

"I'm not . . . no offense, Vince, but it's none of your business."

Chapter 10
February 20, 1944 – Camp Kilmer, New Jersey

I figured we'd wind up at Camp Dix in New Jersey but our train chugged right past it. That disappointed me because I wanted a look at the Navy's Lakehurst airstrip where the Hindenburg Zeppelin crashed and exploded seven years before. They kept repeating the scene in all the movie newsreel intros.

Oh, well. Maybe next time.

We finally came to a siding in a place new to me – Camp Kilmer, also in New Jersey. As we climbed down the car's steps, I got the impression of a city rather than an army base. And brand new, at that.

Instead of standard Army Puke Yellow, the barracks and office buildings were all different colors. The fort seemed to extend for miles and crawled with men in dress brown or olive drab. Plus that, somebody had painted "Kilroy was here," right there on a vertical support on the loading dock.

"Who the hell is Kilroy, anyway?" Nau asked.

"Who give a damn?" Halls said. "Look at this place. Every soldier east of the Rockies must be coming here, every one headed to Europe."

"Man alive," Timmer said, "if Hitler could see this, he'd just pull his armies back inside Germany and try to negotiate a truce."

"Ohhh," I said, "don't count on that, young trooper."

Considering that the United States was moving a whole damned field army across the Atlantic – somewhere close to 200,000 men, not to mention all their food, their artillery, arms, bombs, clothing, fuel, ammo, tanks, planes -- we had to admit it all went pretty smoothly.

Oh, sure, we ran into some snafus. For instance, we got to Kilmer a whole day after they ran out of food on the train.

The boys bitched about being hungry, but it was just a ritual. By then they just wanted the hell off that train. Once out of the cars and lined up on the yellow stripes on the muster ground, The Dick started prancing around trying to send my platoons on his five-mile penalty run.

Fortunately, the major shushed him and Camp Kilmer's cadre routed us to a two-story barrack so new you still could smell pine resin. They had us drop all our gear on our bunks and marched us to a line outside the adjoining chow hall. It was good, solid hot army meat and potatoes and filled the void.

Then they sent us back to the barracks where we could shower, shave and feel human again. It wasn't long after we got cleaned up that one of the boys discovered the camp was named after a World War I soldier named Kilmer – first name Joyce, yet -- who also had been a poet. In the next 20 minutes I bet I heard about 25 soulful renditions of his poem *Trees*. Give me a break.

In the following week, they routed us during the mornings and early afternoons from one processing point to the next. Only one guy in the squad, Frost, fainted during the first assembly-line vaccinations.

After all the morning's processing, Sgt. Bowyer would bellow, "OK! Mandatory formation at the NCO Club!" At Kilmer, you didn't have to be 21 to drink beer and at a nickel a bottle you'd think they all would be guzzling. But most of these so-called soldiers didn't *like* beer. Instead, they'd go to one of the post theaters or recreation centers where the USO held dances.

Torrelli got a lady cousin to set up a bus tour into New York City. The bus actually was waiting outside the main gate with Torrelli's girlfriend as a tour guide when The Dick queered the deal. The bastard was in charge of quarters for the battalion that night. So he inspected our barracks, found something wrong with somebody's locker, and cancelled the whole squad's passes.

Torrelli was a hot-head, so it took four of us to restrain him from beating The Dick to a pulp. The man's pettiness infuriated everybody, but most of us were midwesterners so we didn't know Gotham or what we were missing.

The Dick overheard me and Forster plan a joint long-distance call to Eleanor and Betty. Apparently out of pure spite, he ordered a pair of MPs to arrest us on suspicion of theft of government property. When the MP's learned we had nothing in our possession but our uniforms and gear, they let us go with a warning . . . about what, I never figured out.

But it was enough for me.

Later I cornered The Dick alone on one of the company streets and told him if he tried just any more of his chickenshit involving my men, I'd go straight to the Inspector General.

"Pick on me all you want," I said, "but don't mess with my boys."

"They aren't *your* boys," The Dick sneered. "They're all property of the U.S. government."

"Wrong, Cap'n! They're not property. They're American citizens and you're going to be damned sorry if you don't stop fucking with them." He got red in the face and the veins in his temples bulged. "Just mark my words . . . *sir*." I walked away.

Forster and I finally got our long-distance call through to the girls and, afterwards, agreed it was a mistake.

They both cried as we talked and we couldn't do a thing about it. You know, when your girl cries you want to be able to at least give her a hug or hand her your handkerchief. The only thing I could do was use the orderly room typewriter to write a long, long letter to Betty and a shorter one to Mom and Sis.

Sometime during the week, the New York Port of Embarkation officially handed us over to Headquarters First Army, Bristol, England.

Now that excited me. My favorite boyhood book was *Treasure Island* and so I was eager to see the docks at Bristol where Squire Trelawney, Jim Hawkins and Long John Silver supposedly boarded the *Hispaniola*. I didn't realize the Luftwaffe had bombed whole sections of Bristol into interlocking craters.

With Bowyer's help in supplying some booze to a couple of admin sergeants, we managed to keep the squad together while adopting Wilson and his buddy, Nau, into it. The rough point came when they offered the boys a choice to be riflemen, machine gunners or mortar crewmen. It took some doing, but I persuaded them to sign up for mortars.

Halls, Evans and Whitehorse almost screwed the pooch when they said they didn't like the idea because they wouldn't be close enough to The Action. I shut them up, saying that if they survived two minutes of The Action they'd sell their own mothers for a job in the rear.

Others didn't want the job for the more practical reason that it meant hard work – carrying tubes, bipods, baseplates and clusters of mortar rounds, all 45-pound loads -- plus learning the intricacies of .50 and .30 caliber machine guns. For that matter, I had private doubts whether the choices that the clerks offered actually were real. The Army wanted all the footsloggers it could get because a modern army always seems to be short of riflemen rather than machine gunners or junior grade artillerymen.

But at least it kept the squad together. Only now, since we were becoming mortar crews, we officially became sections rather than squads.

And, I'll say this much for the kids. When we ran them through the short course on mortars, they quickly caught on to aiming stakes and azimuths, as well as to traversing and elevating. At first, they were pitifully slow assembling and leveling a 60 mm mortar. But they picked up speed and retained it even after we pressured them by yelling at the top of our lungs and declaring, say, half the crew to be wounded.

Mastering range cards and determining powder increments took just a bit longer.

"Look dummy, the further forward you incline the tube, the greater the range. The more propellant increments you put on a shell, the greater the range. The card shows you all the combinations for short, middle and long range. Get to know these cards. Now!"

But they were lazy.

Forster shamed them into the chore of digging solid recesses for the baseplate and bipods – something Germans always did. That's why Kraut mortar fire was so precise . . . and lethal.

He told them they'd damn well learn to dig and enjoy it. I backed him up, explaining so many First Division troops dug shallow trenches in Tunisia rather than deep foxholes – and then were squashed like roaches by Afrika Korps tanks rolling over their positions.

On Day Six at Kilmer, we received orders to board the *Queen Mary* to Scotland. The lads knew we wouldn't exactly be traveling in style . . . but, hey, it couldn't be all bad being's how the *Queen Mary* was a luxury liner, right?

They were excited and grinning, but I caught the eye of a transportation NCO who gave me a sardonic look and shake of his head. I warned the boys the trip probably would skimp on luxury.

My God, why did I have to be so right?

Since we now were to be mortar crewmen, we had to trade in our M1 rifles for pissant M1 carbines. But the lighter firearm made sense for men who'd be toting heavy mortar components.

On the eighth morning at Kilmer, we cleaned the barracks, turned in our bedding and repacked our duffel bags. We were on orders, meaning we had to stay in the barracks and could do nothing but smoke, sleep, read or shoot the bull. At dusk we boarded another train which took us and all our gear to a ferry.

Torrelli still was furious about not being able to go into The City – as if it was the only city on earth. As we crossed the Hudson, third in a line of ferries, he tried to point out the sights. But it was a cold, windy, rolling ride. Halls got seasick and upchucked on Nau who swore bitterly at him. All I could see was a great many lights.

Big deal.

But as we drew near the east shoreline, we began making out huge ship silhouettes.

Chapter 11
February 27, 1944 – The Queen

Supposedly for security reasons, it was after dark when all the ferries moored at the Brooklyn Army Terminal – as if they would carry troops to any other location. Torrelli wanted to show us some sight or other, but a line of MPs with nightsticks and holstered .45s blocked the terminal building doors. One barked, "Where do you think you're going, Mac?"

We got the message.

So much for New York sight-seeing.

We formed up and marched for 10 minutes, duffle bags on our shoulders, along dimly-lit puddled docks beneath towering cranes.

When we got to the *Queen*, that enormous overhanging bow blotted out the stars above us. They had us in four columns and it was just a case of following the guy ahead of you as we wound like ants up the gangways and through the massive entry port. Right above the entry, I saw a painted message that Kilroy had been there, too.

One minute later I felt sorry for the poor bastard . . . and for us, too.

We found ourselves in a dim cavernous hold with forests of vertical pipes supporting tiers of five and six stretched-canvas bunks. But stepping inside the *Queen Mary* took our breath away for another reason.

It was hot as hell and the stink was beyond belief – all the sharp nasty odors of close-packed humanity . . . close-packed sweating, farting, vomiting humanity.

That's when I could tell again that Forster was a natural leader. His face tightened at the stench, but before the kids could even start bitching, he browbeat them into keeping together so they could live as a unit.

They kept beating their gums, but followed his lead in trying to make the best of it. Manthei claimed the Army had led us to the Underworld . . . that I was Sgt. Charon who ferried them across the River Styx. Torrelli said we'd found a new level of hell that some other Wop named Dante never got around to describing.

We had to pile everything -- duffle bags, musette bags, steel helmets and all our other gear – either on the bunks or on the deck between bunk tiers. Walking was almost impossible. It was a case of using racks as ladders to climb over obstacles and above the marathon crap games that occupied the only clear deck spaces. Pretty soon you got used to boots stamping the edge of your rack, or even your fingers, as some guy worked his way spider-like from his rack to the latrines – sorry, the swabbies called them 'heads.'

The *Queen* didn't have enough racks, so I had to arrange sleeping rotations for Section Six. And even trying to sleep was a cast-iron bitch. It was so hot we had to strip to our skivvies to sleep, and our sweat soaked the canvas racks right through. Each rack bore multiple man-sized salt ring silhouettes.

One limey sailor told me the *Queen* had ferried soldiers by the tens of thousands all over the world for five solid years and hadn't had a good airing the whole time. The guy, one of those pricks who delights in adding to others' misery, said that when the British refitted the *Queen* as a troop ship, they removed the hull stabilizers to increase her speed.

"So, mate," he said casually, "she rolls a bit, like. Abaht 'alf the troops is seasick all of the time, and all of 'em is seasick at least some of the time. We ain't got the forced-draft blowers to air out the auld bitch and we can't just open 'er up and let 'er air out 'cause all the port 'oles is brazed shut, like. So we're 'eaded for Scotland now. Seven-day run. And then we'll be steamin' back to New York wiv' a lot of ripe Fritz prisoners from Sicily all locked down snug and tight. Then seven days back wiv' 15,000 more of you Yanks and so on. My advice, chum? Don't eat nothink afore we gets to Scotland."

"Thanks, buddy."

"My pleasure, Yank, I'm sure."

I warned the boys of my experience going to Africa in a 100-ship convoy. Half-way across the Atlantic, some poor bastard on our troop ship started clowning around on deck and managed to fall overboard. No vessel stopped to rescue him. Nobody even threw him a life ring.

"Now, boys, we are *not* in a convoy, so if you fall overboard, what do you think will happen?"

"There's no convoy so the *Queen* can stop?" Wilson asked.

"Wilson, do you really think the skipper's going to risk the lives of his crew and 15,000 soldiers for your carcass? No, you'd be taking a long swim."

"Yeah," Timmer added, "a long, long, long, *reallly* long swim."

Fortunately the men got an airing now and then when they conducted topside lifeboat drills. But as icy cold as it was on the top decks, it was all we could do to make the troops return to the Underworld. During one drill, I got to chat with Bowyer. As a platoon sergeant he rated being in a stateroom with a dozen other NCOs. Being a mere buck sergeant, I had to bunk with the troops.

He said once we got ashore he'd put me in touch with a First Division sergeant-major he knew, after that I'd be on my own trying to get a good assignment for an intact pair of mortar sections.

My status as a sergeant ended the third day out. The Dick came snooping below, found a crap game near our bunks. They weren't my men, but he dragged all of them and me before the troop commander, an icy brigadier general. In a summary court martial, the general reprimanded the men, had the money allotted in equal amounts to their separation pay. Then he not only fined me $25 but also busted me to corporal. Apparently it didn't matter that the men weren't my sections or that poker and crap games were underway in all the other holds.

The Army can be like that at times

The Dick smirked as I gave him a murderous look when leaving the general's office. *You'll get yours.*

By the first day out, we discovered that yes – just as the Limey swabbie said – the *Queen* did roll a bit. Being without convoy or escorts, she zig-zagged at 30 knots the whole way in the still-stormy Atlantic. Climbing in or out of a top rack during a 25-degree roll or a high-speed turn was a hell of an agility test.

I was fortunate in having a strong stomach but Halls, Jacobs and Manthei were among those troops who were sick all the time. Timmer at least retained his sense of humor, claimed he had upchucked everything including last Thanksgiving's turkey with all the trimmings. He said he also thought he recognized pecan pie . . . an observation that caused two listeners to start heaving all over again.

Forster got a bit green around the gills, but sturdily maintained that there was no illness aboard at all. "It's just that a lot of people are calling out the name of a missing soldier," he said. "Listen carefully, guys! You can hear them now: 'Raaaaalph! Raalph Braaaack!'"

We NCOs did the best we could for the seasick people. We kept them busy mopping the decks. Otherwise, the pools of vomit made the decks dangerously slick. Mopping didn't do a thing to reduce five years of troop-carrying stench, but the idea was to keep the poor bastards busy so that at least their misery didn't seem to last as long.

Basically, they all went through the same progressive stages of sea-sickness. First they feared they would die. Then they feared they wouldn't die. Then they recovered.

Once we were in the approaches to Scotland's Clyde River, they let us all come topside to air out.

Now scenery doesn't easily impress me, but my God it was beautiful – rugged foothills to the north capped with snow that looked fiery in the sunset. The greens were so incredibly green and the slopes were just about every purple and blue you could imagine.

"Boys," Timmer said, "I think we have just arrived in the Emerald City."

"Well," Torrelli said, "I don't see any Yellow Brick Road, but for damn sure we ain't in Kansas anymore."

Chapter 12
March 6, 1944 – Gourock, Scotland

It was just shy of 1000 hours the next day when they let us sardines start prying ourselves from the *Queen's* forward hold. One of the Limeys told us that even then the *Queen* still was a quarter full.

We straggled out of the gangway onto a ferry boat – the Limeys called it a lighter. It was coal-fired and scruffier than our New York ferry, but we could have cared less. We were in cold clean air and out of all that stink.

The expressions on the faces of the lighter crew showed that despite the sulfurous coal smoke of their own vessel, their noses picked up a good deal of the stench that had impregnated our uniforms.

"We'll give you Yanks a good airing," one of them said, "and you'll be right glad of it."

At least I think that's what he said. Some of us had a hard time with the local accents. Wilson told the sailor that he always thought the people of Scotland spoke English. The tar looked at him with a grin and very slowly and patiently said, "Weel mate, it may strain your credulity a wee bit, but we thought the same thing aboot you bluidy colonials." It gave everybody a chuckle.

In the 20-minute run to the Gourock waterfront, the lighter threaded its way among freighters, tankers and naval vessels ranging from battleships to corvettes.

Even though the bay was almost flat calm, Halls got sick again . . . or I guess I should say he stayed sick. At least this time he could throw up over the railing.

Gourock wasn't what you'd call charming. To begin with, it was an ugly old harbor town. It also had its own lingering stench -- from fires thanks to German bombing.

One of the sailors said the bombers always dropped their loads on the town because they didn't dare approach the overpowering flak from so many ships in the harbor. Our first glimpse of the place was of long rows of scruffy docks and drab warehouses . . . pure paradise compared to the *Queen's* hold. As we struggled ashore with our gear, a British Army band complete with pipers – kilts, rattling drums and all -- played a couple of marches for us, a tremendous welcome even if you don't like the pipes, which I don't.

Some of the boys thought the sentries on the dock looked too short and scrawny for their long Enfield rifles.

"Hey!" Whitehorse yelled. "You think short men can't fight?"

They got the point because nobody in our gang ever dared mess with our Apache-Navajo.

Even ashore, we probably still carried a good deal of the *Queen's* rank odors, but you wouldn't have known it from our reception.

As we tried to relax on the quay – we knew there'd be a long wait because there's always a long wait -- dozens of smiling women descended upon us with cheery greetings that were hard to understand.

They carried pots of hot milky-looking tea and clearly were happy to see us and serve us their national beverage.

And when a nearby squaddy groused that it was "aboot time the bluidy Yanks picked up their end of the stick," a lady volunteer who looked about 70 told him to stick a sock in it.

And as we carried our tea back to sit on our duffle bags, she waved. "Bay-bay, lads. Mind ye tek care, noo." The welcome and the tea gave us all a cheering, warm feeling.

Another lighter tied up at the dock to unload a lot of lady soldiers. Just like us, they wore overcoats, packs and steel helmets beneath which their faces looked tiny, sweet and delicate, even the Brunhildas in the bunch.

They got the same reception from the pipers only this time the band marched as it played. So we got to hear *Scotland the Brave* all over again, or maybe the *Dirge of Hamish MacNish* or some such. As they started the *Lament of Loch Lomand* one of the girls at the back of the group, a tech sergeant, turned around and winced. I went over to ask her whether their group happened to include a 1st Lt. Betty Edwards.

"No, sorry, corporal! We aren't nurses – we're soldiers. We're WACs, typists, encoders."

Just then The Dick showed up to chew me out. "*Corporal* Dudley, there's no fraternization between male and female enlisted personal. Now I want a half-hour of close-order drill for your sections. Leave your duffle bags in line and run your drill right here along this dock. Yes, and keep your packs on. I'll be inside the warehouse here watching."

It actually wasn't a bad idea to get our blood moving after being virtually imprisoned on the *Queen* for a week atop another week on the train.

But from the Roman army to today, it's the mark of a dolt for an officer to criticize an NCO in front of his own men. And he was being such a bastard about it, singling out my sections in front of hundreds of other troops, WACs included, just because he hated my guts . . . or maybe just because he wanted to show the WACs what a big man he was.

So I starting drilling them, calling cadence loudly as if maneuvering a whole company on a parade ground. It was about two minutes before a first sergeant showed up to take in the scene.

He disappeared, reappearing soon with a hard-faced infantry captain and a tall, portly man in a khaki uniform without insignia. The captain, named Freeman, ordered me to stop and asked why I was doing close-order drill during a British Army ceremony. When he found out what was going on, he ordered me to dismiss the men.

"Is this ordinary?" the civilian asked.

"No, Senator. You don't harass the troops when they're in transit and you surely don't interrupt another army's program. Everybody's got enough problems as it is."

"Well, maybe you can put a little salt on that officer's tail."

"Yessir, I will. Meanwhile, here are these WACs that you wanted to greet."

"Ah, yes." The senator began to move among the WACS, shaking hands, introducing himself, grinning and chatting.

The captain inquired about my sections, I explained we were ASTP orphans.

"I'm a regular, sir, and we got these boys pretty well checked out on mortars and I'm in hopes of keeping them out of a repple-depple by getting them adopted into somebody's heavy weapons company."

"How long you been in the Army, corporal?"

"Since the Krauts invaded Poland, sir. I was with First Army in North Africa and got wounded. They bumped me up to sergeant as one of the ASTP cadre at the University of Kansas."

"No, shit? You were at KU?"

"Yessir. Why?"

He gave me a nasty smile. "Well, I just happen to be an ROTC grad of the University of Missouri."

"Oh, crap, sir! I guess we better just disappear into the crowd."

He chuckled. "I won't hold it against you. How come you're a corporal again?"

I could see The Dick watching from a warehouse doorway and nodded toward him. "Because The Dick – sorry, sir – because that captain over there who had us drilling just now, hauled me up for a summary court after he spotted some troops 50 feet from me shooting craps aboard the *Queen*."

"You call him The Dick?"

"His first name is Richard, sir, and I better not go any further into that."

He grinned and then chewed his lip for a minute. "Now look, Corporal, I'm up here to take some of these boys," he waved his arm at a line of soldiers, "down south to the 4th Division. The 4th got here in January and we still are short-handed.

"So, I'm with the 8th Infantry Regiment which is part of the 4th. If your boys can cut it, they might fit in my outfit, D Company, 1st Battalion -- heavy weapons.

"We need two mortar sections yet. But, believe me, if you come with us, you'll work like dogs. Our regimental CO, Col. Van Fleet, is a West Pointer. He demands perfection. So I do too."

"Got it, sir. These kids are real bright – all of them. I'll make damn sure they work into the team. They're already pretty well drilled with 60 mm mortars, and they'd do just fine with the 81. We'll have to work up on radio procedure, but that's about it.

"On the plus side," I added, "about half of us speak pretty good German."

"Really!" he said. "Well, that might come in handy. Cpl. Dudley, have your sections stay in place. I'll look into it right now."

Within the hour, I was marching the boys to a train and could tell them we might have a home.

Forster asked, "What do you mean by 'might,' Sarge."

"Forster, I'm a corporal, not a sergeant . . ."

"I know, but it just seems more natural to call you Sarge."

"Yeah, well . . . back to your question. It's just this: we're joining a rough company in a tough regiment. We'll have to earn our place or they'll ship us off with the rest of the garbage to a repple-depple. That means all of us are going to measure up. Clear?"

"So where are we headed now?" Bull asked.

"Beats the hell out of me. I'll tell you when we get there."

Chapter 13
March 8, 1944 – Devonshire, England

The RAF and U.S. Army Air Corps had pretty well stopped German air raids over England last year. But the British railway system still was under repair, so it took two days to get us from Gourok in Scotland to Plymouth on England's south coast.

But it was a beautiful trip.

Even though far too many GIs acted like jerks, you could tell most of the English still were happy to see us. Whether walking or on bikes, kids or old folks, they smiled and waved as our train passed them and, later, in our truck convoys.

And even though the weather still was a bit brisk, the countryside was beautiful -- neat thatch-roof cottages, little shops in narrow little towns, tree-lined lanes with stone walls, estates that were almost three centuries old, beautiful old churches and, here and there, some real honest-to-God castles. After a week aboard the *Queen*, the scenery was sheer luxury.

"Forster," I said, "with that big nose sniffing out the window that way, you remind me of an old bird dog."

"Aww, Dud. It's the smell of spring. I can tell that it's planting time. Makes me homesick."

That didn't apply in Plymouth, though. One of the biggest ports and naval bases, it was like Gourock in that it still reeked of fire. Looking around as he got off the train, Timmer said, "Jeeze, is this place a dump, or what?"

"Shut the hell up," Forster snapped. "In case you never read the papers or listened to Edward R. Murrow, the Nazis bombed this country for three solid years. Seems to me they're holding together real good. Look at 'em! Skinny as hell because of rationing, but they're walking tall."

"Okay! Okay, Forster. Don't have a shit fit. I'm sorry."

Forster said that since 1941, his folks had been sending food to cousins living outside London. He hoped some time to be able to visit them.

A convoy of deuce-and-a-half trucks dropped us off at another processing center well outside the town. That's where we linked up with Capt. Freeman who ordered us taken to a barracks out on Dartmoor itself – an eerie, craggy landscape dotted with odd granite formations and seemingly hundreds of military camps.

It was almost 1600 when we finally piled out of our truck in front of the Dog Company orderly room. I warned the boys to expect a cool reception.

"Listen, you jokers, the 8th Infantry is one of the U.S. Army's oldest regiments and this bunch has trained together damned near three years. At first we ain't going to fit in . . . not at all. Get it? So quit bitching. When someone orders you to jump, don't argue, don't ask why. Just jump!"

"Yeah, but Corporal . . ."

"Evans! Halls! Try to get this through your thick skulls. You ain't on some college campus now! You're part of a real fucking army headed into a real fucking war."

They subsided.

"So no more dumb-assed questions," I added. "Do as you're told! And the reason for all the orders is to turn you into real soldiers and to fit you into this first-class team."

I stared them in the eyes, one-by-one.

"Now remain at ease in formation until I get back."

When I entered the orderly room with our files, the first sergeant – a blocky, red-faced 30-year man named Svoboda -- congratulated me on what he said was the best dressing down he'd heard since replacements started coming in. Then he said, "I'm putting you men on the second floor of D barracks."

"Sgt. Svoboda, can you tell me the name of our squad leader?"

He grinned. "Yeah. It's Sgt. Allan Dudley."

"What? Who?"

"Congratulations. The captain thinks you got screwed, so he got the battalion CO to give your stripe back. Wants you starting clean. Your platoon CO is 1st Lt. Joe Scott. He's good people." He handed me a set of promotion orders and two sets of chevrons.

"Well, that's mighty damned decent of the captain. Now, can you tell me what we're doing tomorrow?"

"Formation and mile run at 0500. Think your boys can handle that?"

"Yep. We been following that drill since August . . . except aboard the *Queen Mary*."

He looked pleased. He said the captain would introduce us at company formation in the morning after the run. "He'll make a big deal out of it, especially if you keep up. He'll ask everybody to help show you the ropes. And then we're taking a hike. Weapons and packs. And your guys will be carrying mortar components. For the rest of today, I'd just settle them in. Meanwhile, I'll take you around to meet Lt. Scott."

"What's the exec like, Sarge?"

"He hasn't reported in, yet. He's a shave tail named Schiltz."

"Not Parker B. Schiltz."

"Yeah. You know him?"

"Christ on a crutch, yes. We call him The Dick, except that he's no shave tail. He's a captain."

"Oh God," he said. "Another Personnel screw-up."

Before he and I headed off to meet the CO, I filled him in about The Dick and his apparent vendetta toward either me or my section. "He's the guy that cost me my stripe on the *Queen*. And in my book he's worthless as the tits on a boar hog."

"Sounds like a real chicken inspector," Svoboda said. By the time I finished telling the whole story, he was growling and shaking his head.

# # #

Our first hike with the company was a bear. It was 20 miles over some pretty rugged terrain – though not as steep as 14th Street in Lawrence. We still were stiff after a week on trains and a week on the *Queen*, but nobody fell out.

Wilson whispered that we weren't hiking on Dartmoor but on Upson Downs instead, 'cause all we did was hike up and down.

Timmer started off on the president again, trying to imitate FDR's New England drawl. "I hate wawh. Eleanoah hates wawh, too. I don't want ourh American boys in a wawh. But it's good fawh ouwah American boys to get lots of good exawsize."

Bull said Dartmoor gave him the feeling of hiking the foothills around Boulder but without the thin air. We all got a charge out of hearing that Capt. Schiltz – temporarily with the battalion's intelligence officer, the S2 -- only made it half-way, pretending to turn his ankle so he could weasel his way onto a truck back to HQ.

The rest of March was the busiest month I've ever spent. We took one Sunday afternoon off and that was it. During the week, we were lucky to get five hours of sleep a night. When I first roused the guys at 0500, all but Forster seemed stunned. But they got used to it.

I spent too many of my nighttime hours re-reading the sheaf of V-mails that finally caught up with us. Mom and Sis had worked together on a bunch of letters. Nothing came from Betty.

At first, not hearing from her nearly drove me nuts with longing. She had told me that once she passed her RN state boards she would be off to a camp in Wisconsin for four weeks of Army training so I might not hear from her for a while.

I went ahead and wrote a congratulatory note to her anyway, calling her Dear Lieutenant and signing it as "Yr Humble Sergeant" instead of "Yr Humble Servant." I hoped it would give her a laugh.

Forster did receive mail and it got to him just as no mail did to me. The only way for either of us to cope with longing for our girls was keeping busy.

# # #

The boys pretty much heeded my advice, toning down their wisecracks and bitching. Some of the regiment's accents from the South gave them problems.

It took time to dope out that one sergeant came from Texas which he pronounced 'Takes-uss'. He claimed he helped build derricks in the 'all fields.' And he confused my Yankees at first when he demanded that they work fast, but pronounced it 'faced'.

Most of the southerners were solid Democrats and didn't take kindly to Timmer's hatred of FDR. So he shut his yap.

But he and the rest of the section won the old-timers' acceptance by pretending to be in awe about tall tales of slopping through Camp Polk's knee-deep wait-a-minute swamps. Bull was especially good at it, going wide-eyed as he asked breathlessly about water moccasins and was it true an alligator could take off a leg in one bite? *No shit? Did you see it happen? And what about the leeches?*

The old hands went blue in the face trying to look nonchalant about the real and pretend horrors they endured.

The boys actually gained grudging acceptance because though mostly Yankees, they brought lots of fresh jokes from stateside – the book titles, for instance: *Tiger's Revenge* by Claude Balls, *Rusty Bed Springs* by I. P. Nitely, and so forth. The joke about the missing Indian tribe, the *Wehdafkawi*, led to lots of belly-laughing, but Whitehat convulsed all of us when he claimed the Lone Ranger shot Tonto upon learning that *Kemo Sabe* meant 'meathead.'

The story about a missing GI named Raalph Braaak raised a lot of laughs, too.

When stuck with KP, the kids brought bitching to a multisyllabic collegiate level. Frost one day convulsed the entire chow line when he warned the men not to accept any future servings of that four-plus syphilitic, laminated maggot-gagging Spam. Even the Reb professionals were slapping their knees.

Being around the old hands caused one change that I liked.

It hit me when I heard Halls arguing one day with Evans. Instead of his typical down-the-nose remark that Evans' contention was platitudinous, illogical, inane and pubescent, Halls just said, "George, you're full of more shit than a Christmas goose."

#

Being shunted from intelligence to operations, The Dick inspected us from time to time – or I should say he picked on us. And in a way it was good for the squad because little details are everything in a mortar battery.

Even so, The Dick did his best to be a real SOB about it, riding us constantly but often missing things that counted. He was ready to call for a court-martial when he found a box of Kotex beneath the top tray in Bull's foot locker. He was certain Bull was selling the product on the black market. He didn't let up until Lt. Scott patiently explained that though sanitary napkins weren't authorized materiel, they were vastly superior to Army-issue cloth patches for cleaning power residue from mortars.

In fact, The Dick was pretty ignorant about mortars and apparently couldn't be bothered to learn. Like the day we held our first live fire exercise.

Now after every four to six shots, you get a just a brief flare from a mortar's muzzle – about like when you use a kitchen match to light the burner on a kitchen range. It's from a build-up of propellant residue and not enough to do more than singe the hair on your hand or forearm.

But on this particular day The Dick wanted to fire a round at just the wrong time. He poised the shell over the muzzle just as the tube flared. It could have happened to anybody and, in fact, did now and then.

Well, the flame ignited the propellant increments on the shell's fins -- a ferocious, hot, ultra-bright flame right there in The Dick's face.

As with all else, the Army has a standard operating procedure when that happens. You turn 180 degrees, drop the round away from ammunition storage and, critically, drop it on its side. You sure don't want it landing on its nose, otherwise, See you at the Pearly Gates.

Well, The Dick panicked. He just dropped the blazing shell right at his feet and took off like a big bird. So we had this very intense fire about a yard from the rest of the ammo. We all hit the dirt like lightning, but thank heaven the blaze died fast -- propellant fire is like that -- without setting off anything else.

Except me.

When we all arose from our flattened positions, I exploded.

I screamed at The Dick – by then a good 50 yards away – telling him to stay the hell away from my mortars. I swore a lot more than necessary, making me a hero with the boys.

The Dick, however, ran to Capt. Freeman bleating about my public insubordination and Freeman had to back him up.

So at the captain's direction, Lt. Scott issued a written reprimand to me – actually a pretty mild one -- and ordered me to give my superior officer a formal apology in the presence of my men. Which I did, asking his indulgence because I claimed the fire had panicked me.

He knew better. We both did. So did the boys. He shook my proffered hand, but his eyes said Kill.

Later the HQ clerk told Timmer that Capt. Scott gave The Dick his own very thorough ass-chewing. "Sarge," Timmer said, "the clerk told me he wished he could have charged admission. He'd have made a nice little pile of dough."

Fortunately, The Dick couldn't play the chickenshit game of stopping the boys' weekend passes. At my suggestion, Lt. Scott issued no passes. We both agreed they had no time for fun and games until they caught up with the rest of the outfit.

# # #

Two memories stand out.

One day Col. Van Fleet inspected us, doing his impression of a six-foot olive drab pillar of dry ice. Torrelli later claimed the colonel had two facial expressions: Angry and Furious.

The other memory is of Teddy Roosevelt, Jr., the division's second-in-command. I don't know if there was any connection, but Gen. Roosevelt showed up a day after The Dick screwed the pooch again.

This time we were ordered to fire a mission in support of a tank maneuver. Our job was to lower the boom on a make-believe squad of enemy infantry with two make-believe enemy anti-tank guns.

The battalion CO figured, I guess, that The Dick could benefit from some practical experience. So he ordered the company commander to let The Dick oversee the mortar exercise.

Unfortunately, The Dick's contempt for enlisted people led him to ignore Forster's recommendations. He ordered the sections to emplace our mortars by a stand of oaks. Regulations mandate siting the guns a minimum 50 feet apart so that if somebody's return fire takes out one gun and its crew, the others will be beyond the blast radius.

The Dick ignored that SOP – if he ever bothered to learn it -- and arranged the guns about 20 feet apart. I was at the battalion Fire Direction Center and heard the uproar when our mortars didn't fire.

It turned out that The Dick not only sited the guns too close together, but also under trees whose branches lay in the shells' line of fire. When he ordered the battery to fire, Forster countermanded him.

The Dick then demanded that Forster fire and Forster refused again. So The Dick put him under arrest and ran squeaking to Lt. Scott. Hearing about it over the net, I rushed back just as Lt. Scott arrived.

The CO asked Forster why he refused to fire. Forster quietly pointed overhead at the branches and said, "Sir, we weren't permitted time to do our safety clearance. What's more we don't have regulation separation."

Lt. Scott asked, "And exactly why, corporal, wasn't the safety clearance performed?" I smirked inside as The Dick's face turn pink and he literally squirmed.

He leaned close to Scott and whispered. Scott snapped, "Captain! For God's sake, it was a *live fire* exercise!"

Turning back to Forster, Scott said, "Well?"

Forster was smart. "Well, with respect, sir, I'd best not say. I just believe a valuable lesson has been learned by all."

"Okay, Forster. So who emplaced the guns so close together?"

Again, Forster declined to answer.

"Okay, corporal," Scott said. "I think I understand."

He raised his voice. "Let me just point out to everyone here, corporal, that you personally saved these mortar sections from butchering themselves. Nothing, repeat nothing, is more lethal than a tree-top burst."

He emphasized the statement by saying nothing at all for a full minute. Then he said, "So let's just consider this incident closed. Now Cpl. Forster, I'm going to forward a recommendation to the battalion commander that he put you in line for promotion to sergeant."

Scott turned toward his jeep without looking at The Dick whose face now was stark white.

Then he asked The Dick, "Would you accompany me, sir? I'm sure Cap'n Freeman wants to know why the tank squadron didn't get the mortar support it called for. I bet Maj. Cavanaugh at Ops will be interested, too."

We had a very hard time stifling our laughter.

I figure the tale circulated in the officers' mess and I bet that Gen. Roosevelt came by next day to see for himself whether we were a bunch of screwball trouble-makers.

It was raining, windy and cold and again we were firing in support of tanks at about a mile. Forster was standing by the SCR 509 holding the handset to his ear. So this scrawny little guy in plain fatigues using a cane and wearing those old-fashioned WWI puttees came limping up to us through the mud. Nau went to ask his business, saw the single star on the man's stocking cap, and yelled "Ten-HUT!"

Everybody braced, but the general just said, "As you were, men. Just go on with your duties."

Gen. Roosevelt looked nothing at all like his dad, but he did have an ultra-wide grin that never seemed to quit. In fact, even his eyes seemed to smile. Later, Frost said the lines in Roosevelt's face looked deep enough to trap two gallons of water. The old boy had a froggy bass voice and acted friendly though he looked dog tired and his lips were quivering with the cold.

He stayed back as Forster replied to the FDC, "Roger. Two Able Tare guns and 10 dismounted infantry in heavy brush. No danger close. Out."

After a pause, Forster repeated into the mouthpiece, "One round Willie Peter. Out."

When he yelled, "Hang!" Bull poised the shell in the tube's muzzle. "Fire!"

Bull dropped the shell and ducked. As the mortar blasted, Forster called into the handset, "Shot. Over."

He repeated, "Splash. Out," and then seconds later looked up with a grin. "FO says we're dead on, guys."

Then he repeated, "Fire for effect, two rounds per gun. Out." He told each gunner to hang and fire. "Shots. Over," and seconds later, "Splash, out."

Roosevelt, observing down-range through his binoculars, boomed "Great shoot!" A series of *kuh-whupps* came to us. Lowering his field glasses, he turned his grin on Forster. "Corporal, are you always that accurate?"

"Sir, we sure aim to be," Forster grinned, turning to the crews. "Okay, boys. Clean 'em up. They ordered us to head for the barn."

I escorted the general to his jeep which had the legend *Rough Rider* in old-fashioned western lettering on the windshield frame just above the hood. As he sat down in the shotgun seat, he closed his eyes, looking whipped.

When we saluted each other, he said, "Looks like you've got these college kids pretty well drilled," he said. "I'll see that Col. Van Fleet knows."

"Thank you, sir. And if you don't mind me saying this, I'd like to recommend that you try to get some rest."

He gave me a sad smile. "Sergeant, we'll all catch up on our sleep when the Germans surrender."

Chapter 14
April 8, 1944 – Dartmoor, England

On our first Saturday when section members finally got passes, I volunteered for CQ so I could use the company typewriter. I wanted to congratulate Betty who at last wrote, informing me of her commission.

Besides, I didn't want to be around when these boys did their first drinking. I could picture them all getting thoroughly soused and into a brawl and then into the stockade. So I unofficially detailed Bull – the Mormon who didn't drink – and Forster to keep the lads together and out of harm's way.

Trouble was a possibility because they had been taking a lot of ribbing – good-natured, but some of it pretty raw. A few of the old hands ragged them about being ASTP pussies – ASTP standing for All Safe 'Til Peace – sitting in classrooms while the rest of the troops were hiking their butts off in Georgia and Louisiana.

Both Wilson and Nau had been through advanced infantry training at Camp Benning and sometimes called the kids pansies, but if anyone outside the sections started name-calling, both were as ready to start swinging as Timmer and Halls.

In fact, they all had toughened up. Frost and Manthei long since had shed their beer bellies and Whitehorse was down to pure rawhide and bone. They were settling in like soldiers, too. Except for Whitehorse and Forster, all suffered at first from hiking. Yet not one dropped out. And after a month on the moors, they now could hump their loads with anyone else in Heavy Weapons.

They also were following orders without question, and Col. Van Fleet actually gave them a nod and a cold grunt of approval when he watched them run a fire mission under Halls' direction. Capt. Freeman had pulled me and Forster and three other section members out of action as mock casualties.

Anyway, things were quiet until about 2100, when an MP three-quarter ton pulled up bearing Halls, Timmer and Frost and three First Platoon men. They all looked dazed or drunk, and had an assortment of split lips, cut eyebrows and shiners.

The MP corporal, a decent guy, said he didn't take them to the stockade because they hadn't damaged the pub or any other property. Besides, the troops who attacked them had disappeared. He didn't think it would be fair to punish only half the culprits. That's how I could tell he hadn't been an MP long.

"And you say my boys weren't fighting these other guys in your paddy wagon?"

"Hell no, Sarge. Your boys were defending these goofballs who were brawling about some girls in the pub."

"You sure?"

"Damn sure, Sarge."

Just then two jeeps pulled up to drop off Forster, Bull and the rest of the boys. Wilson, Whitehorse and Nau were slightly unsteady and had barked knuckles, but they all seemed in good condition. And they all started talking at once about what a bunch of bastards from the 12th Infantry had done.

"Whoa! Whoa!" The MP warned them he'd already passed the word to me and to shut up before their mouths got them in trouble. I had Forster and his companions steer the tottering combatants to their racks and told him to come back and tell me all about it.

When he returned he explained that the First Platoon trio were in the Admiral Romney Inn, a nearby pub, sharing beers with three local girls. The girls claimed to be widows respectively of an RAF bombardier, a destroyer sailor and a tank gunner in North Africa. It was a story you heard often in England. It usually was true.

Forster said, "I think that the boys were trying to, well . . ."

"Yeah, Mike, I get the picture. They wanted to get their ashes hauled."

"That's right, Sarge. Well, just then this bunch from the 12th Infantry comes in – six or seven of them. Maybe they kind of felt left out because our boys were with the girls.

Well, they started getting nasty, saying the girls were sluts who'd do it for a stick of spearmint. Two of the girls started crying and the third gave back as good as she got. Then she asked pretty loudly if some of these 8th Regiment Yanks wouldn't do something to defend the ladies' honor against those bloody rotten pongos – that's the scientific term for gorillas."

"Thanks, Mike, I'll remember that."

"So, anyway, all three get up from their table and begin squaring off against the guys from the 12th."

Forster said that the pub owner, fearing his establishment was about to be turned to matchwood, pulled a shotgun from behind the bar. Forster laughed. "Sarge, he yells something like this: 'You fookin' Yanks! Noo, ee be teking your fight oot to Dartymoor or I'll be blowing your fookin' arses across t'room. Oonnerstan?'"

Forster said the guys from first platoon very courteously bowed the guys from the 12th out the door and then, as they followed, the 12th jumped them.

"So, we'd been minding our own business. But Timmer says, 'Now, Halls, that doesn't seem quite fair, does it? Come on.' So he and Halls dive into the fray with Frost and, right behind, Whitehorse giving his Injun whoops. The rest of us followed to pitch in but that made the odds too steep for the 12th boys so they took off."

Forster went back inside and found the pub's owner just getting off the phone to the MPs. "When I told him the fight was over he was so grateful he gave me a free pint. By the time the MPs arrived all the guys were pretty well oiled because a couple of the local geezers stood rounds for them, too. And the girls were nursing their cuts and bruises.

When the MPs did come in, the pub owner was very complementary about all of us. Said we were good Yanks what saved him from ruin, so basically the MPs just gave them a ride home. I decided the rest of us had enough excitement and should come back to the post too."

I wrote up Forster's story for the day log. Meanwhile, Sixth Squad – we still called ourselves that, though now we actually were the second and third Sections of the Mortar Platoon – found ourselves to be D Company heroes for rescuing the First Platoon men from those dirty 12th Infantry bastards.

Next morning, of course, The Dick took it upon himself to write up a request for Capt. Freeman to press charges against my boys for fighting.

Sgt. Svoboda told me later that the CO snorted, tore up the papers and said something like "we want fighting men."

Svoboda also said Freeman was taking a chance in doing so. "I heard from regiment that The Dick has a great big 'PI' in his file. That stands for 'Political Influence.' Maybe he's the bastard son of some damned Congressman or something. So regiment is stuck with him, but he's such a worthless pain in the ass that he's just sort of being floated around without a permanent assignment. Of course, all the professionals are afraid he could destroy their careers."

When I passed The Dick the next day I saluted very correctly and then quietly said, "Keep it up, asshole! You're breeding a scab."

He turned white, but that was all he could do.

Chapter 15
April 15, 1944 – Dartmoor, England

The next weekend, I took off by myself. I was worried and wanted to relax and be alone.

See, I knew the kids realized that sooner or later, we'd head into battle. But to them "battle" and "combat" were just words. Yeah, it was something dangerous, but they had no grasp of how dangerous.

They hadn't the faintest idea of the roaring, blasting confusion, the bewildering orders, the screams and shouts, the shock of seeing a buddy's shoulder explode in bone splinters and red spray. They had no idea how many ways, and how easy it was, to get killed or maimed.

They knew Germans were tough. But they really had no idea that "tough" meant steely-eyed, battle-hardened, pitiless killers directing bullet hails and razor-like shrapnel storms at them; that suddenly they might see a Kraut behind them taking aim too late for them to respond.

I was scared for them. I was scared for me. I wanted to find some way to make them understand. I wanted to think.

So I checked out a jeep and took off on a leisurely drive toward Exmouth. I heard it was pretty seaside town, so named because it sat beside the mouth of the Exe River. The real attraction turned out to be driving slowly down country lanes under arching tree limbs forming sun-dappled tunnels. I was losing myself in that beauty when I soon realized I was damned well and truly lost. Country lanes in England twist, turn and fork for reasons that probably confused the Roman Army when it arrived 1,500 years before. But I really didn't give a damn. It was just good to be alone.

On one sharp bend, however, I swerved too late to avoid a spindly looking man pedaling one of those thin-wheeled English bikes.

Forgetting I was supposed to drive on the left, I bumped him with the jeep's spare mounted on the right rear quarter, knocking him and his bike flat. I skidded to a stop and ran back to find a tall, lean old man getting up stiffly and giving me a very icy look. He was limping and the bike's front wheel looked damaged.

I fell all over myself apologizing. I was going to offer to help but the wheel had five broken spokes and a marked bend to the left. "I'm very, very sorry, sir, but I think that wheel is beyond repair."

"Quite." With a glum look on his gaunt face, he added, "And bicycle wheels are frightfully scarce right now, you know."

"Sir, can I at least offer you and your bike a lift to your home? Or maybe to a repair shop?"

He brightened. "Oh, thanks awfully, sergeant. Most kind of you. There's a shop not five minutes from here. I'd be most obliged." He introduced himself as Alf.

I gave Alf a hand into the Jeep -- it was obvious he was in pain. I popped open the jeep's first aid kit and insisted that he take two aspirin to ease the discomfort. Once I hefted the bike into the back of the jeep, he directed me to a shop in a little town about a mile further on.

The shop owner, Williams, looked almost as old as Alf but had at least four times the bulk. They knew each other and he apologized to "Sralfred" that he had no new wheels. "But we do 'ave auld bike parts out back. We might cobble summat together, cannibalize like."

A second bleary-eyed man hanging around the shop muttered about "damned Yanks driving aboot like fookin' madmen" and added that ". . . we ought to chuck 'em oot."

Alf ignored the remark and assured me that he and the shop-owner could take it from there, but I asked to help. It was good to work with my hands to fix something and to chat with people who didn't say "fuck" every third word.

"And, fair trade," I added. "I'm lost. If I help and we get your bike back together and working – with no parts left over -- perhaps you could give me directions how to get back to my regiment."

Alf and Williams chuckled, but the third party repeated his desire to see the Yanks chucked oot. I went to him and quietly explained that I had, indeed, screwed up and was trying to fix it. The smell of liquor on his breath was strong, so I just decided to let it go.

Alf and Williams resumed the conversation by saying that getting lost was common. Many locals had become lost starting back in 1940 when the Home Secretary ordered all road signs removed because it looked as if the Germans might invade.

"All of us was gettin' lost even though we lived 'ere all our lives," Williams said. "So we can give directions. But, mind you, you might find yoursel' drivin' through Manchester or Glasgow or worse."

"Yes," Alf smiled, "the story goes that some of our neighbors have been trying to get home for three years now. And supposedly Mr. Churchill planned a tour here in the West Country, but MI-5 advised against it. Can't afford to lose *him*. National security and all that."

At that point the drunk noisily repeated his opinion about chucking oot the Yanks. Williams' face turned red and he told the man to keep quiet or leave.

"Charlie Williams," the drunk hiccuped, "you can . . . can't order *me* around. I might just give you a punch."

I sighed and got up from the bike. "Sir," I said to the man, "that would be a serious mistake." I raised a fist, "I'd be forced to beat the crap out of you."

He stared at me briefly, but then turned and stumbled from the shop. Once outside he started cursing incoherently about the bluidy Yanks, but the noise tailed off as he continued down the sidewalk.

Williams and Alf apologized, but I just said, "Ahh," and waved away their comments. We spent the next two hours joking. At my urging, Alf sat while Williams and I cannibalized parts. The shop had no wrenches, but spanners, which were the same thing. It had neither sandpaper nor steel wool, but I found a bucket of sand. Using it with pair of gauntlets, I was able polish the worst of the rust from an old front wheel we found overgrown with weeds behind the shop. Williams said he thought t'was off from Mrs. Dawkins's bike, God rest 'er soul.

A few touches of motor oil from the jeep's dipstick actually helped gave the wheel half a sheen. Once we mounted the tire on the wheel and the wheel on the bike, Alf and Williams offered to stand me a few pints at the local pub. I thanked them, explaining that I don't drink. Williams looked amazed. "Durin' the Great War, we 'ad was no such things as teetotallin' sergeants."

Alf grinned and said, "Sgt. Dudler, I'm still a bit stiff from my encounter with your jeep. If you would be so good as to give me and my bike a ride back to the manor, the missus and I at least can provide you a bite of lunch . . . plus a guide."

I thought he was kidding about the manor, but it turned out to be just that – an old ornate three-story stone mansion about a city block long with a circular drive, its landscaping gone to weed. I also learned then that "Sralfred" meant "Sir Alfred" and that I had nearly killed Major General Sir Alfred Abbot-Leigh, retired, MC, DSO, KBE and who knows what all else.

He and his stout little Lady Alice were making their home on the first floor of one wing of Abbot Manor. They had turned over two wings and the second and third floor of their own wing to the Royal Navy as a hospital for wounded officers. Lady Alice offered me tea and apologized for what basically turned out to be spam sandwiches. She said she was very sorry cucumbers weren't in season yet.

"It seems that between rationing and shortages, all we English can offer now is apologies."

I didn't tell her I rate spam over cucumbers any day.

After lunch, Alf offered a tour of the grounds until my guide would arrive. I suggested that, being bunged-up, he should rest. So he and Lady Alice and I sat in his study which looked like it had about 3,000 books. We chatted about the military.

She seemed to know as much as he. She told me he had been medically discharged in 1917 after commanding a regiment, then a brigade and, very briefly, an infantry division in Mesopotamia.

"Yes, very briefly indeed." he chuckled. "One morning a mortar bomb and I arrived in the same place and same time. They had to send us to hospital for sifting, but it didn't work out well.

"I tried to get back into active service when the war started in '39," he added. "They were polite but said that I was far too old and infirm. After Dunkirk, however, they were scraping the bottom of the barrel and brought me back aboard in Planning. So I keep in touch even if I'm no longer on truly active service.

"And if the Huns ever find their way here -- mind you, I believe they'll be as lost as a certain American sergeant -- I'll await them with my old Enfield. I may be crippled and tottery, but I still can shoot."

"So can I," Lady Alice said, "but a .303 is too much for me. So we try to do our bit by lending our home for the wounded. This old place is far too large for us anyway."

I told them I was a rifleman in North Africa and now helped run a mortar platoon. She gave a slight wince and then beamed. He said, "Oh, splendid! Jolly good!" making me feel as if the European campaign might actually succeed now that I was to be involved.

He brought up the impending invasion. I said I had no idea where we would go ashore or when. "Well, if you did, you oughtn't tell me anyway," he said. But then he showed me a big wall chart of the English Channel and predicted we would invade Normandy, secure Cherbourg and Caen, and then break out across France to Germany.

"I think you'll go in June and perhaps even in May," he said. "And you're probably going to spend a lot of unpleasant time in water during the next few weeks."

"Water?"

Lady Alice explained that Normandy was beautiful but had many low-lying areas which the Germans probably had flooded by damming rivers and canals.

"Alice means it's very poor country for armor," Sir Alfred added. "I think your officers, therefore, will want you well-accustomed to swamps and that sort of terrain. Training is the thing, you know."

I nodded and told them of my fear for my men -- that they seemed unable to grasp or even take seriously what they faced.

Lady Alice abruptly got up and left. He frowned. "No innocent can grasp combat until that first few moments," he said. "That's when training must take over. Certainly you experienced that against Rommel. Your training served you there and will serve your lads in France."

He looked downcast. "Allan, the cold fact you must accept is that you will lose some of them. War is waged by spending the lives of young men. We lost our younger son in France in 1940. The elder went down with his destroyer in the Med in early this year."

"Damn, I should have kept my yap shut, sir, I'm very, very sorry to hear that."

"Yes, they were the last of our line," he said with a sad smile. "It's a very, very sorry business. But those are the costs of dealing with creatures such as Herr Schicklgruber. One can hardly describe him as a human being.

"And it was all unnecessary, you know," he added with a rueful grin. "Winston put it best back in '35 or '36 when one battalion could have stopped Hitler. He told Parliament, 'You fear war and so refuse to prepare for war. Therefore, you will have war.'

"Nobody heeded him, of course."

He was quiet for a moment and then asked, "Sergeant, are you a hostilities-only soldier?"

"No sir. I signed up in '39 when Hitler invaded Poland."

"The same as our younger boy," he said.

# # #

Late that afternoon, a dark-headed woman in a blue uniform came into the study and Sir Alfred introduced us.

Katherine had a long narrow English face and deep-set gray eyes. They said she was a leading Wren and then had to explain to me that "Wren" stood for Women's Royal Navy. "Leading" was her rank, a leading seaman being the Royal Navy's version of seaman first class.

As they brought me up to speed, she seemed uninterested and distant -- certainly not particularly impressed with meeting a mere US Army sergeant. She sparkled a bit, however, when Sir Alfred explained how he and I had met, singing my praises for helping repair his bike, and would she please guide me and my jeep back to the regiment?

It was early evening when we arrived back at the regiment. She accepted my offer for a meal in the NCO mess. It was in introducing her to the first sergeant that I learned she actually was Alf's widowed daughter-in-law. It was her husband who was lost in the Mediterranean.

We both told her we were sorry.

She was a bit curt about it. "Thank you, gentlemen, but it's a common story. I do my best not to dwell on it."

Her big eyes widened at the sight of beef and fresh vegetables. "Good heavens but you Yanks have it posh." Then she sighed, "But I've got a feeling that you'd better enjoy it while it lasts."

"You're right, Ma'am," Sgt. Svoboda said. "And I don't think it's going to last much longer."

When I walked her back to her car, I asked her to forgive me for being nosy, but why was she driving for the Navy?

She looked down her long nose as only the English can. Stiffly, she said, "I feel we all, even we mere women, must do our bit. And if Princess Elizabeth can drive an ambulance during London air raids, I certainly can try to help the effort by chauffeuring the wounded one day and flag officers the next."

"Speaking as one of the formerly wounded," I said, "I'm sure they appreciate what you do."

She eyed my scar and said, "Ah. You know what it's like, then." As she got into the car, she told me that her father-in-law felt indebted to me.

"For God's sake, why? I almost killed him."

She explained he was impressed by my eagerness to make amends by helping to repair the bike. She said she also had the feeling that I reminded him of his younger son, William.

"He looked a bit like you, you know – short and stout with an air of pugnacity."

"Of what?"

"Pugnacity. He always seemed ready for a fight."

Somehow her words struck deep. For the first time in years I felt myself get tearful. I looked away and my voice broke slightly. "Well, I am honored," I said. "More than honored."

It was a few seconds before I could speak, and then it came out kind of strangled and squeaky. "He would have made a far better father than mine. In fact, Sir Alfred would be the kind of father I always wanted."

Her eyes softened and she gave me a genuine smile.

"Yes, he's a wonderfully kind man." Then, looking me square in the eyes, she said Alfred and Lady Alice truly meant it when they invited me to visit again.

I promised I would if I had the chance and if I actually could find the manor.

She gave me her card and smiled. "Please call. I can always guide you."

Chapter 16
April 18, 1944 – Dartmoor, England

Sir Alfred knew what he was talking about. Our training not only accelerated but it also, well, dampened.

I think they made us wade every Goddamn bog, pond and creek in Dartmoor. In fact, that whole vista seemed be nothing but steep mounds with hard rocky crests and, between them, saddles with ice-cold streams and freezing ponds, some of them concealed.

I mean literally concealed.

In one of our first field problems on the moors, Lt. Scott ordered us to set up the battery behind a stony hill – a tor, they call it there. So I pointed for one of the guns to be emplaced on a nice flat piece of ground at the base of the hill. It looked ideal -- low enough so the enemy couldn't see smoke or flash – and flat as a pancake. It was even pretty, with a nice stretch of Kelly green grass.

Lance Corporal Laird, our Royal Army guide, murmured that the site might not be suitable. I didn't listen. So, arriving first, Evans -- who was carrying the tube on a sling over his shoulder -- discovered that what I took to be the grass actually was moss, a living spongy lid over a stony pond about four feet deep.

It was something the natives called a quaker because it quivers as you walk across it.

But Evans weighed 190 and he was carrying about 80 more pounds so he broke through. It took him and two other men about 15 minutes of grappling with pitchforks to locate and recover his carbine and the mortar . . . all to Cpl. Laird's ill-concealed amusement and Evans' sputtering curses at me.

Torrelli, jeering from the sidelines, coined the nickname for our section – and later the whole platoon. "I can't believe what I'm seeing," he said. "Groping for a mortar with a pitchfork . . . hell, you guys are nothing but a bunch of mortar forkers."

The nickname caught on instantly, first as an insult in the mouths of every other man in D Company. Then in the battalion and finally the regiment.

We adopted it as our own.

We had no further collapses into the covered ponds of Dartmoor because after that I paid strict heed to Laird's quiet advice. He'd been assigned to us to see that we didn't blunder into the really dangerous bogs.

He told us an ancient local joke about such hazards. A man walking on the moor kicks a top hat that's apparently lying on its brim. As the hat bounces away, the walker hears a voice. "And, sir, whit be you adoin' with me 'at?"

The walker looks down and answers, "Be there a chap oonder neath?"

"Ess, and I be asittin' on me 'oss."

Well, you had to be there.

It was on the moors we first realized how pathetic our boots were. Picture ankle-high lace-up shoes surmounted by a leather collar fastened by dual buckles. The collar reached about three inches above the ankle. As ankle reinforcement, they seemed sturdy as damp cardboard.

Over this we wore khaki leggings – we called them spats – which did nothing but blouse the bottoms of our fatigue pants.

Manthei contended that the spats and collars acted together to funnel water *into* the boots. About five minutes after you began walking through wet brush or grass, your boots felt like saturated sponges tied to your feet.

I vowed that the first time I encountered a German POW with the right size, I'd force him to swap boots. I'd seen their foot gear in Africa and they looked like clumsy black stove pipes, but they were calf-high with no damned laces or buckles. And if any MP – or The Dick – wanted to discipline me for being out of uniform, so be it. I'd rather be a private with dry feet than a sergeant with trench foot.

Now being spring in England, it rained. And rained. And rained.

I'm not talking a 30-minute Midwest American thunderstorm. I'm talking day in and day out of clouds scudding in off the North Atlantic almost at ground level with mist changing to drizzle back to mist, then downpour, then drizzle and back to mist.

Nothing gets so old so fast to a footslogger as the ping-ting-ting of raindrops on his steel helmet. And, no, in the end the helmet doesn't keep your head dry. But the water was just constant. Frost claimed to have found a fast-growing patch of mildew on the wall by his rack and was setting up a pool on how long it would take to reach the ceiling, No wonder every third word in the infantry is "fuck," even among my collegiates.

The Dick, incidentally, came close to getting shot one afternoon. Nau told me that he apparently stamped the accelerator just as he drove past one of the mortar sections, throwing a cascade of cold muddy ooze onto everybody. I guess the roar of the jeep's motor and the sound of its tires in water prevented him from hearing the outraged language that followed him.

A half hour later when he stopped on the way back, the men had regained their temper and politely asked him to lower his speed when driving past troops in the future. Showing what a prince he could be, The Dick smirked that a good soldier always knows how to stay dry. Then he made the mistake of asking directions to battalion HQ. Halls sketched out a route leading toward York or maybe Scotland.

Later I had to lie to The Dick. I told him that Halls was useless with map reading. The Dick was too dim to draw the obvious conclusion about his own navigational haplessness.

In fact, Halls was excellent with maps. The whole gang was . . . and a good thing, because compasses were worthless on Dartmoor. You could just sit there and watch the needle swing 20 degrees out of true. Walk ten steps and it would swing back five. No standard compass deviation existed anywhere on that miserable soggy section of southwest England.

It was just as well, too, because sometimes we operated in small units – some as small as a half section, forcing as many men as possible to master maps. Overall, we were becoming a tough cross-trained savvy team inured to hardship and stress.

Humping 45 pounds of mortar tube or base plate up a mud-slick slope was a bear – not to mention also carrying your carbine and ammunition and canteens and packs.

But if Lt. Scott suddenly ordered us to set up behind a hill to support an infantry attack, we'd scramble and slide back down the slope . . . a scramble by three sections carrying six tubes, base plates, bipods and ammo for six guns. Install guns in baseplates, connect bipods, level the assemblies, get on the collimator sights to place the aiming stakes. And, and as you do it all, you eye the terrain around you because sure as hell you'll get a warning to move the whole platoon because of counterbattery fire from the Heinies.

After one particularly miserable, rainy, muddy exhausting day, Capt. Freeman pretended to take pity and give Heavy Weapons a break.

We were taking off our filthy, mud-caked uniforms after getting back to the barracks early. Torrelli announced that either that God was on Hitler's side or Whitehorse was doing too many fucking rain dances.

Whitehorse gave a rare grin and said, "Now I'm really gonna fix you white-eye bastards." He started an Indian chant.

"Shit!" Timmer said. "We'll have to rename ourselves the Mud Platoon."

The guys tested that nickname, but it didn't have the growling, obscene flavor of "Mortar Forkers."

And they gave the nickname a thorough working-over because the Dick showed up blasting on his whistle. "Orders from Operations! You start a new problem at High Willies Tor – 15 minutes." The tor, the high point on the damned moor, was 11 miles away and pretty much all uphill in a storm at night.

As we started hiking in those miserable boots, we marched to the 4-syllable cadence of "Mortar Forkers," repeated like one of those Catholic litanies. It just seemed to give deep-down psychological relief and the name stuck.

Naturally, The Dick gigged us. Because of all the mud we'd left, the barracks no longer was inspection-ready.

Chapter 17
April 29, 1944 – Dartmoor, England

Dragging in from the moor mid-afternoon Friday, we were -- as our Royal Army comrades put it -- marching on our chin straps. We were dog-tired and depressed after a hard hike bearing a full load plus our mortar components.

Even so, the kids were doing some very energetic cussing at Jacobs, accusing him slacking off and making them carry his share.

"Lousy jerk-off bastard pretended to trip . . . the *real* Mortar Forkers get to hump his load . . . yeah, I'd hang my head too, you gimpy bastard . . . look at that fake limp! Jacobs, you can't act for shit. You'll never make it in Hollywood . . . you'd *better* keep up, buddy, 'cause otherwise I'm gonna be kicking your ass the whole way . . . Stanley Q. Jacobs, you're sleeping with this mortar tube tonight and Halls has a baseplate for your pillow."

Jacobs was limping badly but he snickered at the abuse even as he grimaced at his pain. And I was proud. Half way through the hike, Jacobs hurt his left leg. The medics said he had a serious muscle tear and should be excused from the rest of the hike. But he hiked anyhow. His determination to keep up impressed me.

What impressed me even more was that, without a word from me or Forster, the boys divvied up and shouldered Jacobs' load. They now had the grit to rise above their own discomfort. The original KU college kids now fit well in the 8th Infantry, and pulling level with everybody else in a tough battalion.

Though Forster was still a corporal, the CO had named him acting sergeant. He'd picked me as the platoon top kick, a staff sergeant's slot, though I still was a buck sergeant.

The captain told me battalion HQ now counted on the Mortar Forkers as much as on any of the old hands. The boys now knew to react instantly with the infantry's movements.

If we were practicing an advance, both sections were anticipating leapfrogging the guns forward, alternating with the old hands of the third section. And they responded automatically to displace the same way in retreat, ensuring that at least one section's guns always could be set up, lashing the enemy with steel and burning phosphorous.

They did just as well in half-tracks in which sighting presents special problems. It was nice to ride, but we actually had a lot more to do in half-tracks, especially being on constant alert for ambushes.

Too, you had to keep the vehicles clean and pay constant attention to their tracks. And beyond that, one ammo carrier had to man the .50 caliber machine gun mounted over the cab – and clean and maintain it – and another had the same job with the water-cooled .30 at the rear.

The HQ track also had five infantrymen who, basically were the security element for the platoon. But we trained them as mortar men, too.

Now according to Field Manual 17-27, each section with its two mortars was to move in two half-tracks. But I told the guys that all our hiking in bogs and streams was Col. Van Fleet's way of hinting that we'd probably hit the beach on foot and hump everything ourselves for at least several miles inland . . . and for several days.

Anyhow, as we dragged into the barracks, The Dick strolled in just as Lt. Scott posted new orders. The Dick wasn't happy about it because the orders said as soon as we cleaned ourselves, our gear and our personal areas, we could pick up passes at the orderly room and disappear until 0800 Monday.

I never saw a bunch of whipped doggies perk up so fast. The Dick tried to screw with us by demanding a volunteer to serve as CQ clerk. I looked the orders over and saw, first, that they applied to the entire mortar platoon and, second, that he was the officer of the day, which made it his problem.

So I told him, "Cap'n, the orders apply to every swinging dick in this platoon. You're on your own."

I gave him one of those near-vertical salutes that look like you're thumbing your nose. He started to change color but Forster stepped in and volunteered. "I've got nowhere to go," he said. "So I can spend the night writing to Eleanor. Then I'll dig back into FM 10-5."

It took forever to get a call through to Katherine. By 1630, I had the barracks to myself and was shaved and showered. I stopped my jeep at the mess hall to grab two large crates of gifts I'd accumulated in trade for my beer ration.

It took Katherine about 30 minutes to guide me and my jeep to Abbot Manor.

The general at first was reluctant to accept the food I brought. But when I showed Lady Alice a dozen cucumbers she got misty and said, "Oh, Alf! Look! They're so beautiful."

With them was a Virginia ham, 10 pounds of frozen T-bones, a sack of Idahos, 10 pounds of flour, a bag of Red Delicious apples, a bag of oranges and two 5-pound blocks of butter. Katherine was agog, calling it a cornucopia.

Alf still looked inclined to refuse, but I said the U.S. Army was loaded with a superabundance that the mess sergeants otherwise illegally would sell to some farmer for his hogs.

"Besides," I told him, "it seems to me you folks have carried the load and done all the sacrificing and suffering so far, and now we're finally here to help, so you certainly can share with an ally while we learn from you. It only makes sense." I told them of Forster's family who had sent food to their cousins outside London for years.

In the end, they agreed. Lady Alice urged Katherine to change out of her uniform and to dress for a party. When she returned from her room it was hard for me to miss the swell of her breasts under the thin fabric of her blouse.

Even so, her clothes seemed to hang on her because, like all her countrymen, she had lost so much weight.

The four of us enjoyed the first feast that I bet had taken place in the old manor in years. And I bet ours was the first genuine laughter to echo within those old walls for at least four long years.

We talked well into the evening before I said I must be getting back. All three of them looked up sharply.

Lady Alice said, "Oh, when it's so dark?"

"Oh, don't worry," I said. "I think I'll be able to find my way back without a guide this time."

Sir Alfred stood and said, "Allan, if you're on pass and unless you have some vitally important appointment, we won't hear of it. And actually, it would be hopeless trying to motor back in complete darkness. And we surely need you at breakfast to help us with the ham. You must stay the night in Bill's room. We absolutely insist."

Lady Alice nodded sternly as he spoke. "Quite right. And Sgt. Dudley, it would be wise for you to take cognizance that you have just received a command from a serving major general."

He raised his eyebrows and gave a slight grin. "Ah, yes. Quite so. Failure to obey a direct order would be bad form. A court martial offense, you know. Wicked business."

I raised my hands and said. "I surrender." Katherine smiled and Lady Alice got up to go to the room saying the bed needed to be made up.

"Please don't bother," I said. "I make my own bunk in the barracks every morning. I certainly can do it here if you'll just tell me where . . ."

"Right!" Katherine said, bouncing up. "Please don't fuss, Mother. I'll show Allan where the bedding is. Come along! March!"

I saluted and said, "Yes, ma'am!" She led me to a closet where she found the linins and then walked me to the far end of the wing, once bumping shoulders with me. That and the sway of her hips fully awakened all sorts of rose-colored images in my mind. As we got to the door, she stopped suddenly and I bumped into her.

Without backing away, she turned to me. Red-faced and fumble-tongued, I put my hands on her waist. God, she was so soft! She dropped the bed clothes, shut her eyes and moved against me and we hugged, both trembling.

"Bless you, Allan, for your wonderful gifts. Mother and Father so needed something of the sort. We all did. Thank you. Thank you."

I nodded, unable to speak. Unable to speak because our bodies were pressed together. Unable to speak because I felt guilty -- guilty about Betty -- guilty because it seemed wrong for a guest to be hugging . . . and wanting . . . a daughter of the house.

I backed away from her and stooped to pick up the sheets.

She took them from me and gently pulled me by the hand into the room which looked as if Bill had only left an hour ago. The armoire door was open with a tennis racket hanging inside it. His clothes were neatly spaced.

Hanging above a desk was a photo of two young officers, the taller in Royal Navy full dress. The other lad, the stocky one, wore Royal Army battle dress with lieutenant's pips on the shoulder straps.

"The room wasn't nearly this pulled together when Bill was alive," she whispered, leaning her shoulder against mine. I eased my arm around her. "He was a bit messy," she said. Then, lowering her head and putting her hand to her eyes, "My David was the fussy one."

I pulled her to me again and she cried into my shoulder. I spotted a striped beanie in the armoire. "Was Bill a university student? All of my boys were."

"Yes," she whispered, pulling back. "I'm sorry, Allan. It's just so distressing." With a sniff, she shoved the bed linens back into my hands and bolted from the room. As soon as I made the bed I returned to the study. The missus had retired.

Chapter 18
April 29, 1944 – Katherine

Katherine half-reclined on a couch and stared at the bookcases as Alf and I chatted about Wilson and his bike shop. Suddenly, she stood. "I imagine you soldiers want to talk about military matters and I can't contribute."

We arose as she said, "Goodnight, Father." She met my eyes. "Allan, I do hope you sleep well."

After she left, Alf said, "She's still distraught about David, of course. For a while, things had become much quieter in the Med with the Italian navy out of it. We had hopes. But then at Anzio a glider bomb hit his ship. Beastly things."

I didn't know what to say except that it must be horrible sitting here just waiting for such telegrams.

He nodded. "Exactly right, Allan. Until the Huns invaded France, I never realized how bad it is or how helpless those at home feel. While I was in Mesopotamia during the Great War," he said, "all I had to fear was Turks, Arabs, Germans and my own superiors.

"But Alice was back here with our baby, day in and day out never knowing anything at all about her husband or, indeed, whether he even was alive.

"Well, this time around I was here at home, of course. And when the Blitzkrieg overwhelmed the Low Countries and France and then Dunkirk . . . well at last I grasped her sense of utter helplessness. Perpetual uncertainty . . . seems much harder to bear than battle."

"I never thought about that until now," I said. "I'd guess I'd better write to Mom and Sis much more often." He nodded.

I asked him to name his favorite generals. He surprised me by picking Patton first, then Montgomery.

"But I think Horrocks was a field commander quite equal to Patton," he said.

It sounded to me like he said 'Haw-ducks.' "I don't recognize the name, sir. Who is it again?"

"A major general -- Sir Brian Haw-ducks. He cares for his troops like nobody else. He's always up front at the line . . . well, he was. He was frightfully wounded in Africa and I doubt he'll be fit for action again. I just hope he is."

"Sir, how is that name spelled?"

When he spelled it out, I did recognize 'H-o-r-r-o-c-k-s' from North Africa. And he laughed when I said British pronunciation often was as weird as American butchery of French names.

# # #

The bed was comfortable, but I wasn't sleepy.

Lying with my hands behind my head, I stared at the Milky Way through the window of Bill's room. First I smiled at Alf's discussion of how the English pronounce 'shire' as 'sheer' while Americans do the opposite. From there we moved from "vite-amins" to "vita-mins."

I was trying to avoid thoughts of Betty and reminiscing about how beautiful Katherine was – and how grief still seemed to wrack her. I hoped once asleep I would dream about her rather than beating my father near to death in a West Virginia kitchen. That remembrance still kept coming to mind, but I steered my thoughts away. To Katherine.

As if my fantasies beckoned her, the door opened. In a long, lacy gown Katherine drifted toward me in the gloom as if she were a ghost, a beautiful ghost.

"Katherine . . ."

"Allan, may I please lie with you." She was weeping. I threw the covers back, scooched to make room and opened my arms to her. "Thank you," she said, reclining beside me. "I am so damned alone. I need human warmth."

She laid her head on my shoulder. I kissed her forehead as I covered us and gently stroked her back. She sighed and relaxed against me. "Thank you, Allan."

"Thank you, Katherine. It's wonderful to have you by me like this. Try to sleep."

"No," she murmured. "I want to stay awake to feel this warmth beside me again." Her breathing slowed and she soon slept anyway. I dozed off. Later I awakening to feel her trembling. It was nearly 3 a.m., and the quarter moon illuminated her face, shining with tears.

"Katherine, what's the matter?"

"It was a nightmare."

I kissed her cheek. "Would it help to tell me about it?"

"I cannot. It always awakens me, you see, but I never remember anything about it. It's just pure bloody horror."

"I think I know what you mean."

"Because of North Africa?"

"No, not that."

She raised her head. "What is it, Allan?"

"Oh," I said, "It's hard for me to tell. I've never really talked about it."

But then I told her. About the mewing. About seeing my father, my hero, beating my mother.

"It was savage," I said. "And in a flash it explained so much. I realized he must have been doing it for years. Nothing ever sent me into such a rage."

I told her how, with all my weight, I stamped my bare foot against the side of his knee. How he screeched and collapsed down the front of the gas range, dragging Mom down with him.

"I yelled at him to let her go. He wouldn't, so I kicked him and that only set my bare toes on fire. So I grabbed Mom's marble rolling pin and clobbered his knee with it.

"Well, he screamed again," I said, sweeping the perspiration from my face. "But he kept his hold on Mom, his arm around her neck and his fingers digging into her face.

"He raised his other hand to ward off the next blow. So I just smashed the hand. He released Mom so he could cradle his broken hand with the other. I slammed the rolling pin onto the point of his right shoulder. He yelled again dropping his hand.

"As I hit him, Katherine, I kept yelling 'Why? Why?' I smashed that rolling pin against his face, knocking his false teeth clear across the room. And I kept hitting him – right, left, right, left. Each time I swung I yelled, 'You! . . . Drunken! . . . Pig!' His blood splattered onto the oven door. It wasn't that I wanted to kill him, Katherine . . . I wanted him to suffer."

I told her that in a sense I did kill him. I killed the hero who had taunted and pushed me so much as a boy in football and in studies. In the end, Mom pulled me away leaving him lying there in his blood, moaning.

"As we stood above him, I told her we were leaving for Aunt Sarah's in South Carolina. So I made her to go pack. 'Pack for yourself, Mom, and for Sis. I'll pack for me. Hurry. We don't have a lot of time.'

"I was cruel. After she left, I crammed a tea towel in his mouth, grabbed the front of his shirt and pulled his face up to mine. I said, 'Touch her again – ever! – I'll break every bone in your whisky-stinking body. Here's a sample.' I rapped his nose with the rolling pin. His eyes widened with the pain. 'Now who sounds like a basket full of kittens? Enjoy it? Next time you'll beg to die.'"

I told Katherine how I yanked out the towel and started pouring a jar of his corn liquor into his mouth. "At first he sputtered and tried to spit it out but then he began gulping it and I kept on pouring.

"I jeered at him, 'Yeah, that's what you like, you pig! Guzzle, guzzle, guzzle.' In five minutes he was snoring. I rifled through his secret stash. He had almost $2,000. I left $200 for him and took the rest.

"We were on the road by 3 a.m., but not for Georgia. We headed northwest across Ohio. I had it in mind to get to Seattle. Well, I just drove into Michigan and gave out when we got to the Lake Michigan shoreline. So the next day we caught the ferry to Milwaukee. That's where the rattletrap quit running and that's where we settled."

Katherine whispered, "And you've never told this to anyone?"

"No. Even Mom and I never really talked about it. And I'm sorry to unload on you like this."

"I'm glad you did Allan. I thank you for confiding."

We were quiet a minute. I was still sweating with the strain of it. I murmured, "It wasn't until after we were set up in Milwaukee that I found out the why of it. Mom was protecting Sis from him."

"My God, how awful," she said.

She sighed and snuggled closer. For the first time I became really aware of her body. She was making me aware of it – pressing her breasts against my ribs, pushing her knee up between my thighs. As she breathed gently in my ear, she ran her hand lightly back and forth on my chest. She leaned her head back, eyes wide and looking into my eyes.

"Katherine, I want you. God, how I want you, but I have to tell you there's been somebody else in my life and I don't think this is . . ."

She put a finger on my lips.

"Oh, Allan, do be still. Remember what you said to Father? You spoke of 'all the sacrificing and suffering.' Allan, I have sacrificed and suffered. I am suffering. You have suffered so much and soon will suffer all the more. And not knowing how you are faring, I will suffer too. So now let us take comfort in each other. Let me have you just as you need to have me."

It made some kind of crazy sense. A great excuse to forget, to do what I shouldn't.

We kissed and became more and more heated. She stood and removed her gown. As she lay back, the moonlight transformed her body into an alabaster statue. But she was glowing tender flesh, not stone. I leaned to her. And we embraced again. And shared.

Afterward, we just stared into each other's eyes. I felt a sense of peace I never had known. Sleep crept upon us.

We made love again Saturday night and Sunday night, each time desperately clinging together afterwards.

# # #

I never hated anything so much as having to leave the Manor at dawn Monday.

We said good bye standing in the dark by the jeep, clinging together. I told Katherine I hoped to get away to see her the coming weekend. She shook her head and her words sliced me inside

"We won't see each other for a long time, Allan." A tear rolled down her cheek. "Perhaps never."

"What are you talking about?"

"My passengers think I'm just a stupid empty-headed woman with neither ears nor brains. So they talk. Your forces – all our forces -- are moving to the coast quite soon. The invasion is not far off."

She hugged me fiercely. "Allan, will you please remember me?"

"Oh, my God yes, Katherine. Every blessed minute. I could never forget you. And I will be back."

Chapter 19
May 1, 1944 – Torquay, England

As everybody dragged in and reported in first thing Monday morning I tested Katherine's suspicions by asking the first sergeant to reserve a jeep on Wednesday or Thursday.

No dice.

"Can't do it, Dud," he said. "As of this minute we're all restricted to post. No phone calls, either."

"What's up?"

"I can't tell you except that I think we're about to move."

An hour later, Maj. Cavanaugh – the regiment's ops officer -- gave officers and NCOs in the heavy weapons company a little clutch in the gut. He said the regiment would start a secret movement by convoy after dark. We would be confined at the new location for an indefinite period. "Until we invade . . ." someone said.

The major just frowned and went on. "Meanwhile, the troops today are to pack their dress uniforms and personal gear and belongings in their duffle bags for storage. From this point on, the uniform of the day will be combat gear. Have your mortars and machine guns in your barracks. If you have equipment deficiencies, the time to see the quartermaster is now."

An odd tapping made me glance around the room.

The Dick was rattling the toes of his shoes on the plywood floor, practically a Gene Krupa riff. His eyelids seemed to flutter in time with his toes. The man looked terrified. I couldn't help grinning.

Maj. Cavanaugh looked pointedly at him. "Do you have a problem, captain?"

The Dick cringed. "Nossir."

The major stared at him, then looked back at the rest of us and said, "Good." The major, Capt. Freeman, the First Shirt and I were the only people in the room to have seen combat. Most of the others looked relieved that something was happening . . . finally.

For my part, I was relaxed. I knew terror wouldn't come until the ride to the beach. After that, we'd either be dead or too damned busy to be scared.

"If there are no questions, have your men get packed."

As we all stood, Capt. Freeman said, "Sgt. Dudley, please stick around for a minute."

As the room emptied, he handed me a set of orders, with two sets of staff sergeant chevrons. "Congratulations, Sgt. Dudley. And I've got another promotion order and buck sergeant's chevrons here for Forster. You'll see that he gets them?"

"I will, sir, and many thanks."

"Don't thank me, Dud. You and your men have earned it." The major grinned, extended his hand and congratulated me.

Behind him, The Dick glared at me.

# # #

As the men packed their gear, they unmercifully razzed their new sergeant. "Hey, look who played drop the soap in the shower with the colonel? . . . Yeah, just when I thought things couldn't get worse, Forster makes sergeant . . . Ah, boys, now we're really under the iron heel of a martinet for sure . . . Hey, Sarge! Permission to lick those boots of yours? . . . Mahster! Mahster! May Igor have the privilege of sewing on your brand-new stripes?"

Forster just grinned as he oversaw Bull field-stripping one of the .50 caliber Brownings. "Now be careful, Bob. We don't want any left-over parts."

Bull bowed profoundly, "Yes, majesty. It shall be done."

# # #

About 1700 a deuce-and-a-half pulled up outside the barracks to collect our duffle bags. I organized a relay first from the second floor and then the first. The driver, a black tech sergeant, told us they were being stored in a Quonset hut warehouse. Once we defeated Germany he said he bet the Army would hold us responsible for turning in the contents of our own bags. He said he figured the cost of any missing gear would be deducted from our pay.

"What about the bags of the guys who don't come back?"

"I don't know, Boss."

"Don't call me 'boss,' I'm just a sergeant."

He grinned. "Okay, Boss."

After dark, the same trucks reappeared in the company streets. This time we loaded ourselves, jammed tight because we were in full combat gear, musette bags, steel pots, canteens, helter halves, gas masks and carbines. I rode jammed in the cab between the driver and his relief, a Pfc. It amazed me that every time we came to a major road, we either stopped to let a convoy pass, or else we passed a long column of tape-slitted headlights waiting for us.

"Jesus," I said. "Looks like the whole damn division is on the move."

"Naw, Boss," the driver said. "I figure the whole damned U.S. army is on the move. Seen it the las' three nights. You'll see when we go over this next hill. Look like damn lightning bugs all over the plain." He was right. All southwest England seemed to crawl with dimmed headlights.

"Where are we headed?"

"All I knows is that it's a tent compound somewhere near a little bitty town on the coast called Tor-key."

"You sure it ain't Turkey?" the relief driver asked.

About 0100, our convoy turned through a massive barbed wire gate and rolled down a long gravel street separating rows of 20-man tents. A lieutenant with a flashlight and clip board waved us to a stop. "Name? Outfit?"

"Sir, Dudley, staff sergeant, with Dog Company's mortar platoon, First of the 8th Infantry."

"Good. Here's your new home." He pointed with his light at a cluster of tents. "You and your boys and the next truck go into this area. Now Sarge, move 'em right along because we've got to unload this convoy before daylight."

The boys already had dropped the tailgate were jumping down with their gear, so I herded them to the tents.

We lived there 29 days.

# # #

The next morning we discovered it was a rectangular tent city for the whole battalion, all under a huge umbrella of camouflage netting. It occupied a long gentle rise and we were located toward the summit.

From it, we could see another massive tent city a half-mile to the west. Because a 12-foot double-apron barbed wire fence surrounded each city, both staging areas looked like prison camps. Buttressing that impression was concertina wire filling the 4-foot space between the fences. MPs with tommy guns patrolled outside the fence.

Some of the boys found it insulting and were starting to argue about their rights as Americans.

During one such bitching session, The Dick came into our tent and further endeared himself to the troops. "You men are in the Army. You have no rights." That went over like the proverbial turd in a punch bowl. But the boys decided to handle it their own way. They started debating.

Jacobs informed the captain that rights were societal artifacts, existential entities merely . . . that it would be more philosophically appropriate to adopt an ontological approach by discussing personal liberties. (By now my headache started coming back.) Timmer politely said English pragmatism exemplified by Locke and Hume was the proper guide to attack this issue.

Just then, Lt. Scott came in. Lt. Scott was a nice guy as long as the occasion allowed it and he explained that in the next few days the brass would tell us some of the most important secrets of the war.

"We know the Nazis have spies in England," he said, "and we don't want them to know where and when we're going to land, right?" Everybody nodded. "So these fences aren't so much to keep you in as to keep them out."

The Dick stood behind him in mute disapproval. His attitude was that no officer owed an explanation of anything to anybody.

"Thank you, sir, for clearing that up," I said to Lt. Scott. I gave a glare around the tent but couldn't help breaking into a grin. "These guys kill me, sir. They want to argue about everything. Constantly."

The lieutenant laughed. Forster looked thoughtful. "You know, sir, I believe the compounds have all this extra barbed wire because they'll be cages for all the thousands of Germans that we capture."

The lieutenant, half-way out the tent flap, nodded. "Sgt. Forster, I bet you're right." The Dick just sniffed.

I don't know whether in the end they did turn out to be POW cages, but Forster's explanation made enough sense to calm everybody down.

Soon we did, in fact, begin learning some of the war's most important secrets, including why they didn't want anyone leaving 1st Battalionville.

They briefed us for days on the whole plan: Two airborne divisions parachuting at night behind the mile-wide lagoon that the Germans had created beyond our landing beach; we, the 8th Infantry, landing on the beach, then driving west across the lagoon to link up with the paratroopers at a crossroads village named Sainte-Mere-Eglise.

We and the paratroopers also would make way for a daytime landing by a regiment of glider troops.

Our division's 12th and 22nd Infantry Regiments would land behind us and attack north toward Cherbourg because the allies needed to capture a deep-water port. We also would make room for three more divisions that would attack west to the other side of the Normandy peninsula.

Once we had cleared the peninsula and captured Cherbourg, the whole damned allied army – Limeys, Canucks, Americans, Poles and French, all lined up along the coast -- would attack east out of Normandy, cross France and conquer Germany.

Those were the plan's bare bones.

In the followed days, they plied us with head-swimming masses of detail. The maps they posted for us were 20 feet wide and 10 feet high, depicting a mile and a half of Normandy coast plus the areas inland from it.

They called it Utah Beach.

In the end, we didn't land quite where we were supposed to.

But it turned out, we were close enough.

Chapter 20
May 15, 1944 – Torquay, England

Some G3 major from Division gave us our initial briefing about the landing itself. With his big-toothed smile he reminded me of a used car salesman . . . only instead of having the honor of driving off the lot in a rusty old Hupmobile or Model A, the 8th Regiment would have the honor of hitting the beach first.

Behind me, Halls muttered, "Jesus Christ, how the hell did we get so lucky?"

Timmer whispered, "Do you think that grinning sack of shit will have the honor of going ashore with the rest of us?"

Forster hissed, "Shut the fuck up, you sonsabitches. Now!" The new sergeant wanted his boys to take this seriously.

"Question?" the major said, pointing in my direction. Directly behind me, Whitehorse had shot his hand up. In his slow, flat accent he asked, "Sir, can you tell us whether that Kilroy guy will get there before us?"

I turned around to tell him to shut up and sit down but the major laughed. "Actually, I'm glad you asked that question. Yes, Kilroy may beat us into France – probably will -- but he'll be the only one because we plan to be the first troops ashore.

"Now listen up and pay close attention. First and Second Battalions will land abreast of each other, and lead the way inland. Third Battalion will follow on immediately along with the Third Battalion of the 22nd Infantry.

"We'll all land in LCVPs – that stands for Landing Craft, Vehicle Personnel. You'll soon get to know them.

"With you men aboard, the LCVPs will be lowered from four troop transports. You're lucky being in the first wave, because the follow-up troops get to climb down nets into those same landing craft when they return from the beach.

"You D Company mortar men from First Battalion," he added. "Your half-tracks will come ashore on D-plus One. Until then, you're humping your guns along with the rest of Heavy Weapons." I heard some quiet grumbling but thought it good news that we'd get half-tracks at all.

"Now higher headquarters has issued a couple of very important cautionary notes," the major said. "You'll hear it again from the Navy.

"Before you even think about getting into your landing craft, unlace your boots so you can slip them off easily. Second, be sure to re-fasten your helmet chin straps across the backs of your helmets. Hear that? The backs! This is just in case your LCVP broaches and you go into the drink. Without your boots and helmets, your chances of survival improve. With helmets hanging from your heads and boots on, you have no chance. Period.

"Likewise, we're going to have a drill about life vests. Get 'em on correctly, right up under the armpits, they save your life. Wear 'em wrong, like around the waist, they hold you upside down and drown you."

He turned to the map with his pointer and Forster and I began taking notes.

First Battalion was to land slightly north of Exit 3, a causeway that threaded the flooded marshes behind the beach. The causeway connected to a road which led almost directly west to Sainte-Mere-Eglise.

We'd get on the causeway near a beachfront hamlet named La Madeleine, push through a cluster of 13 buildings called Audeville la-Hubert and a larger settlement, about 30 buildings, named Turoqueville.

Right away it got confusing.

The major was using French pronunciation for the place names.

Now, "Oh-d'vee looBAIR" made sense to any of the men acquainted with French. But to the rest of us ignoramuses, the name looked like it should be pronounced Awdyville la-Hewbert. So for quite a while we were bewildered, looking for map names that he was pronouncing but we weren't seeing.

Later the briefers decided to Americanize the names to Awdyville and Turkoville.

I didn't like Turkoville's looks.

It was a fishhook-shaped cluster of buildings about a mile beyond Awdyville -- the bend in the hook facing our route from Exit Three. If the Germans set up three or four MGs in those buildings and mortars behind them, they could chop up everybody along that entire causeway. Besides, two other hamlets, little clusters of buildings, lay behind Turkoville, looking perfect for retreat and then counterattack – the Krauts' specialty.

Forster raised a hand.

"Question?"

"Sir, I wonder if you can tell us whether the buildings in these villages are stone like so many of the British cottages we see?"

The major said they probably were stone but that we should expect no trouble with La Madeleine or its beach pillboxes because naval gunfire and dawn bombing would blast them apart. The same might apply to Awdyville. Turkoville was thought to be a "probable node of German resistance."

"However," big smile again, "coming ashore maybe 30 minutes behind you will be the division's 70th Tank Battalion." I heard a murmur of appreciation around me. *Don't cheer yet, boys. If these are old stone houses like in Algeria, tank guns won't dent them. Besides, I've got a major general friend who says it's bad tank country.*

"And don't forget," the major added, "that both the British and American Navies will be out there, on call, with guns all the way up to 14-inchers."

Forster raised his hand again. "Just checking, sir, but am I right in remembering that if you call for a ranging shot from a battleship, that they want you at least 2,000 yards from the target?"

Several listeners muttered things like, "Well, to hell with that shit!"

The major blinked and said, "I think you're right, but the Navy will have its own spotters on the beach with us and they'll be working with our forward observers. We'll get into all that detail later."

# # #

After the briefing, Forster and I met with the mortar sections. I told them to pay very close attention to the word about loosening boots and chin straps and to wear their life vests the right way.

"You really think we have to worry about that?" Timmer asked.

Forster said, "Look dimwit, you don't have to worry if you follow those directions."

I put in my oar. "When we landed in Africa, Timmer, a few boats got crosswise in the surf which was really high. They capsized and the troops aboard them went down like stones. Same thing, I heard, in the Sicily landing. They washed ashore a few days later after the crabs and fish had been at them."

Some of the boys swallowed.

"Now, look, we're just one little tiny bit of a whole damned army that's going ashore . . . tens of thousands of men. Some people are going to fuck up. If my boat capsizes and I end up in the English Channel, I want to float. And I don't want any of you water-logged punks pulling me down with you. Clear?"

They all gave me worried looks. "Look," Forster said, "Sgt. Dudley's not trying to scare you, but sometimes you knuckleheads just flat don't pay attention. This is serious. It can save your life."

"Now another thing," I added. "They're saying that once ashore we're facing some garrison troops -- not the best. Well, just you be very, very alert once on the beach. Because even if they're 40-year-old fat-asses, they're still Germans and Hitler has issued at least one eye and one working trigger finger to every one of those bastards.

"After all our training on German rifles and machine guns, you know they have excellent weapons. And, as you know personally, any 10-year-old can drop a mortar round down a tube as long as someone aims it for him."

"Sarge?"

"What, Manthei."

"Why didn't you look very excited about us having tanks along?"

"Oh, it's good news," I said. "But I warn you, in action, tanks need protection from foot soldiers and foot soldiers need to be very careful around tanks. If the tanks are buttoned up, their drivers can't see much. And that includes any GI who happens to fall down or take cover in front of them. The second thing is that tanks draw artillery fire like shit draws flies. You don't want to be close when 88s start hitting them . . . a whole damned turret might land on you."

# # #

We started hearing we would land on D-Day as part of a convoy called Force U. But nobody knew the date other than that it would be sometime soon.

When they ordered everyone to take out $10,000 apiece in life insurance, the boys joked about it. But inside, I think they found it as sobering as when I took out my own policy while on the convoy to North Africa.

They stayed pretty quiet, too, as we paraded through the quartermaster tent to draw all the gear we'd take.

They issued each of us a small sheaf of French francs, carbine ammo pouches to go on our cartridge belts, extra carbine magazines, gas mask in gas mask pouch, a belt of .30-06 for the machine guns, a box of .45 ACP for our pistols, bayonet, life vest, entrenching tool, first aid kit, musette bag, gloves, L-shaped flashlight, shelter half, a canteen of water, three K ration boxes, one blanket, one D ration, Halazone tablets to purify water, two fragmentation grenades, Dramamine tablets to curb seasickness.

They also issued special fatigue pants, shirts, field jackets and raincoats impregnated with some gawdawful smelling chemical that supposedly would retard poison gas. Whatever it was, that chemical stiffened the cloth so that it abraded the skin where it rubbed your wrists, neck and crotch.

Plus that, each of us would tote 45 pounds either of mortar tube, base plate or bipod or an equal weight of assorted of HE, Willie Peter and flare mortar rounds.

They issued the two Mortar Forker sections and the other mortar section two-man carts with solid rubber tires with which we could pull the guns rather than carry them. I worried that the carts would bog down in beach sand. I ended up wrong on that. The beach turned out to be pretty firm gravel rather than sand.

Chapter 21
May 19, 1944 – Tor Bay, England

The reality of approaching combat began to sink in when we took our first familiarization rides in an LCVP. We crammed in three sections as well as the HQ staff together with our mortars and carts – 26 of us -- and took a quick run out into the bay and back.

The boat bounced horribly and the diesel fumes didn't help. What with the mortars and carts, we were so crowded there was no place to vomit except on somebody else's back . . . if they were lucky enough to face away from you.

Fortunately, with any kind of waves at all, you got a regular dousing of cold, salty spray which at least rinsed away some of the used Spam and half-digested macaroni.

The really sobering news was that though the boat's ramp was steel, the sides were plywood.

"What the hell?" Torrelli said when we got back. "Bullets won't have any trouble at all getting through to us."

"Yeah," Bull said, "but since the boat's wood, it ain't gonna sink so fast."

"Oh, well, that's just great," Torrelli said. "So we'll sink slowly and they can pick us off before we drown."

"Jesus Christ on a crutch!" I shouted. "Will you silly bastards stop arguing? Just once? Please!"

"Well, gee, Sarge, it keeps us occupied."

"Well it drives me crazy! If you want to occupy yourselves, go organize a circle jerk."

They had us exercise boarding the ship. And after that, we practiced boarding the landing craft on the ship again and again and again until we could do it in the dark which, of course, was the whole idea.

We also practiced landings from LCVPs at Slapton Sands, a beach located about a two-hour ride and the southwest shore of Tor Bay. The approaches to the beach were pretty well exposed to the swell coming up the channel. So we started speaking of whether we'd take a two-vomit or a three-vomit ride to the beach. Speaking through pale, quivering lips, Frost said that an LCVP wasn't so much a wretched ride as a retching ride.

No argument.

They'd built pill boxes and beach obstacles on Slapton Sands, so we got an idea of what we'd see in Normandy. But what made the guys really glum was hearing how much longer our approach would be to Utah Beach.

# # #

Nau and Torrelli and I watched Timmer unwrap a D Ration. It was supposed to be a high-energy chocolate bar. It looked like tire tread. He tried to bite it.

"Jesus, it's like a damn rock! Are you really supposed to eat this thing?"

"Well, hell yes," I said with a smirk. "It's good for you. The guvmint says so."

Bull suggested cutting off a segment.

"I don't know," Timmer said. "I'm afraid it might break my bayonet."

He began carving at the side of the ration block, slicing off several flakes. He put them in his mouth and munched for a second. He immediately frowned. Then his eyes bulged. Mouth full and running with saliva, he said, "*Holy thit!*"

He spat the black mass into the nearest butt can. "My God, it's awful! Somebody give me a swig of water. It's bitter as hell. It's just like plain old unsweetened chocolate."

"No shit?" Nau said.

"Here," Timmer said, handing it to him. "Be my guest. I don't want the damned thing."

A minute later, Nau spat into the butt can and held up the D bar to the rest of the section. "Any takers? Hearing none . . ." he dropped the D bar into the butt can.

# # #

Lt. Scott and Capt. Freeman and I visited HQ. I wanted to know if we should plan on setting up the mortars right on the beach, or work our way inland first.

They said to hope for the best but plan for the worst -- figure on emplacing inland, but to be ready to fire from the beach if necessary. The battalion S3 told me that if we had to emplace on the beach, we'd find cover behind a very long, low seawall with a high sand berm just inland.

"It will screen you from direct rifle and machine gun fire," he said. "But the Kraut spotters might see your smoke, so they could zero their own mortars on you pretty fast. You've got to be prepared to move at an instant's notice."

"Yessir," I said. *Godalmighty damn, why didn't I just continue being a rifleman?*

Capt. Freeman thanked me and said I better get back to the rest of the Mortar Forkers. We all chuckled as I saluted and left.

As the door shut behind me, I heard them talking about casualties. It was the S2 who said that the G1 at Division was trying to round up a ton of after-landing replacements.

"Already?"

"Damn right. We estimate 50 percent casualties on the beach."

Chapter 22
Wednesday, May 31, 1944 – The *Barrett*

I didn't tell the boys the 50 per cent prediction and tried not dwell on it myself.

Today they announced D-Day would be June 5 and that we would board a Liberty ship, the *USNS Wesley Barrett*, after dark tonight. They took us out there in an LCM, a much larger and steadier landing craft than an LCVP. We mounted an arched gangplank through the *Barrett's* entry port. Guess who had been there first and left us a sign?

Yeah, that SOB Kilroy.

The idea of spending five days aboard another stench barge and then having a one-in-two chance of dying made me shudder. *Why couldn't I at least spend my last week of life with Katherine?*

But actually the *Barrett* turned out to be okay.

Though every bit as crowded as the *Queen*, the *Barrett* was nowhere near so smelly. She was brand new and during her Atlantic crossings she had carried cargo rather than troops. So, all her five holds had faint odors of ammunition, paint and perhaps gasoline or oil, but not human sweat and vomit . . . at least not at that point.

And the *Barrett's* chow was fantastic. In the tent cities, they'd been feeding us steak and pork chops and pie – even lemon merengue pie, my favorite. But those Army grease-burners never could cook for masses of men as well as the Navy's cooks.

Either way, even the tent city eating beat the hell out of regular camp food which leaned heavily on Brussels sprouts, seemingly the only vegetable grown in England at the time. In my opinion, Brussels sprouts made us the gassiest army in history.

We drilled constantly boarding LCVPs. Seven of the boats were stacked on the port side of the *Barrett's* superstructure and the same number on the starboard side plus two more on the stern.

All of us wound up with *Barrett* stripes – two or three indelible black bars across the shins of our fatigue pants. See, the LCVPs were secured in place by dozens of steel cables, all filthy with grease, extending like so many trip wires about 15 inches above the decks. They tripped all of us at one time or another. We had to snicker, though, because even the ship's officers in their neat pressed khakis bore the same hash marks.

During drills we got a good view of the vast number of ships in the bay. I tried counting them and gave up at 150. Capt. Freeman, marveling at the sight, told us this was only one of the many staging areas all along England's southern coast as well as bays and anchorages to the north and even in Northern Ireland.

Evans said we were sitting ducks for German bombers. But the occasional planes roaring overhead either bore the American white star or British red, white and blue roundel. I told him our briefers claimed the allies had total air superiority. "Okay," he said, "but if that's true, why are so many ships towing these barrage balloons?"

"It's just insurance," I said. "And I personally think you should quit worrying."

"Well how can I, Sarge? We could get bombed, drowned, or shot . . ."

"George," I interrupted, "what do you want, an egg in your beer? I figured out when we invaded Algeria that there were just too damned many things to worry about . . . so it's a case of go bug-house nuts, or quit stewing until you get ashore with live weapons and have some control over what's happening. So for now just go play some bridge and take your mind off it."

"Good idea," Manthei said. "As soon as we go below, let's get the cards out."

Unfortunately the weather went to hell and card-playing lost its appeal. See, Tor Bay had a centuries-old reputation as an uneasy anchorage. So the *Barrett* – all 400-plus feet of her – jerked, rolled and plunged at her anchors through much of the day. As a result, by midnight, the seasick troops sealed below decks were throwing up all that wonderful Navy chow. The vomiting soldiers had *Barrett* on her way to matching the *Queen's* stink. At least the crew was able to run the blowers to keep the air circulating.

On Saturday, June 3, the PA system said we were weighing anchor – next stop, Utah Beach! That left us all breathless. For me it felt just like the last time off Algeria. Being below decks, we couldn't see a damned thing, but we could feel the vibration of *Barrett's* engines and now the steady pitch and roll of a moving ship.

A lot of the guys went to Catholic mass. I kind of hovered around the edges, but didn't understand a word. So then I heard there was to be a communion service for Protestants. It looked just like the Catholic service, the priest in his robe droning on, raising the cup and making the sign of the cross. It was in English and kind of comforting. I didn't take communion because of the wine and I really wasn't sure what it was about.

When I got back to my rack from church, Timmer, Evans and Frost were arguing, of course. This time, they were debating the morality of killing Germans.

"Are you jerks fucking serious?" I said.

"No, not really," Timmer said. "But it's something to do to pass the time. Now Evans here claims it's immoral to kill Germans because the Sixth Commandment says 'Thou shalt not kill' so he . . ."

From the top rack, Jacobs interrupted. "That's not correct, boys. The commandment actually says, 'You shall do no murder'. That's a big difference."

"Aw, Stan, that's bullshit," Evans said. "I read it right in the Bible . . . 'Thou shalt not kill'."

"Well, George, I think you got a bad translation," Jacobs said. "My parents were good Jews who made me go to Hebrew school when I was a kid, and so I read it right there in the original language."

"No shit?"

Jacobs first recited the commandment in Hebrew, which sounded to me like a lot of throat-clearing. But then he did a pretty fair imitation of a backwoods circuit preacher, "Brethren, that's the smokin' hot Gospel! Halleluuuuuiah!"

"Don't you mean smoking hot Old Testament?"

"Yeah, of course," Jacobs grinned, "but you got to admit it sounded like pretty good tent revival preaching."

I told them try to get some rest because we'd be hitting the beach in three more hours.

"Now one thing I want all you boys to know," I added. "We need each other where we're going. So I now consider y'all to be my friends, my bosom buddies and members of my military family. Fellas, just call me Dud."

As they all laughed, a new Now Hear This come over the PA.

The storm was so bad and the surf so high it would be impossible to land, so Force U was returning to Tor Bay. The landing was postponed at least 24 hours.

"Where's Whitehorse?" Bull raged. "I'm gonna throw that damn Injun over the side for bringing on all this rain!"

Whitehorse sat up from his rack, raised his arms and said, "Masagwa, white man!"

"What the hell does that mean?"

"Nothing. I just made it up."

Jacobs proposed a theory that the postponement had nothing to do with the weather – that it was a ploy by Ike or Montgomery to make us so fucking fighting mad that we'd go berserk and absolutely steamroll the Krauts.

Bull asked loudly, "Hey Sarge, now that they put off the landing, can we still call you Dud?"

"Hell no. You're not my friends until we're in combat and you can protect my ass."

We tried to settle down for a wait that we knew would be at least 24 hours.

You remember the search aboard the *Queen* for Raalph Braaack? Well, a lot of troops began calling for him all over the *Barrett*, too. Sea sickness was even getting to the craps shooters. I mean, when you're placing a bet and somebody on a rack six feet above you flashes his hash on your cash, it really sours the game.

Makes the dice sticky, too.

The next 24 hours were, I believe, the worst any of us endured shy of combat itself. Everyone was tense and exhausted from seasickness.

Despite the ship's blowers, the smell worsened by the minute.

We thought of asking for the hatch covers to be removed, but the drumming of rain overhead was unmistakable. We'd all be soaked in minutes.

Besides they probably wouldn't do us the favor anyway.

I doubt anyone other than the Pilgrim Fathers ever wanted off a ship as badly as us.

But then at 1600 on the 5th we heard a new Now Hear This. The voice on the PA sounded jubilant even before he gave the news that Force U was getting underway again for Utah Beach. We'd land at dawn.

The yells, cheers and whistles were deafening.

Then the cheering kind of died down.

Everybody obviously thought it would be great to get off the ship.

. . . except that it meant going straight into combat.

Chapter 23
June 6, 1944 – The English Channel

They told us we would board our landing craft at 0230 and that they would lower us into the water about 0330 for the three-hour, 12-mile voyage to the beach. We were not to load our carbines and pistols until we landed.

For the next two hours, I just curled up on a rack, keeping a tight grip as the ship pitched and rolled, and going inside myself to dwell on how much I missed Katherine -- just what I wrote in my last letter to her the day before we boarded the *Barrett*.

Betty kept coming to mind, too. Did my mail just never get through to her? Or had she fallen for some rich doctor? I couldn't think of what to do, but then I quit worrying. Considering 50 per cent casualties, by this time tomorrow I'd probably be dead anyway.

Forster shook me awake.

"Dud. Dud! Wake up for God's sake! They just ordered us to get into the LCVPs."

"They did?"

"Damn right. How the hell can you sleep at a time like this?"

"Nothing else to do. All right, are the boys up?"

"They're up. The rain has quit and they're ready for some fresh air."

"Me, too. Let's go."

As our turn came and we loaded up all that gear and climbed out onto the upper decks, we took some very deep breaths of clean sea air. We also heard a constant, throbbing drone . . . a broad shadowy parade of airplanes flying above us.

Barely looking at each other, the Mortar Forkers and a third section loaded ourselves and then relayed our guns and carts into LCVP 45-4. Lt. Scott, Sgt. Svoboda and The Dick crowded in with us.

I looked at Svoboda and rolled my eyes. The Dick hadn't been with us on any boat exercises. The sergeant frowned and leaned toward me. "Maybe he had a problem with being first on the beach."

As we loosened our boot laces, Whitehorse looked up at the planes droning above us, hundreds of them.

"Jesus, do you s'pose those are bombers?"

"Naaa. They've got to be carrying the paratroopers that they said are landing inland."

"Oh-oh," Torrelli said, pointing forward. "I'd say they're getting a real reception. Look at that."

We could just make out tiny white flashes winking on the horizon. It looked like aerial explosions – probably Kraut antiaircraft fire.

Lt. Scott said, "Can you imagine parachuting, floating down through all that flack? Poor bastards."

"How many paratroops can they fit in one of those planes?"

"I hear it's just under 20."

"Oh, shit! Look at that!"

A small red flash winked and then a thin crimson comet fell in a long arc, disappearing beyond the horizon.

Sgt. Svoboda said, "Well, I think we can scratch 20 paratroopers."

Nobody said a word for quite a while after that.

Frost pulled his St. Christopher's medal from under his shirt and pressed it to his lips.

Chapter 24
June 6, 1944 – Utah Beach, Normandy

We just huddled there in the LCVP swaying side to side as the *Barrett*, rolled in the channel swell. She now was anchored, her lifting cables rattling and banging. The weather had settled, though, and we could make out a blur on the horizon ahead – Normandy.

Then, sounding a bit like God, the PA system boomed. "Away all boats!"

Things started happening rapidly. Electric motors howling, the *Barret's* winches lifted the LCVPs above us one by one and swayed them out over the water. As the first descended from view, a scrawny kid wearing a dark blue helmet climbed into the cockpit of our boat. With him came another sailor to man the boat's .50 caliber machine gun. I was standing right next to his cockpit.

"Sergeant," he said. "I'm yo cox'n. Able Seaman Eddy Billips at y'all's service. Now y'all want to tell the boys to hunker down fur as they can."

"West Virginia?" I asked.

He grinned ear to ear. "Wheeling."

"No shit?" I reached over to shake hands. "I'm from just up river at New Cumberland. Dontcha wish y'all was back in them hills 'bout now?"

"That's the pluperfect truth, buddy. Now they's startin' to raise us, so best hunker down."

Timmer and Nau wailed, "Oh, shit!" when we hit the water. Our boat started rising and falling like a kid's bobber on a pond's ripples. I'd forgotten how scary it was to ride a small craft in open ocean. It was a lot wilder than any run across Tor Bay.

Supposedly we were to stand in 4-man rows, but the boat's motion had everybody lurching and swaying and falling -- and vomiting, of course. Being a shorty, I could barely see over the sides of the vessel and it was scary as hell sometimes to find myself looking upward at waves that seemed about to overwhelm us.

The coxswain steered us in bouncing circles in the dark until all the craft of our wave were in the water. Then they formed a straight line and started the 3-hour run to the beach. About all we could see was an occasional glimpse between wave crests of water foaming along the hulls of the boats either side of us.

During those next gut-wrenching hours we hit every damned wave and wavelet with slam-slam, splash-splash, slam, splash, slam, splash. Thanks to the motor's roar, you barely heard the slam or splash. But you sure felt the slamming in your feet and knees and your hands where you clung to the gunwales. Yes, and spray slashing your face. I tried to keep my knees bent so they'd flex to the rise and fall of the boat. But pretty soon we had other things in mind.

At several points we shipped solid water over the port side and, though the boat had a pump, it couldn't keep up. We started to list, causing more water to roll in. Lt. Scott, Sgt. Svoboda and I had the guys wedge together on the high side while we and Forster bailed with our helmets.

Forster was one strong soldier, but after an off-and-on hour of bailing I saw him just about collapse from exhaustion. He leaned his head on the gunwale and closed his eyes. He got a hard wake-up when another wave slopped into the boat, yanking his helmet straight overboard right off his head.

"Shit!" he yelled. He snatched off Frost's helmet and resumed bailing. As we bailed, I saw The Dick on the deck, knees practically to his chin. I was scared. Hell, everybody was scared. Frost pulled so hard on his St. Christopher medal that he broke the chain and now had it in a white-knuckle grip as he prayed.

But The Dick seemed paralyzed with terror.

That's about when the fireworks began. We all were accustomed to judging the distance of explosions by sound. A nearby artillery burst was a sharp crack that hurt the ears. At a middle distance – say a quarter mile -- it was an echoing bass *ka-thup* and at long range, a mile or so, it was a muted *wumpf.*

The Navy showed us something new.

We must have been about a quarter mile away when a battleship, bow to us, blasted a 200-foot tongue of orange fire toward the land. The heat singed my face instantly and then a second later CRAKK -- the thunderclap muzzle blast jarred us even at that distance. We actually could see the shells glowing cherry red as they soared inland.

"Damn," Nau yelled. He was bailing now. "Had to be a 16-incher – maybe a whole fuckin' salvo. Ain't you glad you're not a Nazi today?"

Amen to that. Kill 'em all.

Right after that, our boat rocked violently and shipped more water thanks to the waves that the battleship's guns generated. By then I knew we weren't going to sink, but bailing kept us busy and kept our minds off things.

Closer in, we passed a cruiser adding to the fireworks with big flashes every half minute from her main turrets and constant flashes from the 5-inch turrets amidships. The glowing shells rose sedately over the water, disappeared into the overcast and then reappeared descending toward land. We were too low to see the shore or to have any idea of whether they were pasting the beaches or something inland.

Next we passed a destroyer steaming parallel to the beach. It had five single-gun turrets and all five would fire at once. Thanks to the roar of our motor, the pounding of the waves and the hiss of our wash, we couldn't hear the shots, but we saw the shells race toward land. Minutes later, Evans slapped at the guys around him and pointed at the destroyer. Fifty-foot water plumes spouted near her. The Krauts were shooting back with something big. *Better the destroyer than us!*

The coxswain nudged me and I stretched upright long enough to be able to see land. We were about 1,000 yards out and the water seemed calmer.

I worked my way through the crowd to the ramp. Torrelli began pointing again – a low procession of bombers speeding north above the beach, red-orange flashes rippling along the shore behind each one. Their smoke soon obscured everything.

By God, maybe that will take some of the starch out of the welcoming committee.

I peeked over the ramp to see that the other boats leading us were almost there. A line of tracers flashed above us. I ducked and then glanced back at the coxswain. He nodded and gave me a crazy grin . . . or maybe it was just a grimace. His gunner started firing the .50 right above us toward shore. The guys ducked and flinched because the big gun's barking muzzle blast shoved needles into the ears. Tracers arced from the shore toward the boats leading us, and those boats were returning fire, too. Four or five yard-high water spouts danced alongside us. Bastards were shooting at us again.

"Men!" Because of the motor roar, they couldn't hear me. I nudged Frost with the butt of my carbine. He turned and I yelled, "Lock and load! Lock and load!"

He frowned and formed the word, "What?"

I fished a 15-round magazine from a pouch on my cartridge belt as another hatful of spray slapped my face. I sputtered salt water and shoved the magazine into my carbine, seating it with a good slap at its base. He nodded and passed the word. By now my face felt stiff from all the caked salt . . . not to mention pure fear. As I worked my way back to the stern, I saw The Dick still huddled on the deck.

Our boat passed others that, now high in the water, were retracting from the beach. The coxswain waved to them and leaned close, yelling, "They's goin' back for another load. Now look out ahead, Sarge. We about to land."

# # #

The LCVP struck bottom and, with the aid of a wave, surged forward another 40 feet. We grabbed our burdens and were braced when the boat jarred to a stop and the ramp splashed down. I hobbled at first. My legs had tightened up during the trip from the *Barrett*.

And I was terrified, my heart sledging in my chest.

But that passed because all in the world I really wanted was to get out of that Goddam boat and onto firm land.

Lt. Scott was right beside me, stepping off the ramp and staggering forward in the following wave that soaked us both to the waist. God the water was cold!

I reached by and grabbed the Dick by his lifebelt, dragging him off the ramp. As he fell into the surf, the icy water shocked him into unfolding himself and getting to his feet. Biggest mistake I ever made. I just should have left the asshole to huddle there.

We had to haul the mortar carts and other equipment through 100 yards of surf. I heard no rifle or machine gun fire. But I was too busy looking for landmarks. Not a one was in view -- except the Douve River's broad mouth which seemed much too close.

Suddenly Gen. Roosevelt was in front of us beckoning with his cane. "What unit, son?"

Lt. Scott and I answered together, "Dog One Eight, sir."

A shell whistled in and exploded about 100 yards away. The Dick squealed. The general ignored the shower of sand and gravel. "Okay, which exit?"

"Exit Three, sir."

"Good." He pointed north with his cane. "Current took us way south. Your causeway is about 1,500 yards north. Look for the first break in the seawall and a big busted-up bunker just inland from it."

"Yes, sir," Lt. Scott said, "we're on our way."

The general waved the cane and called to men emerging from another LCVP. We ducked when another shell hit the beach flinging gravel and sand everywhere. The general didn't so much as flinch.

As we pulled the carts along the beach we saw a cluster of swabbies – they wore olive drab helmets with dark blue bands -- settled with their backs against the seawall. They had on ear phones and were talking into their mikes. Shells burst orange-black on the seawall maybe another mile north of us . . . then another and another; maybe destroyer fire.

We staggered as we pulled the carts. We'd been in the ship so long that the ground rocked beneath us. But Jesse Owens himself couldn't have beat our time to our causeway entrance.

We received no fire other than a few rounds humming overhead. The bombers really had pasted the shoreline. Squad by squad, the riflemen of Able, Baker and Charlie companies mounted the seawall and disappeared beyond the 6-foot sand berm that overlooked it.

Once we got onto the berm, we could see them racing up the causeway and sloshing through the hip-deep marshes either side of it. Now we could hear rifle fire and machine guns.

The S3 had left a runner with orders for us to make immediate radio contact with Capt. Freeman who already was headed inland. The runner and his Tommy gun were guarding two dozen stunned Germans who sat against the seawall hugging their knees. Some of them were wounded and several of them were shaking like leaves on a tree.

They huddled just below a huge concrete bunker that bore several giant black flowers – fist-deep white pits in the concrete with inky spalling that radiated three feet in all directions. Hits from a destroyer, maybe. In the bunker's entry, the lower half of a Kraut lay twined with his intestines in a large pillow of sand. No wonder the Germans looked stunned.

Nau began retching so I swatted him in the ass with the flat of my carbine buttstock. "Come on, Karl. Snap out of it. You're gonna see worse than that before this day's out."

Lt. Scott and The Dick headed inland with Sgt. Svoboda and the mortar platoon's five HQ infantrymen.

About three seconds later, we saw our first dead GI. He had stepped on a mine and it had shredded everything below his waist. His face was pale and expressionless. Even serene. His troubles were over.

We had to ignore him because we got busy, checking both the 509 and 510 SCR radios. Despite the seawater, they emerged from their rubber bags in working order.

I checked in with the captain who wanted us to advance in echelon – one section to set up just inland from the broken pillbox, the other to come all the way up to the causeway exit – almost a mile. I told the captain I'd leave Forster with the beach detail and head to the exit with the other. "But with respect, sir, that kind of strings us out. I'd like to get them further inland."

"Negative, Dud." I could hear background crackling as he spoke. "We need fire support in front of Awdyville. I want your boys dropping shells right now. Those little 60's with the infantry make a nice noise, but they don't get the job done like the 81. So get Forster set up and in touch with FDC.

"You high-tail the other section up here right now."

Chapter 25
June 6, 1944 – Moving Inland

Thonk! Forster's first shot arced downrange above us.

Not for the first time, I marveled at how different a mortar can sound. Up close, it's an ear-stabbing WHAPP. Yet even at 50 yards it's a hollow, almost musical noise, like when you lever a fingertip out of a Coke bottle.

Timmer and Manthei were straining at one cart and Jacobs and Halls were pulling the other. Nau and Evans and I jogged ahead of them, weapons at the ready.

As we trotted, we could hear a steady rumble from the south. "I bet that's Omaha Beach," Wilson said.

"Dammit, keep your eyes peeled to your front and flank."

The causeway's asphalt made for smooth going except when we had to take the shoulders to get around shell holes.

At the half-way point, I had Nau and Evans spell Jacobs and Halls on the carts. We passed a French tank with the Wehrmacht cross on its turret. It looked as if a naval shell had peeled open its front armor. All you really could make out in that twisted steel and eddying smoke was something that looked like half a seat and maybe a clutch pedal

The smell from the tank made me feel a little sick and it just got worse when we passed the first canal in the marsh. A parachute was caught in tree limbs on both canal banks, but its center was under water and its shrouds weren't visible. A paratrooper had to be at the bottom of the canal, drowned.

Other chutes lay like giant handkerchiefs close by and in the distance, but since the marsh was only knee-deep, I guessed most of those paratroopers had survived.

Our causeway curved southwest and the dense brush on its shoulders screened everything from view. But now we could heard rifles popping amid the *tak-tak-tak* of American machine guns and the *braap-braaaap* of German MG-42s. Grenades thumped and we spotted the tops of black plumes, mortar bursts maybe.

"I bet that's in Awdyville," Timmer said.

Just then two men in Kraut uniforms crawled out from the tall brush lining the causeway's north shoulder. They were drenched and their hands were in the air. They weren't wearing helmets.

One yelled, *"Nicht shiessen!"*

Puzzled, Nau lowered his carbine and said, "Did he say 'Don't shit'?"

"No," Timmer said. "Shit is *sheiss*. They're saying *shiess*. They mean 'don't shoot'."

I didn't want to mess with POWs, but Timmer suggested they looked sturdy enough to pull a cart.

"Great idea!" In German I ordered them to take over from Jacobs and Manthei. They gave me blank stares.

Jacobs asked, "*Vwe gavareeteh pa Russki?*"

They grinned, "*Da! Da!*" and started jabbering old home week with him.

"Sarge, want you to meet Alexei and Slawa. They're Ukrainians and they love Ah*may*reekah." Both beamed, nodding vigorously.

"Tell them to start pulling," I snapped. "We got to get to the causeway exit right now. Meanwhile, keep your eyes open. The next ones might not love America."

The Russkies were eager to work with the good guys and so we took off double time, Jacobs, Nau and Halls on the left edge of the pavement and Timmer and Manthei and I on the right, five yards apart.

Rounding the bend, we could see straight west to a scattering of dwellings. The firing had faded. Riflemen were up and moving in rushes toward the village, a machine gun team following. Awdyville seemed clear.

The Dick met us beside a high stone wall just off the exit. "Well, Sgt. Dudley, about time! You need to start showing a little more hustle now that we're in combat, eh? But don't you worry -- the paratroopers already captured Awdyville so we got the Krauts between two fires and they took off. Lt. Scott wants you to set up here and then call for the other mortars to come up."

"Halls!" I yelled. "Get the guns emplaced right behind this wall. And keep your eyes peeled. When Krauts back away, they've got a nasty habit of coming back from another direction."

The Dick yawned, trying to look bored. "Try to calm down, Sergeant."

I ignored his jibes, getting on the horn to the fire direction center when Timmer pointed south, "Hey, who are they?" Several Krauts with rifles were running towards us in the shade of a windbreak.

"Start firing," I shouted,

The two Ukrainians spotted the Germans and started to head for the opposite shoulder of the causeway. They stopped when I screamed, "Halt!" I knelt, cradled my rifle across a cart and started firing carefully aimed shots. One German fell immediately, and then I hit a second who spun and dropped.

"How can you tell for sure they're Germans?"

As I aimed, I snapped, "Well, for Christ's sake, Cap'n, look at their damn helmets! And they're in gray uniforms! And carrying Mausers!"

A swarm of bullets pocked the wall and snapped overhead. They had an MG. I could see the bullets smacking the ground just below the causeway shoulder.

"Oh my God!" The Dick said. His carbine clattered to the pavement and he jittered, almost dancing, his eyes practically popping out from under that shelving brow.

I wanted to tell him to calm down, but had no time. I could see pale flickers, muzzle flashes, as the Kraut machine gunner walked his fire toward us. Bullets zipped and snapped around us, ricocheting off the asphalt. Evans went down. Manthei gave a yelp and fell, grabbing his left leg. "Fuckers hit me!" He tried to stand up and collapsed. Blood pooled on the asphalt beneath him.

Evans didn't so much as twitch. I caught a glimpse of his skull, shattered, brain lying like an orange cauliflower in his upside-down helmet.

Nobody else fired. "Come on, Goddammit!" I yelled. "Get down in the ditch and start shooting! You want invitations?

"Sir," I yelled at The Dick. "They're trying to cut the causeway." He paid no attention, fluttering eyes focused instead on what was left of Evans' face and head.

The Kraut MG stopped. Maybe a jam. I would have given my legs for all of us to have M1s because, at that range, carbines seemed little better than pistols. We needed some muscle.

"Halls!" I yelled. "See where those bastards are?"

"Yeah, Sarge."

"Get busy and drop some HE shells over there before they kill the rest of us."

Just as his first shot went out, the Krauts got their MG going again.

Chapter 26
June 6, 1944 –Utah Beach Exit 3

More MG bullets cracked overhead.

Manthei groaned and cussed "Damn! Damn! Damn!" Timmer and I grabbed his arms and, stooping, hauled him into the shelter of the wall.

Manthie's face was white as The Dick's.

I yelled, "Stan! Quit your cussing and get out your field dressing. Timmer, tie it on his leg right now. Strain it tight as you can." When I glanced up at The Dick. He still was staring at Evans.

"Damn you, Schiltz, snap out of it! We can't support battalion with those bastards attacking us. Can you run and get some help for us? Maybe a squad or even a machine gun team, before the Krauts bring up more."

Ignoring the carbine that he had dropped, he turned without a word and took off at an arm-wheeling, stumbling trot toward Awdyville. Nau and Timmer were shooting offhand at the Krauts.

I yelled at them. "Hey, you idiots! Quit standing upright. You're making yourselves targets, for Christ's sake! Get down! Get flat! You're a smaller target and your aim's better that way."

Halls' first shell landed 50 yards behind the line of Krauts. "Halls! Subtract 50."

I turned back to Manthei. "How you doin'?"

"Doesn't hurt too much, Dud. Just like somebody clobbered me with a ball bat."

"In a bit, it's gonna hurt like hell. When it ratchets up too much, yell to Halls. Have him squeeze a morphine syrette into your thigh. Meanwhile, scooch over to the cart and start stripping rounds out of their cartons when he calls for them."

"Okay, Dud. I'm sorry."

"Sorry? Bullshit! The bastards that did it are going to be sorry."

Halls dropped a white phosphorous round at one end of the Kraut line and several of the *landsers* raced off rather than burn to death. I slapped Manthei on the shoulder and got up just as another shot sang off the pavement between us.

Damn! We couldn't support the infantry before dealing with our own threat.

I couldn't reach Forster by radio. When I got on the Battalion net, they said he already had displaced – Capt. Freeman's orders -- and should be coming up the causeway.

When I told them about the infiltrators, they said they'd try to find some help. Battalion wanted to know how soon we could take a fire mission.

"About one minute after we get these Heinies off our back."

Just then Halls dropped another shell smack dab in the Krauts' midst. They scattered like sparrows.

"Beautiful," I yelled. "Go right 150 mills and add 50 and try another Willie Pete on 'em. Then we can set up the other gun."

Halls had the touch. The white phosphorous blossomed in the top of the windbreak's trees and the remaining Krauts took off like bats out of hell before the snowy burning phosphorous could settle on them. I counted seven of them retreating.

An idea. *Do what Krauts do. Counterattack.*

"Nau and Jacobs! Follow me! Timmer, you're coming, too. Halls! Use the Russkies 'til we get back!"

"Where we going, Dud?"

"Right over where the Krauts were. We'll surprise them when they come back. Halls! Wait two minutes, add 50 and fire another Willie Pete. Then one more minute, add 50 more and one more Willie Pete! Then, same deal, one more after that. That'll keep them away for a few minutes. Then get busy with the battalion's fire mission."

"Got it, Sarge!"

"Okay, let's go! Five yards apart and run like hell!"

I went tearing through the brush like a madman. The ground was spongy, but at least we weren't trying to run through a marsh. I was terrified that the Krauts would reappear before we found cover . . . even more terrified that I was getting us sucked into a Kraut kill sack. But I felt better glimpsing two more Willie Peter detonations. *Should keep them away for a bit.*

Timmer with far longer legs was ahead of me and found us a drainage ditch. It lay at a slight angle to the windbreak and we had to lie with our torsos in mud and legs and feet in water. It smelled like shit, so maybe it was a sewer. No matter though -- the low brush and tall weeds lining the edge of the ditch gave us the cover we needed because we were only about 75 feet from the windbreak. I caught my breath.

"Now listen, men, stay low! Shoot only when I do. I want the bastards so close that we can wipe 'em out before they even know it. Got it?"

They nodded dubiously. "Look, guys, it's a German trick! I've seen them do this. It works!"

Timmer gasped, "Okay, so we shoot when we see the whites of their eyes?"

"Hell, no! Don't shoot 'til you see the *color* of their eyes. Now make damned sure you've got a round chambered."

# # #

Hearts pounding as we waited wide-eyed, we hardly noticed the stench. We could hear our own mortars *thonking* behind us. Also catching our eyes were dozens of troop gliders descending two or three miles further inland.

Nau said, "Sssst!" and nodded toward the windbreak.

Krauts were easing into view and for the first time I got a good look The Normandy Curse – a hedgerow.

What I thought was a windbreak actually was a thick earth embankment – six foot high, equally thick, buttressed by the roots of the bushes and full-grown trees that topped them.

The Germans were slipping one-by-one through a gap in the brush at the top of the embankment. Nine of them formed a staggered line, moving like cats, started heading in a crouch toward Exit 3. They all kept glancing toward the gliders coming down to the west.

Couldn't be a better distraction!

I picked the one carrying the MG and a long gleaming belt of ammo. When they were at 50 feet, I eased my M1 up and put my sights on him. At 30 feet he spotted me but I already was squeezing the trigger. I bellowed "Fire!" and drilled his head, kicking his helmet into the air along with a spray of blood and brains.

Carbines rattled around me and I heard a burst of submachine gun fire as I nailed a second *landser* at the right of their line. Then no more targets.

A potato-masher grenade came twirling toward us, falling short. It exploded, flinging mud everywhere. Nau pulled the pin and released the spoon on one of his own grenades. He counted to three and hurled it to explode at head level just as a Kraut jumped up to run. The pineapple blasted him flat.

We got up, all of us mud-slicked and stinking, looking for more life.

"Congratulations, you're veterans!" I gave them no time to think about their first kills. "Now quick! Each of you grab two Kraut ammo cans and head back. Nau, you too, but stay to cover us until we've gone 100 feet, then follow. We'll cover you."

I draped the ammo belt over my shoulder, pulled the M1 sling over my head and chest, picked up the German machine gun, an ammo can and the spare MG barrel and started loping back to the causeway exit. I thought I'd never get back what with the M1 pounding on my back, the MG ammo belt trying to trip me and twice losing my grip and dropping the spare barrel.

Five minutes later, we emplaced the MG in the ditch by Exit Three. I made Timmer the gunner and Alexei his ammo handler. Alexei showed me he knew how to change barrels.

"Look, Timmer, start firing as soon as they show. And don't wait to see the color of their eyes this time. Okay?"

He nodded jerkily and gave a shaky laugh. "Jesus, when we ambushed those Krauts, I thought you'd never pull the trigger! I was about to get up and shake hands with them."

"Worked. Didn't it? Now keep it at 3-round bursts. We don't have that much ammo."

"Okay, Dud. I got it."

Somebody had dragged Evans to the far shoulder, covering his head with a field jacket. But that didn't hide the broad streak of blood, hair and brains on the asphalt.

Halls was busy firing battalion's mission and Manthie was half sitting and nodding drowsily, his eyes unfocussed thanks to the morphine.

Drumming in our feet and then squeals and clanking behind us -- a Sherman tank came clattering around the causeway bend. It led a long string of deuce-and-a-halfs towing their stubby 105 mm howitzers.

Forster and his boys with their two mortars had hitched rides in the first two trucks.

As they dismounted I glanced up from the handset.

"What took you Mortar Forkers so long?"

Chapter 26
June 6, 1944 –Utah Beach Exit 3

Nobody ever did arrive from battalion to help out.

Timmer and Alexei with the MG, and Halls with his tubes, beat off three more attacks. The rest of the Forkers fired missions for battalion and I kept busy running between the MG and the mortars.

Three hours later they ordered us to displace forward, so that Kraut infiltrators became somebody else's worry.

It was the first of five or six times that we displaced forward during that very, very long day, always leap-frogging other mortar sections. Mobs of wounded and prisoners streamed past us toward the beach – paratroopers, ordinary infantrymen, bandaged faces, torn uniforms, limping or hobbling, nursing their arms in dirty slings or even web belts.

Except for their coal scuttle helmets and *feldgrau* uniforms, the Krauts shuffling past looked about the same – filthy and tired with skin showing through tears in their garb and lots of bloody field dressings. One or two *landsers* glanced at us and gave rueful grins. *We've been there. We're out! Your turn now.*

Another Kraut was different -- a young one with cornsilk hair and virtually invisible eyebrows. He glared at us with pure hatred.

Twice we passed GIs just sitting in the rubble, staring into the distance with nothing registering.

"That's the thousand-yard stare, boys," I said. "I guess we'll all get a touch of it now and then."

"Damn!" Timmer said. "What causes it?"

"You'll find out. It's just how you get if you've been through a bit too much to handle. . ." I paused, barely hearing a harsh sigh amid the rumble-grumble of fighting to our north. "Hey! Incoming! Down! Get down!"

God, I'm glad I heard it. German mortar shells started falling about 50 yards away near a POW column. They all dived to the ground – and we rolled into our own mortar pits. I alerted FDC via the handset.

The shells were big – probably 120 mm – so their explosions were shattering, but not loud enough to drown the slap and slash of shrapnel hitting the broken buildings and shattered trees around us.

Between impacts, I yelled for everybody to lay their tubes flat. A hole or two in the tube, and a mortar can be almost as dangerous to its crew as to the enemy.

The mortar attack went on for about 15 minutes. Apparently FDC triangulated the Kraut tubes because pretty soon we heard some real artillery come over with a locomotive roar. I suspect it was naval gunfire -- maybe 6-inchers or 8-inchers from a cruiser. It seemed to come in salvos – clusters of shells roaring overhead to someplace inland.

Four more Kraut mortar shells crashed in and someone landed on me, knocking my breath out.

As the firing died, I pushed him off and peeked out of my mortar pit. My new neighbor was a German private whose drawn, dirty face looked about the same as I felt.

I grinned and asked, *"Wie gehts?"*

He replied with a veddy posh British accent. "Well, ectually you know, under these rahther trying circumstances, it's going about as well as one would expect."

"Damned good English," I said. "Are you sure you're in the right Army?"

"Thanks awfully," he replied, beginning to giggle. In 10 seconds we both were roaring almost hysterically with laughter. We shook hands and then I told him he ought to head on to the beach.

"Oh, gladly," he said. "And thank you, old chap, for letting me share your shelter."

"Foxhole," I said, as he got up to rejoin the prisoner column. Looking puzzled, he turned and repeated "foxhole?" Then he became a correct German soldat again because he was getting some dirty looks from a Kraut sergeant.

Meanwhile the Mortar Forkers were darting some very curious glances at me as they emerged from their holes.

"Who the hell was that?"

"Frost, don't be so nosy. It was my fourth cousin 18 times removed."

"If you say so . . . Down! Down!"

The Kraut mortar teams laid into us four times more and finally quit about dinner time.

By then most of us would have been content to just sit and stare.

Battalion had lots more work for us, though.

Chapter 27
June 7, 1944 – Audouville-la-Hubert

"Go ahead, sir. Have a sip."

Forster offered his canteen cup to Capt. Freeman when he squatted down beside the little blue flame of a captured German sterno cooker.

I grinned wearily.

It was about 0300 but the Navy kept the night alive by firing intense blue-white flares above the Normandy coastline. The flares swung side-to-side under their little parachutes, making shadows around us oscillate and creating the scary illusion of movement in destroyed tanks, crushed cars and the empty windows of shattered buildings. In the shifting shadow of his helmet rim, Freeman's baggy eyes appeared and disappeared. His face was drawn and he yawned and asked, "Sgt. Forster what's really in that cup?"

"Well, sir, being's how we spent most of the night doing fire missions, I needed a little pick-me-up."

"Don't tell me you're drinking booze."

"I wish, sir," Forster laughed. "No, Sgt. Dudley and I just melted some of those D ration segments in boiling water. We thought you might want to try a sample of it."

"Wasn't my idea," I said.

The captain laughed. "Sergeant, I was under the impression that it's contrary to army regulations for enlisted men to poison their officers."

"Oh, Cap'n," I said, "that's just an old wives' tale. Army regs say we can poison officers just as long as we only use official Army rations. Besides, Forster managed to scrounge some sugar from this little store that we're leaning against, so this drink ain't quite so bitter. Kind of like chocolate milk . . . real, real *thick* chocolate milk, you understand. And you might say it's . . . well, tangy, I guess." I extended my cup to him.

The sip turned the corners of his mouth down. "Good God, Dud! It's tangy all right. Whew! Tastes like you brewed it from old dog turds."

Forster and I chuckled and sipped again. "How we doing, sir?"

"We're doing fine. All the talk about 50 per cent casualties was way, way off . . . so far, at least. Word is that we lost less than 200 killed out of the whole division. Thanks to you boys and the paratroopers, we didn't have much trouble with the Krauts outside of Awdyville. But in Turkoville they're putting up a hell of a stiff fight. Turned out to be first-rate troops there – German paratroops. *Fallschirmjaeger.* But with tanks and artillery, and the 82nd Airborne behind them in Sainte-Mere-Eglise," he said, "we'll take Turkoville come morning and be able to relieve the 82nd."

"Mike," I said. "I need a minute alone with the captain."

As Forster got up and moved off, I said, "Sir, I've got to ask you a hard question."

"What is it, Dud?"

"When that Kraut squad with the MG showed up on our flank yesterday morning right off Exit 3, I asked Cap'n Schiltz to bring us some help. He immediately took off for Awdyville."

"Yes?"

"Sir, did he relay that request to anyone at battalion? Because nobody ever showed. Wasn't anybody available?"

The captain's eyes took on an anthracite glitter. "I'll check into it. Immediately. Meanwhile, keep quiet about it."

"Hey Mike," he called, "come on back over here."

As Forster returned and sat down, Capt. Freeman said he wanted us to know that things had been chaotic because the division was forced to attack in disjointed directions. Now the battle lines were beginning to coalesce a bit.

"Even so," he said, "things still are kind of fluid. You never know when some Krauts might pop up out of the bushes – like they did with you guys yesterday."

He said Maj. Cavanaugh, battalion's operations officer – the S3 – wanted one mortar section under his direct control.

"So, even though Lt. Scott commands the mortar platoon, he'll run 1st Section for the S3. If need be, he'll call on you guys in 2nd and 3rd sections. But for the most part, you'll be under battalion's fire direction center, just like you have been.

"Soon, each section will have its own half-tracks and will move with the headquarters 'track. Dud, you'll be in charge of the HQ track under Capt. Schiltz."

I took in a sharp breath.

He held up his hands in a defensive gesture. "I know. I know," he said. "Can't be helped. But battalion, in effect, will command you and I'll be with the battalion CO. Main thing, Dud, is to keep both sections running smoothly. I'm depending on the two of you. Now, I can't say everything I'd like to, but I'll try to smooth things for you."

"That's okay, sir," I said. "We'll do our best."

"I know you will."

"Now," he asked, "are you and your men set for this morning? The battalion's going to assault at 0430."

"We're ready, sir," I said. "We had to send one dead and one wounded to the beach -- Evans and Manthei. Manthei took a bullet in the thigh and I'd bet he's out for months if not the duration.

"We also received our ammo resupply," I added. "We've got our guns behind good cover and we've got our own MG-42 with a few thousand rounds left. And, sir, I'd like to unofficially change our TO&E a little bit. I'd like to swap our carbines for M1s."

"Why?"

I spent some time reviewing our trouble with the infiltrators of Exit Three. "That MG-42 has been a blessing for us, but as far as I'm concerned, trying to defend ourselves with carbines at 300 yards is impossible. At that range you might as well throw rocks."

The captain smiled. "Dud, I'm not authorized to change our TO&E. But HQ has a pile of M1s from our casualties. Send a couple of your boys with a cart and help yourself. But keep your carbines handy because you should have your half-tracks late today or early tomorrow. With their machine guns you'll have all the security firepower you need."

He mused for a minute. "By the way, Dud, I hear you did a hell of a job organizing that little counterattack of yours yesterday. I think I'll put you in for something."

"Thank you, Cap'n. Oh, one other question."

"What?"

"Being's how we're shorthanded, can we keep these two Ukrainians?"

"What are you going to want next, Dud? A tank platoon?"

"Well, hey, sir! That sure couldn't hurt none."

"Yeah, keep them for now."

"Thanks, sir. And can I count on you to run some interference for me with The Dick about the Ukrainians?"

"I will, but for Christ's sake find some American uniforms for the bastards."

"Yes sir," I said, glancing down at my feet. "One of them already has GI boots."

He looked at my Wehrmacht boots, snorted and left.

Chapter 28
June 7, 1944 – Turqueville, Normandy

We had continuous fire missions starting at dawn. They kept us so busy that we didn't notice The Dick was gone.

Not that we missed him or even gave a damn. Firing several hours of missions eats up attention as well as energy.

First you fire for registration. Then, once you're on target, the command is "Fire for effect!" That means four rounds each out both the section's guns. And if that doesn't do the job, then it's "Fire for effect!" again, and again the same drill. A full day of that, and you get a bit punchy – for sure not as bad as being a rifleman, but it still wears you down.

We liberated uniforms from two dead GI's to outfit Alexei and Slawa who, incidentally, turned out to be an artist with the MG-42. We also managed to scrounge more Kraut ammo for it.

I was in love with that damned MG. It was so simple to use and no damned headspace adjustments or headspace wrench to mess with. As for changing barrels – it was a 5-second process with the MG as opposed to a 5-minute job with American 30's.

# # #

Battalion ordered us to displace by stages to the north of Turkoville. As we started pulling the carts out onto the road, the cobblestones made our carts and their handles vibrate so much that our hands went numb. But when we turned into the village's main drag, we stopped dead and forgot about it. That same stink of burned homes hit us, but it was the sight that stopped us.

"Damn," Forster said. "Looks like a tornado just about wiped it out."

To me, the town looked crushed. Several skeletal sections of masonry reached two stories above a street filled with broken bricks and shattered stone lintels. Soot and dust coated everything and furniture and lumber smoldered. Debris flows buried some sections of the street five feet deep.

A stocky bow-legged old man with a fierce-looking white moustache watched us from the doorway of a shattered shop. The splintered door hung by a single hinge and a chain of bullet holes pocked the facade. The sign and windows were broken and most of the second story had collapsed inside the first. Beside him, an old lady wiped her tears. Even so, he stiffened his thick old shoulders and snapped his hand up in a perfect open-handed French salute. I ordered both sections to stop and come to attention. We all saluted.

Forster yelled, *"Lafayette! Nous voila!"*

The old man's eyes crinkled. He raised his cap and yelled, "Oui! Oui! OooRAH!" There was more, but I couldn't get it.

His cheer kind of gave us a lift.

"What the hell did you tell him, Mike?" We picked up the cart handles and started yanking the carts over the debris.

"Something I read," Forster said. "When Gen. Pershing showed up in Paris with the first doughboys back in '17, he said those same words. It means, 'Lafayette, behold us!' He was saying we were repaying the debt we owe France for saving us in the American Revolution."

"That's great," I said. "But I'd like to know how those poor old folks are going to live in this fucking mess."

Forster just shook his head

To maintain distance between sections, I ordered Forster to stay in place until we reached the end of the block. Timmer, Bull and Evans stayed with him.

Even with the Ukrainians' help, we were having a hell of a time getting the carts over the rubble.

"I'll be glad when we get the half-tracks," Jacobs said as he and Borodin and I lifted our cart across a splintered 8x8 beam.

We passed the burnt-out Sherman close at hand. The turret sat askew above a softball-size hole in the tank's hull. "That's what an 88 does, boys," I said. "It penetrated, blew the turret right up in the air and it came down six inches off center."

"It's a coffin now," Nau said.

"I bet," Halls said. "Makes me glad I'm not in armor. You can't dig a foxhole in steel."

A man and woman, each carrying a little girl, picked their way past us through the rubble, barely giving us a glance. The woman kept wavering as if she was losing her balance. The child's little fists were buried in her mom's hair. Jacobs offered a D ration to them, saying *"Chocolat,"* but they ignored him.

A bend in the road brought us abreast of a brick building that was only half destroyed. Seated on the front step in front of an open front door were two little girls I guessed to be five or six. With them was an even younger boy. They were grimy and seemed to be in shock.

Jacobs said, "Shouldn't we . . .?"

"No," I said, "we've got to keep moving. The engineers coming up behind us will give them a hand."

We turned north onto the main road, keeping our ears cocked to the machine guns that were stuttering in the direction of Sainte-Mere-Eglise. The noise competed with the rattle of our carts on cobblestones.

Coming toward us was a long column of German POWs, hands on their heads.

We had just got onto clear pavement when the engineers showed up behind us with a dozer tank. They started pushing debris to one side of the street. Two engineers went to the children and lifted them indoors before the dozer got to the street in front of the house.

In an hour, the dozer cleared a broad path for the POWs being herded by men with minor wounds. But then guards at the rear of the column started shouting, "Make way! *Raus mit euch*!" Out with you!

The POWs pressed to one side of the opened road to let a convoy of meat wagons pass – a long line of olive drab trucks. All sizes – panel trucks, three-quarter ton -- some bearing bullet holes even in their big red crosses. One dribbled a trail of blood.

After the ambulances passed, the POW column resumed trudging toward the beach. They looked whipped and kept dropping their hands and the guards kept motioning with their rifles and shouting, *"Hände hoch!"* Some of the Germans looked really old, maybe 35 or even 40. Most were our age, though. Two old *Landsers* nodded to us and grinned. *"Ami! Krieg ist fertig, nicht wahr?"*

Evans asked, "Did he say 'Army'?"

"Nope. 'Ami' for 'American.' 'Ami' for us and 'Tommy' for the English. Then he said, 'The war is over, not so?'"

"Yeah. Over for him."

Alexei cleared his throat, and spat towards the POWs. Then he yelled *"Svolochi! Sukini sini!"*

Most of the Krauts just glanced at us and then stared straight ahead. Jacobs answered my look. "He called them bastards and sons of bitches."

# # #

We were just emplaced outside Turqueville when a sudden howl startled us. Six or eight smoke trails raced above us coming to earth in a field a half mile northeast with gut-shaking explosions. The blasts threw up enormous smoke and dust clouds. Alexei and Slawa, eyes like saucers, yelled. *"Katyusha roketa!"*

"Holy shit, what was that, Sarge?"

"I don't know . . . maybe those Moaning Minnies or Screaming Meemies we heard about."

More rockets roared above us, each a tongue of flame trailed by the same yellowish smoke. Through the explosions, closer now, I heard a tinny voice through my handset, "Mike Fox 1, this is Fox Dog Charlie 1, adjust fire. Over."

The fire direction center's routine calmed me. "Fox Dog Charlie 1, this is Mike Fox 1, adjust fire. Out."

"Nebelwerfer launchers. Direction 4800, Distance 2,800 yards. No danger close. One round Willie Peter. Fire when ready."

I repeated him and yelled the info to Halls on the mortar's sights. Yelling "Willie Pete" to Jacobs, he adjusted the elevation and traverse. "Hang!" Jacobs placed the shell's base above the tube, holding it. Halls called "Fire!" Jacobs ducked, releasing the shell. The mortar's WHAPP! seemed muted in the howl of a new flight of rockets.

"Shot, over," I said into the handset, Alexei and Slawa crouching, looked eager to pass ammo.

"Shot, out."

Five seconds later I called, "Splash, over."

A few seconds later I heard, "Splash. Adjust fire. Right 380, subtract 400. Two rounds Willie Pete. Over"

We went through the same routine, expecting the order to fire for effect from both guns. But FDC just said, "Mission complete. Over."

"Mission complete?"

"Yeah, great markers for the fly boys. They'll take it from here."

"Cease fire," I said. "Planes coming."

We soon applauded a noisy ballet by the Army Air Corps.

Three Thunderbolts took turns pasting the area where the smoke trails had sprouted. Smoke and hedge rows and trees hid the target from us, but not from the pilots. One attack produced an explosion roiling far above the trees, giving birth to several more smoke trails which soared in crazy spirals like giant fizzled firecrackers.

Forster suddenly yelled at Nau and Frost. "For God's sake, you men are supposed to be security, not gawkers at an air show. Look to your fronts and your fire lanes."

A squad of dusty riflemen had wound onto the road from a nearby farm and joined us watching the Air Corps at work.

Their corporal accosted me. "Hey, Sarge, I've got replacements for the 12th and we're way off track. We're supposed to be headed toward a place called Montebourg. Can we take a look at your maps?"

I showed him Montebourg and our location. "Good thing you were off track," I said. "Otherwise, you'd have been where those screaming meemies hit."

"Thanks, Sarge. We'll be taking off."

They spread apart and moved out, heading to cross through the smoke over the beaten zone. Battalion ordered us to displace north of town and for me to meet with Lt. Scott. As we saddled up, Chuchecko muttered something to Borodin and Borodin nodded wearily.

I asked Jacobs what they were saying.

"Oh, it's Russian slang. Kind of their equivalent for, 'Pickin' 'em up and layin' 'em down'."

Chapter 29
June 8, 1944 – Sigeville, Normandy

Lt. Scott's briefing took three minutes and what he described didn't sound like a lot of nice neat phase lines on a map.

The 22nd Infantry still was attacking north along Normandy's shore to destroy Kraut artillery that was firing at troop ships and supply vessels in the English Chanel. So far the Kraut gunners had sunk a pair of destroyers, but had hit no troop ships.

The 12th was on the left of the 22nd, pushing north toward Cherbourg, and butting against very tough dug-in opposition in Montebourg. Casualties were heavy. And now, having broken through to the 82nd Airborne at Sainte-Mere-Eglise, the 8th Infantry was wheeling north too, taking out the Krauts who were harassing the left flank and rear of the 12th.

Forster asked what would cover the left flank of the 8th Infantry.

"Mainly water," the lieutenant said. "The Germans flooded the Douve River to block us. It didn't work, but now it works against them, blocking any tanks they'd try to bring up behind us. They also flooded much of the Merderet River which is to the west, on our left. It's not much more than a glorified creek. But being flooded, it's a half-mile wide in places. North, where we're headed, it runs between real steep banks so Kraut tanks can't cross it. But it does have two bridges, one's a railway bridge – too narrow for panzers -- the other is a two-lane stone bridge that might support tanks."

He said the whole 4th Division's fighting front -- from the beach to the Merderet -- was five miles wide.

"We've got a lot of power packed in that zone and the Navy's guns are on call when we need them. But First Battalion now is the division's left flank and for now Dog Company's mortars are Battalion's main punch."

"The Merderet isn't enough obstacle to protect us from snipers and patrols, is it?"

"Nope. Battalion scouts will keep it under observation, but Dud, you and Mike are going to have to be on your toes the whole time."

"Any word, sir, on how soon we get our half-tracks?"

"I sent Cap'n Schiltz and a party to the beach to find out."

# # #

We wanted to stage north on the Montebourg road, but couldn't. It not only was the main supply route for both the 8th and the 12th Regiments. So MPs kept non-essential traffic off the road. Troops and ammo had northbound priority and POWs and ambulances had southbound priority.

We fell into the non-essential category.

The MPs were routing refugees east of the road, so I decided we'd use farm lanes west of the road to pull the carts, even when tanks and half-tracks sometimes damn near ran us down.

It wasn't the brightest decision of my life. The countryside was fairly open and somewhat rolling, with heavy brush and woods along creeks and banks of the Merderet. Good cover for Krauts.

And that's where we came to grief.

I was taking my turn at a cart, listening to Alexei humming some Slavic march or other. Then the rhythm changed -- *pang-pang-pang* – bullets hitting the cart's steel side, snapping past our ears and slapping through weeds and grass.

They slammed Slawa aside like a rag doll and Wilson's feet were knocked from under him. The *braaap* of a German MG caught up with us as we dropped. I heard Timmer say, "Ouch, dammit."

We all went prone at the lane's edge, firing our M1s toward the brush along the Merderet. But it was sunny, making it impossible to spot muzzle flashes as aiming points. You could only guess where the enemy MG might be.

Fortunately, Forster -- set up 500 yards behind us – saw what happened and popped a line of three Willie Peters into the brush along the Merderet. Burning phosphorous spooked several Germans into the open. We nailed two of them and three more raised their hands.

Wilson shouted, "You bastards! You shoot us and then expect to be treated nice. Well, fuck you!" He shot all three Krauts. Then he dropped the M1, rolled onto his side, face contorted. "Now, somebody come bandage me."

A bullet had drilled his left ankle and another ripped his left calf wide open. "Jesus, Charley, I'll put field dressings on it. We'll get you up to the road and catch an ambulance."

"GOD! It *hurts*!"

"Well, hell, did you expect it to feel good?"

"Go to hell, Dud!"

As I injected morphine beneath the skin of his thigh, I said, "It's against regulations to talk to your sergeant like that, asshole. Now that'll take the edge off." I pinned the empty syrette to his shirt pocket.

Bull and I got him up onto his good foot and, with his arms over our shoulders, walked him 200 yards – him hissing all the way -- to the Montebourg Road. We flagged down an ambulance and they let him ride shotgun. His head already bobbed drunkenly. He smiled and again said, "Go to hell, Dud."

"See you there, Buddy."

When we got back to the cart, Alexei was cursing, crossing himself and weeping over Slawa. But he also was ready to resume pulling. Timmer had a nasty furrow sliced across the back of his thigh. As I helped him with a field dressing, I remembered Sgt. Bowyer's prediction back at KU that half of them would be killed.

I didn't feel like I was a very good job of nursemaid for my college kids.

Chapter 30
June 9, 1944 – Opposite Neuville-au-Plain, Normandy

Forster and I were getting the sections ready for another foot march and we were worried.

Since wading ashore three mornings ago, none of us had slept more than four hours. Some of the guys had the staggers, like cows with milk fever. Cigarettes and crappy-tasting ration coffee was all that kept us going. I'd fallen asleep twice myself on my feet.

Firing mortars more or less continuously for three days wears you . . . ducking below the muzzle every second or two, the constant WHAPP two feet from your ears, needles jabbing your eardrums, breathing cordite fumes, constant jarring and battering by the concussion.

And we were even more short-handed.

Late yesterday, Torrelli was hanging an HE round when we heard "clank." He collapsed beside the mortar as he dropped the round down the tube. A sniper had drilled a 7.92 mm hole through the front of his helmet. He was stone dead.

Nau bent over to pull Torrelli away from the gun and another shot tore his throat open. All we could do was fire a machine gun in what we hoped was the sniper's direction while blood spewed from Nau's neck in finger-thick gouts. He was gone in two minutes.

Not that any other outfit in the division had it one bit easier.

The 8th, 12th and 22nd -- pushing hard to secure the beachhead for the new forces now pouring ashore behind us -- had been butchering Germans and being butchered by them three solid days and nights.

So about dark the two of us said "Thank God" in the same breath when The Dick – after a 24-hour absence -- arrived with our half-tracks. As Forster got the mortars and radios their crews into the tracks, I checked the vehicles' weapons and motors.

The Dick protested. "Sergeant, we've got to move out now! Those are the orders. What the hell are you doing?"

"My duty . . . sir!"

The motors were fine, oil up to the line. The tires were inflated properly and drive wheels and bogies lubed, tracks tightened and so on. But the .50 caliber on the HQ track was inoperable because some jerk had assembled it without buffers. And the water-cooled .30s on tracks Two and Three had no tube connecting their water jackets and water chests.

It took 15 minutes to scrounge the double tubing for the .30s from the engineers' ordnance NCO. Then, trying my best to ignore the odors, I stole a working Ma Deuce from a disabled Sherman.

The Dick climbed up beside me as I mounted the .50 on the track and fed ammo into its tray. He told me he intended to destroy me.

I turned to him in disbelief. "What?"

"I said I'm going to destroy you, Dudley.'"

As he jumped down and stalked away. I called to him. "Better bring some help . . . sir!"

The threat, Forster later told me, probably arose because Lt. Scott, forgetting rank, reamed The Dick for accepting the tracks without fully checking them out. Forster also said Capt. Freeman walked in on the conversation just as The Dick started blaming me for not being at the beach to assist him.

Freeman asked Forster to leave and then flayed The Dick, asking why he took so long getting the tracks. He threatened to bring formal charges against him if he didn't shape up.

I don't know why they couldn't just relieve the sorry bastard right then and there. We sure as hell didn't need him.

But at least he stayed out of the way, sulking in the shotgun seat of the HQ track as we headed north.

Chapter 31
June 10, 1944 – Approaching Fresville, Normandy

About the last thing I wanted this morning was to crawl on my belly on a muddy forest floor. But, like Whitehat said, "It's enemy country, Dud. We'd best stay low."

He and I wiggled five yards apart through the brush at the crest of the low ridge. Every time I crawled beneath a bush, I'd get a cold little shower on my neck and back, left-overs from the night's rain. So my back was thoroughly soaked and my front thoroughly plastered with mud and leaves as I eased my way around the broad base of a giant oak.

We wanted a good look – a good *safe* look -- at the valley lying across our path.

It appeared a bit more than a mile wide -- maybe 2,300 yards at a stretch. Through the morning fog I could just make out a dense wood at the crest of the ridge on its far side. A third of the way across the valley a narrow stream in a deep wooded gully fed into the flooded Merderet gleaming far to our west.

"See anything?" Whitehat said.

"Not yet." As I slowly scanned the stream's trees and thick brush, the picture in my captured Kraut binoculars looked peaceful.

The problem was the gully's banks.

From my vantage, the gully looked 10 to 15 feet deep and maybe 50 feet wide. It was no problem to see the inside of the gully's north bank. Nobody there. But it was impossible to tell whether anyone crouched out of view against the near bank.

Anyway, no movement, no people, nothing looking out of place. I was about to stand up when Whitehat said, "Whoa! I think I got a mortar tube 'bout 100 yards off our lane." His eyes were good, but after a look through the binoculars, I said, "It's a stump, not a mortar. Mortars would be back of those woods across the valley."

And that's when I glimpsed a thin cloud of smoke rise from the gully. "Wait! I do think some dumb Kraut down there in the gully is having hisself a morning smoke. I bet he's part of an MG crew." The smoke faded. "But I still can't make out anybody for sure."

Mortar platoons had no business scouting, but thanks to constant combat and casualties, battalion didn't have any spare infantry right now.

The sun was high enough now to begin warming us and the birds were singing. We could hear artillery thumping off to the northeast, but everything seemed quiet here. The problem still was that no solid front line existed. The square-heads could be anywhere.

Taking one final scan with the binoculars, I spotted something else several hundred yards from us in the lane crossing the valley -- a cluster of potholes. Maybe mortar registration craters.

We crawled back to the half-tracks in the lane on the ridge's reverse slope.

"Gee," Frost said, "you boys look like you been in a hog wallow."

"Go fry it," I said, passing him to go to the HQ track. For the second time I tried to awaken The Dick who was sprawled, snoring in the shotgun seat. This time it worked. "Sir, I don't like it," I said. "I keep remembering Sgt. Bowyer's axiom: 'The easy way is always mined – or registered.'"

Behind me, Halls said, "Jesus, I don't want to head out there – not without a couple of tanks."

I said, "Well, we got no tanks, so we'll head back the way we came and find some way to work around east of this valley."

As soon as I spoke, The Dick decided he'd now pick up the reins of command. He boasted he'd take the HQ halftrack right across the valley to show us it was safe. He sneered at me. "It takes courage to run a war, Sergeant."

I know I turned red, but I kept my temper. "Yes, sir. But don't you think we ought to call operations or at least Cap'n Freeman about this? If you drive out there, you're taking a chance."

He sneered. "Just watch, Sergeant. Watch and learn. Watch and learn."

He directed the driver to head up the lane, cross over the ridge and follow the lane north to cross the wooded ridge across the valley. The poor driver looked terrified as he steered the track over the ridge. We pulled the other two tracks to the ridge crest.

Halls said, "What an insufferable sonofabitch."

"The dumb bastard has no business doing this," Forster said. "And all our food and extra ammo is in that track."

The Dick turned out to be right. The lane was safe.

For about 300 yards.

That's where an explosion took out the left front wheel, causing the track to slew into the ditch. Four Krauts jumped into sight from the brush along the gully. The Dick jumped out of the shotgun track's seat, and began running up the lane toward us.

As the Germans knelt to fire, Forster cocked the .50 atop his track and fired at them. The sound panicked The Dick. He dived off the side of the lane and the Krauts made a mad dash back toward the gully.

Forster walked his bursts to them and tore them apart. They went down like rag dolls. He continued shooting, flailing the brush along the creek.

I made him stop and we backed our tracks back down behind the ridge. Not five seconds later, the first Kraut mortar round landed just about where Whitehat and I had reconnoitered. We drove the tracks about a quarter mile and halted so I could get on the horn to Ops.

"Sir, this is Sgt. Dudley with two of Dog's Mortar sections. Uh, we got us a mess here."

The ops officer, Maj. Cavanaugh, demanded to speak to The Dick, forcing me to say he couldn't come to the phone because he was under cover in an exposed position. "Explain!" he said.

So, between mortar explosions 300 yards away from where we had parked earlier, I told him as tactfully as possible what had happened.

"Sergeant, do you think you can rescue him?"

"No, sir. Not without exposing the other tracks . . ." Just then Forster began signaling that he'd spotted the Kraut mortars. "Wait, sir. If we can get ten minutes of help from the artillery, say some 105s, I think we might be able to get him back."

The major checked and reported the FDC said all his 105s were tied up. How about some 155s from Division?

"I think 155s would be great, sir."

We spotted for FDC and the ranging shot tore in and exploded just shy of the tree line. With FDCs' help, we were able to call in a thundering, plowing barrage that splintered the trees on the ridge. Many of the shells were exploding in the treetops so we figured the Kraut mortar crews had their heads down.

Forster drove his track back to the ridge crest and he and Halls resumed hosing the brush along the stream with his track's .50 and .30. Whitehorse and I took our track down the lane first to check the HQ track's driver.

He was still in the cab, badly wounded. Whitehorse and I got him into the back of our track along with all the spare ammo. We poured gasoline on the rations and radios, set the fire, and barreled back up toward the ridge.

On the way, we stopped and spotted The Dick hiding among reeds in the roadside ditch. We persuaded him and ride back with us. Just after he climbed into the shotgun seat, the first mortar shell fell behind us, shrapnel flailing the back of the track.

Once under cover behind the reverse slope, I found Whitehorse half sitting against the gashed sides of the track. Slicing through the track's panels, shrapnel had ripped him wide open, strewing his guts across the floor and the wounded driver. Feebly, he was trying to pull the steaming, ropy mass back to himself. "Hell of a mess, Dud. I don't think they can put 'em back."

"Jesus, Charlie! Hold on! We'll get you to the medics."

He ignored me and his eyes fluttered as he jerked his head toward the wounded driver. "Finished him, too."

He died.

"Watch and learn, you stupid asshole," I snarled at The Dick as he vomited beside me. "Watch and learn."

I had Forster sight in on the gully's far bank with his machine gun while I prepared to drop HE right and left inside the gully with my mortar. The Dick ordered me not to fire because we'd be wasting ammunition.

I shoved the handset at him. "Here! Ops wants to speak to you!"

As he undertook a one-sided conversation, I got busy walking HE mortar rounds right and left in the gully.

A half dozen Krauts bounded up the far bank and began running toward the woods. Forster was ready for them with the .50 caliber.

Then The Dick, white as a sheet, told me that we were to report to Operations.

# # #

I wasn't included in the conversation. But afterward, Capt. Freeman and Lt. Scott came to see me. They seemed uneasy.

"Look, Dud," the captain said, "the major was real pleased with the way you handled the situation back on the ridge. Real pleased. In fact, he's going to recommend you for a battlefield commission."

"Whoa! Wait just a minute, sir, I wouldn't know how to be an officer. I'm just a transplanted hillbilly from West Virginia."

"Oh, bullshit, Dud. You know how to handle troops in combat. But here's the thing: regiment has to approve it and regiment's real busy right now being's how we're up to our asses in Heinies. Matter of fact, we have a real acute need for mortar support."

"So for now, until it's all official, we want you to run the two mortar sections yourself. In effect, you already have been. We'll pass the word to your boys."

"But," the captain added, "we're still stuck with Cap'n Dumbshit until we can either shoot him or foist him off on the Finance Corps or a mess kit repair battalion. "We can't have him whining around battalion HQ and we can't send him back to division without officially charging him with something. And nobody's got time right now to write up the charges and specifications.

"So for the next three or four days we need mortar support and we also need him out of the way. You're stuck with both jobs, Dud. Just ignore him as much as you can."

"Yes," Lt. Scott cracked, "consistent with military courtesy, you understand."

I just stared at them for minute. "Very well, gentlemen, this strikes me as being a monster FUBAR. Do I have any choice in this matter?"

"None whatever," the captain said cheerfully.

"Well, Cap'n, since I'm an officer-to-be, can I speak frankly?"

"Of course," he chuckled, "consistent with military courtesy."

"With respect, gentlemen," I grinned, "this is a huge pile of shit that you're dumping on me. So can we at least get a new unshredded halftrack so we'll have a place to keep The Dick out of the way . . . in a manner that's consistent with military courtesy?"

"Yeah, you'll get a new track," Capt. Freeman said. He turned to Lt. Scott. "You see? I told you he'd figure it out right away."

Chapter 32
June 10, 1944 – Vicinity Fresville, Normandy

We could only drive about 5 m.p.h. as we wove along the flare-lit road among burnt-out tanks, bodies, piles of shattered brick and stone, walking wounded, crushed trucks, ambulances and the heart-breaking trickle of civilian refugees. I don't know how the little kids could bring themselves to wave at us, but now and then they did.

I wanted us in place before the next POW parades started at daylight.

Battalion ordered us to set up near Fresville – "Freeseville" to us -- a cluster of farm homes on the highest piece of ground for miles, a whole 80 feet above sea level.

The whump-thump of big artillery around us was constant. The north horizon flickered like heat lightning – flashes from cannon barrels, flashes, of exploding shells.

We parked herringbone style east of the Fresville slope and radioed battalion that we were ready to shoot. They had targets about 2,500 yards north near Ecausseville (we called it Becauseville) and the same distance northeast near Emondeville (Edmundville).

We also were to cover the two bridges about 1,000 yards west over the Merderet – the railway bridge and, a quarter mile north of it, the stone span that might or might not be armor-capable.

We fired for registration near Edmundeville when an observer tipped off the FDC to a German motor patrol sniffing around the stone bridge.

We reversed the tubes and our ranging shot landed in the stream beside the bridge. The FDC asked us to add 100 yards to the range and fire one more round. It landed on the pavement just beyond the bridge, so the FDC ordered us to add 50 and fire for effect. Over a space of three minutes we dropped a dozen eggs on the bridge's west approaches.

It was the first time that we saw HE shells explode at night. The wind was wrong so we couldn't hear the impact. But one after another, crimson halos blossomed in the night, instantly spreading and disappearing. It was wholly different from the flash and black smoke plume you saw in daylight.

"Beautiful fireworks," Timmer said. "And scary. A perfect circular shrapnel whiplash. Don't want any of them blooming here."

Just after we finished firing, a tiny bright blue dot appeared in the woods across the river. It instantly swelled to softball size, cracked over our heads, dwindled and disappeared toward the beach.

"Holy shit, what the hell was that?"

"Maybe an 88," I murmured. "I hear they're so fast the air friction makes 'em white hot, but they look blue to whoever's on the receiving end."

"Well damn," Jacobs said. "Let's just hope their FOs didn't spot our muzzle flashes."

Two more high-speed rounds passed so close over us that we could feel the wind.

With his eyes so wide they gleamed in the darkness, The Dick said, "What are you taking about?"

Jacobs said, "When mortars fire at night, you get quite a muzzle flash. It's not right at the muzzle but four or five feet above it. We usually don't see it 'cause we're ducking, but if the Krauts are looking this way, they might spot it."

"Well, then we've got to move," The Dick said. "Let's displace. Right now!"

"Sir," I said, "the land around here is so flat, our flashes are visible wherever we are. Besides, we can only move on order from battalion or Cap'n Freeman. Anyhow, the Krauts can't get a bead on us from a few flashes because of all the other artillery firing . . ."

"Dudley, shut the hell up! Get on the horn to the captain and get permission!"

Another 88 cracked over.

His voice squeaking, The Dick said, "Damn you! Do it this minute!"

I rolled my eyes in the dark and picked up the handset but the FDC spoke first. "Mike Fox 1, this is Fox Dog Charlie 1, adjust fire, over."

I responded, "Fox Dog Charlie 1, this is Mike Fox One, adjust fire. Out." FDC had a new mission near Edmundville. I began reciting the data for Halls in my track and Forster and Timmer in the others.

As Halls reoriented our gun northeast, The Dick got up on the cab's running board and aimed his carbine at me. He screamed, "You stupid bastard, I ordered you to get permission to move!"

Jacobs, Alexei and Halls looked at me with their eyes wide. I just shook my head and relayed FDC's target data. I told The Dick, "I can't, sir. We've got a fire mission!" He jacked a round into his carbine's chamber. Then FDC gave the order to fire.

We fired.

So did The Dick.

His first shot smacked open the steel gate in the back of the half-track. The second caught me in the right chest and spun me out through the gate onto the road.

I don't remember landing, but I found myself staring at the stars and it felt like I'd had the breath knocked out of me. Then, when I took a deep breath I heard a bubbly wheeze. It was a minute or two before I realized it was a hole in my chest. I couldn't help but grin at an old British Army joke: *A sucking chest wound is nature's way of saying you have been in a fire fight.*

But then I got serious.

Oh God. Katherine! Am I a dead man? Can Katherine handle this?

I heard the motors of both tracks roar. The one from which I fell pulled away from me. I tried to yell 'Wait!' but nothing would come out. Then the second track headed right for me.

Suddenly, Jacobs was beside me, bending down, grabbing my arms, pulling me to the side of the road. It hurt like hell. It also hurt when he sat me up and tore my shirt away. "Hold yourself upright, damn it!" As he tied the dressing front and back, the track started to accelerate away from us. Jacobs yelled, "Hey! Goddammit! Wait!"

A big orange blast blossomed in front of the track. The vehicle's steel body didn't quite shelter us. I felt something whiplash my leg. Jacobs gave off a choking gurgle and dropped me.

I heard screaming and wondered if it was me.

Okay. Guess this is it.

I figured I was a dead man.

Another blue comet streaked over, so fast and so beautiful against the starry sky.

Then I seemed to die.

Chapter 33
June 11, 1944 – LST 327, Utah Beach

Somebody lifting me? Somebody cussing? It's still dark. This don't seem like heaven – could be hell.

"Ahhhhh! Damn, that hurts!"

"Don't worry, Dud. We're going to take good care of you." It was Forster. I felt the prick of a morphine syrette in my left thigh.

"Mike, the fire mission? D-d-d-done? So cold."

"Dud, I told you don't worry. Cap'n Freeman's here. He's taking care of that sumbitch. Won't be bothering you again."

"How's Jacobs? He was bandaging me."

"They already took him in an ambulance."

"Hurt bad?"

"Don't know. I didn't see him."

"Mighty proud of you, Mike. Proud of all of you. Come a long, long way from KU. Look out for the boys, Mike."

"You know I will, Dud."

"Think I'll sleep. . . ."

# # #

Riding in a stretcher isn't as bad as taking a beating, but comes close.

My right chest registered every step the stretcher bearers took and when they stumbled, it really zinged. I could tell the poor bastards were whipped. They stumbled a lot and were breathing hard. And though I was shading my face with my left arm, I could see the guys carrying the foot of the stretcher having to keep regripping the handles.

"How long you been doing this . . . ?" I was going to add ". . . without rest?" but it hurt too much to talk any more.

"All day, Bub. But don't worry, we'll have you there in a minute."

"Not worried. No rush. Where we headed?" My throat was so dry and scratchy it was hard to get the word out.

"Out here onto this here great big old boat."

I pulled my arm down from my eyes, and saw the mouth of a cavern loom over the men at the foot of the stretcher. Huge clamshell doors yawned either side.

They slowed as they sloshed through water and they took me up a ribbed ramp into the cavern. After the sun in my face, it was hard to see. I heard a woman . . . a no-nonsense voice, like Mom's. "Right over here, men. Help me get him onto this rack. Gently, now. Don't jar his chest tube."

They were slow and gentle, laying me on my left side with my back propped against the wall, or bulkhead, or whatever the Navy calls it.

"Thanks a lot, fellas."

"Good luck, buddy."

She told them to take a break and get some coffee. "Really can't, ma'am. Got too many more of 'em out there on the beach yet."

She paused to look at the card on the twine loop around my neck and then at me. "Ah yes, Sgt. Dudley."

"Friends call me Dud."

A brief smile as she draped a brown Army blanket between me and the hull and eased a pillow under my head. "How are you feeling?"

"Woozy and thirsty. Hard to get my breath. What happened?"

"Gunshot and some shrapnel. You need some surgery when we get to England. But you should recover nicely."

"I bet you say that to all the guys."

She chuckled and disappeared, returning soon with four bearers and another stretcher. They put their man into the rack below mine and then hung a bottle of blood for him from the rack above mine. I caught a glimpse of half his face. Bloody dressings swathed the rest of his head.

I looked at her. "He okay?"

"He'll be fine," she said in case he could hear, shaking her head to show me the man was bad off. She disappeared and returned with a steel cup, a glass straw sticking out of it. "Orange juice," she said.

I raised up onto my left elbow, but my right arm was strapped to my chest so she had to hold the cup. Though it hurt my chest to sip, I drained it in about five seconds.

"Thanks, Miss. Is this an LST?"

"Yes, sergeant. And we're leaving for England soon."

"Do you happen to know an Army nurse, a Lt. Betty Edwards?"

"I'm sorry, no, not on this ship. Now I have to go help with other patients. Try to rest."

"I will."

I did.

Ship motion awakened me later. It reminded me of when I was a kid getting a 2-penny elephant ride at a circus -- slow, ponderous and dignified. The ship rolled a bit, but nothing like the *Queen*. The guy in the rack above me said he was getting seasick. I told him that if he upchucked on me I'd kick his ass overboard.

With the bow doors closed, the lights seemed stronger and I could see us wounded stacked in tiers of three, lining both walls of the tank deck.

Because I was lying on my side, about another 100 men were in my field of view, each cocooned in his brown blanket in a stretcher on the deck itself. Some looked okay, but others looked butchered – arms and legs missing, gaping face wounds. Medics and doctors constantly moved up and down the aisles between the stretcher rows, bending, kneeling and then standing back up.

Sometimes they'd draw a blanket over a man's face.

After an hour passed, you could tell we now were well into the English Channel because the ship began to curtsy to bigger waves. It gave me the impression of a very fat, dignified duchess paying her respects to King George.

At times the motion hurt me a bit, but it apparently was agony for some of the other wounded. One man not far from me screamed with each movement. I think they quickly gave him some morphine.

Later a doctor came by and asked how I was. About five minutes after I told him I was thirsty and it was getting harder to breathe, they put a needle in my left arm and connected a bottle of clear fluid to it.

I think they must have slipped me a Mickey Finn, because I don't remember another thing about the trip.

Next thing I knew somebody said we were at Southhampton and that they'd soon be taking us by railroad to hospitals.

The apes who lifted us out of the railway cars in Salisbury were very, very careful because a little old Scottish nurse with beady black eyes was there to oversee every move. "Noo, men, ye'll no slam this Yank aroond. Ye ken he's no a crate of rations."

I winked at her and she said, "Aye, lad, 'twont be lang afore we have ye in fine fettle."

Once at the hospital they just flat cut off my uniform tatters and spent a lot of time cleaning me up. No wonder. I remembered I hadn't had a chance to do much more than shave and wash my hands for at least a week and I was caked in mud and sand.

One of the nurses wondered aloud why I was wearing German boots. I said, "*Ich weiss nicht.*" That got a double take from several people, so I said. "Relax. I'm American. It's just that German boots are better than ours."

And then they took me into surgery. Somebody put a cone over my face and told me, "Count backwards from 100." I barely got to 99.

Afterwards I was woozy and had strange dreams about beating the hell out of Dad, stealing the car and running away with Mom and Margaret. In the dream my sister looked a lot like Katherine. And for part of the way, Jacobs, Halls, Slawa and Forster were jogging beside us, pulling their cart and cheering us along.

And Slawa kept saying "Now I am one GI son of bitch, da? And I can live in Ah*may*reekah, da? Yes? Okay?"

Chapter 34
June 17, 1944 – Odstocks Hospital, Salisbury

I awakened in the dark to the roar of wind-driven rain lashing the Quonset hut's corrugated steel.

A nurse was going bed to bed, lighting her way with a flashlight. I didn't care about her. I felt smug about being warm and dry and not having to sleep in the downpour.

Then I started remembering that I was in a hospital. And why.

She took my temp and checked my pulse. She had me sit up so she could peek under my back bandages. Then she peeled back the chest bandage and took another look. "How am I doing?"

"You're getting along fine, Sergeant. Yesterday, you had a little temperature, but it was normal today and it's normal tonight."

I told her it was nice to hear an American voice among all the Limeys and asked how she was holding up. She rolled her eyes and said she could do with a good night's sleep. "It's getting so we can't sleep during the day because of the German rockets."

"What do you mean?"

"I guess you haven't heard one yet. We call them buzz bombs. They look like little planes that fly over. But then their engines stop and they fall to earth and explode."

That was the first I'd heard about the German V1 rockets that a few days earlier started coming down all over southeast England.

The first one I heard came later that same morning . . . a loud, ragged growl first in the distance, then passing overhead, then nothing. And after that a big explosion.

Not as thunderous as a Screaming Meemie, but a damned good-sized blast anyway.

Later in the day a surgeon in a dripping poncho came in to examine me. He said I was lucky -- that the bullet through my chest missed the shoulder blade on the way out. Plus that three shrapnel wounds in my left leg were basically like three knife stabs. No major damage.

"This chest shot is a serious wound," he said. "But it's nothing like getting hit in the shoulder. You know in the cowboy movies when Roy Rogers gets shot in the movies, it's always in the shoulder?

"Well Sarge, that's just the purest Hollywood bullshit. A shoulder hit can take months and maybe three or four surgeries – and even then you might never have full use of the arm.

"But you're recovering very quickly. You'll be in fighting trim by September. Maybe even August."

"Oh, great!" I laughed. "Just what I didn't want to hear, Doc."

They encouraged me to start walking.

At first the pain in my thigh was agonizing and I asked for a cane, but the pain which the cane caused in my right chest and back convinced me to continue hobbling.

One morning, I asked to call Abbott Manor in Devon but they put me off. The next day, my nurse said some people wanted to speak to me.

"Who's that?"

"Two investigators that say they are from CID. But I don't know what that means."

"Well, miss, it means that they are detectives from the Criminal Investigation Detachment of the Military Police.

"Are you in trouble?"

"No, but I think somebody else is."

Chapter 35
June 26, 1944 – Odstocks Hospital, Salisbury

The first thing they told me was that anything I said could be used against me in a court martial.

The warning came from a pair of warrant officers from the Criminal Investigation Detachment.

As Tweedle Dee and Tweedle Dum sat there with their note pads I asked, "Well, sirs, am I going to be court-martialed?"

The younger one said, "We'll do the questioning."

The elder, looking pained said, "We don't think you're going to be court-martialed."

"Well, sirs, am I under arrest or accused of something?"

The younger took a deep breath and said, "No. We're here to ask you about the events of Saturday, June 10. And we're required to give you that warning before we can ask you anything at all."

The older one said, "It's just a formality."

"Who requires this formality?"

He sighed. "The Articles of War."

So I told the pair to ask away and they wanted to know what had passed between me and a certain Capt. Richard Schiltz. I didn't think it was the best choice of words.

"Well," I said, "what passed between us was a 110-grain round-nosed copper-jacketed bullet from his carbine that hit me in the right chest and bored its way out my back."

They both blinked and glanced at each other.

"It was his second shot," I added. "The first missed my hip by about an inch and struck the back gate of the half-track. After that, everything's pretty foggy.

"It was not an accident," I added.

"You're saying he shot you deliberately?"

"Exactly. And then, I'm not sure about this because I was flat on my back on the road after he shot me, but I believe he started to drive our half-track away. And then I think it was hit by a German mortar round, but again I'm fuzzy about all that."

"Where was he standing and where were you when his carbine discharged?"

"I was in the back of the half-track on the radio telephone with the 1st Battalion fire direction center. His carbine didn't just discharge. He fired it at me after threatening to shoot me."

They waltzed me through the story about six times.

Yes, Capt. Schiltz gave me a direct order to request permission to move the sections. No, I knew of no immediate threat to us. Yes, 88 cannon rounds were going over us, but the target seemed to be well to the east. And, yes, I was unable to follow his command because I was receiving and relaying commands from an officer of superior rank in the battalion FDC.

I expressed the opinion that Schiltz was in sheer panic generated by his own cowardice. No, I did not know whether anyone at FDC overheard his order, but members of my section certainly did – Timmer, Jacobs, Halls and Chucheko, though Jacobs might be dead and Chuchecko had very little or no English.

And I had no witness to prove it, but two days earlier Capt. Schiltz promised to destroy me because my actions supposedly had got him royal ass-chewings from his commanding officer, Capt. Freeman.

"Did you ever threaten the officer in question?"

"Yes, after he damn near got us killed during training, I told him to get the hell away from us or I'd kick his ass."

"Describe that incident."

I took them through the time when The Dick dropped a live mortar shell, propellant flaming, near stored mortar ammunition. I also filled them in on his orders for the battery to fire when it was located under tree branches. The two men looked at each other.

"Can anyone vouch for what you're saying?"

I told them that if Capt. Freeman, Lt. Scott and Sgt. Forster were still alive they could verify my statements.

The investigators could not or would not answer my questions either about the sections or whether Jacobs had survived.

After the interview was over, I asked what would happen next.

"We don't know," the older one said. "We're only investigators for the judge advocate general."

"So I'm not under arrest or anything?"

The older one heaved another sigh. "Look, son. Something pretty rotten happened and the Army just wants to get to the bottom of it."

"And you can't tell me how my boys are doing? This is driving me nuts."

"We honestly don't know. Our only real knowledge of the case is based on what we were told to check, and what you've just told us today. We're going to type up a statement to the effect of what you've told us and have you sign it.

"After that, our report and your statement will go together to the judge advocate. Other investigators are in Normandy looking into the case in the 4th Division. We're sure you'll hear more later on."

The younger office added, "Right now you can say a prayer for everybody in Normandy because they're recovering from a hell of a storm."

That afternoon I was able to get a call through to Abbott Manor.

Chapter 35
June 27, 1944 – Odstocks Hospital, Salisbury

The British, God love them, do have a way of keeping unwanted people at an arm's length.

A starchy male voice that I didn't recognize answered at Abbott Manor and said neither Sir Alfred nor Lady Alice could come to the phone. And Leading Wren Abbot was absent, thank you, engaged in her duties.

His frosty tones indicated hell probably would freeze over before he would report my call to any member of the household.

I decided to lay it on thick. "Very well," I said, "would you then convey my respects to Maj. Gen. Abbot-Leigh and give him a message for me?"

With tones of doubt about whether any message from me was worthy of the general's attention, the speaker assented. "Would you please tell him that Allan Dudley called. I'm a U.S. Army staff sergeant and . . ."

"Good heavens, Sergeant, why didn't you say so? They talk about you constantly. I regret Sir Alfred is away from the manor but he should return tomorrow morning. May I have him ring you?"

"Most kind of you, but I'm afraid I don't know the number here. I'm at Odstocks Hospital in Salisbury."

"I will give him the message immediately he arrives. And, again, my apologies. You can't believe how many try to bother the general and Lady Alice."

"Thank you kindly," I said, "and give my best regards to Lady Alice and Leading Wren Abbot."

# # #

Next morning, I received a letter in a grimy envelope. The single sheet of note paper inside was even grimier thanks to several oily fingerprints.

It's what happens when you're trying to write with a pencil stub on the hood of a half-track. But at least the news in the letter was half good.

Hey Dud –

We hope you recover fast because we want you back. We hear they still plan to bump you to 2nd lt., but I guess they first need to know whether you're still alive. The Dick is gone. We don't know any more than that. Rumor has it that he's going to get a long tour of duty in the stockade at Ft. Leavenworth. We hear Wilson's ankle is a million-dollar wound and he's stateside for good. No news so far about Jacobs.

The rest of the gang is okay which seems like a miracle when you consider that Charlie Company got ambushed and took just about 50 percent casualties. (Too bad The Dick wasn't with them.) But then the rest of the battalion and the tanks ripped the Nazis apart. We fired so much the tubes were nearly red-hot and we were all walking around like we were punch drunk. When we cleaned the guns they were so hot the Kotexes came out charred. We're still at it, but we're told the beachhead finally is secure.

We got some replacements and they scare me. One started to drop a round into the tube nose first. I had to keep Halls from snapping his neck. But they're shaping up. Halls tells them what The Dick said: watch and learn. Well, don't pinch the nurses. You ain't an officer yet.

Mike Forster

Acting Assistant Chief Mortar Forker

# # #

Mike's note dropped me straight into the dumps. It was good to know he was okay. But when I folded his letter back into its envelope it hit me how much I missed them. I thought it would even feel good to hear those damn bridge players arguing again about doubles and redoubles, whatever the hell they are.

I moped around until time for my therapy routine and the nurse, a little red head, chewed me out for being so lackluster about it. The chest wound required arm exercises that hurt my chest like hell at first. But the more I stretched and reached, I could feel my strength increase and the pain begin to ease. The hole in my ribs where they put in the chest tube was closed and healed and I had a star-shaped scar southeast of my right nipple.

Anyhow, I was in robe and slippers leaving Therapy for my bunk in the Quonset hut, when somebody standing in the intersecting corridor shouted "TENN-hut!"

I turned to see Sir Alfred, tall and lean in full uniform, red cap band and tabs and all, returning a salute as he marched toward me, a white-coated doctor following him. Seeing him pierced my depression like sunshine through fog. I came to attention and tried to give Sir Alfred a precise salute.

"Welcome, sir," I said. "It's wonderful to see you."

He returned the salute, turned to dismiss the doctor and then shook hands with me. "Allan, considering what you've been through, you look quite well." Other patients in the corridor passed us with wide eyes; generals just don't shake hands or pass the time of day with enlisted people.

Sir Alfred lowered his voice. "Don't be put off by all this finery," he said, pointing a thumb to his uniform and ribbons. "First time I've worn it all in weeks. I thought it might encourage the authorities here to let me spirit you away. The surgeon commander has given permission to take you for a drive if you feel up to it."

"Lord yes, sir. I'll go get into my uniform. Is Lady Alice along?"

"Sorry, Allan," he said. "She couldn't come along since this is official business, you see. And Katherine couldn't come because she's doing chauffeur duty today."

He drew me to one side. "Er, Allan, there's more to my being here. I don't wish to presume, but I can put in a word with the MO and, if you're agreeable, I feel certain the U.S. Army will let you transfer to the manor for the remainder of your recuperation. We've a full-scale hospital there, you know of course, even if it is Royal Navy instead of U.S. Army."

Seeing Katherine in my mind's eye, I didn't hesitate. "I'd love to be at the manor," I said. "I'm pretty well patched up. All I need now is exercise -- you, know, therapy, for my recovery. I'll go get my things."

"Oh, don't bother about that," Sir Alfred said. "I'll have Clay collect them."

"Who, sir?"

"Cpl. Clay, my batman. You've already met him on the phone. He'll clear out your locker. Why don't we just walk out to the car if you can manage?"

When we got to the car, Sir Alfred opened the door for me.

"Sir," I scolded, "generals shouldn't open doors for mere sergeants."

"Oh, stuff and nonsense," he said. "Besides, you're out of uniform. Nobody can tell." Then, his hand still on the door, he gave me a flinty look. "Allan, before Clay returns, I must speak to you about Katherine."

Standing there about to climb into the back seat, I tensed. *Oh God, he knows about us.* "Sir?"

"Alice and I suspect you and Katherine have found comfort together. Wonderful. She needs all the support she can get. She's had a horrible time."

"Well, yessir, losing her husband . . ."

"That's only a fraction of it. She's under our roof not only because she is our daughter-in-law, but she now has not another living soul in the world."

"Lord, sir, I didn't know."

"Right. Her brother was a corporal in my son's company. They got the hammer the same day."

"My God."

He paused, looked into the distance and swallowed.

"Then last winter she returned one day from driving some admiral to his club only to discover that her family died in one of the last air raids. She arrived just as they pulled her parents and sister from the rubble."

"Oh, my God!"

"Yes," he said. "You see what I mean, Allan, about all that has befallen her. Now . . . Allan . . . I don't want to seem officious, but please understand that Alice and I regard Katherine as our daughter. She is all that is left to us, and we are the mere vestige of what remains of her people. With this in mind, I strongly warn you not to hurt her."

"Sir Alfred," I said. "With respect, that is the least necessary warning I have ever received. I never would do a thing to injure Katherine – especially not having heard everything else that has happened to her."

"Indeed." he said. "I'm very glad to hear you say that.

"Lady Alice and I will hold you to it."

Chapter 36
June 28, 1944 – The Manor

The view through the car windows was downright depressing. Though the wind had eased, the clouds were low and rain still fell in sheets. Sir Alfred said the storm had done tremendous damage to the artificial ports on the Normandy beaches.

"I'm told supplies are down to a trickle for the moment." He said. "But, Allan, your forces have done a prodigious job pushing the Nazis back on Cherbourg. They made way for more divisions to come ashore. In fact, I'm told they have secured the whole peninsula except Cherbourg and are about to take it, too."

He kept talking about the war, managing to interrupt my thoughts about Katherine.

He said his main worry about the invasion was over – that the Germans no longer had any hope of driving the allies off the continent. "But they do have us stalled right now." He said the British and Canadian forces had failed to advance as far or as quickly as Ike and Montgomery had planned.

Just then we heard the discordant buzzing roar of a V1 rocket somewhere overhead in the clouds.

"And *that* business is causing difficulty," he said. "The rockets have no tactical value, but they're a very real strategic threat. The British people stood up to the blitz, but it's asking a bit much of them to start putting up with these devilish things blasting London anew. It's forcing Winston to put a lot of pressure on the military.

"But the essence of it is that we're in Europe to stay, and sometime soon we'll break out into France – and then it becomes a race to see whether we get to Germany before the Wehrmacht can."

At the general's direction, Clay drove us on a short side trip to see Stonehenge.

We stayed in the car, eating cucumber sandwiches and drinking hot chocolate as I marveled at the eerie sight. In the rain and fog, the monument looked ghostly. It filled me with questions, but Sir Alfred said Stonehenge was a stark mystery.

"We know it was here when the first Roman Legions arrived almost two millennia ago," he said. "And there's been speculation that it might some sort of temple built by the Druids."

"Druids?"

"Yes, some ancient religious wallahs – sun-worshippers and that sort of thing -- but that's all anyone knows about them."

"May be," I said, "but they sure seemed to know their engineering. Those stone blocks are huge!"

As Clay put us back on course for the manor, the place-names tickled me – Middle Wallop, West Wallop and Over Wallop – leading me to ask whether they had an Under Wallop or maybe a Hard Wallop.

Sir Alfred became slightly stiff about my attempt to be funny. But I got him to chuckle when I told him of training at Camp Leonard Wood where we encountered Missouri town names such as Cabool and Quarrels – and Versailles which the natives pronounced "Ver-sales" rather than "Vair-sigh" – and how one could pronounce "Missouri" ending either with an "uh" or an "ee" depending on I didn't know what.

Then he laughed aloud when I told how American soldiers butchered the names of towns in Normandy, such as Awdyville lah-Hewbert.

# # #

By the time we got to the manor, I was a bit wobbly. I gave my respects to Lady Alice and asked if I might retire early.

I awakened in the night to find Katherine nodding in a chair beside my bed. I sat up and kissed her awake and then we cuddled on the bed for the longest time, just holding each other.

"I think they know about us," I said.

"You mean Sir Alfred and Lady Alice?"

I nodded and said, "He was getting very fatherly and being rather stern. I wouldn't want him mad at me."

"They're the dearest of people," she said. "I was so distressed when you left and they were so supportive . . . and then even more so when Clay told us you were in hospital. Are you in much pain?"

"Not now. Not holding you like this. As far as I'm concerned we could lie like this for a year or two."

"Will you be going back?"

"I don't want to think about it, but probably."

She said nothing but snuggle closer. "I missed you so very, very much," she said. "And . . ."

"I know," I said. "The constant worry and never knowing. And I think I missed you just as much, fearing that you'd forget me."

"Oh, Allan! You must never, ever fear that. Never!"

At length she said, "It's been torture for both of us but for now it's over. We're here together. That's all that matters."

"Exactly how I feel," I said, suddenly surprised tears were rolling out of my eyes.

"Now, here with you, I feel alive . . ." and I couldn't talk any more. I started shuddering and weeping.

She pillowed my head on her bosom and we both wept there in the dark, clinging gently and sweetly . . . just being . . . and not thinking about the future.

Chapter 37
Thursday, June 29, 1944 – Convalescence

The next morning at breakfast, Katherine announced that she was applying for a month of leave. She said it should be no problem since she'd had none since the start of the war.

"Splendid," Sir Alfred said. "Perhaps I can wangle extra petrol and you can show Allan some of our countryside."

I grinned at that. "Sir Alfred, that sounds wonderful – just as long as it's not Dartmoor. I've seen more of Dartmoor, foot by foot, than I suspect most of His Majesty's subjects have. And I don't really want to see any more of it."

"Katherine, you could show him the Downs in Sussex," Lady Alice suggested. "They are quite lovely this time of year."

"If we can get enough petrol," Katherine said. "And, come to that," she added, "if rationing is too tight, I suppose we could do some bicycling."

"Capital idea," Sir Alfred chuckled, "but beware of GIs in their jeeps. They're a dangerous lot."

# # #

In the end, we just strolled. About half the time, the Devonshire weather was beautiful. We carried military ponchos – the British call them rain capes -- to keep from getting soaked in the showers that often processed across the countryside.

One day we reached the crest of a hill and the view stunned me. I told her it made me think of Sherwood Forest and Robin Hood. "It's as if his ghost is here," I said.

"Exactly," she grinned, "along with Friar Tuck, Little John and Maid Marion."

"And seeing this reminds me of something else," I said. "It was some little verse Mom used to read to Sis. Something about: 'I can see rivers and trees and cattle and all over the country side.'"

"Of course," she smiled. "Stevenson. *How Do You Like To Go Up In A Swing.*"

She recited it. '. . . Up in the air and over the wall, 'till I can see so wide . . .' Memories flooded back. Of Mom and the hero turned dirty bastard father. I shook my head.

"Is that the same Stevenson who wrote *Treasure Island?*"

"The same. Have you read any of his other works?"

"No. I'm afraid I'm just a country boy. Got through high school and that was about it. But I did enjoy studying German at that university. I'd like to maybe go back some day."

She had studied French, so she laughed delightedly when I told her about how us Yanks butchered place names in Normandy.

On those walks we were gradually discovering more of each other. I was a bit surprised that though she seemed gentile and polished – I think the Limeys call it "posh" -- she was not one of the gentry. Her father had been a factory craftsman and her mother a seamstress. They had scrimped and saved to send Katherine and her siblings to good schools and, in Katherine, it showed.

One Saturday a heavy shower surprised us and I actually found that I could run after a fashion, so Katherine and I trotted to shelter in a little stone cattle barn. Her hair was soaked into strings around her face but she seemed more beautiful than ever.

Then things became a bit gloomy.

"Allan, you mentioned before that there was someone else in your life."

I nodded. "'Was' is the word, Katherine. We had some dates at the university and went to a USO dance. We became fairly close. She was going into the Army, too, as a nurse. But I've heard next to nothing from her since then."

"Do you love her?"

"I liked her. But it was nothing like the way we feel. Or at least the way I feel."

She looked out the window for a long time. "How *do* you feel, Allan?"

That was a hard answer for me.

"Katherine, it's a very, very selfish feeling. I guess I'd say I need you and I want you. And I don't mean just in bed, though I love that, of course. I mean I just want to be with you in every way for every minute. And I hope that you want me now and that you'll want me when all this is over."

She turned her face away. "Oh, God!" and she began crying almost convulsively. I tried to put my arm around her, but she stood up and pulled away from me.

"Katherine! Don't do that to me!"

She turned and with both hands gave a despairing gesture. "Why ever not, Allan? When you recover you'll do exactly the same thing to me. You'll turn away. You'll leave me. You'll be gone, just as you left in May. And next time perhaps they'll kill you. You just said that when you fight you think of yourself as dead already. Oh, my God, I didn't want this again!"

It hit me how she must feel – a mirror of my own desire not to go back into combat. I just stood there helpless. "I hate seeing you feel this way," I said. "It makes me feel evil and small. I don't know what to do."

She turned back to me, still in tears with a wretched look on her face. "Don't you see? You've already done it. No, that's unfair. *We've* done it, Allan. The two of us together. We're in love and I fear it and I hate it."

"There's only one thing to do."

"What?"

"Start making plans for when the war ends."

She stared at me. "You're bloody mad."

"Well, maybe so," I said, handing over my handkerchief. "But I didn't think proper British ladies were supposed to say 'bloody'."

She gave a wry grin and guffawed as she wiped her eyes. "Well, ever since I met you I've hardly been a proper lady, have I?"

"Oh, I don't know. You're one gorgeous doll and your manners make me wish I had better manners.

"Very well, sergeant. What shall we do after the war?"

"Well, how would you feel about being an Army wife and living in the states?"

"Allan Dudley, are you proposing to me?"

"Yes . . . yes, I guess I am. How about it, Kid? I'd get down on one knee, but it's still kind of painful right now. And I guess I'd better see about going to town to get a ring."

"You're quite serious, aren't you?"

"Completely serious, Katherine. Being an Army camp-follower isn't a glamorous or an easy life, but you do get to see lot of beautiful countryside – on the other side of the pond." I was about to say, 'Who knows? You might be an officer's wife.' But I kept it zipped. She already was an officer's widow.

She didn't say yes.

But as we strolled home, she clung to my arm and rested her head on my shoulder.

When we walked into the Manor's drive, I said "Oh-oh."

A Military Police jeep was parked out front of the manor.

# # #

Once inside, we found Sir Alfred and Lady Alice entertaining a giant MP corporal trying with fingers the size of bananas to cradle a delicate flowered tea cup. With him was an MP captain overwhelmed in the presence of a major general.

He jumped up and handed me a folded sheet of paper.

"Sgt. Dudley, this is an order from Supreme Headquarters Allied Forces In Europe to appear on Monday, July 10, to give evidence in the trial of Capt. Parker B. Schiltz. Are you now sufficiently recovered from your wound, or does it prevent you from giving evidence?"

"Is the trial here in England?"

"Yes. In Bristol."

"Then as long as I can get transportation . . . ."

He and the general answered at the same time. "We'll get you there." Then they both laughed.

# # #

By July 10 I felt fairly well recovered. I had discarded the sling. I still had a mild ache in my chest and back, but the shortness of breath was gone even when I did some hard walking.

A general court martial was something new to me. I didn't realize regulations prohibited me from meeting with or speaking to any other witness. I wanted to catch up with the boys, but only saw Forster far down a corridor and later glimpsed Halls.

The JAG officers running the prosecution were furious that the CID investigators who interviewed me never had returned to get my signature on my statement. It turned out that the written statement based on the interview was accurate. I signed it after making and initialing a few minor corrections.

Learning I'd never been a trial witness, the JAG officers explained that The Dick's defense attorney probably would question me at length and try to upset me by being sarcastic and abrasive.

"The main thing to remember is that even though he's an officer and he ranks you, you mustn't let his rank sway your answers. He probably will try to sway you, but you need only answer his questions as truthfully as possible. He'll probably try to speed up your answers to trip you up. But just remember that even if he tries to rush you, there is no rush. None at all! The court wants the truth, not a lot of drama."

Other than that, it was a case of wait, wait and wait until my turn came which wasn't until Day Three.

It wasn't until after I took the oath that I got a good look at The Dick.

His face seemed to have melted slightly, just enough to droop from his facial bones. His eyes seemed more hooded, so he looked a bit like Boris Karloff, that actor who played the Frankenstein monster.

He wouldn't meet my eyes.

Chapter 38
July 11, 1944 – Court Martial

I was nervous, of course, before they called me to testify, but my old man unwittingly prepared me years before when he bragged about snaring witnesses.

"The stupid bastards keep looking at the jury or the judge, looking for sympathy or approval. And they always answer too fast. If you're ever on the stand, kid, take your time. Count to ten before you say a word."

What really made me nervous was that the tribunal consisted of five officers – headed by a crotchety-looking full bird infantry colonel who looked like an eagle about to close his talons on a bunny.

As soon as I was sworn in, Capt. Johnson led off with questions for the prosecution. "Please state your full name, rank and unit."

"I'm Allan Gregory Dudley, staff sergeant, currently assigned to Abbot Manor Naval Hospital. My unit is Company D, First Battalion, Eighth Infantry Regiment, Fourth Infantry Division."

"Very well. Now please tell the court what happened to you on the night of Saturday, June 10."

I knew I'd get this question some time or other, so I had the answer ready. In a low, quiet tone, I said, "Sir, what happened was that Capt. Schiltz threatened to shoot me and then he carried out that threat."

"And by the words 'Capt. Schiltz' I take it you are referring to the defendant?"

Keeping the quiet tone, I said, "I am, sir." I pointed at Schiltz. "I mean that officer at the defense table, Capt. Parker B. Schiltz."

"Thank you," Capt. Johnson said. "Let the record show that Sgt. Dudley pointed at the defendant as he identified him by full name and rank." He then turned away from me to face Schiltz and asked, "Sergeant, what do you mean by the words, 'then he carried out that threat'?"

"Sir, what I mean is that he fired two shots at me from his carbine. The first one struck next to my right hip, hitting the rear gate of the halftrack I was standing in. Then he fired again and the bullet struck me right here . . . in my right chest."

"Sergeant, how much time elapsed between the first and second shots?"

"As long as it takes to pull a trigger on a semiautomatic firearm."

"So there's no way this could have been an accident?"

The defense lawyer jumped up. "Objection: the question calls for a conclusion on the part of the witness."

"Objection sustained."

Capt. Johnson begged the court's pardon. "Sgt. Dudley, where was Capt. Schiltz when he fired at you?"

"I couldn't see his feet, but he appeared to be standing on the right side running board of our section's half-track."

"And was the half-track in motion?"

"No, sir. We were parked ready to carry out a fire mission."

"Sergeant, was the motor running?"

"Yes, sir, so as to keep the radios powered."

"Now was anyone standing beside Capt. Schiltz or was anybody in the half-track's cab?"

"No sir. Three members of the section were in the back of the half-track preparing to fire our mortar."

Memories of the night overtook me for a moment. I had to duck my head and take a deep shuddering breath.

"Sergeant, are you alright?"

"Sorry, sir. Yes sir, I am. I've just never been in a court like this before and it makes me jittery."

"I have just a few more questions." He pointed his index fingers at his own temples. "Now, think carefully. Did you see anything or anybody jostle or bump against or jar either Capt. Schiltz or his carbine, or both, causing him to fire?"

"No, sir. Capt. Schiltz had his carbine at eye level, the butt against his shoulder, aiming it at me. No one was near him."

"Now, sergeant, according to the record, you testified . . . 'Capt. Schiltz threatened to shoot me and then he carried out that threat.' So, what was the nature of that threat?"

I took another deep breath. "Sir, I think his exact words were, 'You stupid bastard, I ordered you to request permission to move!' That's when he shouldered his carbine and aimed it at me."

We proceeded from there with Capt. Johnson directing me to review what had happened before Schiltz's order. I kept my eyes strictly on the captain, never looking toward the judges or Schiltz.

Then it was the defense attorney's turn.

"Sgt. Dudley, are you a good soldier?"

"I try to be, sir."

"Do you obey orders?"

"Yes sir."

"Well, then, why didn't you obey the order from Capt. Schiltz on the night of Saturday, June 10?"

"Sir, I couldn't. I already was relaying fire mission orders from the FDC – the battalion fire direction center. As far as I was concerned, those orders from higher authority took precedence over Capt. Schiltz's orders which would have delayed our mission."

"Don't you think that the officer on the ground knows better than someone on the other end of the radio?"

"Which officer on which ground, sir? The FDC director sure was on the ground."

He started getting snide. "Is that analysis based on your years of vast experience as a staff sergeant?"

Stick to the truth. "No, sir. I've only been a staff sergeant for two months."

"Exactly how long have you been in the Army, sergeant?"

Gotcha. "I was sworn in about 1030 hours Wednesday, Sept. 13, 1939, a week after the Nazis invaded Poland." I heard a rustle from among the tribunal. The defense attorney looked like he had taken a gulp of battery acid.

"Then how did you come to make that judgement, sergeant?" He was really sounding caustic now.

I looked at him but directed my words to the infantry colonel. "Sir, I did not make a judgement. I carried out orders from a veteran major at FDC. He needed our mortars to support the battalion's riflemen. To me, that's all that counts. Besides . . ."

"Thank you. No further questions."

The colonel looked at Capt. Johnson. "Redirect?"

"Thank you, sir. Sgt. Dudley, you said the word 'Besides' but did not get to finish that testimony."

"Yes sir, I wanted to say that the fire direction center knows a lot more about what's going on the ground than any of us around a mortar, especially someone who's worried about nothing but his own skin."

The defense attorney exploded like a Screaming Meemie and the colonel cleared the court.

It was an hour before I was recalled to the stand. The colonel, looking daggers, warned me to be very careful in my testimony, to cite only facts, not my personal opinions.

Capt. Johnson, who had a faint smile on his face, asked me what Capt. Schiltz did leading up to his demand to move the battery.

"Nothing, sir." I explained that he had said or done nothing for hours. "But when one of the troops said our gun's flashes might make us targets, he immediately demanded that we move. And, when I kept relaying orders from FDC, he threatened me."

The defense attorney objected that my testimony was hearsay and the colonel sustained him.

Capt. Johnson didn't seem fazed. "Well, sergeant, don't you agree that the flashes from your guns might cause the Germans to target you?"

Another chance to talk to the colonel.

"I suppose it could, sir. But since it was night and the terrain was flat and 88 rounds already were zipping right over us, it didn't much matter where we would relocate. Our flashes still would be visible . . . along with the flashes of all the dozens of other artillery pieces that were firing in the area.

"What was most important is that the men in our rifle companies are targeted every damn minute – sorry, sir – every single minute by rifles, mortars, MG-42s, and heavy artillery and those screaming meemies. The infantry needs all the help we can give, no matter what the risk to us." I heard another stirring from the tribunal's judges

"Where did you get that Purple Heart, sergeant?"

I told him what happened in North Africa. He took me through my combat with First Division. He wound up by asking how much longer I would be on convalescent leave.

"The docs think I'll be ready to go late this month, sir."

"And will you be return to your company?"

"I sure hope so, sir. We came across together in the *Queen Mary* and humped together all over Dartmoor, so I miss them."

He turned away toward The Dick's table.

"Your witness."

The Dick's lawyer didn't want anything more to do with me, so I was dismissed.

Chapter 39
Friday, July 15, 1944 – SHAEF HQ

They isolated me from the other witnesses for two more days. But when the tribunal handed down a guilty verdict, we had about an hour to shake hands and reminisce.

The guys were headed back to Normandy to help prepare for the break-out into France.

"Right now," Forster said, "we're trying to capture St. Lo and the Krauts are doing all they can to keep us from it."

"What's St. Lo?"

"Just a town, but it's got five highways radiating out of it and the brass wants those highways. And what makes it hard is all the damned swamps and hedgerows in front of it."

Capt. Thompson congratulated all of us and explained that The Dick's conviction would be appealed as a matter of course.

He told me he thought I ought to go to law school when the war ended.

"You did a great job of playing the tribunal," he said. "The colonel was impressed. I wish more witnesses were as professional as you."

He said he thought The Dick could be busted to private, sent to the Leavenworth Disciplinary Barracks, and lose all pay and privileges. "Attempted murder is a serious charge," he said, "and for an officer to be convicted of trying to murder an enlisted man is far beyond serious. He could be in prison for decades if not life."

Even cleaned up and in dress uniforms, the boys all looked about a year older, with tired eyes and deep parentheses at the corners of their mouths. Forster now was an acting staff sergeant and Halls had been promoted to sergeant.

They told me Jacobs still was alive but in serious condition from extensive shrapnel wounds to his legs and gut. He had not been able to come to court, but had given a deposition.

Forster said the explosion that injured Jacobs and me was not a mortar but a *panzerfaust*, the Kraut version of the bazooka. A six-man German patrol had ambushed us as during all the distractions after The Dick shot me.

As we chatted and waited for a jeep to take me back to the manor, a major came out of G1 and asked all of us to accompany him.

They took us to an inner office where the tribunal president himself greeted us. He actually smiled as he called me to attention. He had an underling read a citation about our action at Exit Three, and then pinned a Bronze Star with V for Valor on my breast pocket.

Then he handed me a set of promotion orders and a small black box containing two gold bars.

"Congratulations, lieutenant." The guys clapped and then we all shook hands even though I felt dazed.

The colonel dismissed us, telling me I'd better draw some pay from G1 because now, being an officer, I'd have to buy my own new uniform.

"You at least need a new hat and jacket," he grinned. "With bars on your shoulders and officer's brass," he said, "you sure don't need those chevron shadows on your sleeves."

By the time I drew $100 in pay, the MP jeep was waiting for me, so we all shook hands again.

"Don't defeat Germany before I get back," I said.

"We won't, Lieutenant," Halls said, with undue emphasis on my new rank.

"Guys," I said as I got into the jeep, "My first order is for you Mortar Forkers to keep your heads down."

We all saluted and the MP and I headed back to the manor.

Chapter 40
July 15, 1944 – Abbot Manor

The MP driver, being a cop, drove like a madman. Over most of the lurching route, I braced to ease the discomfort by clinging with both hands to the jeep's side curtain strut. I could have ordered him to slow down, but I wanted to get the manor as fast as possible.

As I climbed gingerly out onto the driveway I congratulated him of qualifying for the Indy 500 and asked whether he had some place special to be.

"Damn right," he said. "I've got this chick in . . ." suddenly he clammed up.

"Don't worry," I said, "until I get the uniform I guess I'm still an enlisted man so I won't turn you in."

"Thanks a lot, sir. I'm going before a promotion board next week."

"Well, then don't get yourself busted for speeding on the way back to Bristol, corporal."

"Right, sir. And thank you."

As he drove off, I found that being addressed as "sir" rattled me a bit. It put me on opposite side of a line where I stood from the day I enlisted; really since the day Mom and Sis and I fled Dad.

But for the moment I was more concerned about seeing Katherine and the general and Lady Alice.

I didn't tell them about my commission, fearing it would dredge up distressing memories about their sons and Katherine's late family. But during dinner the general made it clear that he knew. With a slight smile, he kept probing with questions like, "Now, after the verdict Allan, did anything *special* happen?"

I told them that I had received the bronze star and was starting a second row of fruit salad. They congratulated me. But the general kept at me. "Yes indeed, Allan, but did anything else of note occur?"

When I finally spilled the beans everybody seemed delighted and Katherine asked why I was still in a sergeant's uniform.

"Well, I've got to go out and buy my uniform and I really didn't want to bother with it today because I wanted to come right back here. And I'm not even sure where to buy it. I guess I'll have to find a PX somewhere."

"Oh, pish-posh," the general said. "We'll take you to my tailor first thing tomorrow. We'll make a day of it, all four of us. Lunch in Exmouth. Or a picnic if the weather's fine."

I explained I was concerned about the cost, never having bought a uniform . . . and would the general's tailor, er, be up to date on American officers' uniforms?"

He laughed, assuring me that Goldsworth & Sons had made officers' uniforms for about 300 years. "And you needn't worry . . . they won't try to outfit you with a kilt or put you in a dragoon's pelisse."

He said they could outfit me with summer khakis and winter uniforms plus fatigues for 10 pounds which would leave at least 10 pounds of my draw.

So later I drew him aside and asked whether one might find a jeweler in the neighborhood of Goldsworth's.

He gave a big grin. "Now, sir, is this something you wish to keep confidential for the nonce?"

"Well, I don't know Katherine's ring size," I said, "so I'd better have her along, hadn't I?" Then a thought hit me. "And I suppose, Sir Alfred, since you, in effect, are Katherine's father that I really ought to ask your permission – and, well, your blessing."

"Ah, just so. Well, Allan, you certainly have both from me and my wife. We both are in hopes you don't take her away to the States too soon. Now, regarding the ring . . ."

He recommended consulting with Lady Alice. It turned out she knew Katherine's ring size and thought it best that I buy the ring and present it to Katherine in private.

"Excellent, my pet," Sir Alfred said. "So during Allan's fitting in the morning, you and Katherine can pop along to do some shopping and he and I can stop at Ira's. And then if the weather's right, we can picnic and you and I can just stroll away . . . "

Katherine interrupted us. "What are you three scheming about?"

Lady Alice said, "Why, dear, we're just making plans for the morrow. If it's raining we can go to a nice pub. But if it's fine, we can picnic and perhaps do some punting. So I think we'd better pack a lunch . . ."

"Punting?" I interrupted. "Like in football? You know, real football like we play in America."

All three laughed. They explained American football isn't true football, you see. Besides, a punt is not an athletic tactic, but a shallow boat which British men propel with poles on a shallow waterway while their ladies relax in the bow reveling in the peace and serenity of it all.

"So," the general asked, "what in heaven is a punt in American football?"

My explanation became confusing because it meant covering downs, first-and-ten advancement, drop kicks, field goals and, of course, punts.

Together with my attempted wit about soccer vs football -- succeeded in diverting Katherine from further questions.

Later I asked them to explain cricket to me. It was incredibly confusing, so I said it sounded to me like a primitive form of baseball.

"Not at all," the general drawled, "It's a very sophisticated form of war."

Chapter 41
July 16, 1944 – The Return

I expected the fitting to be a case of pulling one or two uniform jackets and pants off the rack and shortening the cuffs – maybe a 20-minute process.

Instead they minutely measured about everything but my ears. Since I was a protégé of Sir Alfred, they said they'd be ready for the preliminary fitting after tea.

From there we headed to Ira's and where I picked out a nice engagement ring – nothing huge or conspicuous, but with a Florentine accent on the band.

Then it was a case of trying to spot Lady Alice and Katherine among the shoppers. Somehow, I glimpsed Katherine's gorgeous curving smile in the crowd before I saw her face or figure. We just seemed to gravitate, because an instant later she was waving and her smile broadened, giving my heart flip-flops.

When we met, she grabbed my upper arm and pulled us together and the day became wonderful . . . and what's more the weather actually was warm and sunny. So the general drove us to a nice park beside a little stream.

I had a bad moment as we got out of the car because a lot of brush edged the stream, reminding me of the Merderet where the Krauts ambushed us. Katherine sensed something upset me, but one look at her face and everything was fine.

As Katherine spread the blankets I lifted the ponderous wicker basket from the car's trunk – sorry, the boot, the limeys call it. As Lady Alice pulled food packets from the basket, I asked whether ants were a problem at English picnics.

Oh," she grinned, "ants sometime invade picnics like a lot of little Nazis. But today I petitioned Buckingham Palace for a royal intercession to protect us from the insects."

King George VI apparently favored her petition because, except for a solitary little scout or two, the ants kept their distance.

After we ate, Sir Alfred – having taken a snort or two from his flask -- lay back on the blanket and began snoring. Lady Alice gave him five minutes and then prodded him. "Come along, Alfred. We must walk or you'll just take root here beside the shrubs. Children! Do take care of the basket, please, won't you?"

"Charming," Katherine said, grinning as I gathered the plates and silverware and she knelt to replace them in the basket. "I think she wants some time alone with him," Katherine said.

"No," I said as I grabbed the mustard pot and the half-empty jar of gherkins. "She wanted me to have a few moments alone with you."

She looked up surprised as I knelt beside her.

I took her hand.

"Katherine, I don't know any proper way to put this, but I am in very much in love with you and I'm asking if you will consent to become my wife." I opened the ring box and presented it to her.

"Oh, Allan," she said, bending to lean into me. "I don't know. I love you. I do love you, so. But I don't know . . ." She put her head on my shoulder. As my arm went around her, she wept.

When Sir Alfred and Lady Alice returned, we were sitting side-by-side near the stream. I imagine I looked glum. Katherine's eyes were still red and damp.

"Why whatever's the matter?"

"Oh, Mother. Allan has asked me . . . well, I guess we're engaged. And it terrifies me." She burst into tears.

Lady Alice leaned to put a hand on her shoulder, glanced at me and said, "Allan, why don't you trot along with Alfred? Katherine and I will talk."

"But . . ."

"Allan," she said with a dismissive wave, "Go away."

I did.

Chapter 42
Saturday, July 13, 1944 – Exmouth

"I don't get it," I told Sir Alfred. "She said she loves me – said it twice. But then she also kept saying, 'I don't know . . . I don't know.' It's got me in a bind. I don't know what to do."

We walked for two minutes before he responded. "I'm taking so long to answer because we're talking about women and that's a subject on which I really never know what to say. No man does."

After another lengthy pause he said, "See here, Allen, it's part of a woman's wonder and mystery. At times they can just explode, flinging around jagged emotions like so much shrapnel. That's when one must take cover and stay alert.

"But this is different," he said. "I think Katherine's terrified. And who wouldn't be? She's lost almost everything to this beastly war and now a man who is going back into the heart of it – a man for whom she obviously cares deeply -- wants her to marry him. It's got her in a cleft stick.

"I think it's quite wonderful that she ever could love again," Sir Alfred added. "And I'm inclined to say you shouldn't worry, Allan. But I do think you should consider delaying the wedding until you return."

"Why is that, sir?"

"Well, first of all, the priest has to read the banns of your marriage at least three Sundays in a row."

"The what?"

"The banns – it's the public announcement of a couple's plans to wed. It's a church custom inherited from medieval times to prevent the occurrence of irregular marriages. Nowadays, it's just a formality really, but the church has its ways, you see."

"Good Lord," I said. "In the States, all that you need is a negative Wasserman and a justice of the peace."

"I daresay," he grinned. "But all of this ties to another fact. I just this morning learned that your troops are closing on St. Lo. The Canadians and British have consolidated their capture of Caen and the build-up of the armies' supplies is just about complete. And what all this means, I think, is that soon the allied armies will attack out of Normandy into France. And doubtless they'll call you back to duty, probably before the banns can be read three times."

"General, couldn't we just get married in a civil ceremony?"

"Allan, you must remember that on this side of the pond, church and state are almost one. And even if they weren't and even if the banns could be announced before your recall, I'd not like to see such pressure put on Katherine.

"Give her time, Lad. She has suffered that much. She loves you, but you see that implicitly means a great deal of pain – yes, and fear -- for her, too, not to mention constant anticipation of more grief."

# # #

When we got back to the manor, I asked Katherine to walk with me.

During the drive, she had been remote, conspicuously looking out the window and avoiding my eyes. And as we began walking, she still was stiff and formal. She let me hold her hand, but it felt cool and lifeless with no return pressure.

I apologized for rushing things.

"It looks like I've been thinking only of me," I said. "I want you to be my wife and I want to live the rest of my life with you. But I've got to face the fact that I may not have much life left and most of what remains probably would be apart from you."

Her hand gripped mine. "Oh, Allan, please don't say such things. I beg you. Please!"

"I won't say them again, Katherine. But I've got to face facts. I'll say this much -- if you love me and you're willing to be my wife, we can wait to take that step until you feel able to do so.

"And, my dear, if that means putting off our wedding until the war is over and I come back from it, so be it."

My words made no sense to me, though they seemed to be the right thing to say. Married or not, after I left we would miss each other equally. And if I were killed, I thought she'd mourn me just as much, freshly widowed or not.

But nonsense or not, I didn't care. I felt that we already were husband and wife in all but the legal sense. And if delaying the wedding would make my absence somehow easier to bear, fine by me.

"Now one thing, Katherine, after the war ends, I'm going to get real impatient if you want to wait more than three weeks for us to marry."

"Why three weeks?"

"Well, silly, that's because they need three weeks to read the bands or whatever they are. After that, Babe, no excuses!"

She giggled. "It's 'banns,' silly, not 'bands'." Then she turned, gripped my face in her hands and said, "Dear man," and pulled my face to hers. As I embraced her, she pressed the side of her head to mine and we just stood there.

"Thank you for understanding," she whispered at last. "I do love you Allan and I do want to be your wife – but not 'til we can be wed with the fair certainty of at least a few years together.

"So, Allan, I accept your proposal and your ring."

Chapter 43
Sunday, July 16, 1944 – Goodbye

Sir Alfred pulled me into the library late the next afternoon and got out his old Michelin road map of Normandy, now a bit tattered because we had folded and refolded it so often.

With his fountain pen, he sketched a rough triangle formed by the coast and the allies' front lines.

"The British and Canadians have Caen here on the coast to the east and your American forces soon are capturing St. Lo to the west – so you see the allies will occupy a pretty straight east-west front. It's about 25 miles long, extending between these two towns. That's a tremendous front for Rommel to defend."

"Rommel, eh? That's the bastard who we were facing with First Division in Tunisia. He really clobbered us at first, but we learned."

"Indeed. He's a daring and energetic commander and the German soldier always knows his business."

He paused. "But we have them heavily outnumbered in artillery and troop strength. And our air forces not only have driven the Luftwaffe from the sky, but also now are playing hell with the Wehrmacht's supply lines.

"So I think sometime soon, we're going to attack somewhere along that line and burst out of Normandy into the rest of France.

"The supply build-up is nearly complete," he said. "God knows that's critical since we still haven't captured Cherbourg and, even if we had, I feel the Germans have thoroughly wrecked its harbor, so it'll be no use for months."

He stepped away from the map and looked at me.

"And there's something much more personal," he added.

"The MO at our little naval hospital here got a call today from the MO's office at Odstocks Hospital. The U.S. Army there want to see you for an full physical examination as soon as possible. Now I think I could delay things for a bit . . ."

I shook my head. "Thanks, Sir Alfred, but there's not much point in it. Thank you for all your kindness, but I'd better pick up my uniforms and get over there. I think I'm in good enough shape now to command a mortar platoon."

"I expected you'd say something like that," he said.

# # #

I was fearful that Katherine might not come to me during the night, so I simply knocked upon her door.

She looked at me in surprise as she opened it.

I took her hands in mine.

"My darling, I'm sorry to intrude, but I wanted to spend some time with you because I leave Monday for Odstocks. I don't know whether I'll be back. I'm fit now, so probably not."

She held her hand up to her throat. "So soon?"

"Afraid so. And I just wanted to see you and sit with you and talk with you . . . just be with you. Oh, hell, I don't know how to say it, Katherine. I just know I'm going to miss you terribly and I want all the time you can give me in this last weekend."

The tears were streaming down her cheeks.

"Allan dear, I'm yours and you are mine. Let's make love and dream together of better times to come."

It was my life's shortest weekend.

Chapter 44
July 17, 1944 – Cleared For Duty

After picking up my uniforms (which fit perfectly), I reported to the surgeons at Odstocks.

They thumped my chest, listened to my heart, looked at my shrapnel scars, took my temp and pronounced that I was fit. They told me I was to return to active duty in Normandy starting Friday.

Then I walked into the U.S. Army's little Personnel section at the hospital.

The paper-pushers weren't at all friendly. I heard a couple of not-so-discreet murmurs about "deserting" to a British hospital, an act that apparently threw a monkey wrench into all their precious SOPs.

But since they all were enlisted people and since the hospital director had cleared my temporary transfer to the manor, there wasn't much they could do face-to-face.

The top kick in charge, however, started trying to give me a bad time, He told me that this week they were dispatching 28 other recovered wounded to Normandy and that he was detailing me to deliver them to Southhampton where all of us we would report to a Replacement Depot.

I ordered him to back off.

"No, Sergeant, you're definitely not sending me to a damned repple-depple. You're cutting me a set of orders First Battalion, Eighth Infantry Regiment, Fourth Infantry Division. And you're going to do it now."

"Hey, I can't do that. It's against regulations. And I should point out that if you don't report to that replacement depot you could be charged as being AWOL."

"Sergeant," I snapped, "I could give a rat's ass about that. And I should point out that you appear to have abandoned all your military courtesy."

The sergeant looked boiled. "Sorry . . . sir. But, being's how you're a mustang, a former sergeant . . ."

"Look, sergeant, if you don't like me, tough crap. But you will respect my rank and uniform.

"All that matters to you, sergeant, is that I'm an officer. The fact that I also was a sergeant last week doesn't cut any ice. It only means that I'm not a Ninety-Day Wonder and I know when a multi-striped desk jockey is trying to give me the bum's rush.

"Now here's the deal, mister. I'll ride herd on these recovered wounded to get them to the repple-depple. But that's it. You cut those orders or I'm going to make life hell for you."

"Oh! And how do you plan to do that?"

"Sir!"

"I'm sorry . . . sir."

"It so happens that my father-in-law is a major general in Plans and Logistics at SHAEF and I know – believe me, I *know* – how desperate they are for replacements and it's only going to get worse.

"So, I can sure inform him about this comfy little detachment of 10 able-bodied walking, breathing paper-pushers headed by a lard-assed 6-striper. Just about any infantry battalion would love to have you boys because they're so short of riflemen to send out on night patrols.

"And besides," I added, "maybe it's time that you took a few of the risks that landed so many people in this hospital."

The sergeant looked as if he had just swallowed something square and thorny.

I grinned. "Don't forget what the Army always says, Sergeant – every man is a rifleman first."

We had a brief very staring contest before he sighed and gave in.

Chapter 45
Friday, July 21, 1944 – The Road Back

I held a quick formation of the men the hospital was releasing.

They turned out to be a grab bag – several ground-pounders, a pair of medics, two cannon-cockers and a Signal Corps man, an MP sergeant, three armor troopers and a Quartermaster Corps Pfc. who limped, but who kept forgetting which leg hurt.

A corporal in the group told me that the man with the limp was a goldbrick doing his damnedest not to go back into a battle zone.

"What's the big deal?" the MP asked the corporal. "He's just a damned feather merchant in Supply. He don't have to go up on the line."

"He does if he's with my outfit," I said. "It's a pretty dangerous job in the Eighth Infantry. Col. Van Fleet doesn't want the line troops to get low on ammo, or food or water. He wants them resupplied before they're low. And Supply has to bring it all up to the line because he doesn't want any riflemen leaving the line."

I told the MP and the corporal to straighten the guy up. I sure as hell wasn't going to let any healthy soldier goldbrick his way out of his duty . . . especially if I couldn't back out of mine.

# # #

I got back to the manor that evening. We had a quiet parting dinner and then Katherine and I went for a long walk. We were arm-in-arm and hardly spoke.

Once I said, "I don't know. 'Mrs. Dudley,' doesn't sound very classy to me. Maybe I could change my last name to Fotherington or Pettingill something like that."

She laughed and said, "Hush, leftenant. I think Dudley would be a lovely last name. I look forward to being Mrs. Dudley."

"I'm glad of that. Very glad."

It was a good memory to take with me the next day and to treasure in my mental bank vault for the months ahead.

# # #

Once we got to Southhampton, I was able to funnel my little gang into a large crowd of other recovered wounded returning from other hospitals. We also found ourselves among a company of green replacements straight from the states.

The scars we showed made the new guys' eyes go wide. And it wasn't long before the veterans began telling them what combat was like. But what really rattled us all was getting a good close look at what lay in store for at least some of us.

Now the deal was that we were supposed to leave England and cross the channel by LST. But it didn't work quite that smoothly.

When our LST arrived, it was teeming with wounded. Stretchers carpeted not only the interior tank deck, but also the upper deck Walking wounded packed the gun tubs and even the bridge wings and they were sitting against the bulkheads and crammed into the crew's quarters.

My platoon, as I now thought of them, was one of many detailed to help carry stretchers off the LST to the railway siding. I know officers aren't supposed to do this kind of thing, but I helped carry stretchers. So did lots of other officers.

You wanted to help. Many of the wounded were so broken and maimed. And it was a slow process. You try to be extra careful moving somebody whose shoulder and arm is gone, or who's missing both feet, or whose half-bandaged intestines are pulsing away in full view.

Two sights especially struck me.

The first was Betty – yep, 1st Lt. Betty Edwards.

At first I wasn't sure it was Betty because she looked like she had aged 20 years. She was pale, gaunt and hollow-eyed. Blood was spattered across her face and the breast and left shoulder of her fatigue jacket. As I helped carry a stretcher past her, she looked up and met my eyes but I didn't register with her.

On the next trip into the LST, I wanted to say hi and ask why she had never written, but the answer lay right there on the deck and she was kneeling above him.

He had maybe half a face, the other half had bone splinters standing up from something that looked like one of the roasts mom used to fix for Sunday dinner. She was starting a new bottle of blood into his remaining arm and she was speaking to him in low, gentle tones. He couldn't see her, but I hoped the poor bastard could hear her.

The other sight was an Able Company sergeant I recognized. I spotted him because of the 4th Division ivy patch on his left shoulder. He was drowsy with morphine but recognized me as I picked up the foot ends of his stretcher.

"Hey, Dud. You on your way back?"

"Yeah, Harvey. How are my boys?"

"Not sure. Ain't seen much of them, but we sure been getting some good mortar support.

"Trouble is, we was beating our heads against those goddamned hedgerows ever since we landed. First north to capture Cherbourg, then west to clear the Krauts out of the peninsula, then south to capture St. Lo. Nothin' left there but a fucking brick pile and we still ain't captured it. The Krauts just don't never quit and they never quit counterattacking, either. You gotta respect the bastards.

"And them hedgerows, Dud. They was a cast-iron bitch – even when you got tanks. Got a deal so that now our tanks could kind of auger through them -- beautiful to see until the Krauts lower the boom with their mortars. That's how I finally got hit – hit bad, in my legs."

"Okay, Harvey," I told him. "Thanks for the briefing. Now try to sleep. They'll take you to a good hospital and get you fixed up. They're real good to you."

"Okay, but you watch out, Dud. The Krauts got some new tactics. They send an armored vehicle at you. Everybody fires away at it and it backs off. Then while you're all slapping each other on the back, them 120 mm mortar shells start landing in your lap. Sometimes they use 20 MM antiaircraft guns and they just explode a fella. Keep your head down, Dud."

# # #

We spent much of the day exhausting ourselves by off-loading human wreckage, including a goodly number of chopped-up Germans who looked and acted just like chopped-up Limeys, Canadians and Americans – dirty, pale, whipped and either unconscious or gritting their teeth and writhing in pain.

I'd heard of war being called slaughter, but I saw it concentrated for sure on that LST. And then came some punctuation.

Once we carried off the last casualties – including the fresh corpses – we picked up what little luggage we had. But when we returned we found the LST's crew using high-pressure hoses to flush out the vessel, tank deck and top deck alike.

It was amazing how red was the water that first gushed down the ramp.

Then, the vessel's skipper said we couldn't leave for another three or four hours because he had a steering-gear problem and the medics, nurses and doctors had to replenish their supplies.

We just curled up with our bags right there on the docks. The concrete pavement and wooden pilings and rails were unsympathetic surfaces. But most of us slept like rocks, glad of the exhaustion . . . it kept us from dwelling on the human wreckage we had handled.

Chapter 46
July 22, 1944 – Utah Beach . . . Again

LSTs are slow as the itch, so it took about four plodding hours for us just to work down from Southhampton past Portsmouth, around the Isle of Wight. Then once out in the channel, it was another six hours to Normandy.

Being an officer, I got to stay on the bridge out of the rain and that's where a signalmen told me the vessel's standing joke.

The initials LST stand for Landing Ship, Tank. But like every item of military hardware, the nomenclature was reversed to suit an alphabetical listing. You know, as in "Coat, Field, Man's, Winter, OD in color, 1 ea.", and so on

So the vessel was labeled LST for Landing Ship, Tank.

But the crews told me LST actually stands for Large Slow Target. Slow indeed, but far too fast for my taste. I kept hoping it was all a bad dream and I'd wake up snuggled sweetly with Katherine and a peaceful day ahead of us.

I asked the ship's skipper, a pudgy lieutenant looking about 19, why we and the three other LSTs with us didn't have destroyer escorts.

In his slow Carolina drawl, he told me no U-boat had dared enter the English Channel since well before D-Day. He claimed British and American destroyer-aircraft teams had become so adept that the Kriegsmarine had diverted its subs to other areas.

That was good because the channel certainly was loaded with rich targets. Through the rain and fog I could make out cruisers and battlewagons at anchor, perfect submarine targets -- firing salvos inland. Big tenders and oilers were tied along some of them.

I kept saying "wow" when a battleship fired a salvo, but the lieutenant boasted that the LSTs, virtually unarmed, were the real weapons.

"Suh, these ships are an enohmous pipeline providin' ammo, food and gasoline foh yoah ground troops – and, o'coahse, carryin' yoah wounded back to England. If we was to stop ouah runs, y'all at the front would be arunnin' out of ever'thing mighty fast."

As we arrived off Utah Beach I got an idea of what he meant. In the mist you could see dozens of the blocky vessels side-by-side, bows on the beach, like so many taxicabs parked at Union Station. Dozens of other LSTs were anchored off the beach waiting their turns.

As a hospital ship, we had priority and got ashore as soon as one of the other LSTs used its stern anchor to pull back from the beach. Among those pulling out were four LSTs like ours -- with huge red crosses on their sides; more wounded headed to England.

"It's been a very bloody couple of weeks," the lieutenant told me. "First Corps finally captured St. Lo last week, but the butcher bill has been terrible. We been awful, awful busy with casualties."

Because the tide was in, we were able to march right down the ramp and onto the shingle practically dry-shod . . . except for the rain.

My jaw dropped at the changes in Utah Beach. It looked like a mile of seawall was gone and the German bunkers appeared to be little more than mounds of scrap rebar and broken concrete dotted about in a massive transportation hub.

Since D-Day, Army engineers widened the old single-lane causeways into modern highways crammed with 2-way truck traffic. Areas inland from the beach had become a gargantuan supply dump – no, a supply metropolis. Literally wherever I looked I saw huge stacks of artillery shells, half-mile lines of parked cannon, tanks, jeeps, all cloaked with camouflage netting.

The same netting arched over enormous piles of rations and rows of tents.

"Jesus, what a bombing target," I said to an MP who was directing truck traffic. He just laughed.

"Naaaah. The Krauts sometimes try to send over a plane or two at night, but that's it. Ack Ack from all these ships keeps them at a healthy distance. The Luftwaffe don't count for much here. The Air Corps and the RAF are running the show now."

Man, was I happy to hear that. In Tunisia and Algeria, the German fliers made life miserable for us, shooting up American convoys right and left. Back then, you didn't dare walk to the latrines -- you dashed, but not before looking for some place to take cover.

It took about an hour to turn in my charges to their repple-depple – a soaking tent city located uncomfortably next to a fuel dump with gasoline drums stacked about three stories high.

The orders that the hospital jerks cut said I had to rotate through the repple-depple, but I just hiked until I found a weapons carrier headed for 4th Division.

Chapter 47
Night, July 22, 1944 – Reunion

At Division HQ, I hooked a ride with a supply sergeant and by nightfall found my way to Capt. Freeman's desk in the battalion HQ tent.

By the light of a Coleman lantern, he was resting his elbows on a rickety little field desk holding his face in his hands. A half-finished letter lay on the desk by a stack of sealed envelopes.

I guess he heard me approach because in a dead voice just audible over the rain he said, "What?"

"Lt. Dudley reporting back for duty, Cap'n."

He raised his head, rubbed his face and finally turned. His cheeks and eyes seemed to have sagged, making him look about 60.

"Oh, hey. Dud. You're back. You okay?"

I had planned to joke that I could use another two or three months of convalescent leave. But seeing his face, I just said, "I'm fully recovered and doing fine, sir."

"Good," he said. "Pull up a bench and set a spell. I'll be with you in a minute."

He dipped his pen in the inkwell and resumed writing.

"I'm sending a letter to Lt. Scott's parents," he said as he wrote.

"It'll be one of your new duties in taking over the mortar platoon. You've got to try to tell the bereaved how great he was and . . . aw, shit, I don't know. How do you find the right things to say after seeing that the Krauts had turned him into a slab of ground beef mixed in olive drab tatters?"

He rubbed his eyes and peered at me. "You want to comfort them but you know there's no Goddamned comfort. Their boy's dead. Gone. But still . . . you try."

"God, sir, I'm not much of a writer."

"You'll learn, lieutenant."

"Have casualties been heavy, Sir?"

"Well, Dog Company's been fairly lucky," he said. "The rest of the battalion has been chewed up pretty good, especially Charlie Company. But the old hands are teaching the new ones what the Krauts have taught us . . . and now we're teaching those bastards a thing of two. Hang on a minute."

His pen scratched steadily on the paper for five more minutes. Then he blew gently on the letter and set it aside to dry.

"Sorry, Dud, not much of a welcome for you. I'm damned glad you're back but it's kind of bad timing for you." He looked at his watch.

"Let's see, it's almost 2200 hours. You've got about 30 hours to get to know the whole mortar platoon before we attack to break out of Normandy.

"If I were you, I'd start right now. You'll get a full briefing with all the other officers and NCOs right back here at 0400.

"And it won't be just a routine go-get-'em bullshit session," he said.

"Now that we're holding the Peries-St. Lo Road, and we're out of these damned hedgerows, we're getting ready for the big push." He showed me a map and I recognized a section of the front line from Sir Alfred's road map.

I saluted but he already had picked up another piece of paper and was dipping his pen into the ink well.

As I turned away, he said, "Oh, one thing about writing these letters, Dud."

"What's that Cap'n?"

"Sit ramrod straight when you write."

"Sir?"

"That's so's your tears don't fall on the letter. Makes the ink run."

Chapter 48
July 23, 1944 – Preparing

Forster's welcome was a bit warmer than the captain's – but only a bit.

"Sorry, sir," he said, rubbing his eyes. "We're all pretty whipped and discouraged right now. We captured Peries three days ago -- about the time that the 30th finally captured St. Lo. It took a lot out of everybody."

He shook his head slowly and rolled his eyes. "God, you can't believe these Germans! Every damn time you turn around, the bastards come up with something new and it's back to the drawing boards.

"Anyway, we captured Peries but then the higher-ups made us all pull back about 2,000 yards because something big supposedly is in the wind."

I told him about the mile on mile of trucks and tanks and artillery I saw when I came ashore. "It looks to me like we're planning something big alright," I told him. :Maybe it's the break-out into France."

"I'll believe it when I see it," Forster said.

"We been butting our heads against these fucking hedgerows and then had to work through the swamps. But we busted through the last ones at Peries and -- Bam! -- we lose Lt. Scott and then they make us walk it all back."

"What shape are the Mortar Forkers in?"

"Pretty good, sir. We've gotten replacements for replacements and they've worked in pretty well."

"Replacements for who?"

He got out the roster. "Well, of course, you know about Whitehorse, Jacobs, Manthei and Torrelli."

"Yeah, and Nau and Wilson. And Borodin."

"Right," he said. "So Chucheko was wounded pretty badly and is gone for the duration. We got him sworn in and tried to get him shipped to Ah*may*reeka, but I don't know if it happened.

"And Frost got hit," he said, "but not too bad so we think maybe he'll be back pretty soon.

He listed four replacements who had been killed or wounded plus new replacements for them.

"So far, meanwhile, Timmer, Halls, and Bull and I haven't gotten a scratch . . . so far."

"So, Mike, how's your current crop of replacements working out?"

"One of them – a guy named Best -- is the worst I've ever seen. No kidding. He's either too dumb to learn or so terrified that he can't think.

"The others – here's the list – are Nelson, Purcell, Rosedale, Fayette. Stechley and Armor. All of them were green as grass. Straight from basic when they showed up. Didn't even have their carbines zeroed in.

"But we've worked 'em in pretty good. Fayette and Purcell are good with the machine guns. Not as good with mortars as the old KU crew, but I've got Timmer, Halls and Bull training in each section getting them up to snuff.

"Creed still is running Third Section and he's a pro. No problems there at all."

"Okay, Mike. You know about the meeting at 0400."

"Yes, sir."

"Say, do you hear much from Eleanor?"

"Yeah, she seems to write every day. I get her letters in batches every week or so. How about Betty?"

"She never wrote after she graduated at Camp McCoy. I found out why when I saw her yesterday with the wounded on an LST. She's gone off the deep end as a Florence Nightengale . . . and I'd say the guys she helps are lucky.

"Meanwhile when I was convalescing, I met somebody – an English war widow, a Royal Navy staff car driver. She also lost her parents and brother and sister in the blitz. Anyway, we'll get married . . . if I make it through this alive."

"Well, Dud – sorry – well, lieutenant, let's both work on that."

"Damn right, Mike. And it's Dud when we're alone." I reached to shake hands.

"Well, I've got to go look up Halls and Bull."

"I'll have one of the boys guide you. It's good to have you back, Dud."

"Thanks Mike. I just wish it was good to be back. At least the rain has quit."

"Yeah. For now."

# # #

I wrapped up my visit with Third Section well after midnight and crawled into the shotgun seat of the HQ halftrack and tried to doze.

But too much detail about the mortar platoon kept crawling through my mind. So I sat up and started jotting down all my impressions to help crystalize them in my mind.

Section leaders Forster, Norton and Creed – Creed an old-timer, lifer who's been with 8th Infantry since '41. Competent. Not impressed with a mustang lt., not defiant, either . . . just watching and waiting to see whether I turn out to be another 90-day blunder or somebody work working with.

Norton, a replacement, seems somewhat tentative but Forster says he's learning to lead.

Forster says the supply NCO needs shaping up. Been some stupid delays. What the hell's it going to be like if we ever do break out and start moving 30 miles a day? What shape are these half-tracks in? Check tomorrow.

# # #

Finally, I gave up trying to sleep and started writing my first letter to Katherine.

Darling –

It's hard to say how much I miss you. I'd be lying if I said I was thinking about you every minute. There's too much to learn and do every minute. But when I raise my eyes from paperwork or from somebody who's giving me an excuse, I see your beautiful gray eyes and lovely smile. It's sheer disappointment not to be able to hold your hands – or to hear your voice with its veddy British accent, or to hug and hold you.

I told you a lot about me. There's still stuff I'm sure I overlooked. I want you to meet Mom and Sis. I know they'd be nuts about you – especially Mom. She's tough like you and sweet like you. I've written to tell her and Sis about us but there hasn't been enough time for a reply to reach me. I also sent her your address and I bet they'll both write to welcome you to her side of our little family.

I must go to an important meeting. Something big is in the wind. I'll bet you read news about it before this letter reaches you. Just remember that whatever is going on, I'm thinking of you. And smiling.

All my love,
Dud

Chapter 49
July 24, 1944 – The Cobra FUBAR

The sky still was dark and it was sprinkling when Forster and I ducked into the captain's tent to join the rest of Dog Company's officers and NCOs.

The battalion ops officer gave us an exciting and scary briefing.

"Men, about dawn we start Operation Cobra, our break-out into France. Once we break through the Germans, we'll be out into open country and finally away from these Goddamned hedge rows for good."

Everybody in the tent gave approving nods and mumbles and seemed to hold their breath.

Even Sgt. Pointer looked excited. I never knew his real name but we called him Sgt. Pointer because it was his job to tap the rubber tip of his 3-foot pointer on the maps at every place that Maj. Cavanaugh mentioned. Sometimes he tapped so fast on so many villages and hills and objectives that it kind of made your head spin

"Operation Cobra will kick off with a gigantic aerial bombardment all along the St. Lo-Peries line. First, about 500 fighter-bombers are going to attack that zone with everything they've got."

After that, he said, about 1,800 B-17s would pulverize that same 4-mile front and everything for 2,000 yards south of it.

Somebody said, "Holy shit!"

"Yeah, you bet," the ops officer said. "It should put our friends in the Panzer Lehr Division into a long deep sleep. The heavy bombers ain't the most accurate, however, which is why we pulled our troops back from the line.

"Anyhow, after about two hours of bombing, the artillery will spend *another* hour chewing up what's left and then we'll move out with armor and infantry, once again supported by artillery and fighter-bombers on call – exclusively for 4th, 9th and 30th Divisions.

He looked at me. "Lt. Dudley, because of your convalescent leave, you're new to the air-ground coordination we've worked up. Cap'n Freeman probably already has clued you to some extent.

"Just for now, Dud, it's like this: these P-47 Thunderbolts carry bombs, rockets and eight .50 caliber machine guns and they are on call just like the family doctor . . . but none of that take-two-aspirins-and-call-me-in-the-morning crap."

We all chuckled.

"A Kraut tank shows up, you call the regimental air controller and within two minutes a pair of Thunderbolts hammer them. And believe me, Lieutenant, I'm not handing you the old rah-rah.

"You need to take out an artillery battery or a hard-to-reach machine gun nest? You call for help and you get help . . . fast."

The other officers and NCOs were grinning and nodding as he spoke. B company's commander, Capt. Michaelis, raised his hand and interrupted.

"If you'll pardon me, sir," he said, and turned to me. "Dud, just two days ago – and this is no bull -- we had a Panther tank show up on our flank. He was barrel-assing toward us between two hedge rows.

"I thought we were sunk because he also had some infantry with him.

"Well, we called for help and hunkered down to do some praying. But I didn't have time to do a full Hail Mary because in about one minute" -- Michaelis threw his hands in the air – "BLEWIE!

"They blasted that son of a bitch and now it's half gone and lying in a 40-foot crater. The Kraut infantry took off and we didn't lose a man. I've seen some Tigers that looked they've had better days, too."

Looking slightly pained, the ops officer said, "Thank you for that valuable testimonial, Captain."

Everybody chuckled again until he said, "All right, now, let's move on. And please pay close attention."

He said that the 4th Division and the 30th would assault first, the 9th Division waiting in reserve to exploit any breakthrough.

We all looked at each other and the maps Sgt. Pointer had been tapping. I didn't like it.

Once through the German line, the assault lines showed arrows driving off in all directions just like we did on D-Day . . . literally north, south, east and even back behind us to the west into Brittany.

And so while we were racing past the Krauts' left flank, what would stop the Krauts from assaulting *our* left flank?

# # #

Cobra didn't work.

Not that day.

At dawn the sky still was overcast and word came down that because of the clouds, the airstrike was cancelled.

But as usual, some stupid bastard didn't get the word.

First there was the faint drone which got louder and louder until it sounded like thundering doom itself was coming to crush us. Who knows how many B-17s were approaching?

Then the ground under our feet started quaking as the bombs began going off in succession.

At first they sounded just like chains of railway cars slamming together when the brakes go on -- but then all the explosions merged in one solid bellowing roar that never seemed to end.

It did, of course, but we received no orders to move out because the whole thing was a monstrous fuck-up.

We heard later that about a third of the bombing force never received the recall order.

They flew over and bombed through the clouds, for Christ's sake, probably hitting a few Germans. But a lot of their loads fell short, killing and wounding a lot of 30th Division assault troops.

The higher-ups tried to down-play it all.

"Don't worry, men. We'll do it again when the weather clears. Clear skies and all 1,800 bombers this time.

"Them Norden bomb sights are precision instruments, you know. If they can see it, they can drop a bomb into a target as small as a rain barrel."

Sure.

If they can see it.

And that turned out to be a mighty big "If."

Chapter 50
July 25, 1944 – Cobra

The next day dawned clear as a bell and noisy as hell.

First, dozens of fighter-bombers combed over the area south of the St. Lo-Peries Road, bombing and strafing. The forward observers in tanks, half-tracks and even spotters in little Piper Cubs flying overhead directed them where to strike.

Then the same deep roar of doom grew from behind us again as the first waves of 1,800 B-17s came over us from the north. The fighter-bombers disappeared. The heavies flew above us in a deafening, rigid procession, four miles wide, dropping their loads on that 4-mile stretch of road and the Panzer Lehr Division dug in south of it.

Supposedly, all we had to do was stand there at ringside holding our ears and watching as the bombs blasted out 100-foot fountains of earth, dust and smoke into the air.

Just like yesterday, the earth literally started quaking beneath our feet.

Some of the observers seated themselves atop the cabs of trucks and half-tracks watching in awe what was happening a mile away. Others peered through binoculars at the planes. Through the roar and thunder you faintly heard some of them pretending to do play-by-play sports reports as the bright dots fell from of the planes' bellies. But the bombs fell so fast you didn't see them as they neared the ground. All you really saw were leaping towers of soil and smoke.

I stood in the .50 caliber machine gun ring mount above the shotgun seat of the HQ half-track. My feet felt the bombs' vibrations even through the seat cushions. We all were tense, trying to relax until it would be our turn to follow the tanks and infantry.

But I was doubly tense. I'd heard what happened to the 30th yesterday. And in Algeria and Tunisia I'd been close enough to bombing to feel and see what happened when bombs fell short.

And they began doing exactly that, exploding closer and closer to us. The earth no longer trembled. It was slamming our feet.

Maybe the Norden bomb sight was perfect – drop a bomb into a pickle barrel and all that. So what? Once 900 bombers dropped their loads, the dust and smoke obliterated all the targets, including the road itself.

From better than two miles up, the follow-on 900 bombardiers couldn't see diddly. They were able to aim only at the thick smoke and dust that a nasty south breeze was slowly drifting north . . . toward us. And with it, the bombardiers' aiming point crept in our direction. Finally, those damned bombs started landing right before us and then among us.

Fortunately, I saw the explosions starting to creep toward us.

I ordered all our half-track drivers to haul ass at least a mile further to the rear. Then I bellowed for everybody else to quit watching and start digging in.

Sending the half-tracks back violated my orders from battalion, but it's a damned good thing I did it. In fact, I should have ordered the whole damned mortar platoon to ride in the half-tracks because the next 15 minutes were catastrophic. It was the one time I ever felt sorry for Germans. If they were under that kind of barrage for two hours, God alone knows what it must have been like.

Concussions from the explosions around us felt like Joe Louis, Max Baer and Jersey Joe Walcott slamming my head from all sides . . . with bare knuckles. The concussions bludgeoned us inside our chests and stomachs like so many body blows. I felt helpless as an ant on a rush-hour highway. Nothing before or since ever terrified me so completely.

The bombs literally dug men and their weapons out of the ground . . . fragments of a foxhole's two occupants flung east and west in a blast plume, then falling to be buried by yet more earth – all in a graveyard marked by shattered tree trunks, pieces of cattle and chunks of ancient stone houses.

And no last rites.

One stick of bombs marched so close past us – maybe 50 feet – that it threw a blanket of dirt over me and one of the new men, Fayette. I was screaming for Katherine and cringing face down in our foxhole when that brown avalanche flumped onto us. Reeking of explosive, it filled our fox hole -- and our ears, noses and mouths.

In panic, we forgot the bombing and desperately pushed up and out of the dirt before we suffocated. I no sooner got my head into the open when another wave of reeking soil fell over us. Fortunately, those bombs were further away and it was only a six-inch shroud of cordite-infused earth.

By the time it was over, the B-17s killed a third of us and destroyed half our mortars. Baker Company, right in front of us, got plastered just before us losing more than 30 men.

I didn't hear until the following year how bad the Air Corps hit the rest of the battalion or the outfits east and west of us. The final word was that the fly boys inflicted about 500 casualties among the fighting troops, killing an American general for good measure.

As the smoke cleared, Timmer pushed himself up into view. He looked like some filthy mushroom. Then Bull and Halls struggled into sight. They couldn't hear and were bleeding from nose and ears. Fayette and I could barely hear. Forster was staggering and deaf and his eyes were so filled with dirt that he looked like he was wearing a whore's make-up.

It took a full Jerry can of water to flush the soil from our ears and eyes and rinse the mud from our mouths and nostrils. We all had to strip to shake all that crud out of our clothes.

Halls muttered something about murdering the first Air Corps pilot who happened to show up.

Some of the replacements – Nelson and Purcell -- survived. Various fragments of Best and Stechley were scattered around what had been a field.

We never found a sign of Creed, Norton or Armor. A 20-foot crater yawned where Creed's foxhole had been. So the original 12-man Mortar Forker section from KU was down to four of us staggering like drunks and another, Frost, still in the hospital,

Once the bombardment ended, our artillery began shelling the area south of the Peries-St Lo Road.

The bombed zone literally looked like moonscape – all interlocking craters to the horizon. Where once we'd seen woods and orchards, there was nothing but stinking powdery dirt dotted with huge tree splinters, upended artillery pieces, butchered cattle, fragments of soldiers and low mounds of stone that had been farm homes.

The follow-up shelling was loud, of course, but to our damaged ears it was muffled.

I got all the men together who could walk and tried to hurry them back toward the half-tracks. But it was like trying to trot in a freshly-plowed field. With each step, your foot sank a good six inches into granulated earth.

The drivers were trying to come to us, but because the roads were absolutely destroyed, their front wheels kept sinking to the hubs.

Once I got to the HQ track, I got on the radio to Capt. Freeman, saying we were all torn up and needed to refit and reorganize. I couldn't believe it when he relayed the word that the attack was going ahead as planned.

"Are you bullshitting me, Sir?"

"I said to move up. We're attacking as soon as the artillery quits."

"But, Sir, we've only got four guns . . ."

"No buts, Dudley. And stop shouting! I'm not deaf. Baker Company got clobbered, too, and they and the tanks are attacking by 1100 hours. If you think you're in bad shape, imagine what it's like for the Krauts. Move as far forward as you can right now and get ready to take fire missions. We've got to break through!"

I couldn't believe it and the men couldn't believe it either when I told them. They had the staggers as bad as I did and still were trying to overcome the shock.

At least we didn't have too far to move too far. The supposedly-destroyed Germans somehow rose out of the soil and rubble fighting like demons.

That devastated landscape turned out to contain riflemen, machine gun nests and small and large anti-tank guns and hard-bitten, really pissed-off veterans who knew how to work those weapons even if they, too, were staggering and bleeding.

Except for Forster, the platoon's senior NCOs were either dead, missing or wounded. I divided us into two sections, each with two guns, Forster heading one and me the other. We attacked that morning, firing for all we were worth.

Our armor and foot soldiers made an initial advance and then seemed to run into a stone wall that they had to break apart piece-by-piece, advancing a few hundred yards at a time, losing men every yard. It was hard for us mortar men to know what was going on because we kept receiving orders to fire on positions that were closer to us than others we had hit earlier.

It turned out the battalion by-passed some German positions and needed us to keep the Krauts' heads down.

I had to send two half-tracks to the rear for more ammunition and replacement mortars and replacement humans. They returned with two new guns and lots of ammunition but no people. The infantry got first dibs on replacements.

But even cut down to 16 men from a full-strength 32, the platoon managed to carry out our missions. I was pretty confident there'd be no counterattacks, but after dark I kept three men on watch, changing with sleepers every two hours. That way everybody but Forster and I at least got a little sleep. He kept an eye peeled on the tracks' machine-gunners who were acting as our sentries.

A column of wounded moved north past us paralleled by an arriving column of replacements, ammo trucks and more tanks.

I sat in the HQ track drinking coffee and, working from a long list, starting to write letters by candlelight.

Dear Mrs. Creed:
I'm sure you have learned by now that your husband Arthur lost his life in action against the . . .

As I wrote, I found myself wondering what I'd write about some of other casualties whom I had only met and never got to know.

Chapter 51
July 27, 1944 – Breakout

As the day dawned most of us had a problem putting one foot in front of the other. Forster still seemed in fair shape. As for me – well, the platoon's Old Man felt like a real old, old man.

We fired missions all day yesterday and often during the night because our tanks and infantry still were attacking against very tough resistance. But thanks to their progress, we advanced our guns 1,500 yards.

They notified us that 4th Division now was transferred to V Corps from VII Corps. Big deal.

I already was so mired in missions and administrative crap that I asked Capt. Freeman if I could quit being an officer and have my stripes back. Maybe you get to give orders when you're an officer and the mess hall food is better. But in combat you don't find many mess halls and you're so busy you feel like the proverbial cat in a room full of rocking chairs.

Anyway, Capt. Freeman didn't bother to say 'No.' He just snorted and said I'd be in command anyway, so I might as well get paid for it. What made it tough was that I didn't have a top kick who knew all the short-cuts. He was just more fertilizer scattered somewhere in the Air Corps' freshly-plowed fields behind the Peries-St Lo Road.

Without him, I had to do every job and learn those jobs while doing them. You can't delegate when there's nobody to delegate to.

Meanwhile everybody in the platoon did double duty because we were trying to fire six mortars accurately with about half our usual manpower. Constantly taking mission orders from FDC, I still had to rotate two halftracks back and forth to headquarters to keep food, water and ammo flowing to what was left of us.

It also was essential to arrange some kind of rotating minimal rest for the men. Even 15 minutes of sleep made a hell of a difference to a guy who starts snoring the instant he ducks to fire a mortar.

Meanwhile we had to keep displacing the guns because some Kraut Davy Crockett kept doping out where we were. About every hour or so, he'd drop 120 mm mortar rounds in our neck of the woods. Oh, and meanwhile, somebody was supposed to maintain an operations log of all our missions.

I just kind of let that one slide.

Fortunately, two lightly wounded men rejoined us. We also received four green-as-grass replacements. For two cents I would have sent them back because they just added to our grief. Somebody had to train them. And that mainly was me and Forster.

And these guys weren't even from the bottom of the barrel. At first they looked to me like they came from some dank spot way down beneath the barrel.

One exception – a real little guy who looked about 12 and was so shy he almost couldn't say "Yes, sir." His name was Maus and he pronounced it 'moss.' But I gave it the German pronunciation, 'mouse,' because it seemed to fit. That was before really I noticed that he had a long upper lip which gave him kind of a stubborn look.

And, man, in the end did he turn out to be one stubborn little killer.

Another replacement, Kennedy, was a giant who looked about 30 and had about the same IQ. Then there were two ordinary wise-guy American high school kids, Edwards and Leland. They were the types who think they know everything and the world is no sweat. They also were kind of skittish about hitting the dirt, see, 'cause they didn't want to get muddy.

Herr Davy Crockett soon taught them a thing or two.

After concussion tossed them a couple of times and they got a few cuts and bruises from flying sticks and stones, they'd go to ground flat as a pair of weasels, even on the fringe of a manure pile behind a stone barn. They even dropped when Kraut artillery passed far above us toward our rear or when our own shells passed above us in the opposite direction.

That's what it's like at first. The big shells sound scary but you soon sense whether you or someone a quarter mile away is the target. Meanwhile, amid all that din and even half-deaf, you absolutely must keep what's left of your hearing tuned for the telltale whisper of approaching mortar rounds.

Anyway, we had to teach them all -- monkey-see, monkey-do -- in the fastest, meanest and least-forgiving school of all . . . combat.

And with lots of shouting.

"The main thing, Maus, *always* drop the shell down the tube tail first. Drop it nose first, it'll go off inside the tube and kill you. And if it don't, *I'll* kill you . . . second main thing, when you drop the shell, duck below the bore . . . the bore, goddammit! That's the hole you drop the shell into. That's where it fires out of . . . What's that, Kennedy? Jesus wept! Did you think the damn shell just *disappears*? . . . No! It's flying down range thataway to land on the Krauts . . . let me worry about the aiming . . . Edwards, just drop it and duck down and don't ask questions . . . We'll tell you about it if you survive and if we get some quiet time."

"If you fail to learn, men, you don't get an F like in a school. It's a D. Get it? Guess what D stands for."

Late that afternoon, after moving his section's guns for about the umpteenth time, Forster came wobbling to me with a grin on his grimy mug. He still was shouting because he still had trouble hearing.

"Hey, Dud! We're having to raise the range again. We're firing at almost 2,500 yards. I think the boys are starting to crack through the Krauts. If it keeps up like this, Operations is going to order us to advance pretty soon."

Then he sagged down on the running board of the HQ track. "But I don't know if I can handle any more, Dud. I'm so damned tired I fell asleep on my feet earlier."

It suddenly struck me that his smooth 21-year-old face was showing a lot of age. Beard stubble couldn't conceal brand-new tension lines just past the corners of his mouth, or the sagging eye pouches and a new network of crow's feet.

I handed him my cup. "Here, Mike, gulp down some cold coffee. You remind me of Gen. Roosevelt back on Dartmoor. Like he said, we'll get our rest when Germany surrenders."

"Well, he's resting for sure."

"What do you mean?"

"Oh, you were gone, I guess. He had a heart attack and died a couple weeks ago."

"No shit! Well, right now that seems like an easy way to go."

"I hear you," Forster said.

"But in the meantime, Mike, we've got to keep plugging away. We're whipped, but we can't be as tired as the survivors in Able, Baker and Charlie."

Chapter 52
July 28, 1944 – On The Road

When you're just a lieutenant running a platoon – or even the remnant of a platoon – your world's focused down so tightly that you don't know what's going on around you.

Oh, I knew we were advancing because we were putting more powder increments on the shells and inclining the guns further forward. And then we were displacing forward. But it wasn't until two or three years later that I learned the big picture of what happened around us.

All I knew was that at 1000 hours we received orders to mount up as part of an attacking arrowhead. The 8th Infantry Regiment would be the point of the attack and the 9th and 30th Infantry Divisions would cover its flanks.

Supplying the punch right at the point would be an outfit from the 2nd Armored Division. The Mortar Forkers' job was to make life hell for German antitank gunners.

A tanker truck arrived, a gift from Capt. Freeman to fill up our half-tracks and extra Jerry cans. We loaded the half-track beds with all the ammo they could carry and so everybody had to hang their musette bags, shelter halves and ration cartons outside of the tracks' sides. It made us look like a convoy of traveling surplus stores. I forced everybody to check the vehicles' track links to make sure they were tight, but not too tight.

We test-fired the tracks' machine guns and then followed a guide from Operations who worked us into the advancing column.

I did my best to keep us well behind the tanks. They look like iron monsters, but when an 88 hits them, they explode and burn and everybody around them catches hell. That's why the Krauts nicknamed Sherman tanks Ronsons.

That nickname was almost as bad as what we called our half-tracks – Purple Heart Boxes. They were just trucks with tank tracks instead of rear drive wheels. They provided no overhead cover at all, of course. And the supposedly armored sides were too thin to keep out anything but flying mud and gravel. They sure couldn't stop an ordinary rifle bullet, let alone shrapnel.

Even so, it felt so damned great to be riding away from that hell-hole. I didn't speculate about what the next hell-hole would be like.

When we were halted, the replacements – who still had good hearing – said a lot of firing was rumbling behind us and way off to our left. But we were rolling south in the clear on nice asphalt leaving behind that gawdawful moonscape.

The countryside was fairly flat with little villages and lanes as quaint as those in England. At that point, the homes were whole and people waved from their doorways and roadsides as if we were a parade. It felt so normal I started day-dreaming a letter to Katherine and wondered if we'd ever get mail.

We saw almost no live Germans. But we passed burned-out German trucks and tanks by the dozen and mile after mile of roadside slit trenches – the Krauts' only resort when our air forces attacked. And as we rolled past some of them, the smell told us the trenches had become graves waiting to be filled. Sometimes, the smell of rotting corpses was beyond belief.

The engineers had pushed many of the wrecked trucks and burned-out tanks off the road, but occasionally we had to dodge a wreck or two still standing in its own circle of blackened pavement.

We heard little shooting ahead of us because we were behind the German left flank and P-47s were on call to blow apart Kraut roadblocks and to blast any armor or artillery they spotted.

Now, yes, Field Manual 17-27 stresses that cross-country travel by mortar teams is not sight-seeing -- that everybody in the tracks must be on constant alert for the enemy. I violated orders again, telling everybody to sleep when they could. And some of them actually did manage to sleep, even lying on rattling ammo crates and jouncing Jerry cans reeking of gasoline.

Three times that afternoon, the column stopped and we parked herringbone fashion off the road, taking fire missions from battalion.

It was exciting. For the first time we were out in the open and could see the fall of our own shots. Granted, even in flat country you can't see much at 1,000 yards, but as those black smoke plumes burst into view we cheered as if somebody scored a touchdown.

That's about the time we discovered we had a genius in our midst.

Maus, the shy little guy, hadn't said a word during our helter-skelter combination training-combat sessions. But when he helped in crewing one of Timmer's mortars, he obviously watched and listened carefully.

I walked over during a break in the action when he happened to look up at Timmer. "Can I ask a question?" I almost laughed because Maus sounded like a real tissey-prissle, talking soft-like, almost like a girl.

Timmer, as exhausted as the rest of us, gave Maus a dull stare. Then he shook his head and seemed to awaken. "Sure. Just as long as it ain't too complicated. I'm a little past thinking."

Maus told us he just wanted to make sure that he understood what we were doing. And then he came off not only sounding prissy, but just as dry as one of our training officers back at Camp Kilmer.

"It seems to me that we're controlling three variables," he said. "The first is direction, expressed in mills, north being zero clear around to 6,400. Second is power, a function of the number of propellant increments we put on each shell. Third is the inclination of the gun.

"Now if I'm correct, the gun's angle of inclination and the explosives' power together control the shell's range. You know, the less the tilt, the less the range and vice versa. So by altering those two variables once we have the direction, we can place the shells' point of impact pretty precisely. But I'm not quite clear how much reach these mortars have."

Timmer and I just stared at him. Finally I asked Maus, "Are you a college kid?"

He looked surprised and said, "Well yes, sir. I was a junior minoring in math and science at a teachers' college."

"Math, eh?" Timmer yawned, scratched his stubble and turned his red, baggy eyes to me. "Dud, you think maybe we got us a new gunner here?"

"Maus," I said, "you're now going to undergo initiation to a very exclusive club: Mortar Forkers International. Come with me."

He looked bewildered as I marched him back to meet Forster. As we walked I said, "Where were you in school?"

"Sir, I was at Pittsburg State Teachers College."

"Oh? Pennsylvania?"

"No, sir. Kansas – Pittsburg ending in a 'g' not in 'gh'."

"You kidding? Kansas? Well, this outfit started at KU – the University of Kansas. There were 12 of us then, but now only five originals are left. I'll introduce you to Sgt. Forster, our second-in-command. He's a Kansas farm boy."

Forster, once an easy-going guy, gave Maus a brusque welcome. Combat hadn't exactly transformed Forster into a professional soldier, but he had become the next best thing: an ice-cold expert killer.

He began bringing Maus up to speed on radio procedure. Maus had a question that had come to mind in all of us from time-to-time: namely, when you're firing by command and neither seeing nor hearing your own shells land, are you actually hurting people?

"Hurting them, hell," Forster said. "We'd better be butchering the dirty bastards."

Maus blanched a bit but said nothing

"When you've been on the receiving end a time or two, Maus, you'll get it," Forster said.

Next day, Foster told me Maus adapted to aiming and firing a mortar fire like a duck takes to water. I still had my doubts. He spoke with such a gentle lisp that he just seemed soft.

But then, the third day out, some dumb Kraut starting shooting at Forster's track while we were firing a mission. Maus grabbed the .50 over his track's cab. He remembered to cock it twice and, in three bursts, walked the rounds right across the German's position, sending him to Valhalla.

I'd figured him to be too slight to control a .50. They have a lot of muzzle jump and it takes a fair amount of weight or strength or both to manage them.

Maus had the strength. In fact, he had a lot of muscle in that wiry little frame, having been a champion lightweight wrestler in high school. So instead of being a mouse, Maus was shaping up as a warrior just like our first little guy, Whitehorse. Some of the boys took to calling him Mighty Mouse.

It was puzzling that someone so new to the Army could become so effective so quickly. But combat makes you or breaks you. Whenever we had a minute, you'd see Maus with his nose deep in FM 17-27, absorbing it like a sponge.

When he finished that, I lent him my copy of the infantry manual.

Within two more days we had him running one gun, using that dolt Kennedy as his one-man crew. I mentally marked him down for promotion if he survived. When I wondered aloud how he could manage a moron like Kennedy, he said, "Oh, it's simple, Sir. He loves killing Germans so he just needs very, very clear guidance . . . plus hope."

"What? Hope that he'll survive?"

"Well, sir, I suppose. But his real hope is that he'll get lots of beer soon and I promised that when we find some I'll make sure he gets his share plus my share, too.

"Great work, Maus. Promise him my share, too."

Chapter 53
Saturday, July 29, 1944 – Into The Jaws

As I said, I had no idea about the big picture, but the operations briefing last night clarified things, as usual producing both good news and bad news.

The Ops officer displayed his big map as usual, but he had to man the pointer by himself. A Screaming Meemie had given Sgt. Pointer a million-dollar wound to the states. Timmer wondered aloud whether the Krauts amputated Pointer's pointer.

Ops himself wore a dirty field dressing on his swollen left cheek. By now the bloodstain was black and his uniform looked like mice had nested in it. Battalion and regiment had taken some heavy artillery hits and for the second time since D-Day. The headquarters staff was thinned out a bit.

Join the crowd.

He told us the good news was that the B-17 carpet bombing and the three-division assault and break-out had created a yawning gap in the German line. Patton's Third Army now was pouring through that gap into western France, pushing in all directions, especially east across France toward Germany and north into the German defenders' rear. He said resistance was minimal at this point.

"The bad news," Ops added, "is that having created that gap for Patton, now it's our job to keep it open. We're on the Germans' left flank and we must keep pushing the Krauts back to the east. We don't want them cutting Patton's supply lines. We've got to hold the shoulder of that gap . . . at all costs!

"Now we're hoping the Wehrmacht will retreat. It would make good military sense for them. But we have to assume the worst – namely that they'll attack to close the gap so as to cut Patton's supply lines.

"So we're being sent out to keep the door open, as it were. We're going to take the shoulder of the gap and we're going to hold it. The shoulder is this northwest-southeast line." He began running the pointer back and forth on the map. "It extends from Villedieu (tap) in the north through St. Pois (tap) to Mortain here (tap) to the southeast."

I raised my hand.

"Sir, what do we know about the forces we're going against?"

He paused, absently bouncing the pointer's tip on the floor. "The intelligence is pretty sketchy. We know we're still dealing with elements of the Panzer Lehr Division."

"Elements? That sounds kind of vague, sir."

"Yes, Lieutenant. Like I said, it's pretty sketchy. But I can tell you this. We've been fighting hardened Wehrmacht troops, not the second team. We've inflicted very heavy losses on them, but they're very tough veteran soldiers. They're going to stay tough."

# # #

Naturally, we called the three French towns Villy-do, Saint Poise and Morton. But our lousy French pronunciation wasn't funny for long, especially since in the next three days we virtually obliterated those towns in order to push the Krauts east, away from Patton's Parade.

Our initial probes with armor and infantry produced nothing but counterattacks. So then our air and artillery pounded the towns to rubble and then blasted the rubble. Then the infantry had to push in to capture them in vicious fighting against very adept defenders. Some of the Krauts surrendered. Most wouldn't. It didn't do to think what happened to the villagers in their cellars.

All we knew was that the FDC kept us Mortar Forkers so busy that we had to get three whole new basic loads of ammo.

In honor of what we seemed to be doing every minute around the clock, Timmer one afternoon coined a term. He said we had a special form of combat psychosis that he called Thonk-Happy.

He said the word Thonk is the noise a mortar makes when it fires. Actually, if you're doing the firing, your ears are only a foot or so from the gun's bore. There, the sound is a very hard WHAPP! You get the *thonk* when you're 30 feet away.

Anyway, Timmer said the tip-off to Thonk-Happiness – these were his words, not mine -- entailed a soldier walking in a permanent deep crouch, dropping his face to his knees every five seconds, while dipping his right ear to shoulder and using the left hand to cover the other ear.

He said we'd need our own special ticker-tape parade when we got home. It might even lead to a new dance step, the Thonk Trot.

Actually, we were just plain whipped because we still were at little better than half-strength.

See, a mortar crew normally is six men. The sergeant tends the phone or radio, two gunners lay the gun and fire it per his shouted directions, two ammo carriers strip the required shells from their cardboard tubes, and add or remove increments from the shells per the sergeant's directions per the range card data. The driver keeps watch, mans the machine guns just in case, spells anybody that needs a break, treats anybody who's wounded and does anything else that needs doing.

It might sound like a lot of people, but when you're firing missions throughout the afternoon or night it's not.

With half the platoon dead or in the field hospital, the sergeant may be scrambling back and forth among three guns with a minimum 50 feet of separation.

Meanwhile, there's maybe only one of us at each gun where he's doing everything -- the laying, firing and ripping open the ammo tubes.

So when they call to fire for effect, you've got to hang and drop four rounds from each gun as fast as possible. With the platoon's three remaining mortars, that puts 12 rounds on the target within the space of a minute – a living hell for the enemy.

But it also demands a heck of a lot for even a 2-man team . . . not to mention cleaning the gun when there's five spare minutes. And when it's time to displace – for instance when Kraut artillery starts screaming in nearby – everybody has to scramble to set up the battery in a new and temporarily safe location.

Then the guns have to be leveled and staked again before you can fire Round One.

So we were just plain numb stumbling tired.

We bitched, of course, but that's just how you cope. We knew the infantry squads and tankers had it much worse. And it showed. Seeing the 35 men left standing in a 2nd battalion company, Halls said he thought our whole regiment must be little more than a shell.

As Patton's Third Army troop convoys and ammo and gas trucks rolled south through the gap, convoys of wounded rolled back north into Normandy from Villedieu, St. Pois and especially heavily, starting Aug. 7, from the area around Mortain.

Well before dawn the morning of Aug. 7, the Krauts launched their assault toward Patton's supply line.

As usual, they managed to do the unexpected and were damned clever about it.

Chapter 54
Monday, Aug. 7, 1944 – The Shoulder

Darling Katherine:

I'm very, very sorry I haven't written more. We've been on the go day and night, literally. I'm healthy but tired-out. Right now it's late at night and I'm stretched on my stomach on the front seat of our track. My writing pad is on the floor beneath the brake pedal and I'm scribbling by the light of a tiny birthday candle stuck to the clutch pedal. I'm tired but healthy. Wait! I wrote that. Sorry. Anyhow it's . . .

My driver – up in back doing sentry duty at the .50 caliber – started pounding on the cab roof. "Sarge! Sarge!"

"Pvt. Armor, I'm a lieutenant now, remember? Why're you making all the racket?"

"Sir! SIR! Listen!"

At first I hardly heard it -- just a dry rattling, like the snapping of tiny twigs well off to our southeast. It soon swelled into loud, intense small arms fire in the direction of Mortain, third tap on the map. We heard faint thumps -- grenades or mortars. I pinched out the candle and wiggled my way out of the track cab.

Not hearing artillery, I was inclined to think it was just some infantry company with a bad case of midnight nerves.

But about a minute later battalion radioed us that a big Kraut assault was underway. "Looks like they want to break our hold on the gap's shoulder. Have your troops on full alert."

No problem. The noise had them wide awake. Just before dark, we had circled the mortar platoon wagons, seven half-tracks nose to tail 50 feet apart in a 200-yard circle. The tracks' left sides faced inwards so the drivers would have a tiny bit more protection in case of a surprise.

The firing to the south spread and intensified into a genuine roar. We also heard occasional whiplash cracks that sounded like tank guns. Signal flares and illumination flares popped to the southeast and artillery flashes began dancing along the horizon.

I took off to do what I called my nightly bed check. I damn well wanted everybody awake and alert.

They were.

The old hands were up, going through battle preparations. It was almost a ritual. Nodding at each other maybe, but not talking. Groping in the dark to make sure machine gun belts were clear and grenades were handy. Making sure carbine magazines were full. Dabbing a speck of graphite grease onto the bolts' camming lugs. Racking the action back and forth. Tapping the bullet points in M1 clips against rifle stocks.

The replacements took their cue, keeping quiet. Wiping down their weapons' actions.

It was so dark I practically had to grope from track to track. As I approached the rear of the first track, the pintle mount of its .30 caliber squeaked and I could hear the ammo belt clack against the bed's steel side. The gunner, silhouetted against the stars, aimed the weapon at me and quietly called, "Wandering world wide."

I gave the response, "Thicker than thieves." The idea was that even a German speaking excellent English would have problems with tongue-twisters involving "W" or "th" sounds.

Everybody was wide awake. And cold, too. Nights were getting chilly. At Forster's track I got on the radio and checked in with FDC.

"Nothing new, but stay awake. We might need you at any time."

By 0115 I was back in the HQ track sharing coffee with Armor who now was behind the wheel. I said, "Shit!" when I realized his boots probably were resting on my letter to Katherine. "Say, Eddy, would you mind reaching down and handing me the notepad that's under your clodhoppers?"

He started to reach, but then dropped his coffee, cocked his carbine and aimed it out the front window over the hood.

"What the hell, Armor?"

"Not sure, sir. I just thought I glimpsed some . . ."

With a flash and a roar, the half-track 50 feet in front of us exploded. Seconds later its gas tank went up in a ball of orange flame – 60 gallons of blazing gasoline turned night into day.

Somebody yelled "Panzerfaust!" and the .50 caliber above us began blasting toward the woods, the big empty casings clanging onto the hood and the top of the cab.

Through the slamming of the .50 over our heads, I heard an MG42 began its *braaaap-braaap* off to the left. Armor yelled, "Ouch! You sonofabitch!" He had one of those new full-auto carbines and he emptied his clip at somebody in front of us. The muzzle blast was almost as long as the hood and as blinding as the gasoline fire.

I jumped from the cab, blundering into a German who was running past the track. We both recoiled and as he started to raise his Schmeisser, I bellowed, "*Zurück! Zurück!*" The command 'Go back!' confused him just long enough for me to plug him in the chest with my .45. Rounding the front of the cab I stumbled on Eddy's victim, a Kraut officer, head shattered, lying between us and the blazing track.

The fire revealed a rush of maybe a dozen Krauts toward the center of our circle. They had infiltrated, attacking by stealth without an artillery barrage. But I don't think they planned for the burning track because the blaze illuminated them so clearly the gunners couldn't miss.

Gunners on the north tracks cut down the Krauts with short, aimed bursts. Two men with chemical fire extinguishers and more than their share of guts hosed the burning track before its ammo store cooked off.

Through the stammer of machine guns I yelled, "Armor! You okay?"

No answer. The driver's side door had about a dozen punctures. The crown of Armor's head lay in his door's window.

I climbed up into the track bed and manned the .30, but kept it trained to the outside. I tried to stay low and warned the .50 gunner to do the same so the fire couldn't silhouette us.

Battalion called wanting to know what was going on. I let them know and said we could handle it.

"Can you fire missions for us?"

"Yessir. So far they haven't hurt us that bad."

"We may need help. The fuckers are all over. Kind of like the Alamo. We think we can hear tanks. See if you can put up some flares for . . ."

The transmission cut off.

I got on the platoon net. "Forster, Battalion wants light and their radio's dead! Fire three parachute flares 1,700 yards, 2100 to 2900 mills. That ought to silhouette the nasties for them. Repeat as soon as the flares die out."

Gunfire spread and got closer again, Forster called back asking if the Krauts might have infiltrated the whole regiment.

But Battalion got back on line and then Regiment came on the net advising that the attack seemed to be a general assault toward Avranches, behind us on Normandy's west coast. The Krauts were attacking toward Patton's supply line. They said the attack seemed to consist of small mixed infantry-armor battle groups.

"They've got to come through us and we've got to hold," they added. "No retreat."

Hearing that, I detailed the HQ track's two remaining infantry men and two of our ammo carriers to dig a pair of foxholes outside the perimeter's south face.

I gave them both our bazookas with five rockets apiece. "Guys," I said. "You're our anti-tank teams. Get out there in the dark 200 or 300 yards or so and dig in. Dig deep 'cause when the Kraut infantry attacks again, we'll likely be shooting your direction and we don't want to kill our tank killers. If it's Kraut infantry, stay down and keep quiet. Let 'em through. If the armor shows up – no, *when* the armor shows up – that's when you start shooting."

One of the men was Maus. I could barely see his face in the dark. "So, Lieutenant, we're the forlorn hope, eh?"

"No, Maus. Right now we all are."

Feeling miserable about putting them out on their own, I remembered Sir Alfred's words that combat means spending young men's lives. I turned to leave, but then stopped. To keep from sounding emotional, I used the harshest voice I could.

"Men, a tank's front armor is thickest and bazooka rockets tend to glance off unless they hit a flat surface. So shoot them in the sides. The tanks' backs are even more vulnerable than the sides, but I'd rather you hit 'em in the sides, because by the time they pass you so can hit them in the rear, they will have killed all of us in the tracks."

# # #

Kraut assault teams tried to overrun us three more times. The attacks – especially the last one which came in platoon strength out of the woods to the north – scared hell out me at first. It was too much like what happened to two squads of us one morning in Algeria.

Fortunately, however, a circle of half-tracks each mounting a water-cooled .30 caliber and a .50 caliber machine gun is a much more formidable obstacle than two dozen riflemen in foxholes. We also were able to drop some HE and Willie Peter rounds into the woods, causing tree bursts which seemed to break up the attacks.

Tanks roared and crashed past us through the woods twice, but seemed blind. Fine with us.

Then about 0400, a tank gun south of us outside our perimeter fired into our bivouac. A rocket zipped west to east in the woods. It worked. The tank's ammo cooked off, white-hot internal explosions blasting out through its turret hatch. It was just like a damned Roman candle. Each interior flash also shown through the driver's slit and machine gun sponsons. The glare revealed the big oblong turret and long gun of a German Panther.

A second tank to the rear, a much lighter Panzer 3, began lashing the perimeter foreground with its machine gun.

Then, as its main gun blasted another of our tracks, sparks suddenly flew from its mantle. Seconds later, it began shuddering as its ammunition load exploded too, hurling the turret upside down 20 feet away. The blaze lit us up like day, making us perfect targets for the next tank that was coming into view.

The bazooka teams killed it first.

# # #

Fighting near us died as the sky began to pale, but south of us it only intensified. Tank rounds and panzerfausts had destroyed three of our seven tracks, but we still were able to fire mortar missions several times during the night.

The sun was just clearing the horizon when the medics and I pulled Armor from the cab of the HQ track. He still was breathing when they got his plasma bottle going.

I just leaned into the cab to retrieve my writing pad from the floor when D Company's new executive officer, Lt. Charlie Mason, drove his jeep into our perimeter. The fresh young West Pointer looked as unshaven and grubby as I felt. As we saluted, he took in the still-smoking tracks and the scorched circles in the grass around them. He started counting German corpses and gave up.

"Looks like you need some new tracks, Dud."

"Yep, Chuck, and two new guns. We also could sure use some replacements. We're down to 14 men to communicate with FDC and fire four mortars."

"We can't help you there, but I think I can get you half an infantry squad to handle your MGs. And we've got an ammo truck on the way along with your beer ration."

"The boys will appreciate that – especially Kennedy."

"Who?"

"One of our recent replacements. He doesn't have the brains to wad a shotgun, but he loves beer and hates Germans. He killed two of the infiltrators last night with an entrenching tool."

"Whoa! Sounds like he earned his beer."

Just then I noticed a little soldier walking toward us from the woods. Mud made his uniform unrecognizable and his helmet was missing.

But he was carrying a bazooka.

It was Maus. "So did this guy," I said.

"Lieutenant, is it okay if I come on in?"

"Hell yes, Maus. Where are the other three?"

"They didn't make it, sir. After we got the second tank, some infantry hit us."

"I'm sorry to hear that. So who got the third tank?"

"I did. By then I was hiding behind a real thick tree."

"You guys did a hell of a job. Go sack out."

"Yessir," he said, trudging toward Forster's track.

Mason looked at me, eyebrows raised,

"That's Mighty Maus, the survivor of two bazooka teams we sent out into the woods." I pointed. "They accounted for those three tanks."

He nodded. "And what's that?" he said, looking down at my hand.

I held the writing pad up to take my first look at it. Between Armor's blood, spilled coffee and boot prints it was a mess.

"Well, sir, it was a letter to my fiancé. But before I can re-do it, I've got some other letters to write."

Chapter 55
Aug. 8, 1944 – Assault

Lt. Mason said G2 predicted the Germans would lie low during the day because the Air Corps would be working them over.

"Jesus, I hope you're not talking about B-17s."

He gave a rueful laugh. "Nope, Dud, these will be fighter-bombers. They can see a lot from the air that we don't, so they're going to spend time looking for tanks and artillery. But we probably can expect the enemy to resume the attack tonight."

He drove off promising he'd try to get us some replacements and at least two new mortars.

As I started touring the tracks, two men from second section got my attention. Standing in the morning shade beside their track, they were beckoning and laughing. Being dog-tired, overwhelmed and worried, I was a bit short with them

"What the hell do you want?"

One pointed to the side of the track bed and said, "Sir, would you just look at this?"

"What, for God's sake?"

"Well, Sir, it seems the Jerries gave our track a new firing slit."

I looked closer and then gaped. "Wow!" A three-inch hole yawned in the steel wall of the track's bed, razor-sharp petals pointing outward toward the woods.

"Jesus, looks like a 75 hit, or even an 88."

"Sure looks that way, Lieutenant."

I walked around to the other side of the truck bed and found the corresponding hole. Peering through it to the track's interior, I saw a matching hole in the half-track's mortar. One of the men waved to me through the hole in the opposite side of the bed.

I circled back to the pair. "It's Leland and Edwards, right?"

"Yessir," Edwards said. "Sgt. Forster says he figures it was the first shot from that Panther. It went clean through without exploding. We didn't even notice till we got back from the fire."

"You two are the ones who doused the fire?"

"That's right, sir." He tilted his helmet up off his head. "We lost our eyebrows." Their faces looked sunburnt.

"Well, you do look a bit crisp around the edges. What made you take on that fire?"

"Sgt. Forster was busy shooting Krauts with the machine gun and he suggested that we take some fire extinguishers and see if we could douse the blaze before it started cooking off mortar shells. Said that they'd be a lot more dangerous to us than a squad of Nazis. And we were wondering, sir, would it be dangerous to fire our mortar now that it has a hole through it?"

"Guys, does a cat have an ass?"

They both laughed with just a touch of hysteria. "Good one, Sir," Edwards said. "So, we should just ditch it?"

"Yep. But keep the base and tripod if they're still okay. We'll probably need to do some cannibalizing later on."

I called FDC to let them know a third mortar was beyond repair. "Are you still operational?"

"We are, sir," I said. "But now we're down to three guns."

I ordered everybody to get some sleep because we might have a busy night. Forster and I decided to split the watch and he lost the toss.

With a rag I wiped Armor's blood from the driver's seat and floor of the HQ track, lay my aching body along it and the shotgun seat and was asleep in about four seconds.

In another hour we all were awake.

The Krauts assaulted again.

And again.

Chapter 56
Aug. 13, 1944 – Aftermath

They told us this morning what we figured out for ourselves a day ago. Over five nights, the Germans had killed a hell of a lot of GIs, but they never really got their counteroffensive rolling.

During the day, American fighter-bombers paralyzed their tank and truck traffic. At night, the Krauts tried to flood northwest through us, but kept running into outfits that refused to quit or run. Both the 9th and 30th Divisions set up hundreds of little strongpoints that fragmented the German forces – especially the 30th on Hill 217 outside Mortain.

The bulk of 4th Division was in reserve, but 8th Regiment -- including Dog Company's mortar platoon – provided other strongpoints that butchered our share of the Krauts

So now the Germans were retreating, headed east into a death trap -- British and Canadians on the north, Patton's forces attacking from the south.

Meanwhile, we who held the line from Villedieu to Mortain, were told to stand down, dress our wounds and wait for orders.

When I passed that word to the Mortar Forkers, they just stood around staring at each other. Finally Forster said, "Okay, you heard the man. Take it easy. Just pillow your aching head on one of these nice soft cow pies. Get some sleep."

One-by-one, the men began collapsing against the tires and running boards of the tracks.

"Sgt. Forster," I said, "set one man to keep watch. Relief every two hours. I'm going to headquarters and see what I can find out."

Before I actually walked into headquarters I could hear it. The HQ tent resounded with snores. A lone sentry was pacing outside and slapping his cheeks.

"S'matter," I asked. "Mosquitos?"

"No sir, I'm just trying to keep myself awake." Inside, a Signals corporal wearing ear phones snored thunderously, head cradled in his folded arms beside his own radio set.

"What's going on?"

"Nothing," the sentry said. "I get to roust out my relief in an hour, and then I'm going to sleep around the clock. If the Germans attack, I won't give a rat's ass . . . sir."

He saluted me. I waved and stumbled a quarter mile back to what remained of the mortar platoon. A set of boots propped in the shotgun seat window showed somebody had stolen my place in the HQ track. So I just crawled under the back of the track and collapsed on the ground.

Afternoon sunlight in my eyes awakened me. I tried to pull my helmet over my face to shade my eyes, but a bunch of stiff papers fell out of it onto my cheek. Letters. Mail had caught up with us and somebody had put my letters in my helmet.

I reached up to grab the track's back bumper and, with a long groan, pulled myself upright onto my butt. I moaned as I pulled out my canteen. Somebody thought that was funny, I guess, because chuckles erupted. Forster, sitting 10 feet away, was grinning at me, too, as I chugged some water.

As I rubbed my eyes and face, I asked, "What's so damned funny, Sergeant?"

"Oh, just the sounds you're making, Lieutenant."

"What time is it?"

"Sir, it now is 1600 hours."

"Damn, Mike! Why didn't you wake me?"

"Because *I* was sleeping. Regiment's orders. They say we're just going to set for a few days, read our mail, catch our breaths, shave, get resupplied, do repairs, train replacements, get drunk or whatever else we want to do, consistent with military courtesy, of course."

"Well, hell. Then I guess I'll just read my mail."

# # #

I saved Katherine's letters for last.

Mom wrote that Sis really had grown up and was quite the young lady now. Come September she'd be a high school sophomore and she now belonged to a very wholesome church youth group. The kids were learning ballroom dancing.

Wholesome? Yeah. I'll bet the boys' thoughts ain't so wholesome.

Mom said Sis already knew how to jitterbug and was angry that it was impossible to buy hose. You couldn't find rayons in the stores, let alone nylons. Sis's hair still was curly, but now in the past year had become darker.

Thinking of her dancing brought back memories of bouncy curls on the grinning pixie who stood on top of my feet as I tried to foxtrot to the radio broadcast.

Mom wrote that lots of the girls in the youth group spent their days at the church babysitting toddlers whose parents worked in defense plants. Little ones and teens alike also were starting to harvest vegetables from the church's Victory Garden.

Finally she said my old man at last had located her and Sis and sent her all kinds of nasty threats about prosecution and lawsuits and worse.

That dirty bastard! If I ever get home . . .

But she also said I was not to worry. She had a protector, a kindly gentleman – she underlined that word – who was a former cop. He was middle-aged widower on the security staff of the aircraft assembly plant where she was installing electronics in bombers.

Alfred, his name was, had taught her how to shoot his .45 pistol that he brought home from World War I where he was a military policeman.

It scared me at first, but now he says I'm a dead-eye shot at 15 yards. All I have to do when I aim is think about That Beast. I wouldn't really shoot him, of course . . . unless he tried to beat me again or to get his filthy hands on Margaret. Then I'd plug him right between those evil blue eyes. The only good thing about him is my two children, bless you both.

Speaking of eyes, Alfred tried to re-enlist in the Army after Pearl Harbor, but his vision never had fully recovered from when he got gassed in France. So he was 4F besides being too old to go anyway.

But because he was a city policeman here before the war he now works as a DAC, a Department of the Army Civilian, in security here at the plant. He's keeping an eye on Margaret and me. He put me in touch with one of the company lawyers who filed a restraining order or writ or something that prohibits you-know-who from coming within a city block of either of us or our home or my place of work.

Her news gave me a lot to chew on, but it was nothing compared to the bombshell I opened next, Katherine's most recent letter.

Dearest Allan:

I start by saying I love you, I miss you and I fear for you. I also have news you may not welcome. I think I'm starting a baby, our baby. I know we have committed to wed, but I don't know that you expected to be a father so soon. I can end it but I really don't want to because it's a part of you that I would have always. Yet the little mite is yours, too, and so I want you to tell me how you feel about it . . .

I didn't even finish reading. I startled everybody by jumping up and yelling "Yaaaa-hooo!" I ran to battalion where I grabbed a jeep and drove to regimental HQ. It took about 15 minutes to find the chaplain and five more to explain that I wanted the Red Cross to get a message – a phone call, not a folded piece of yellow telegram paper – to Katherine Abbot at Abbot Manor, East Devon.

My message was simple.

Katherine. Wonderful news. Suggest naming our child after your folks. All my love, Allan.

I asked the chaplain about the chance of a three-day furlough. He just shook his head. "Sorry, son. This is a blessing, not an emergency. No furloughs now."

I shrugged. "I figured as much, but I didn't think it would hurt to ask." He congratulated me and gave me a handshake.

For the first time since my return from England, I felt fully awake and lively. The news about the baby seemed to wipe out the news about my old man. When I got back to our bivouac, I didn't want to do a damned thing. I flopped down on the bare ground, extending my arms out like Jesus on the cross. I just stared up at the scattered clouds, letting my imagination roam.

See, I know babies. I helped raise my little sister from infancy. It had been wonderful to walk her, to bathe and feed and burp her . . . such a sweet, wonderful thing with all her gurgling and laughter. And the baby talk, too. I could speak Baby even better than German. Here I was, commander of killers, and all I wanted to do was daydream about holding my child.

Somebody came over and stood beside me. First he shuffled his feet. After I ignored him for a full minute, he respectfully cleared his throat.

"Will it wait until tomorrow?"

"Oh, sure. Yessir."

"Okay. See me first thing. Right now I'm enjoying my future."

"What's that, skipper?"

I tilted my head up to meet Halls' eyes. "There's a good chance we'll all get killed before this is over, right?"

"Yeah. I hope not but I guess so."

"Okay, I just got news today that I'm going to be a father. So I'm lying here soaking all that up. In my mind, I'm giving my boy his bottle. Or helping my little girl get all dolled up as a princess. Or having Pretend Tea with her. I might not ever get to do those things, so I'm doing them now in my mind.

"So take off, corporal. I think my boy and I might go out for a while to play catch."

Chapter 57
Aug. 20, 1944 – Resting

I should have kept my mouth shut because during the next week everybody from Col. Van Fleet to Maus and Kennedy had to congratulate me.

Not that we had time for frivolity. The sound of the guns had moved beyond what was left of our hearing and we were supposed to rest. But the Mortar Forkers worked like dogs.

We received replacements for our destroyed half-tracks and got the damaged ones repaired. In some cases, they still had blood stains and sloppy paint jobs over the patched bullet holes. The guys thought, and I agreed, that patching the bullet holes was a waste of time and sheet metal. "They're going to look like sieves anyway after we meet the first Jerry MG, just like before."

But at least the engines were tuned up with freshly sand-blasted spark plugs.

Meanwhile, the XO of the repair battalion just about ripped us a new one, demanding that drivers start downshifting the tracks in order to slow them, rather than ride the brakes. "Look, half-tracks is heavy as hell and you bastards keep hitting the brakes so they's all wore out by the time you really need 'em. Then where is you? So ease up, dammit!"

Replacements started showing up and Frost rejoined us, scarred but restored. Three new men actually had some training on mortars. Most of the others had only been through shortened basic training.

Forster got Timmer and Maus to set up a rifle range, so the new guys got to zero in their carbines, and a chance to fire at least a few bursts with both the .50 and .30 caliber machine guns.

Forster also drilled the new men on strict radio procedure. He really had turned out to be a gem. He was tough, making the new men learn while overriding their gripes. But he also helped them work through their New Guy Bewilderment.

Most important, he forced the old hands to welcome and help the new guys. Most old-timers, having lost buddies, want nothing to do with replacements -- the cherries, as they called them. But Forster made damn sure the old hands, even his own friends, genuinely welcomed the new guys and helped them learn the ropes.

The thing was, I could delegate to Forster. Hell, I could lean on him because he anticipated everything. He wanted the outfit to work because he wanted us to survive.

So I campaigned hard for Forster, explaining to Capt. Freeman how reliant and loyal he had been. The captain forwarded a request to promote Forster to platoon sergeant, and he got his new stripe.

Then that dirty bastard farm boy turned around and betrayed me.

Just after Frost returned from convalescence, Forster brought him and Halls to my tent one night and demanded that I let the three of them teach me to play bridge.

"You're bug house nuts," I snapped. "Why the hell should I learn that pansy-assed game?"

Forster looked at me very sternly. "Sir, we understand you plan to stay in the service after the war. And if you're going to succeed in your military career, you've *got* to know bridge. All officers must be good bridge players. It's part of their social life . . ."

"Oh, bullshit!"

"No, sir," Frost said. "Ike himself plays bridge. Honest injun. He loves it."

"Ike? You mean Gen. Dwight D. Eisenhower? How the hell would you know?"

"It's the truth," Frost said. "He toured our hospital in England and when he came into our Quonset Hut he asked whether anybody came from Kansas. Well, I held up my hand and told him our little outfit started out at KU. He gave that big grin of his and wanted to know all about it. Told us when he was at staff college at Ft. Leavenworth, he and some classmates always used to drive down to KU on Saturdays to the football games.

"Then when I told how we had a marathon bridge tournament on the train all the way from Lawrence to Camp Kilmer, his face really lit up. He wanted to know if any of us had master's points. I bet he and Bradley and Monty are playing bridge this fucking minute."

It took an hour for them to grind me down.

I admit I came to enjoy the game, because it was just a complicated form of Euchre. Maybe it was beginners' luck or just that they rigged the deck, but once I got the rudiments of bidding, I did pretty well.

# # #

Our rest, such as it was, lasted 10 days. And just before they sent us back into action, Gen. Barton – the division commander – paid a visit to the regiment as part of an inspection tour.

We were all lined up at attention in uniforms that at least were clean if not in good repair. His jeep stopped first in front of the regimental command group. Then he surprised us by stopping in front of D Company. I mean, normally, the guys with stars drive by to take our salute, look stern, and then head straight to the O Club for a couple of scotches.

But Gen. Barton dismounted from his jeep and walked over to receive Capt. Freeman's salute. They shook hands and chatted for a minute and then Freeman made a half turn and bellowed, "Lt. Dudley! Post!"

"Good God," I muttered, "what do they want with me?" As I trotted away from the platoon I swear I heard a snicker. Stopping before the captain and general, I gave a snappy salute, "Lt. Dudley reporting, sir!"

Both looked at me with flinty eyes. They exchanged looks and Gen. Barton's moustache twitched. "Lieutenant, I have a tactical question."

"For me, sir?"

"That's what I said, Lieutenant. Now pay attention. You're the dealer and your hand has seven spades but only six to 10 points. Got that?"

"Wha . . .?" It took second to reorient myself from mortars to bridge "Uh, yessir."

"What's your bid?"

"Uh, sir, I – well, I guess I'd bid three spades."

"You guess?"

"Sorry, sir. I would bid three spaces. Definitely."

"Lieutenant, how can you justify an opening three bid without enough points to open with a one bid?"

"Well, sir, the boys tell me it's a special situation – a pre-empt, a very strong defensive move. And if your partner has opening count, you may have a slam.

The general gave a tight grin, "The boys?"

"Yes sir. My platoon sergeant and two other men are avid bridge players. They conducted kind of a mutiny, forcing me to learn bridge. They said if it's good for Gen. Eisenhower, it's good for me – that it would help my career now that I'm an officer."

The general's shoulders started shaking with a phlegmy cough deep in his chest. He sounded like he had a hell of a cold, but a grin cracked his face as the cough became a chuckle. He turned away, hawked and spat and then he and the captain laughed aloud together. The general reached to shake hands. "Lieutenant, I hope maybe we can have a game before all this is over."

I tried to give an aww-shucks grin. "Sir, I'd be honored. But I kind of think I'd be better safer trying to repel a German assault."

He stopped smiling. "How are your boys doing?"

"Sir, we're rested and ready to load some Nazi asses with shrapnel."

"Replacements?"

"Like everybody, sir, we're short-handed. But we've trained the new men like mad. Got their carbines zeroed in. They're green, but they know mortars now. We're not as ready as we could be, but I think we can handle it."

"Glad to hear it, son. We need you and your boys." He and the captain chuckled again as I saluted, did a snappy about face, and marched back to the platoon.

When I got there, I met Forster's eyes. "Mike," I whispered. "how the *hell* did the general come to know that I've been learning bridge?"

He grinned. "I have no idea, sir."

"You lying bastard!"

"Thank you, sir."

Chapter 58
Aug. 23, 1944 – Paris

Our rest ended when we took off for Paris in a driving rain.

My driver asked, "What's going on, sir?"

"Purcell, we're riding to the rescue, just like the cavalry saving the wagon train."

Our briefer said the French Resistance had attacked the Nazi garrison in Paris and was holding its own, but they were in jeopardy because Paris still was 12 miles deep in German territory.

We kept rolling all night, our ponchos flapping in the wind as the rain dripped from the rims of our helmets. We stopped to refuel the next morning, and rolled on, supposedly to break through to rescue the Maquis. But it didn't work out that way.

Thursday night we bivouacked within sight of the city, ready to attack the next morning. When we probed toward Paris at dawn, the Germans were gone. We motored north and then east around Paris while the 22nd Infantry drove into the city to a thunderous welcome and to receive a formal surrender by the German commandant.

Our column passed around the north suburbs of Paris, encountering no opposition. It was exhilarating to know Paris was free now, but it presented me a problem – the same problem a lot of officers faced.

As I shaved, Timmer and Halls came to see me, both looking as spic and span as is possible in combat gear. Timmer spoke first. "Say, Lieutenant, what's the chances of getting a pass to go into Paris? I mean, just think about all we've been through."

"Yeah, I think we're about due," Halls said. "We've been shelled and bombed by our own bombers. We fought through the damned hedge rows." Nelson was with them, grinning in anticipation.

"And please don't forget the Mortain battle," Timmer added. "We really could use a little relaxation – and maybe even a bath – maybe a bubble bath with some of them Paris beauties, if you know what I mean."

I rinsed the lather from my face. "You poor guys. You make my heart pump piss. You've just finished sitting on your asses for 10 solid days. You even got to swim a little. You get into Paris and you're gonna catch some Kraut's clap or a whole flock of crotch crickets."

I said that in our briefing last night, Regiment announced there'd be no Paris passes. No more rest, either, because we could give the Germans no rest. We'd had some time off and now we had to pick up the chase. Patton was swarming across central France, the British and Canadians were speeding across northern France toward Holland. We in V Corp were headed for Belgium. Paris was only a side-show because of a call for help from Gen. DeGaulle.

"Look, guys, the only reason that the 22nd got into Paris was that Gen. DeGaulle asked for some Army units to make a show of force so that the Communists in The Resistance wouldn't try something funny."

After I explained all this, Timmer said, "Well, that's all well and good, sir. But we haven't even *seen* any real dames since we left England except for some farm wives -- and they were fat! -- let alone kissed any of them. And now we hear those ground pounders from the 28th Division get to go into Paris and make time with the ladies."

"Well, if it's any comfort, Timmer, they get to lookee, but no touchee. Some of the 22nd marched right down the Champs de Elysee, but they didn't stop at the sidewalk cafes or stop at any cat houses. They went through that town like a dose of salts and are taking up the chase – with us – now that they came out the other side.

"And, boys, I do hate to sound like Scrooge, but it's my duty to point out that we're in France to fight Germans, not to get laid. Our next stop is *Deutschland*. For us it is *Deutschland über alles*."

"Awww, sir," Halls said. "Look at us. We started this campaign with 12 men. Five of us have been wounded and . . ."

"Yeah," I said. "I'm aware of that and I've got the scars to show it."

Halls shut up, but Timmer picked up the argument, "Yes sir and six of us are dead and . . ."

"I know," I added, "I've been writing to their families."

Timmer shut up

"Look, guys," I said, "if it's any comfort, SHAEF G2 claims that the Wehrmacht has had it. They say the war is damned near over. I don't believe it myself. But I'll tell you this. Once the Krauts do surrender, I'll do everything in my power to get all of you not just a pass but a two-week furlough to Paris. There! How's that?"

Timmer gave me a cold look.

"It ain't going to help if I'm already dead. And I'll believe the Germans are defeated when we hear a broadcast from them saying exactly that."

"Yeah," I said. "I hear you."

# # #

As we left Paris behind, the guys had to admit that the motor march through France still was nice going. We were moving in swift columns, clearing up to 100 miles a day. One infantry officer leading our column told me that they could tell instantly whether Krauts still occupied a town along our route.

"If the people are out to greet us with flowers and wine, we know the Germans are gone. We can just ride right on through. Trouble is, it's always a big party. They keep clogging the streets and trying to give us their wine and pretty soon you've got a hell of a traffic jam and half the guys are drunk.

"But if there's no sign of people, then we send in tanks with several squads of infantry."

The regiment itself moved in three battalion columns, so that if 1st Battalion was going through a town, 2nd and 3rd would pass north and south of it. That way we flanked any German force that tried to make a stand.

Twice in the next three days, the FDC called on us for support. The new guys in the mortar platoon got some practice under very close supervision.

What I liked most was passing the farms. They were nothing like the typical farm you'd see in Ohio or Michigan -- house, barn, windmill and silo and maybe a fenced-in front yard.

Instead, French farms looked like little fortified villages – clusters of maybe a dozen stone homes and barns often enclosed by stout stone walls six or eight feet high. The walls had big heavy double doors studded with bolts. But as we went by, the doors always were wide open and all the families were out waving and cheering. And the kids were all bending over picking up ration candy that the boys tossed to them.

"If these folks farmed in Kansas or Oklahoma," Forster said, "they sure as hell wouldn't want those walls. They'd block the wind and you need that wind on summer nights. Otherwise, you get no sleep at all."

Several times we passed small groups of unarmed German troops sitting by the road wearing soft caps rather than helmets. Who knows? Maybe they were Russians or Ukrainians waiting for a ride to the POW cages. Anyway, they always grinned, waved and begged cigarettes.

A couple of times, too, we encountered genuine Krauts under guard. All of them seemed to be veterans and some were those stiff-assed SS types. We stopped opposite one cage and strolled over to practice our German under the close eye of MPs. The Krauts were dirty, tired and unshaved, but standing proud, statue-straight. If they were dejected they didn't show it. Most of them glared, looking as if they were ready to pick up their weapons and start shooting.

Afterwards, Halls was furious. "I offered one of those SS pricks a cigarette and he accepted it, but he acted contemptuous about it. Even when I gave him a light. So I asked if he couldn't at least say 'Thanks' and he just turned his back on me. Maybe we've swept up these assholes, but they don't act defeated to me."

I had to agree because the closer we got to Germany, we began seeing fewer and fewer ersatz *landsers* relaxed along the roadside. And we began seeing more and more caged POWs who acted very stiff and arrogant – cold and correct at best and surly and churlish at worst.

I started wondering whether Timmer might have a better bead on things than SHAEF.

Turned out he did.

Chapter 59
Aug. 26, 1944 – The Race

Northeast of Paris, we linked up with some of the 22nd Infantry and found them to be one very disappointed group.

Yeah, they got to do a foot parade through Paris, marching to roaring cheers from thousands of Parisians.

But the infantry had to stay in company mass ranks, meaning that only the guys on the two outside files got targeted by girls. And the police kept most of the people of Paris from mobbing the troops as happened to the doughboys in 1918.

Halls and Timmer still felt aggrieved, again grousing to me that they were certain to get killed before getting so much as a kiss.

"Then you should know St. Peter will check you right through the gates," I told them, "because you will not have sinned."

Once we passed Paris, place names on the road signs started to ring bells.

All of us were born at the end or just after World War I, but we sure remembered the stories about the Second Battle of the Marne and the carnage that Germans and Americans inflicted on each other 26 years ago at Soissons and Chateau-Thierry.

Crossing that same terrain in 1944 was much easier. We had virtually no casualties. The speed of our advance didn't permit the Germans to establish a solid line anywhere in France. And for the most part, we outnumbered their battle groups.

So it was a case of a column preceded by two or three tanks with troops riding them, or two or three deuce-and-a-half trucks that were following the tanks, maybe a tank destroyer or two plus us bringing up the rear. We were sweeping up or simply crushing Wehrmacht rear guards. And we then punched through some stiffening resistance to cross the Aisne River.

The Meuse River, a much wider stream, had us all worried. But with aerial and artillery support our engineers quickly bridged it and we got across before the Germans could make a stand.

Not that anyone was handing out prizes, but despite all the ballyhoo about Patton, 4th Division actually won the race to Germany.

First to cross the line was one of the 22nd Infantry's foot patrols which passed through Echternacht, a little town just this side of Germany's border with Luxembourg. The next day the whole 22nd occupied the place and set up a military government. Then they started probing the Siegfried Line and actually got through it – but ended up being called back.

We of the 8th Infantry were further back, rounding up Germans in a host of small Belgian towns including two – St. Vith and Bastogne – that a few weeks later would become big news. Sometimes, Germans were waiting patiently to surrender. Usually they were service troops or clerk typists who had neither desire nor the training to fight as infantry. They met us with helmets off and *hände hoch*.

A couple of times, the infantry passed those guys back to us and we didn't know what to do with them but hand out cigarettes and practice our German while waiting for the MPs to show up. These same Krauts warned us that the SS and Gestapo had rounded them up from rear areas and sent them forward as delaying forces. They said the Wehrmacht was massing troops behind what they called the Western Wall – the Siegfried Line.

They didn't delay us a bit. But we kept slowing down anyway and coming to a series of complete stops.

One major delay was the Belgians themselves. They seemed hysterical at being liberated from the Germans. It was against SHAEF orders for us to get down out of our vehicles and fraternize with them, but they just swarmed right into the tracks and the trucks.

I was riding shotgun in the HQ track going through some little burg and a girl who looked about 18 got up on the running board and leaned through the window. She said something about tray sheik, grabbed my face and gave me a kiss and held it for dear life. But Katherine and the baby were very much on my mind so I didn't reciprocate.

Well, not much.

I mean, I didn't want to be so rude as to push her off a moving half-track.

The men, women and kids all were skinny thanks to near starvation. But they insisted on kissing. Yep, the men, too. They kissed us on both cheeks as did most of the women. But like the honey who smooched me, some of the younger ladies were, shall we say, more forward. The cheering Belgians brought wine with them, but worst of all they packed the streets and slowed us to a crawl.

Worse, the lack of gasoline also slowed us down. On Sept. 2 we ran dry. The whole damned Army was running dry.

The S4 told us that even though the port at Cherbourg now was open and even though they were building a gasoline pipeline under the English Channel, it still took too much gasoline to convoy gasoline to the Army all the way from Normandy.

The Red Ball Express would deliver truckloads of jerry cans full of gasoline and we'd fill up with enough fuel for the regiment to move 20 or 30 miles the next morning and free another town. Five miles later we'd run out again.

Part of the problem was the tanks. They used about four gallons to the mile, but nobody wanted to proceed without them. Vulnerable though they were to panzerfausts and to German Panthers and Tigers, they still were fantastic for taking out machine gun nests and even whole battle groups.

Oh, and the jerry cans themselves were piling up in the wrong places. The Red Ball express would drop off, say, 50 jerry cans of gasoline to us and go on to the next unit. We'd empty the cans into our vehicles and carefully stack the empties by the road. Then we'd move on.

But after dropping all their loads, the Red Ball drivers often were forced to head back to Normandy by a different route, so the empties just sat there until the local farmers helped themselves. So after a while, the Red Ball truckers had a hell of a time getting enough jerry cans to fuel us.

But then, Germans themselves began slowing us down.

The Wehrmacht was regrouping behind their borders and soon resumed fighting in the same old way. We'd attack. They'd retreat. And then they'd shell and mortar the hell out of their old positions just as we occupied them. Then they'd counterattack from other directions with mortars, tanks and infantry.

Once we Mortar Forkers got near the border, we not only were in constant action, but we also had to dismount and displace constantly because heavy counter battery fire – mortar and artillery both – began searching very noisily for us.

We almost lost Forster when a counter attack came up *behind* us – 180 degrees from where the Germans were supposed to be. The Krauts had a way of doing that.

Forster was on the phone to FDC when he spotted a smoking potato-masher grenade arcing toward him. He actually caught it in mid-air and hurled it back. It exploded in air 20 feet away.

As Forster rose from ducking, Fayette -- on duty at the water-cooled .30 – hosed the brush and trees from which the grenade came. Perhaps a half-dozen Krauts began firing back. Fortunately, they didn't have an MG-42 with them while we had not only Fayette's .30, but the .50 caliber on the front of the track. With the two gunners flailing the undergrowth, the surviving would-be ambushers cleared out.

Forster and Fayette just stared at each other and then said a collective, "Whew!"

And meanwhile up at the head of the column, the 88s were beginning to set the Shermans ablaze, so FDC had us begin trying to shell the 88s.

Chapter 60
Sept. 3, 1944 – Crawling

Dear Katherine –

    I only have time for a brief note. We've outrun our mail again, so I haven't heard from you about the baby. I hope you're not suffering in the mornings. Mom told me that was the worst time for her when expecting. The weather here was beautiful until this morning when it began to rain. But I have a good rain cape as you Limeys call it, so I'm staying warm and dry. I must go. Please give my best wishes to Sir Alfred and Lady Alice.

Love,

Allan

    I snorted as I gave my letter to the orderly. I was neither dry nor warm. There's just no way to stay dry when it's pouring and you're riding in the open cab of a half-track.

    To begin with, rain is clattering through the front windows at whatever speed you're going. We can't have windshield glass because it shatters when explosions occur nearby.

    And naturally, the track that we're following is throwing up rooster tails of muddy water creating a slimy mist which comes right into the cab.

    Meanwhile, the wind of the track's 20 m.p.h. speed is lashing rain down on you through the machine gun ring mount over your head. Or if you're in the back of the track, you're taking 20 m.p.h. rain in the face and the cold water is trickling down your neck.

    Oh, the poncho hoods? Well, they're actually are big enough to entirely enclose your helmeted head, but the helmet forces the hood wide open at face and neck so, before long, you're soaked.

    Some news correspondent, no doubt sitting at his portable typewriter in a nice warm room and hearing the rain drum overhead, wrote that it's the infantryman's lot to suffer.

    No shit.

    Maybe the writer was Hemingway who we hear is a buddy of the old man, Gen. Burton.

    Well, if he did write it, he probably typed it while boozing and partying with girls in Paris with the rest of us enroute for Germany.

# # #

    Once we would clear a Belgian town, the lack of gasoline often forced us to bivouac just beyond its outskirts.

    When that happened, battalion would clear us to issue 3-hour passes so small groups of the guys could walk in and visit the shops.

Even when it was quiet, the ground-pounders would stay on the perimeter facing Germany. And us Mortar Forkers stood by at our dripping guns, just in case.

The battalion was pushing foot patrols out front and we heard they often caught sight of Kraut patrols. But kind of by a gentlemen's agreement, each usually left the other alone. Occasionally we'd hear sporadic shooting.

More important to us for now was Halls and Purcell returning from pass in one of the little burgs to report that some of the bakers had gone back into business.

"They won't accept our French francs," Halls said, "but they'll barter. So you can get some very nice pastry for a pack of cigarettes. Great change from C Ration crackers."

Forster later told me he traded two little cans of his C-Ration instant coffee for a shave and haircut.

"But as soon as the barber found out how lousy it tasted, he said nix to any more of that. You want a haircut, Dud? Better bring a couple packs of Lucky Strikes or Chesterfields. Right now I think they're the only legal tender."

The rain finally stopped and instead of cold, cold rain, we started getting some nice crisp autumn weather. It was beautiful during the day with the maples and birches changing color. But it was damned chilly at night if you still were damp from the rain and huddled in a half-track.

I went into one town – a tiny place consisting of two parallel streets with some connecting alleys. I just went door-to-door asking for someone who spoke either English or German.

Finally, an elderly lady greeted me with a clear, smiling "hello." It took about two minutes to explain that I would pay for a hot bath. She smiled, "Yes. I fix for you." She told me she'd have to heat the water on a wood stove so I should come back in an hour.

So I wandered about, exchanging friendly nods with residents. And when I returned she charged four packs of Luckies, It was worth it -- a long, hot soaking bath in a giant old tub. She threw some kind of special soap into it. God, it was wonderful! I just lay back in the steam and suds, even falling asleep for a while.

When I got out to dry off, the water was the color of tea – real murky tea. It was the first chance I'd had to bathe since leaving Abbot Manor in Mid-July. Oh, of course, I'd been soaked by rain occasionally, but for seven weeks none of us had found a chance to really scrub or to soak off the grime.

The real surprise was that she had laundered my fatigues. They were badly wrinkled from the hand-cranked wringer she used. They still were damp and a couple of buttons were broken. But they were clean. I gave her two more packs of Luckies.

As I walked past Purcell back at the bivouac, he sniffed, and then pretended to follow me with his nose.

"What the hell you doing, Purcell?"

"Sniffing that perfume, sir. Was you in a whore house? And can I have the address?"

I laughed. "No, this is a nice respectable village. I hate to disappoint you, but I bet there ain't a whorehouse within 20 miles. I just got me a nice long hot bath."

It was the last chance to clean up for a long, long time.

# # #

The deeper we inched into Belgium, the more forbidding it seemed.

Now I have to explain this part of Belgium is very rough countryside. Sure, there are lots of little villages, but they're scattered amid very dense woods and very sharp hills.

In fact, the nearer we got to Germany the more the terrain reminded me of the hill country back in West Virginia and Pennsylvania – hill after hill after hill, all covered with real dense woods, and often featuring occasional granite outcroppings forming sheer cliffs.

At home we used to say that us hillbillies only get to see the sun two hours a day. Well, that's how it looked in southern Belgium, too, and it all seemed uphill toward the German border.

And if the woods looked sinister as we approached them, our patrols started running into brick walls.

A squad would go into the woods and come back quickly with one dead and two wounded. The Krauts weren't assaulting, but they attacked anything moving toward them. The gentlemen's agreements were cancelled.

Fayette sneaked off with one patrol, because he wanted a souvenir Luger. When the patrol returned, he was muddy, wide-eyed and shaking.

Forster chewed him out and turned him over to me. I asked him if a Luger was worth his life. "Stupid move, soldier. I'm thinking of changing your name to Pvt. Dumbshit."

"You're right, sir," he said. "I wouldn't do that again for all the Lugers in Berlin. Lookit, sir!" He showed me two bullet holes in his field jacket and another level with the knee in his left pant leg. "Never again, sir. I swear. Never again."

The infantry officers were looking grim.

They told me that the war of movement – fancy high-speed flank runs with tanks and motorized infantry -- was definitely over. It wasn't so much being out of gasoline, but that the Germans now had a solid line again, and all assaults wound up an infantryman's battle.

"Even if we'd had the gasoline," the S3 told us, "we no longer can loop around strong points. The roads are few, far between and little better than 2-tracks. Besides, any forest *is* a strong point. Tanks aren't much use in them. Even a tank can't push over an oak that's three feet thick.

"So it's going to be inch-by-inch like Normandy until we break through to Germany. We've got to go in and root the Krauts out of very strong natural defensive positions that they've made even stronger."

He told us our mortars would be very much in demand and in the woods they could confer a special advantage.

"If we're dropping HE on a wooded objective," he said, "the shells explode in the treetops and that subjects the Germans to shrapnel. No problem if you're in a bunker with a good roof, but it's slaughter if you're in a."

We soon found out that tree bursts – like all other combat techniques -- work both ways.

Chapter 61
Sept. 16, 1944 – The Siegfried Line

Bull and Halls groaned in unison and Maus and Forster just looked grim when I told them the S3 started his briefing by saying that he had some good news and some bad news.

"Guys," I said, "you'll be happy to know that the 12th and the 22nd broke through the Siegfried Line. Our brother regiments not only broke through, but they also spread out behind it. They're holding it wide open for a follow-on assault into Germany."

"Well, gee whizz and wow," Frost said. "I can hardly wait. Next stop Cologne, right?"

Eyeing my frown, Forster said, "Something tells me it's not gonna be that simple."

"Right," I said. "The bad news is that Montgomery's operations up north in the Netherlands have left no assault forces down here to pour through that gap. Monty's got most of the gas, too, so there's no fuel for our tanks down here to drive through the hole, either."

"Oh, that's great," Forster said. "So now I guess the 12th and 22nd are left high and dry."

"That's right, Mike" I said. "And the worse news is that the Krauts have begun attacking their flanks and infiltrating behind them. So guess who's going to the rescue?"

"Oh, shit!"

"Yep, the 8th Infantry is gonna head south and seal off the leaks so that the 12th and 22nd can pull back out. Shouldn't be too bad, because even though the Krauts are harassing our buddies, they don't have the forces to do it in strength.

"I don't care!" Bull said. "I don't like this. All of a sudden the Krauts are putting the pressure on us instead of vice versa and, if you'll notice, we're looking pretty thin on the ground here, too."

"Well, thank you for that analysis, corporal. When Gen. Eisenhower and I have breakfast in the morning, I'll be sure to apprise him of your views.

"But listen," I went on. "It really shouldn't be all that bad. The Krauts are still off balance, so we're going to clobber them from behind and keep them off the backs of the 22nd and 12th. The S3 says we'll probably meet minimal resistance."

Maus said "Minimal? How minimal is it to the guy who steps on a bouncing betty?"

# # #

"Well Jesus wept, will you look at that!"

Rosedale, one of the ammo carriers, laid both his web bags with their mortar shells on the flat top of a waist-high concrete pyramid. "These damned things are lined up just like a company on parade."

We were standing in the front of the Siegfried Line. The pyramids – designed to hang up tanks – stood four feet apart in a perfect row following the curve of the slopes out of sight into the woods far to our right and far to our left. And it was just the first of four parallel lines, 15 feet apart, each succeeding line of pyramids being slightly taller than the ones to its front.

"So these are the dragon teeth," Leland said. "Looks like they've sure been here a while. They've got some kind of moss or something on them."

"It's lichens," Maus said.

"Dammit," Forster said, "this isn't a botany lesson. Come on, We've got to get set up."

We led both mortar teams through a 60-foot gap the engineers had blasted and then bulldozed through four lines of dragon teeth. We were carrying our gear just behind a platoon of infantry that was passing among the first pill boxes spaced out checkerboard style starting 200 yards further into Germany. Also concrete, they looked a bit like upside-down coffee cups, each having two firing slits. The slits looked pocked and chewed and some were blackened. They'd taken a lot of rifle and artillery fire, plus flamethrower blasts.

Because the only clear zone for our mortars was on the crest of the ridge itself, right in the front of the Siegfried Line, we suspected we were in full view of Kraut forward observers. So we dismounted the mortars from the half-tracks and dispersed the sections about 400 yards apart, each pair of guns split at least 50 yards apart. Forster was in touch with the guns on the platoon net while I prepared to take orders for us all from FDC.

I ordered Maus to set up one gun beside a pill box 100 feet to the south and had Forster emplace gun his near another pill box close at hand. We didn't like being there because we felt so exposed.

The problem was that the German border – and the Siegfried Line – extended for miles along the crest of a steep ridge frowning down on the borders of Belgium, Luxembourg and Holland. The forward slope of the ridge was so heavily wooded that it afforded no clear zone where we could fire. So we had no choice about where to emplace.

As Leland and Rosedale started digging right in front of the pill box's west face, I ordered the tracks back down into the woods.

Forster said, "Lieutenant, how 'bout we check out the entrance in the back of the pill box. If they start shelling us we could dive in and be safe from anything – even an 88."

"Sounds good, Mike. But first make damned sure it's not booby-trapped."

He and I peered into the back of the concrete box. The steel door in the rear yawned open and was perforated by a dozen bullet holes. "Looks like a rusty cheese grater," Forster said. Peering inside, we dimly made out large piles of MG brass and a jumble of empty ammo boxes.

"I think I could carefully tie a cord to those boxes," Foster said, "and just pull them out one-by-one and that way . . ."

Just then we heard a hollow *whomp* from the other pill box.

"Goddammit!" Maus screamed, "I told him not to go in there until we checked it out." Leland had crawled into the other pillbox. Pale smoke was rising from it and Leland's lower legs and boots protruded from the pillbox entrance, just like the Wicked Witch of the East

"Is he okay?" I called.

Maus bent to look inside, stood up and raised his hands and dropped them to his sides. "Yeah, he's okay. Stupid bastard's dead."

He turned back and shouted to the rest of his crew. "Okay! Come on! Dig! And keep digging!" They did.

"Pull him out and get a dog tag," I yelled. I turned back to Forster. "I think we'll just forget about using the pillbox, okay?"

"Damned right," he said.

# # #

We were just about to start firing our first mission when Purcell shouted, "Down!"

The Krauts' first four shells blasted in quick succession in a damned diamond pattern around us. More started coming down before we could move. As the shells slammed around us, I cowered on my side, my left ear pressed to the handset while I tried to tell FDC we couldn't shoot right now.

The tinny response came back. "Roger that. We'll try to get some help."

Trying not to inhale the dust that the explosions whipped over us, I watched Forster's face contorting about three feet away. He had fingers in both ears. But every time a mortar shell exploded and its shrapnel slapped into the pill box above our hole, he winced. Some of the shrapnel ricocheted onto us from the pill box concrete. Having ricocheted, it wasn't lethal. But it stung like crazy and was blistering hot.

I'm sure I was wincing, too, because Forster gave me a wry grin. I could see the line of Purcell's shoulder just beyond him. As more and more dust and dirt fell on us, he looked more and more like a pile of soil. I prayed that the Krauts wouldn't have any white phosphorous shells handy.

Which gave me a real nasty idea. I decided that with the next mission, I'd plan on mixing in two or three Willy Peter rounds. They'd force any Kraut who'd taken cover to dash right into the shrapnel storm.

Over the noise of the Kraut mortar bursts I heard something new – a high, echoing crack. It sounded like tree bursts, but there weren't that many trees where the Kraut mortars should be.

The mortars stopped falling around us and FDC came on again.

"We just sent them a Peter Fox treat. That ought to clear you. Proceed with fire mission as soon as possible." We got up gingerly and started firing, ready to go flat in case the Krauts started again.

It never happened. When I asked FDC what a Peter Fox treat was, all I got back was, "Disregard -- slip of the tongue."

We stayed on call, having to fire several missions when the Krauts tried to get frisky with our withdrawing ground pounders. As a company of the 22nd filed out past us and down the ridge, they looked thoroughly pissed off. Their captain stopped to thank us for the support, but he was in a foul mood.

"We blew right through these bastards last week. Mark my words, we're going to have to do it all over again. Next time it's gonna kill a lot of us."

It was a week-long operation before we were able to get back to our tracks and to establish a line along the German border.

Chapter 62
Friday, Sept. 22, 1944 – On Defense

"Okay, guys, I've got some good news. As long as Monty has his dick hanging out half-way across Holland, we're digging in down here to the south and going on defense."

Foster piped up. "So then this means all the talk about the war ending by Christmas . . ."

"Yeah," I said. "It's just talk. We're going to stabilize the line and hold it. And the other good news is that even though the Krauts are defending, they ain't attacking."

I stood up. "So what all this means is that now we've helped our buddies in the 22nd and the 12th, we're going camping outdoors for the autumn and probably the winter . . . in the snow and mud."

The boys all gave me a glum look. "Okay, sir" Forster asked. "So how soon do we get some cold weather gear?"

"Well, S4 claims they're working on it."

"Sure," Halls said. "And the first snow pac boots that arrive in theater will go on the feet of those rear echelon assholes."

"You might be right about that," I said. "But instead of bitching, I'd recommend that we scrounge some real shovels and start digging deep bunkers and roof them with thick timbers. Get you some straw for the floors, too -- or lumber -- so you can make an elevated floorWith autumn rain and snow, you're going to have pools and ice rinks inside those bunkers."

# # #

So we started digging in. We felled trees to cover our bunkers. We split logs to make floors for them. We scrounged ponchos to cover the roofs and then shoveled dirt over the ponchos. The thicker the roof the better it serves as a bursting pan for incoming artillery

When the rains started, they showed us to be amateur roofers. We got a constant drip-drip-drip inside the bunkers. Pools formed under our log floors and the water rose.

The bunkers were absolutely miserable – but a little better than being out in the open. At least the autumn sights were beautiful, the turning maples looking like golden lightbulbs against the dark green pines.

The Krauts shelled our neighborhood sporadically, but they didn't waste much ammo on us because their shells plowed deep into the mud before exploding. Unless you were close by, they weren't too much of danger. We were hardly shelling either because very little ammo was getting up to us. At one point we were limited to 10 mortar shells per gun per day, and two belts per machine gun per day.

One night I was sharing coffee with Halls at platoon HQ – which was my bunker about 50 yards behind the center mortar section. A line of men from Able Company had just filed past us toward Germany. The brass from division on down wanted patrols and lots of them.

"You know, Dud," Halls said, "I've got to thank you – sorry, I should be saying 'lieutenant' . . ."

"Yeah? What about?"

"Well, you remember back at Camp Kilmer when two or three of us didn't want to be in mortars because we wouldn't get to see any action?"

I nodded and grinned.

"Well, I thought you were being a panty waste. I'm sorry. I really thank you for insisting on mortars. Honest to God. I really pity the infantry," he added, shaking his head.

"Late each day," he said, "those poor bastards slop through the mud right past us into the woods, like these guys just did. The leader lets me know whether they're headed left to that burnt-out farm, or right to cross the creek, or straight ahead to scout the village on the crest of the ridge . . . or whether they're just going to hunker down to ambush some Kraut patrol.

"Anyway, during the night we'll hearing some firing or a grenade of two. Maybe they'll call us for a few rounds.

"Then before dawn, they call and let us know they're coming back in. Pretty soon somebody in the dark calls out the password and then they come dragging back past us. They look like whipped dogs. Their eyes are all sunken and they're caked with mud. Each boot looks like it's carrying about 10 pounds of mud and it seems like almost every time two of them are helping somebody whose leg or arm or head is wrapped in a muddy, bloody field dressing. Or else they're shy a man.

"Anyway, I just wanted to say 'Thanks' for setting us straight."

# # #

Once we got settled, I went to FDC to find out what they meant by Peter Fox treat. The major looked alarmed and just gave me the old runaround. When I asked Capt. Freeman, he said it was top secret and that if told me he'd have to shoot me.

"Cap'n," I said, "come on, now. That's bullshit. When I was a mere sergeant, I was cleared to hear all the damned top secret details about our invasion plans. So I figure that as an exalted butterbar I'm cleared for this, especially since it's some kind of artillery . . ."

"How the hell do you know that?" he demanded.

"Know what, sir?"

"How do you know that it's artillery?"

So I told him about how FDC called in some kind of howitzer strike that sounded like air bursts. And after that, somebody at FDC called it a Peter Fox treat. "So it sounded to me, Cap'n, like it could have been a timed-on-target barrage. But the shells didn't go off all together. Three or four detonated in succession. Doesn't make sense, sir."

Freeman swore me to secrecy before letting me know that Peter Fox was just a nickname for an invention officially called Pozit -- a top secret fuse for medium and heavy artillery. Gunners could set the fuses to detonate the shells any given distance above ground rather than on the ground.

It took two seconds for the beauty of the proximity fuse to dawn on me.

See, a shell exploding on the ground – especially muddy ground -- digs a hole and sends its shrapnel skywards from the crater. If you've taken cover in a foxhole or just behind a fold in the earth, the explosions may terrify you and jar the hell out of you, but the shrapnel misses you.

But if you get the shell to explode 60 or 70 feet above ground, the shrapnel rips straight down into your old Aunt Sally of a carcass at better than bullet speed – unless you're lucky enough to be inside a stout masonry building or a bunker with a good, thick timber roof.

But the point was that now 155 or 105 howitzer crews could achieve that aerial burst just with a simple fuse setting. It didn't matter if there were trees or not. Likewise with Long Toms and those big bastard 8-inch howitzers.

Unfortunately, in another month we would be in a thick, wooded hell, a killing zone, where the trees enabled Germans to give us tree bursts all the time.

Chapter 63
Nov. 3, 1944 – Hürtgen Forest

I shivered uncontrollably in the dark but at least I could huddle with the lower half of my face buried down inside my jacket. The driver, though, had both hands on the wheel forcing him to embrace the sleet and freezing rain whipping through the track's window.

The guys in back had it no better. A big piece of canvas they rigged as an overhead cover rippled and flapped in the wind so that icy rain tore right in to soak them.

We were on the move. The whole damned Fourth Division was pulling out of line in front of Monschau, moving north and then turning east to attack and capture the Hürtgen Forest.

Rosedale yelled to me from the track bed. "Hey, Lieutenant," he yelled to me. "How do you pronounce the name of this forest? You know, it's got a U with them two dots over it."

"You just purse your lips and give it an 'ew' sound," I said.

"I can't purse my lips. They're too cold!"

The driver broke in, "Then warm your lips on the lieutenant's ass."

I mumbled an obscenity through my jacket.

A light flashed in front of us. Then our lone taped headlight – the other burned out long ago – revealed a soldier clad all in white waving his arms angel-style. I recognized him as a battalion master sergeant.

"Whoa!" he yelled. "Stop here! Dismount and start unloading!"

We all clambered down from the mortar platoon's half-tracks into thick mud under a crust of icy snow. As cold as I was, I was grateful for my Kraut boots. My toes may have been cold, but at least the boots didn't leak.

He pointed to our left. "Sir, get your guns and gear unloaded and off to the side of the road into that area that's taped off. Don't let your people wander past the tapes. The Krauts planted mines all over the place. In about 10 minutes Baker Company will head up front. You'll follow right behind and I'll send a guide who'll take you to your positions."

Shivering and bouncing up and down on our toes was no fun, but it beat the hell out of riding in an ice-glazed half-track . . . until Rosedale spotted the bodies. Off to one side of our square, what looked like a good two dozen pairs of booted feet jutted out from under an ice-covered tarp.

"They ours?"

The sergeant shook his head. "Nope. They're mixed 9th and 28th Divisions. Been getting the crap shot out of them."

One of our replacements, a brand-new guy from New Jersey, yelled, "Well, fuck this shit! They coulda dumped them somewhere else! Jesus! This is bullshit!"

Forster snapped, "Shut the hell up, Sklar! Haven't you ever been to a funeral before?"

"Well, hell yeah, sarge, but this . . ."

"Damn you, it's just like a funeral," Timmer said. "These boys are waiting for a decent burial. If you don't like it, shut your hole and look the other way."

# # #

Baker Company filed past and the guide didn't keep us waiting. We followed Baker's trailing platoon along a badly rutted muddy two-track that trended upward through two steep turns. It was so damned dark we could see little but the snow on the ground and yard-thick tree trunks either side of the two-track.

After what seemed like a quarter mile, the guide separated us from Baker by veering off to follow a long strip of white tape over a sharp rise.

We passed a line of 11 bodies, Americans. They seemed to be a whole squad machine gunned before they'd even been able to get to their positions.

"Poor bastards. It's just like a damn firing squad got them," Halls said.

Once we crested the rise, we had to half-slide down a second steep snowy slope, clinging to trees and boulders to keep our footing, and up another slope just as steep. It seemed like about a half mile. Then the guide whispered, "We're here, sir. So long."

"Dammit, don't leave us until we're situated," I said. "We can't even see what the position is."

"Sir, there's supposed to be a liaison guy here from the 28th Division."

"Bullshit, there's nobody here! So what's the lay-out?"

He raised his arm and pointed in the darkness. "Sir, it's a slit trench that leads uphill thataway. It's zig-zagged so when a Kraut mortar goes off in one section of the trench, it doesn't hit the guys in another. Just be damned sure nobody uses any lights."

"Wait a minute . . ."

But he was gone.

Teeth chattering, Forster, Halls and I had everybody stay in place while we scouted the trench. The minute I stepped into the trench, I felt ice break beneath my boots and I just sighed -- we'd all have icy wet feet in minutes.

We found a bloodied American corporal, literally frozen stiff, who might have been the liaison type.

The snow made it possible to see the trench's outline well enough. It seemed about 150 yards long, one end at the military crest of the reverse slope of a long hill. And the whole thing was in a narrow clearing. Against the sky, we made out the tops of very tall densely packed evergreens on all sides.

We set up the guns at both ends of the trench and in the middle, and spotted the .30s at regular intervals. Forster and I got under a poncho with his flashlight and compass so we found that our trench lay northwest to southeast.

Relying on ponchos and flashlights again, we at least got our guns leveled. I reported in to FDC on the radio but told them we were useless until we could get aiming stakes in the ground. They gave me our position's grid coordinates and warned me to be alert for German patrols.

The remainder of the night passed quietly – except for chattering teeth and the sound of mud sucking at boots, butts or knees or whatever other parts we rested in the trench. The snow and rain let up at dawn, but it stayed cold – right about freezing. That dawn also marked the start of what Forster later said was one of the shortest duty tours on record.

As the sky brightened, shelling began going off in the tops of the trees south of us. The detonations looked like clusters of miniature orange sunrises. All hell broke loose on the ground in the same area, too, with the *braaaap braaap* of MG 42s and the rattling of American 30s. Red, green and white tracers ripped back and forth in the woods. We couldn't do a thing to help because we had no idea which were the Germans or where they were.

The fireworks enabled us to see that our trench lay in a cleared alley – perhaps a fire lane. The nearest trees were maybe 50 feet from our trench, too damned close for comfort.

Timmer, at the upward and far end of the trench got on the radio. "Skipper, I think we got company. Looks like a line of ghosts moving in the woods just opposite us . . . Krauts in white."

"How many?"

"Maybe six. Maybe more."

"Okay. Tell your boys to stay low and keep an eye on them. Don't shoot unless they're in pistol range. Don't use the machine guns unless you absolutely have to. I'd just as soon the rest of the Kraut regiment don't know we're here yet. And whatever you do, don't fire any flares. They'll illuminate us better than the Krauts."

As the light strengthened, we got a good look at our surroundings and they were bad. A huge block-long slash pile of limbs and shattered three trucks lay in the woods immediately south of us. It looked absolutely impenetrable and would make a great shelter for a Kraut assault team. I asked Forster to assign two men to scout the area.

And Halls didn't help my sinking feeling when he sloshed up to me.

"Hey, Dud? Notice something?"

"What?"

"Well, sir, the snow kinda camouflages it, but if you look carefully, the ground all around us looks like a moonscape – big craters with smaller craters inside them, and soup bowl craters, too, from mortars. They're really zeroed in on us. And the way the trench edges are collapsed, I'd say the Krauts have pounded the bejaysus out of this position."

"Yeah, I see that."

"Well, sir, I think whoever the hell was here before us got the shit kicked out of them. And I bet we're next on the target list."

But the day stayed quiet, even though we heard the stammer of machine guns work up to a crescendo in the distance. FDC ordered a dozen fire missions, but then had us stop. Battalion said the fighting was too confused. The Germans had counter-attacked. Some units were falling back but others weren't . . . or couldn't

# # #

Just after dark, a fusillade of explosions detonated along our trench – potato-masher grenades thrown from the woods to the south where the slash piles were. Kraut grenades aren't as powerful as our pineapples, so when we threw our own grenades back, I think we gave better than we got. They charged us three times, but using pistols, carbines and even entrenching tools, we beat them back.

After the last assault, the cordite smell still strong, I made my way up the trench. We'd lost two men killed and at least six wounded, two seriously. One lightly wounded man bragged to me how Cpl. Maus stopped one Kraut.

"The bastard came barreling right into the trench with us, you know? I dasn't shoot 'cause I might hit one of our guys, but Mighty Maus there just yanks off his fucking helmet and bashes the Kraut's face with it. Knocked that big bastard back against the side of the trench so I could plug him with my .45."

Four dead Germans lay huddled at or just beyond the edge of the trench. We helped ourselves to their white helmet covers and divvied up their white jackets and pants. The more we blended with the snow, the better.

Chapter 64
Sunday, Nov. 4, 1944 – Hürtgen Forest

At dawn Forster came down the trench to meet with me. "Well, maybe I've got good news. I think I spotted a great target." He said he'd wormed his way to the actual crest of our hill to see the top of a higher wooded hill about a mile northeast. He pointed it out on our terrain map.

"Dud, I saw people moving up there. I bet it's them that called down all the fire on the woods behind us last night."

"Well, Mike, they've got our position zeroed in so if we hit them, we'll catch hell. But they ain't paying us these big salaries here to just sit on our asses. Make sure all your people are ready to take cover."

I called it in to FDC, giving the map coordinates. They ordered us to do a fire mission on what they agreed must be an important Kraut OP.

We fired three registration rounds. Saw them bloom *ka-whuff* on the hill's crest and then fired for effect – four rounds from each of the six guns, Willie Peter mixed in.

About five minutes later, concussion knocked me flat as a huge blast of black smoke erupted between the two guns at the center of the trench. It so stunned me I couldn't do much but turn over and curl up in the slush at the bottom of our trench. The next 15 minutes are a blur but I knew the Kraut gunners were getting tree bursts off to our sides because people near me grunted or screamed when either steel or wood shrapnel slapped into their backs.

The barrage was mortars because there was none of the rushing howl that preceeds howitzer shelling. Just sudden thunderous blasts that tore us apart. I got enough of my wits together to try to report it to FDC but shrapnel shattered the radio.

When the shelling quit, I staggered upright and stared stupidly at a 10-inch wood splinter as thick as a fountain pen sticking right through my left hand, glove and all. Thinking I was the only survivor, I came very close to falling apart. But a few heads began peeking above the edges of the trench.

All our guns were destroyed. Forster waved with his left hand. His right sleeve was torn and bloody. Halls, Timmer and Maus survived, all with minor wounds like mine. Frost was badly hurt and shrapnel had torn Sklar into three distinct pieces. The man who hated the sight of corpses now was a corpse.

One by one, I shuffled through the slush to the other radios -- all destroyed. Forster reported 12 survivors, all wounded, three seriously. Too, all of us were soaked and freezing.

"Mike," I said, "we've got to abandon ship. Now."

He just nodded and started to organize us. I don't know why the Krauts didn't assault us because they could have wiped us out in two minutes. Maybe they felt the way I did – the position was too damned dangerous.

If they'd had a patrol out, they could have ambushed us as we worked our wounded up and down those Godawful slopes back to the two-track.

I was deeply ashamed about our defeat until we actually got to the two-track. It was crawling with wounded and defeated men.

Carrying our wounded was nearly impossible because tank treads had chewed the road, one side of a rut being almost two feet higher than the other, now frozen brick-solid. The footing was incredibly difficult for the stretcher-bearers and agony for the wounded.

Forster and I had to rig three rifle slings behind our necks and over our shoulders to carry the foot of Frost's stretcher. I couldn't grasp with my impaled left hand and Forster's right forearm – spitted with a 2-foot splinter -- was useless.

We were almost unable to stand by the time we got back to battalion. The S3 told me Baker Company had started an assault and took 40 per cent casualties. Among the dead was Capt. Freeman who had gone up to support Baker with Dog Company's machine gun teams. Those men also were dead.

"Christ," I said. "Dog's practically wiped out?"

"You're in command of what's left . . . at least temporarily."

"Great." I said and showed him my hand. "I need to see the doc. All of us do."

"It'll be a while," he said, grimacing at the splinter. "The docs are kind of busy right now."

My hand was so cold it was numb. "Sir, do me a favor."

"What?"

"Just grab this splinter – right here by my palm – and yank the damned thing out."

He did and I hardly felt a thing except that my glove was filling with blood. So I just went on. "Sir, we're also going to need replacements and all new equipment. Every damn thing -- radios, guns, machine guns, the whole fucking shebang."

"Dud, just get your people to the aid station and wait to get treated. When you get your hand cleaned up and bandaged, we'll go over everything."

"Sir," I said, "I don't think you have any idea of what this place is like."

"Dud, I know exactly what it's like. But Division and Corps don't," he said bitterly. "They don't come up here much. They just radio orders to us because it's too cold and muddy here and they might catch cold. And they know we don't have champaign or steak for them, either."

# # #

A week later, Forster's arm was still in a grimy sling and we both were hacking and coughing with the galloping crud. The whole Army seemed to have it. Pointing to the map Forster said, "Dud, this is impossible. It's an impenetrable mess. I don't think Division has any idea what it's ordering this regiment to do."

"What is it, Mike?"

"The place they want us to site the mortars. It's behind about a 1,000-square-foot pile of tree splinters, each one about a foot thick and maybe 20 feet long. And about 150 yards beyond it are three Kraut bunkers with MGs. A fucking mouse couldn't get through there alive.

"But the main thing, Dud, is there's no goddamn overhead clearance. Even if we could emplace, we wouldn't dare shoot. It'd be suicide. There's little enough left of us as it is."

He was right. Timmer, Halls and Maus were all that was left -- each with one gun and two green-as-grass replacements. In fact, we were all that remained of the battalion's heavy weapons company.

Forster said. "If they want mortar support, they're going to let us find our own sites . . . maybe where the shelling has cut the woods down."

It took a bellowing 10-minute argument for me to get G3's permission to for us pick our own emplacement. With Freeman dead, he was trying to run our show without knowing that much about it. Halls found the right sit later -- a stretch of blasted land in the forest's south flank. It was in the defilade shadow of a 50-foot granite cliff. No trees overhead and it didn't look like counter battery fire could drop closer than 100 yards from us.

It was freezing, snowy and muddy – so muddy that as we fired at first, the recoil pushed the guns' baseplates and bipods deeper into the ground. That threw off our aim. So we had to anchor the bipods and base plates on thick logs. But there was no shortage of timber in the Hürtgen.

Our site was within sight of the main supply route.

"God this is sickening," Timmer told me. "One minute you see a half-strength infantry company follow a couple of tank destroyers up the MSR. Then you hear the fight. Then the mortars and the Kraut counterattack. A couple of hours later, the remnants drag back down the MSR on stretchers. And you can smell the smoke from the burning tank destroyers."

We got new replacements and so did the infantry companies. But . . .

Maus came to me about it. "Sorry to bother you, Dud, but this is driving me nuts. These kids show up with four weeks of basic and that's it. They know how to salute and that's about it. So, okay, once they get their wits about them, we can train them on mortars pretty quickly. But all they're doing in infantry squads is walking up and getting killed. Some of them hardly know how to load their rifles."

We continued like that for five solid weeks. We emplaced forward again and again, losing seven replacements who hadn't learned to duck or shoot, nothing compared to the toll upon the infantry companies.

Corps wanted to capture Hürtgen Forest and the Krauts wanted to keep it. I never understood why the generals committed us to such a bloodbath for that 10 square miles of worthless woods.

Finally, the artillery and what remained of the infantry killed what was left of the Krauts dug into the cellars of an obliterated village called Grosshau. That so-called victory brought Fourth Division – now a shell of itself -- to the east edge of the forest.

Then they pulled us out.

Roll call was kind of depressing. It produced six responses – six out of an original platoon of 40.

Flogging our memories and comparing notes, Forster, Maus, Halls and I figured that maybe 10 lightly wounded people would link up with us some time in the future

Compared to some outfits, we were lucky.

We were wool-gathering about what to do when we heard the Division was being trucked north to Luxembourg.

The trucks carrying 1st Battalion made a pretty short convoy.

Chapter 65
Dec. 15, 1944 – A Short Break

Climbing the narrow outside staircase was pretty tricky. Maybe six generations ago someone built it for little Napoleonic-era folk. But this 20th century American had to place his big feet sideways on the very short stair treads.

The treads were icy, too. But the delicious aroma of breakfast ham seeping outdoors beckoned so strongly that my eagerness made me stumble. As I recovered my footing at the door, a gasp of female anguish made me forget food. I opened the door and ducked inside the little kitchen.

"Jenkins!" I bellowed. "Get your muddy fucking boots off that lady's table. Honest to God, you have the manners of a dog!"

At least it wasn't rape

The section's newest replacement gunner tilted his chair forward, dropping his feet to the floor with a double thump. He looked up at me in anger and doused his cigarette butt in a delicate tea cup, eliciting another feminine gasp and making me boil. I don't know a thing about dinner China, but I do know my Mom loves delicate things, and I assumed most *hausfraus* felt the same.

"Dammit Jenkins, the lady of the house got out her best dishes and cups for you. She's treating you like an honored guest but you're using her china like it's a barracks butt can!"

I bowed to the grandmotherly woman at the stove. *"Bitte, verseihen Sie uns."* Please forgive us. She returned a tremulous smile as a tear rolled down her powdered cheek.

I glowered back at him. "Jenkins, your pass is revoked as of now. Hike your ass back to your gun and eat some C rations. And next time you want a nice home-cooked breakfast, try acting like a gentleman instead of a hog. And start by taking off your boots outside!"

Jenkins snarled, "Yes, Sir!" and clumped out the door into the snowy morning. I heard him stumble and half fall down the stair.

"What a jerk," I said, stepping back out to the porch to shuck off my boots. As I came back to sit at the table, I apologized again. And meant it.

This little Luxembourg hamlet had opened its homes to our mortar sections. It gave us the first chance in six weeks actually to be both dry and warm. Yet Jenkins acted like a conqueror instead of a guest.

When the trucks dropped us off yesterday, we emplaced the guns in three sections a half mile apart northeast of the village.

We were supposed to support the remnants of Easy Company, all of 95 men, covering about three miles of the west bank of the Sauer River, the border between Germany and Luxembourg.

That averaged about one rifleman to defend a frontage a football field long. Not that it seemed to matter, because it was supposed to be a quiet sector where we could rest and refit from Hürtgen.

I was issuing the men 12-hour passes. For a few packs of cigarettes, a guy could soak off a month and a half of mud, shit and blood. If his nightmares weren't too bad, he could catch some shut-eye between honest-to-God clean sheets on an actual mattress. By this morning, though, at least some villagers started grumbling about us.

The mayor, in whose home Jenkins bunked, was upset. He said that for two years, the Nazis had forced the villagers to quarter German soldiers. But he claimed the *landsers* were polite, quiet and very neat and clean.

In his odd mixture of German, Dutch, English and French, he said that Americans not only were very noisy and disrespectful, but also filthy and smutty.

It took work, but I finally got across to him that the German boarders were garrison troops.

By contrast, my boys had been through six months of combat, having to live in mud like pigs, while battle killed their friends right and left. And if they talked loud it was because their ears and nerves were shot. Too, probably a third of them had walking pneumonia.

I apologized again for Jenkins, a clod by nature, and said that after my turn for a square meal and a snooze, I'd send guests who were university men – muddy and loud, yes, but polite and cultured. The mayor brightened at that and so did Frau Mayor when he explained.

When I dragged myself out of bed at dusk, I released Halls and Forster. They were overdue. Sleet and freezing rain had iced their helmets and greatcoats. Their faces were raw from the wind and they were chilled to the bone. And now it was snowing from clouds so low they cloaked the treetops.

The only winter gear to reach us so far were big goulashes that fit over our boots.

So to survive the cold, we wrapped scraps of blanket over our heads before we put on our helmets. Some of us had captured German snow camouflage capes, and some had mere rags for makeshift gloves. The Army actually had issued World War I gear to some of the replacements – thin wool uniforms that literally were moth-eaten. And the 25-year-old leather of the doughboy boots cracked at the instep, so that icy water seeped in.

As Halls and Forster took off, they waved and grinned. Reconciling myself to a cold night with half the section, I checked in by radio with FDC and with the other two mortar sections.

Maus, in charge of the first section a half mile northwest reported talking with a jumpy Charlie Company officer.

The Krauts – who normally set up a few listening posts on our side of the river -- suddenly seemed to be patrolling very aggressively.

He also said an Easy Company patrol returning the east bank claimed to have seen stacks of rubber rafts plus dozens of artillery pieces set up in battery ready to fire.

I passed the word to Timmer who was heading the section to the south. I also alerted the S3, Maj. Cavanaugh, who said this was the second call he'd received about the rafts. He was passing it on to Division.

Unfortunately, Division G2 didn't bother to pass the word to Corps or, if they did, Corps took no notice.

Maybe they were playing bridge back and sipping champagne in their plush chateau HQs.

The night just grew colder and snowier.

We had nothing to do but stamp our feet and flog our arms and chests with our freezing hands.

Chapter 66
Dec. 16, 1944 – Hornet Nests

It came as a cold shock at 0530 when artillery fire erupted behind us to the south. Screaming Meemies tore above us headed west, landing with their thunderous explosions to our left rear. The frozen ground literally bucked with the impacts.

Definitely not patrol action.

Artillery flashes flickered through the trees as battle roar rose and drummed in a giant arc around to the east and then northeast. It sounded just like the assault we heard at Mortain back in July – thumping artillery, the crack of tank guns, the popcorn sound of distant rifle fire and rattle and stammer of machine guns.

Then the Krauts turned on the lights.

They angled antiaircraft searchlights up into the clouds, creating a glow for their assault troops and tank drivers to see the way. In fact, it became bright enough that we could make out faces and even the dials on our watches. We clearly saw Halls and Forster still pulling on their gear as they galloped to us from the village.

They found me cussing a blue streak because the Krauts were jamming our frequencies with Third Reich marches. Through *Die Fahne Hoch* and the *Horst Wessel Lied* I couldn't contact FDC or Maus or Timmer and it scared me shitless. So I had no idea what was happening. Or where.

"Now what do we do?" Halls asked.

I took a deep breath to steady myself. "Guys," I said, "I think this is where unofficial Rule No. One in the infantry applies -- do something, even if it's wrong.

"So, men, we got us two half-tracks here, each with two machine guns, maybe 30,000 rounds of ammo plus two mortars and their ammo. We'll move forward toward Easy Company and maybe see if we can fill one of their gaps. At least we can give some fire support with machine guns and if we spot targets on our own, we'll mortar the bastards."

We mounted up and traveled no more than 500 yards along a fire break when an Easy Company sergeant with a squad of riflemen flagged us down. They were headed away from the river.

"Sir, am I glad to see you! I got orders to set up a road block and we don't even have a machine gun. We got nothing but rifles and two bazookas."

"A roadblock?"

"Yessir. My cap'n told me the Krauts are pouring across the Sauer in at least battalion strength. Maybe regimental. He thinks it's a multi-division assault. The bastards overran all our outposts."

"So what road are you supposed to block, sergeant?"

"Any one that I can find," he said. "The captain is doing the same with two other squads. And he sent us and another squad out to block any road, paved or dirt. He said we can jam up the Kraut columns right back into Germany. Maybe give our reserves some time to organize and come up. Sets them up good for air attacks tomorrow."

With clouds low and snow falling, I doubted we'd have any air support. But I just said, "Okay, sergeant, let's find us a road."

# # #

We proceeded down the firebreak. The sergeant knew his business. He had a point man 100 yards out front and one on each flank. About 20 minutes later, the left flanker came trotting back breathless. He said he'd climbed a wooded rise overlooking a westbound road filled with traffic . . . Kraut traffic.

Forster and the sergeant went to the ridge, and checked the road. They came back to report infantry on foot plus two self-propelled guns, some horse-drawn artillery, and some Kraut officers in two American jeeps. Right now the column was shuffling at a crawl.

"Sir,' the sergeant said, "it's a damned shooting gallery. We can set up a hasty ambush."

Forster stood beside him nodding. "I couldn't believe it, Dud," he said, "but they've got no flankers out. No security at all. We could dismount the mortars and bring the tracks up overlooking the column and hose the hell out of them and then mortar them when they run to ground north of the road. And we'll be getting tree bursts."

"Yeah, but it's gonna be like kicking a hornet's nest," the sergeant said. "So maybe we give them a hotfoot first. We could hit them SP guns with bazookas. That'll start a hell of a fire and block the road for tanks and trucks for hours. And maybe it'll panic the infantry."

"Let's get moving," I said. "Forster, I'll take the HQ track to the left and you take t'other to the right – 200-yard separation. Halls, you're back here with the mortars. Start firing right after we do. Now listen, Forster, the instant the bazookas blow those self-propelled guns, take out the officers in the jeeps."

The sergeant sent his two bazooka teams sneaking down the ridge. As they crawled into range, I ordered Jenkins to get on the HQ track .50.

"Jenkins, your first job is to kill all the officers you see."

With a wolfish grin, he looked at me. "*All* the officers?"

"No, wiseass, try to concentrate on the German officers – at first anyway. Shoot me and you lose your stripe."

"Jeeez, what a killjoy."

The Germans, a bunch of kids, were singing some marching song as they waited to move. Minutes later, the bazooka teams kicked off what I called Operation Traffic Jam.

# # #

Both SPs exploded in blinding flashes which quickly changed to billowing orange gasoline flames, turning the cloud bases crimson. And Jenkins and I joined in from our track. The man was a crud. You wouldn't invite him to tea or even a beer blast in a bowling alley, but he sure had a fine touch with a .50.

With him on the .50 and me on the .30, we plowed that road with cascades of bullets. Tracers ricocheted crazily as the slugs ripped through the troops' ranks. They didn't know what to do, so we were able to kill them by the dozens . . . maybe the hundreds. The dumb brats in their sharp gray uniforms just fell over like so many toys. We and the mortars killed the horses pulling supply wagons.

"Listen to them Krauts scream," Jenkins said, with manic laugh. "They're calling for their mothers. Jesus!"

Long since then, I've read that little pockets of Americans here and there upset the Krauts' complicated timetables. Sounds neat and tied up, but ambushes are strictly slaughter. By rights, the *landsers* should have run like rabbits, especially once ammo in the SP guns started cooking off in big nasty fireballs.

But as the sergeant predicted, it was like kicking a hornet's nest.

Tough NCOs in the column organized bases of fire with some of their MGs. Now green and white tracers joined the mix and 7.92 bullets began taking out our boys by twos and threes. Meanwhile, some clear-headed *feldwebel* got a group of survivors to spread out and start working around our flanks.

I had to start shooting to our left as Kraut squads began climbing up our ridge through the trees. I couldn't see the other track, but I had to believe the same thing was happening there.

Soon, an MG burst tore through the side of the track bed, shredding Jenkins' lower body.

As he collapsed, his body dragged gun's breech end down, firing tracers straight up into the clouds. It took a second to unlock his dead hands from the spade grips. After I pulled his body aside, I started sweeping the big gun over the Krauts' firing line.

Halls' mortars kept sounding *thonk-thonk* behind us. He had switched targets away from the road. Using low charges at a very high angle, he started dropping the rounds into the trees on our flanks.

It seemed like seconds later that Forster fired a flare to break off the action. A panzerfaust had taken out his track. So we got the hell out of there in my track, carrying Forster, Halls and his guns, and five survivors from the Easy Company squad. The Charlie Company sergeant wasn't one of them.

We made our way west on 2-tracks through the woods for about three hours before we heard machine guns again and saw a billowing orange blaze dead ahead of us.

It was another American ambush. They'd set up in an L along a nice paved road. A half-dozen trucks were blazing amid the litter of bodies in *feldgrau* uniforms.

But our timing was bad. Just as we arrived to help, the Germans began counterattacking with mortars and MGs and the ambushers were retreating because their ammo was running low. We also were down to maybe 2,000 rounds, so we couldn't do much more than half-cover their retreat.

We did our best until a burst of machine gun fire sounded close behind us. One of the rounds hit Hall's helmet, tossing it 20 feet in front of us. A very American-sounding voice said, "Okay, cowboys. Drop them shootin' irons and reach for the sky!"

Oh shit!

We turned around slooowly, hands up.

We were staring down from the track at a squad of *landsers* standing in a semicircle, covering us with submachine guns and rifles. A couple of them were grinning and bouncing potato-mashers on their palms.

Chapter 67
Dec. 17, 1944 – POWs

It's impossible to describe the instant deep internal chill of finding yourself a POW. The shock rockets right to gut and heart.

Smirking at the look on our faces was a tall Wehrmacht lieutenant in scruffy white overalls, duckbill cap tilted at a dramatic angle. He stood at the center of the white-robed German squad.

He repeated, "I said, 'Reach!' You boys understand?"

The slamming of my heart made me gulp, but for the benefit of my men, I tried to keep it light. "*Herr Leutnant,*" I told the Kraut, "I beg your pardon, but I think maybe you've watched too many Tom Mix westerns."

"Oh, no, Lieutenant," he said, now with a genuine smile. "I myself have read all your westerns . . . *The Virginian,* and every one of the books of Zane Gray and Louis L'Amour. And in English, not translation. I'm very sorry the both authors died."

Forster piped up with a grin, "Sir, didn't you even watch any Hopalong Cassidy movies?"

"No, sergeant." The officer chuckled, pointing his Luger negligently in our direction. "For me no Hollywood, Just the reading." He kept up the conversation we jumped down from the track and his men kicked our weapons aside. Then they searched us, stole our watches and billfolds and lined us to head down to the road.

"Head 'em up, move 'em out. Is that not the right phrase, lieutenant?"

"Yup, partner."

He chuckled again and fell into step beside me. Leaning close he said, "Sir, I give you good counsel to keep your men very correct around our major. He is very furious at what you made here and he is a very hard man. He has no sentiment. He is not chivalrous like your good Texas sheriffs."

# # #

About five minutes after we got down to the road, I saw what he meant. The major, a little guy with Himmler-style glasses, looked to be in a rage because so many of his troops either lay dead on the road or still were tossing and screaming in agony.

Picking his way among the bodies, he walked up to us, his face working. He turned to one of our guards armed with a strange-looking weapon, and pointed at the two wounded sitting on the pavement beside us.

"*Schiessen sie!*"

I was mentally translating the unbelievable command when the guard fired a burst through the head of first one and then the other.

First I gagged. Then I blared, "You bastard! Why the hell did you do that?" A guard hit me in the center of my back with his rifle butt, knocking me to my knees.

As I glared up at the major, he raised his eyebrows. "*Leutnant*, be very careful how you speak of officers of the Wehrmacht. Very careful."

He pointed to the two bodies. "This is only logical. You have many long hard kilometers to march. We cannot carry those wounded men who cannot march." He nodded to the other guards, pointing around us at other wounded Americans, turned about and walked away. The guards casually began murdering the other wounded.

Twenty minutes later, the Krauts had two dozen of us marching east along the road's shoulder opposite the direction of their column of troops, tanks and guns. Two guards were behind us and two limped on either flank. All of them seemed lightly wounded.

# # #

As the day drew on, Halls seemed to slip completely down into the dumps. His head was lowered and he was muttering. Instead of walking he was shuffling in his goulashes, often stumbling. I didn't feel much better. Forster, though, still was furious at the murders. "We've got to escape," he murmured.

"Yeah, well . . ." The flanking guard next to me whirled his weapon toward Foster snarling "*Ruhig!*" Quiet! As he turned, however, he flinched and nearly fell.

I asked, "Comrade, are you wounded? *Haben sie Wunde?*"

He turned away, saying '*Ruhig!*" again.

The guards apparently needed frequent stops, often walking us off the road so they could rest in the edge of the woods. The German column itself now had begun moving steadily thanks to the urging of NCOs who were shouting and blowing whistles.

But traffic jammed again when what looked like German staff cars began passing the column by driving down the shoulder. The passengers wore peaked officer's hats and overcoats with fur collars. They glanced incuriously at us.

Once they passed, the guards just kept us in the edge if the woods. Forster murmured, "Our guards either are hurting or goldbricking."

"Or both," I said.

The guard who snapped at us earlier, dropped his pants to the knees, revealing a good-sized puncture high on the fleshy inside of his right thigh. He was trying to re-tie a handkerchief around the bloody hole.

Remembering the conversation with the Afrika Korps medic back in Algeria, I whistled and told him, "*Comrade! Du bist ja ganz glüchlich, eh?*"

Forster peered at the injury, pointed a bit higher and joined in, "Wow, *mein Freund!* You came close to losing the family treasure."

The other guards laughed and the Kraut gave a sickly grin as he kept messing with the blood-soaked handkerchief.

"That won't work," I said, standing up and reaching for my first aid pouch on the back of my cartridge belt.

All the guards raised their guns, but relaxed when I ripped the big field dressing out of its foil pouch. They raised their gun muzzles again when I started walking toward the wounded guard, but I held my hands well above my head, displaying the dressing.

I knelt in the snow before the Kraut, placed the dressing against the wound and motioned with my head for one of his buddies to help pull the ties around his thigh and knot them.

"There!" I said, standing up. "That's better isn't it? *Besser, ja?*"

Groping beneath my shirt, I brought out my last pack of Luckies and offered them to the guard and his buddies. The guard put a cigarette in his mouth, hitched up his pants and then produced a stolen Zippo. He lit my cigarette and then his.

As he raised his suspenders to get his pants back in place, we smoked, chatted and relaxed. It was the comradely air I wanted, hoping now they'd see us as ordinary working soldiers, not inconveniences to be shot out of hand.

"Wie heissen Sie?"

He introduced himself as Bodo. Leaning wearily against a tree, he said he didn't want to fight any more. I nodding and said I understood -- that I was glad to be a POW. No more war for me, brother.

I asked whether he had a girl and he grinned and showed me the photo of a sturdy-looking blonde having more than her share of bosom and jaw. I gave a low whistle of appreciation. Forster asked if he could see it, and gave out with a deep "Wow. Looks like Betty Grable."

Bodo nodded vigorously. *"Jawhol!* Great legs."

I asked if I could have my wallet back to show him Katherine's picture and the photos of Mom and Sis. He persuaded the guards to return all the wallets. I asked if he could give me the name and address of a nice German girl and he actually apologized when he said that was impossible.

Finally, I got him to tell me about the ugly-looking weapon he carried. It looked like it was assembled from parts in a junkyard and had a funny little pin jutting beneath the sight parallel to the barrel.

He called it a *Sturmgewher* which I translated to myself as "attack rifle" and pulled out the magazine to show me the stubby bullets – far shorter than the Wehrmacht's regular long rifle ammo. God knows he carried enough of them in the rifle's big curved magazine. As we'd seen, it could shoot either as a rifle or a submachine gun.

Our guards let us chat as we resumed our march through the falling snow toward the German border. We even sang *Silent Night* once and they sang *Stille Nacht* along with us.

Chapter 68
Dec. 18, 1944 – Escape

Our chance came about dusk the second day. They'd fed us nothing and we were hellishly cold even though the snow quit. "My God," Forster said, "It's colder than a witch's tit!"

"Tell me about it," Halls said.

"I already did."

"Shut up!"

I said, "God, why are you always arguing? Both of you shut up."

We still were on a road bisecting thick forest. As in France, the Krauts had dug roadside slit trenches about every 200 feet. Perhaps a mile ahead the road bent upward to snake around a large, cleared hill with barn-sized rock outcrops.

I don't know who he was, but I'm forever grateful to the commander of some American howitzer or Long Tom battery that started firing salvos of 155 mm shells at the column.

It started with the silk-ripping roar of the incoming registration round. A brilliant light flashed in air about 200 yards ahead of us and maybe 70 feet off the ground. For the barest instant, it lighted its own ball of silvery shrapnel slicing down into the column.

Air bursts! Pozit fuses.

Forster, Halls and I and two dozen other guards and POWs dove off the road into the ditch and the slit trench.

"Dud! Halls! Over here!" Forster spotted a corrugated drain beneath the road. Like crabs on a beach, we scrabbled into it. Bodo, eyes like saucers, tried to join us. His got his head and shoulders just inside the culvert, when the next blast made him convulse and scream. Shrapnel pulped his exposed back and legs.

Halls yanked the *Strumgehwer* from Bodo's death grip, reversed the weapon and shot him in the face.

"Poor Bodo," Forster shouted over artillery bursts.

Halls said, "Hey, screw it." Halls twisted in the claustrophobic drain to yank ammo from the German's corpse.

"Good job, Halls," I yelled. "When the barrage stops, we run for it. If you see them, grab a couple more of these weapons."

With each blast, shrapnel smacked the road over our heads. The exploding shells alternately sucked air in and out of the drain, making us feel like we were in a pulsating hurricane. Then in the dark we felt warmth, liquid warmth, beneath us.

"God almighty," Halls yelled through the noise. "I thought I was pissing myself but it's blood!"

"Blood?"

"Yeah! Got to be. It's from the road. It's running two inches deep, for God's sake!" He tried to raise himself up from it, but the culvert had too little room.

"At least it ain't a manure pile," Forster yelled.

"And be damned glad it ain't your blood," I bellowed.

In the subfreezing temperatures the blood in the drain rapidly chilled to cherry-colored slush. But even though it was horrifying and soaked and chilled us to the core, the screaming above us between blasts muted any bitching.

When the bombardment ended, we gave the gunners two minutes to resume shooting – an old mortar battery trick designed to catch people emerging from cover. When they didn't, Halls used his feet to push Bodo's corpse out of the drain's mouth. Then we backed out of the drain and started crawling for the woods.

Dusk is the worst time of day for vision and the smoke from burning vehicles screened us. But even if it hadn't, I don't think anybody would have given a damn. A quarter mile of that column looked like a snake flattened by a cement truck – except snakes don't scream or claw at each other.

Halls grabbed a rifle lying beside a screaming *landser*. I picked up a *Sturmgewher* and ammo pouches. But then I jumped, terrified, when a minced Wehrmacht officer beside me mewed, just like a kitten.

I panicked and jumped up and ran like mad.

Forster passed me while Halls lumbered along in the rear. Three other Americans came with us. We ran deep into the woods and then, after hugging and slapped each other's backs, turned west and kept marching.

Over the next week we came across four other escaping American POWs plus a Kraut deserter who was quivering like a tuning fork. He couldn't seem to talk. After we searched him, we didn't care as long as he stayed out of our way.

We came across four battle sites and were able to relieve some Kraut corpses of zip-up snow overalls. We also found rations – mostly brick-hard German black bread. Some butter would have been nice, but it kept us going. We also liberated some handy pieces of Kraut gear – a kind of a scarf covering head and neck, the Kraut version of a balaclava.

I kept hoping to shoot a deer, but I think the battle around us made them take cover. A couple of times we steered past what sounded like platoon-size firefights.

Chapter 69
Christmas Day, 1944 – Almost Free Again

Dawn found us huddled half-way up a knoll trying not to freeze in a beautiful Christmas scene pine grove – clear air, perfect blue sky, brilliant sunshine on snow-laden branches, and bitter, bitter cold.

"I don't know the temp," Forster said, "but when your breath freezes on your stubble like yours is, Dud, you figure the mercury's mighty low."

Just as we got up to move out, a burst of machine gun fire made us flop face down in the snow.

"That's a Tommy gun," Halls said. "You can't mistake that. These are Americans." He stood, hands up and waved. "Don't shoot! Don't shoot! We're Americans!" They fired another burst at us anyway and we also heard a couple of M1s bark.

The guys all started yelling. I bellowed, "Shut up! I'm the officer. I'll speak for us."

I stood up, hands up. "Hey! Please don't shoot. We're Americans – escaped POWs trying get back to the 8th Infantry. And do you have any rations? We haven't had much to eat except some fucking black bread."

They rose out of the snow and brush and shocked me by shouting *Hände Hoch!* Some very serious eyes in grimy unshaven faces were trained on us. So were their rifle muzzles. The sergeant leading the patrol wouldn't listen when I told him we were from the 8th Infantry.

"Bullshit!" he said. Keep your hands up and your yap shut. We're within an inch of shooting you right here."

"Why, for Christ's sake? I command the mortar platoon in Dog Company, First battalion, 8th Infantry. The Krauts captured us and we escaped during a barrage. We've been hiking through the woods four days now."

"Sure! Keep your damned hands up and you can tell it all to the MPs and CIC."

That was it.

He wouldn't listen to another word and he ordered his men to shoot if any of us tried anything funny. One of them tried to argue saying we sure sounded American.

"The jokers is wearing Kraut gear and was carrying Kraut weapons," he said. "That's evidence."

I asked, "Evidence of what, sergeant? I mean, if we were Nazis infiltrating as Americans, wouldn't we be carrying American equipment?"

"Shut the fuck up!"

They kept us covered, hands on our heads, for the two hours it took to work back to their HQ, 2nd battalion 12th Infantry.

The patrol turned us over to some surly MPs who herded us into a barbed wire cage separate from their Kraut POWs. It had no roof, so we spent the whole night hugging ourselves and constantly rocking up and down on toes and walking in circles to keep our feet from freezing.

When they gave us each a box of C rations in the morning, Halls complained that the food looked as if was packed during the Civil War. Our MP guard said that if Halls didn't quit bitching, he'd do a Gene Krupa drum roll on his head with a night stick.

Halls shut up.

It wasn't till late that day that we heard what was going on.

It seems that when the Krauts began their offensive, they infiltrated some English-speaking troops in captured jeeps through the lines. They also dropped in some parachutists all supposedly to create chaos behind allied lines. It led everybody to interrogate anybody else that he didn't know.

We even heard that some GI stopped Gen. Bradley's jeep. The man demanded that the general prove that he was American by naming the capitol city of Illinois. When Bradley answered "Springfield," the guy started arguing that it was Chicago, but let the general go on anyway.

To the extent of that confusion, the German plan worked.

It took me at least 20 minutes to stop shivering when the 4th Division counterintelligence interrogator finally brought me into his heated tent. It was great to feel warm again – so great that I didn't want to leave even after convincing him we were neither deserters nor Kraut agents.

"I hope you'll talk to those bastard MPs about keeping us out in the open all night."

The CIC officer smirked. "Lieutenant, you're lucky as hell that patrol didn't kill you. The whole army is in a rage."

He said a Kraut tank column way to the north captured a supply convoy of Americans at a crossroads. "So then they lined up all the drivers and passengers in the snow, mowed them down with machine guns and then used pistols to finish off the wounded. As a result, we hear a lot of the troops say they're no longer taking prisoners. So you're lucky. Merry Christmas."

"Thanks. Peace on earth, good will toward men, right?"

"Yeah, sure. Now tell me about the Kraut major who ordered your wounded murdered. No idea what his name was?"

"Nope, but I'd recognize the little bastard in a minute. He looked a lot like those like those pictures you see of Himmler."

# # #

They ran us past the medics who found that all of us had touches of frostbite and that our feet that were on the verge of losing lots of badly puckered skin. That's why it hurt so much to walk.

Thanks again to the MPs who kept us outdoors all night.

The field hospital sent us to a rest station. We went in through the tent flap to see dozens of guys lying on double bunks and on the floor, all with their feet propped up. At first I wondered why their boots were still on but then Halls turned to me, horrified. He whispered, "Oh, my God, look! Their feet are black."

So they were. The toes and the balls of their feet were black and so swollen they looked like hideous clown shoes, relieved only by the little cotton balls nurses had wedged between the toes. I instantly recognized the smell of gangrene. I'd encountered it in North Africa. And, damn him, one of them was mewing from the pain.

"That's from deep frostbite," a nurse said. "Why are you boys here?"

Forster turned to leave. "Let me out. I'm ashamed to even be in here."

"Wait," I said, grabbing his arm. "Nurse, if we could just get some dry socks, we'll get out of your hair."

She just pointed through the tent flap at another tent. We hurried off to it, finding inside large piles brand-new winter foot gear. The supply corporal in charge looked harassed. "Look, Sir, all this stuff just got here. Straight from the US of A. So help yourself but please ask your guys not to leave your crappy old boots and socks behind. I got enough worries."

"Fuck your worries," I said. "Boys, help yourselves."

Dry shod at last with new socks, dry boots and snowpacs to go over them, we reported to battalion headquarters.

The whole regiment was changed.

We found out that Col. Van Fleet had received his star and now was second-in-command of a division. Fourth Division itself had a new commander because the docs had shipped Gen. Barton stateside with double pneumonia and a suspected heart attack.

In our battalion, all but one company commander was dead, yet to be replaced. They said Maus, now a sergeant, was in command of the half-strength mortar platoon.

But several NCOs and clerks were giving us funny looks.

Finally I spotted and waved to Svoboda, now a sergeant major. When he saw me his eyes about popped out of his head. "Dud – sorry, lieutenant -- what the hell are you doing here, sir?"

"We were captured and then escaped. I thought you'd be happy to have the Mortar Forkers back . . . what's left of us."

He pulled me aside to his desk and whispered. "Who all is with you?"

"Well, Forster and Halls plus some riflemen from another division. What's the deal?"

"Keep your voice down, sir. Now didn't Halls and Forster testify in The Dick's trial?"

"Yeah, why?"

"Well, Dud, Capt. Schiltz is back, only now he's a fucking major and he's been looking for you guys. All of you."

"*What*? The bastard's supposed to be in prison."

"Yeah, well. It didn't quite work out that way."

Svoboda explained that The Dick's father-in-law was a powerhouse on the Senate Armed Services Committee and a close political buddy of the Secretary of War and supposedly a friend of FDR.

"So do they all take hot soapy showers together?"

Whispering fiercely, Svoboda said, "Lieutenant, please shut up and listen. The politico jump-started The Dick's automatic appeal and somehow got his conviction set aside on some technicality. So now the prick is back in theater with 4th Division HQ, freshly promoted to major in the Inspector General's office.

"Sir," Svoboda said, "he's got a hard-on for the people who testified against him and he's in a position to screw up the careers of a lot of officers who are brand-new and don't know what happened. You got nobody in the regiment or the division to run interference for you."

"Maybe I could just shoot the son-of-a-bitch."

"Hell, then it would be you going to Leavenworth for sure. But I've got an idea. How about we get you and your boys transferred the hell out of here? New divisions are coming into this theater every damned day. They're green as grass and they need some experienced hands."

"Well, okay, if you say so, Sar' Major. And thank you. By the way, has the mail caught up with us?"

"Hell, no. This Kraut attack fucked up everything. All we can do is send letters and pray we mail from home maybe by 1947 or 48 – 1950 for sure."

"Well, will you make sure they forward it to us?"

"Damned tootin'. Meanwhile, I want you guys to disappear for an hour while I crank out some orders. I'm going to ship you to 9th Army's main repple-depple – the 18th. When you get there, look up John DeCoursey. He's the sergeant major and he'll take good care of you.

"After that, all you got to worry about is Germans."

Chapter 70
New Year's Eve, 1944 – Heading North

Svoboda got us away from 4th Division and The Dick by detailing us to ride shotgun in a hospital convoy of wounded GIs.

It was a long, hard haul – especially at first because the roads were nearly destroyed, horribly rutted with enormous chuckholes and washouts at low points, all resulting from snow, ice, tanks and trucks.

What's more, we were headed straight west, which meant we had to cross the line of march of Patton's Third Army which was surging straight north to attack into what everybody was calling The Bulge.

We did everything on that convoy.

We tried to steady the stretchers against the rocking and bouncing going over rotten roads. We relieved exhausted drivers. We helped medics and nurses with plasma bottles and whole blood. We pushed trucks out of snowbanks. We stole gasoline for the trucks. An armor captain and I had a screaming match when he refused to give us right-of-way . . . at first. We did what we could to clean the poor wounded bastards who couldn't keep from fouling themselves. We pulled blankets over some faces.

"Honest to God," Forster told me at one point. "I think nurses and medics have the toughest jobs of all other than the infantry. I mean, how in hell do you look down into the eyes of somebody who's all broken up and try to cheer them?"

"Yeah, I know. You see nurses and medics – all of them just flat whipped – constantly trying to boost the patients' morale."

A surgeon ordered me to help one nurse who was looking after amputees. Most of them were fuzzy with morphine. But one of them knew that he'd lost both legs and he wanted to kill himself. Right now.

"Don't hand me a lot of shinola, Nurse. Just gimme three or four morphine syrettes and I'll end it myself."

"I can't do that and I won't do that," she said. "And you don't really want to do that."

"Yes I do, Godammit," he bellowed. "I'll do it as soon as I can and nobody can stop me. I'm not gonna go back to my fiancée only half a man."

"Shut up," I yelled. "You're asking this nurse to commit murder. Now just shut your hole."

"What are you gonna do, Lieutenant," he jeered, "court martial me?"

"No, but I'm not gonna have her court-martialed which is what you're asking her to risk. You'd damned well better get off her back or I'll slap the shit out of you. She's here to help you, not kill you. And, my friend, as long as you keep talking like this, you *are* half a man – a real gutless wonder."

"Easy for you to say," he sneered.

I told him his fiancée wasn't worth having if she didn't love him, legs or no. We argued furiously for about 10 minutes before the morphine that the nurse gave him finally started taking effect. The nurse then went to help other men in the truck and to have a good cry.

After that I spelled a driver and got a bad case of sweaty palms because from the cab I saw green, white and red tracers racing upward and bouncing back and forth in the darkness . . . not within a quarter mile, but close enough.

Once we got west of the battle zone, though, the roads smoothed and the artillery noises subsided to a rumble.

I got a good look at a driver's maps and saw that we were moving in a large arc, first west back into France and then north to Reims where we'd deliver the casualties. Then we'd have to hitch our way east back into Belgium. Our destination was the 18th Replacement Depot at Tongeren.

Once we helped off-load the wounded at Reims, Forster told me we'd be headed through some areas where his Dad had been during the First World War – St. Quentain, Cambrai and Leige.

I didn't give a rat's ass about the area's history, but the map at least gave me an idea of where we would be going. The convoy's nurses, medics and drivers invited us to join in their version of a holiday dinner – C rations, some captured champagne, and to sing *Auld Lang Syne*. Meanwhile, artillery kept grumbling in the distance, creating more casualties.

They let us share their bunks for the night in the unheated trucks. I slept spooned with a nurse who'd be cute if she'd been able to shower and get a week to rest. Sex was the furthest thing from both our minds.

The next morning, giving me a bleary-eyed look, she said I snored. She gave a snort when I said she did too.

# # #

The next day, we thumbed a Red Ball Express ride right to the barbed wire gate of the 18th Replacement Depot. The repple-depple was an enormous tent city with icy graveled streets and long, long lines of lost-looking souls, brand-new to Europe and wearing brand-spanking new fatigues and overcoats.

They'd glance at us, do a double-take and look away. Then they'd keep glancing at us in our torn, blood-stained uniforms, dented helmets and deep-lined unshaven faces. We must have looked scary. Halls snapped at one of them, "What the hell you staring at, boy?"

The kid went pale and looked away.

"Hey, they're looking at us like we're something that just crawled out from under a rock," Forster said.

"Well, so what?" Halls said. "If I could find a nice warm rock, I'd move right back in under it. I just hope to hell we can get some new uniforms. I've been wearing these same fatigues with that anti-gas impregnation shit since they issued them to us back on Dartmoor."

"Yeah, and you smell like it, too."

"Oh, Dud, for God's sake just find that sergeant major, will you?"

It took about an hour to run down Sgt. Maj. DeCoursey. He was lean, ramrod straight, had a white crew cut and looked like he'd been Jersey Joe's sparring partner – flattened nose, scarred eyebrows and a cauliflower ear. His voice had the gritty bass of too much whiskey and too many cigarettes. I guess we looked worse than he did because when he saw us, his eyes bugged out.

"Jesus. Beg pardon sir, but Svoboda sent you raggedy-assed bastards to me? What am I supposed to do with you?"

"Well, sar' major," I said, "we wouldn't mind if you just discharged us from the Army. But since you probably can't do that, maybe you could let us see the medicos for a little help for our feet. And then maybe you could send us to some outfit that needs some experienced mortar men."

He reached out behind a tent flap and brought in several snow-covered bottles of beer. "Here's your New Year's drink," he said, "now tell me what the hell brings you to me."

For the first time in my life, I took a swig of beer. It was all I could do to swallow it. I almost puked, then handed the bottle to Halls. I don't know how people can drink that stuff. In my book, it's pure panther water.

Anyway, we went through the whole dog and pony show, the shooting (I even had to show him my scars), the court martial and the reappearance of The Dick who we now called Major Dick.

DeCoursey, elbows on his desk, mulled things over. "I think I've got just the ticket for you. The 84th Infantry arrived from stateside and came ashore last month at Normandy. And now they'll be part of Ninth Army attacking the north side of the Bulge.

"So how is the German attack going?" Halls asked.

"It had folks worried and looked like touch and go for a while, but Monty's taking charge here on the north side of the Bulge and I hear Patton's attacking from the south, so it's going to work out."

"Yeah," Halls said, "Patton'll cut 'em a new one."

"I think you're right," the sergeant-major said. "But for now, let's get you over to the depot's hospital. They aren't a casualty station, so they'll be happy to have something to work on besides VD."

Chapter 71
Jan. 11, 1945 – 18th Repple-Depple

The hospital treated our feet which meant a full week of rest. They issued us new uniforms and full winter gear and we also welcomed Timmer, whom Svoboda forwarded to us.

I told Timmer I was glad to see him and happy that he was beyond Maj. Dick's reach. On the whole I would rather have received our mail. Though I didn't hear from Katherine, I sent her a letter every day.

Darling Katherine --
I want you to know I've been reassigned. It's quiet here and they're giving us some rest. We all sang Auld Lange Syne on New Year's Eve and it made me cry. Next year you and I can sing it together in a nice dry quiet building somewhere – even if it's that cow shed where I first proposed to you.

By the way, I don't think I ever told you that I'm an old hand at changing diapers. I think you British call them nappies. Dealing with a dirty diaper sure is not a pleasure, but it beats the kind of work we do over here. I miss you so much, Katherine Dear. I'm aching to get this fight over so I can hold you and our baby and kiss you again.

# # #

It was dusk and freezing when the four of us paused in front of a battalion tent. Forster said, "You remember that little 10-second lecture you gave us back on Dartmoor about not fitting in?"

I chuckled, nodded and said, "Well, get ready to start fitting."

A major and corporal leaning over maps behind a long table looked up as we processed in. As Halls, Timmer and Forster joined me, we saluted.

"Lt. Allan Dudley reporting, sir, along with the NCOs from my old mortar platoon."

The major gave us a very correct salute.

But instead of saying, "At ease," he reached across the table to shake hands with each of us. "I'm Bill Welsh and this here tall drink of water is Cpl. Charlie Vanderboom. I just call him Broom."

Broom laughed, pointed to the major and said, "And I just call him 'Sir'."

I introduced us. "Major, we heard you need some experienced hands and we are that. I also want you to know we're not here to make waves in your command, but to fit in quickly as possible and to help out any way you need."

"Good to know," Welsh said. "Well, tell me about yourselves."

I kept it short, sketching our story, starting with me in Algeria, then to meeting the boys at KU, the *Queen*, joining 4th Division, the formation of the Mortar Forkers, Utah beach, Hürtgen Forest, and being captured.

"After we escaped," I said, "we were pulled out of the line for a debriefing and medical treatment with a short rest. They sent us up here because they said the 84ᵗʰ Division is brand-new in theater and doesn't have many combat-seasoned officers or noncoms. That's pretty much it, sir."

Welsh listened intently, arms folded and one finger to his lips. He gave a little smile. "Well, I bet there's more to it than that. But I don't care.

"Fact is, we sure are brand-new. All of us. We all trained together and we trained hard as hard as we could. The boys are in great shape but we haven't run into the Germans yet. So there's a lot to learn."

"Beggin' you pardon, sir," Forster said, "but that first contact can be a hell of a shock. I think having good mortar support would help a lot to settle them in. And thank God we don't have the ammo shortages that we did back in July and August."

The major quirked an eyebrow. "I hadn't heard about that, sergeant."

Timmer said, "Sir, we were short of everything – gas, bullets, artillery shells and mortar shells. Had to make every shot count. So we got pretty good – especially mixing and matching HE and Willie Peter rounds."

"Okay, gentlemen," the major said, "grab a chair. I want to hear about that and I especially want you to go over fire control and direction procedures so that we get them down pat.

"Oh, I almost forgot," he added as he sat down. "Even though we're a bit past the First, Happy New Year to all of you."

"With some hot chow," Halls said, "I'll drink to that."

The major smiled. "We're a little low on anything hot right now, including chow. But in a few minutes, sergeant, you'll be able to have that drink. Once we finish here, courtesy of the Royal Army we can toast the arrival of 1945."

"How do you mean, sir?"

"Ah, I guess you haven't heard. SHAEF loaned the 84ᵗʰ Division to the British Army's XXX Corps and in XXX Corps everybody is allotted a daily tot of rum."

"The other good news," Cpl. Vanderboom said, "is that the corps commander also is supporting us with British armor along with British artillery which we've heard is excellent."

The major, who was the battalion exec, decided I would work with him in the fire control center, while Forster, Timmer and Halls would backstop the mortar sections.

After our briefing, chit-chat or whatever it was, Maj. Welch offered us our tot of rum.

I passed.

I'd heard that they didn't call it Demon Rum for nothing – that it was very strong liquor and, after my one taste of beer, I wasn't about to sample it.

Chapter 72
Jan. 15, 1945 – The Siegfried Line Again

I was trying to warm my hands around a steaming canteen cup of coffee when a voice broke into my day-dreams about Katherine. "Wotcher mates!" Speaking was a runty British sergeant with a lantern jaw. He was crunching to us across the debris-strewn street.

Timmer called to him, "Hey, Sar' Benson! How's it hanging?"

"To the right, you know. To the right."

Timmer introduced Sgt. Benson as being in charge of our neighbor -- the nearest mortar section of the Royal Army's 43rd Division. When Benson saw my rank, he braced and saluted, "Sorry, sir. Didn't realize an officer was present."

"Relax, sergeant. Even though Congress has seen fit to make me a gentleman, I'm still a sergeant at heart and one of these original Mortar Forkers. Pull up a brick and join us." He grinned and sat down with us. We were sheltering in the covered entry of a half-shattered home, part of a tiny burg on the boundary line between the 43rd and our division.

Sgt. Benson carried a cuppa he called it – an enameled cup of tea with milk and probably laced with rum. Their cups retained heat a lot better than our aluminum GI versions. He squatted down with us, "Nice little fire you blokes have here."

"Yes, thank God," Halls said, launching into how cold he was. Halls griped constantly and Forster usually kept his complaints to himself. But today, seated on an ammo crate and holding his hands over the fire, Forster was grousing too. "I thought I was used to cold weather. Nothing's colder than Kansas in January, but by God this comes close."

Sgt. Benson said, "Ah, give over, Yank. The Met call this a Russian high pressure. It's a bit parky, but it'll pass soon and then thaw and we'll all be up to our goolies in the muck."

Forster grinned and looked at me. "Okay, Dud, you've spent time among the English. So did Sgt. Benson just agree with me or insult me?"

We all laughed. "I'll translate," I said. "He said to quit bitching. It's a bit cold, but this cold snap will pass soon and then we'll all be crotch-deep in mud. But, Sgt. Benson, you boys got to admit that when the sky is clear like this, the flyboys are flying overhead and shooting up the Krauts."

Sgt. Benson nodded. "Too bloody right, mate. But I tell you, this cold isn't bad compared to what we faced in Norway."

"Norway!" Forster said. "You were in on that?"

"Yeah," Benson said. "My battalion's been about everywhere. First Norway. France. Pulled out at Dunkirk. Then Greece and Crete. Then North Africa. Sicily and now this. We've been just about everywhere but Burma."

"Good God," Timmer said, "you've been in almost constant battle."

I interrupted, "How many men do you have left of your original company."

"I heard Cap'n Soames say we had 370 per cent casualties in five years. Everybody's been wounded. But to your question, sir, I think 18 members of the original company are left out of the original 110 blokes. And 43 Division itself seems to be about one-third strength.

"Damn! Aren't they getting you replacements?"

"Sorry, mate, there's no fresh fodder left. Blighty's just about empty, so we make do with what we've got"

"Jesus," Halls said. "And you've been at it for five years?"

"I'm in my sixth. I signed up in '39."

"Just like Dud here," Timmer said, nodding at me.

The sergeant gave me a grim smile. I asked him, "How do you think these new boys in the 84th will do?"

He sipped his tea. "The men appear to be tough and disciplined right enough. But saving yourself, sir, I think the officers are gormless twats. They'll make a dog's body of any job. So Fritz will cull the 84th. Any roads, in the end, it'll be us sergeants and corporals pulling them through."

Timmer said, "Gormless twats, eh? God help them. That makes them all sound like Maj. Dick."

Sgt. Benson grinned, "Maj. Dick? You must tell me this story."

Halls grinned back. "Okay, I'll start. It's the story of an officer who's a perfect coward."

"Oh," Benson said. "Windy bastard, was he?"

"Windy?"

"Sorry, mate," Benson said, his face grim. "Means cowardly. Worst insult in the Royal Army is to suggest someone is windy."

"Well," Halls said, "The Dick for sure is as windy as a hurricane and tornado combined. He's so windy he shot Dud here because . . ."

# # #

Snow and sleet sifted down on our tent fly as Maj. Walsh and I began setting up for our first mission as a fire direction center.

As we poured over the maps for about the fiftieth time, a company of infantry, ponchos glistening and heads lowered, marched past us in the slush toward the front. We were just about to dismiss our forward observers when one of them looked over my shoulder. "What the hell's going on now?"

Three Sherman tanks were clattering and squeaking up the road toward us, a jeep in trail, hanging well back to avoid a plastering from the tank tracks' muddy rooster tails.

What made it odd was that the middle tank had no turret. Three men stood in the turret ring, peering forward with binoculars toward the combat zone. One wore an officer's cap and two wore berets, so they obviously were British.

Maj. Welsh and I dismissed the FOs and stepped out into the road. I held up my hand to stop the parade as it approached.

I said, "Welcome, gentlemen, but you should know we're quite close to the FEBA."

"The what, sir?"

"Pardon," Maj. Welsh said. "The lieutenant here was using American shorthand. Forward Edge of the Battle Area. If you proceed 300 more yards, you'll likely come under German shellfire. Meanwhile, may I ask who you are and why you're here?"

Looking down over the tank chassis to view us, a Limey captain saluted and grinned. "Thanks awfully for the warning, major. Didn't realize we were quite that far forward. We're here to sniff the battle zone."

"Sniff?"

An elderly looking officer in a cap with a red base just like Sir Alfred's lowered his binoculars and gave us a broad smile. "Right. British slang for taking a shufti – a reconnaissance. We must see the objectives before issuing attack orders. We pay these visits because our headquarters are too far in the rear to be in the picture."

"Pardon me, sir, but who are you?"

"I'm Brian Horrocks, commander of Thirty Corps."

Holy shit, a lieutenant general!

We came to attention and gave very correct salutes. "Apologies for stopping you, sir. We don't get many generals up here – or colonels, for that matter."

"Yes, I see."

I broke into the conversation. "Sir, I give you greetings from Maj. Gen. Alfred Abbot-Leigh, my father-in-law to be. He told me that you either are a British version of Patton or that Patton is an American version of you."

Everybody in the tank laughed delightedly. The general pulled his lanky frame up out of the turret ring and, using the tracks and suspension wheels, descended painfully to the road.

The captain followed. Meanwhile an odd couple alighted from the jeep, a rangy American lieutenant colonel and a short spindly soldier with the six stripes and diamond of a first sergeant. They waded through the slush and mud to join us.

Walsh led us to the tent fly, but Gen. Horrocks grabbed my arm, holding me back. He gave me a hard look and said, "I was not aware Sir Alfred and Lady Alice were parents of a daughter."

"Beg pardon sir, Katherine is their widowed daughter-in-law. Their older son was her husband."

His eyes widened and he shook his head. "Good God! He and Alice lost David, too? Bad business. I didn't know. Was out of touch in hospital more than a year. I must write straight away. But congratulations on your impending nuptials."

Talking with a lieutenant general made me nervous, doubly so because his narrow face had an icy expression. But when he smiled, which he did readily, that together with snow white hair made him grandfatherly. He spoke with little of most generals' loftiness. He also seemed like an ordinary human because, like most of us, he winced when incautious movements made his wounds hurt.

I told him of my jeep accident with Sir Alfred and sketched our conversations including my initial mispronunciation of his name.

That produced a smile. "I'm afraid I have a fresh surprise for you in that connection. For some reason, from Monty on down, they've taken to calling me Jorrocks – and I suppose that's one of the more polite epithets the troops award me."

As we neared the tent, he stopped again and faced me. "Now sir, your major said few high-ranking officers visit the front?"

"Sir, you're the first one ever I've seen. Except for recuperation from a wound, I've been in this theater since D Day. Oh, I was in Algeria before that and I did see Gen. Patton there two or three times."

"At the front?"

"Damn right, sir."

"Good show. So then you're quite new with 84 Division."

"Yessir, three of my sergeants and I were just transferred to provide the 84th with some experience."

"Yes. I should think 84 Division wants leavening and will be glad of having some old hands." He turned to Maj. Walsh and the lieutenant colonel. I did a double-take because Frank Bowyer, the old sergeant first class from KU, winked at me over the colonel's shoulder.

"Gentlemen," the general said, "I sniff the battlefield, as I put it, because starting with President Roosevelt and with Prime Minister Churchill, there's tremendous pressure on all of us to attack. The pressure for offense worsens as it pushes down through army, corps and division staffs . . . and then, of course, to regiment and battalion. Finally it lands full force on the wretched company commanders and platoon leaders who must put it all into effect.

"Now I want this clear. I'm disappointed that American corps and division staffs and even regimental and battalion officers rarely visit the front. The result is they often order attacks against objectives that are mere words on a map. They neither see it nor the conditions troops face. Consequently, they often haven't the faintest notion of what their orders actually require.

"At of this moment," he said, "that will change in 84 Division and will remain in effect as long as it's part of Thirty Corps.

"Especially in this beastly weather," he added.

He paused. "Now, major, when is the last time the troops up here had a hot meal?"

"Sir, we usually don't get hot meals on the line."

"Indeed?" the Gen. Horrocks said, turning to the lieutenant colonel. "Yet I recall your battalion headquarters just 15 minutes back offering us a generous breakfast, didn't they?"

Looking queasy, the colonel said, "Yes, sir." Behind him, Bowyer didn't exactly smile, but managed to look amused.

"Right," the general said. "Perhaps you would care to explain why the battalion doesn't provide hot meals to its fighting soldiers." He stressed the word 'fighting.'

The colonel began a USDA-certified Class A bullshit excuse about exigencies and, er, shorthandedness. The general interrupted politely.

"Colonel, I can't help thinking that it would be better were you to ensure hot food for your fighting troops rather than explain why they have none. Surely the exigencies in providing hot meals would be less onerous than the rigors those soldiers themselves face. Wouldn't you agree?"

The colonel jerked his head and said, "Yes sir." Bowyer grasped his mouth and turned away.

"Then, Colonel, I recommend you see to it."

The colonel and Bowyer came to attention, saluted and trotted through the rain and mud toward the jeep. "Oh, Colonel," the general called.

"Sir?"

"Kindly let regiment know we'll call on them within the hour."

"Yessir!"

Gen. Horrocks turned back to us and asked how we liked working with British troops.

Maj. Walsh said he regretted having no experience so far with the British.

"I only have a corporal's perspective from North Africa," I said, "but the British and Aussies seemed tough and expert. When they were on our flanks, there was nothing at all to worry about. My only problem was finding it harder to understand British English than German."

He chuckled and asked, "How do you think the men of 84 Division measure up?"

"Sir," I said, "I think they're in excellent physical condition and they trained together. So they're close knit -- a team. When they meet the Krauts, it's going to be hard going at first. But they'll learn quickly."

"Right," the general said. "The German are experienced and battle-hardened. And their counterattacks always are absolutely vicious."

Chapter 73
Jan. 18, 1945 – Carving Into Germany

I don't know how – or even if -- Gen. Horrocks did it, but when the 84th attacked, several senior officers were up forward with them. Something we'd never seen before.

What's more, the intensity of the troops' training showed – or at least what I saw in the battalion we supported. They'd really drilled hard on standard U.S. Infantry fire and movement squad tactics – scout group scouting, rifle group ready to assault the Heinies, gun group setting up a base of fire.

They made it work in their assault through the outer layer of Siegfried Line pillboxes.

Backing them up was a veteran British tank regiment Gen. Horrocks assigned to the division, the Sherwood Rangers Yoemanry. We nicknamed them the Robin Hoods.

Horrocks also threw in some flamethrower tanks and flail tanks -- Shermans with a rotating drum that slapped the ground with chains, harmlessly detonating mines lying in the infantry's path.

The 84th's progress came thanks in part to the flamethrower tanks that could jet out a 200-foot blast of blazing jellied gasoline.

"I think our boys have done remarkably well," Maj. Walsh told me. "But I've got to admit that those flamethrower tanks induced a good many Germans to surrender rather than be broiled alive. It's too bad they didn't survive."

"Who, the Germans?" I asked, thinking someone had slaughtered prisoners.

"No, the tank crews," he said, solemnly. "Some 88 battery nailed them and they were immolated in their own fire. They had to know they'd be very visible targets, but they went ahead anyway. Pure guts."

He credited our forward observers with quickly calling in mortars and Limey artillery onto the 88s – and later onto German strongpoints.

"With Timmer, Halls and Forster goosing the mortar sections," he said, "it only took seconds to register on a target. If anything, the British artillery seemed even faster."

I was on edge, remembering the scary rhythm of fighting Germans. Counterattacks – the Wehrmacht specialty – would hit just as the 84th captured any part of the German line.

But then I got a call back from Forster that was sheer good news. "Hey, Dud, it looks like their junior officers and NCOs paid attention. The minute Able Company captured its initial line of pillboxes, the sergeants and corporals started screaming like banshees. 'Dig in, damn you! Dig! Dig!'

"Well, they just disappeared into the earth like a bunch of badgers. Most were in cover when the Kraut mortars started landing. When the Kraut counterattack hit, they blew it apart

# # #

Later, Halls called me sounding almost hysterical. "Dud, you won't believe this! But our mortar just stopped a King Tiger tank."

"Bullshit, Halls! Mortar shells don't hurt tanks."

"Dud, this Tiger was in defilade where the Limey anti-tank guns couldn't touch him. He was headed in our direction about ready to roll over a squad of infantry. So we started dropping Willie Petes on him. And Dud, honest to God, after three hits, the crew just fucking bailed out."

"You're kidding!"

"I am not! We think the phosphorous either got inside through their vision slits, or else the smoke was asphyxiating them. Either way, that abandoned tank's still sitting there with its hatches open and engines running. The infantry is all around it. Now I can see some officer with them. I think he's calling for help on a walkie talkie.

"Oh! Oh! Now the Krauts are trying to take out the Tiger. It's those damned blue 88's. Whoa, Dud, and they're starting to drop mortars on us . . ."

A blast of noise in my ear and then I heard only static.

# # #

Once things settled down, Bowyer paid us a visit. He and I worked our way forward to the gun sections. On the way I got a good look at the troops.

When we got to Forster's gun, Bowyer congratulated him. "Man, you boys don't look green now, do you?" He wasn't talking about the mud on their uniforms. It was the hard, alert look in their eyes.

"Nope," I said. "Like my granddaddy used to say, these boys have seen the elephant."

As we made our way toward Halls's section, a corporal behind a pillbox yelled, "You better look out. There are Krauts just over that hill." He nodded with his head toward a low rise to the east.

"Yeah, well, we're checking on our mortars. Maybe we can put a little salt on those Krauts' tails."

He grinned, "Oh, are you with the Mortar Forkers?"

"Yeah."

"Well, sir, you tell them they've done good – real good."

The nickname tickled Bowyer.

We found Halls and his men in good shape. "Hey, Dud! Hey Sgt. Bowyer! Good to see you. Shrapnel took out our radios and we need new ones plus more ammo, but we're doing okay. We been firing missions for two platoons that lost their 60's."

He pointed. "There's the Tiger that we stopped. Looks like somebody started to whitewash it. That's the phosphorous ash there laying lay across its turret and glacis."

"It's still smoking."

"Right, Dud, but that's because the Krauts hit it in the butt with 88s and burned it up."

# # #

When we returned, Maj. Walsh had moved the fire direction center forward so that it now was about 200 feet from the main supply route. It gave us a first-hand view of the assault's price – something I could have done without.

Trucks and Jeeps bearing blanket-shrouded forms made a slow bloody parade past us to the nearby surgical hospital which was inside a half-destroyed factory. I kept praying silently that one of those jeeps wasn't bearing any of my boys. Only four Mortar Forkers left out of the original dozen . . . 67 per cent casualties, not to mention the attrition among our 30-some odd replacements.

The MSR made me think of high school science anatomy lessons. The eastbound side of the route was just like an artery carrying nourishment, replacements and ammo to the body, the division.

The westbound half was an intestine carrying away waste.

Chapter 74
Feb. 8, 1945 – Moving To The Roer

Maj. Walsh felt, and he was right, that the battalion FDC no longer needed a spare lieutenant. He and The Broom and two other men were doing just fine.

"Heavy Weapons lost its exec," he told me, "so we can assign you to replace him. You'll be working directly with your boys again."

And that's how I wound up at Dog Company HQ – a freezing hoed-out pillbox with several sets of radios. It was about 100 yards back of the line. I hardly shook hands with the CO before a chunk of shrapnel zipped through the door, laid him out cold and took out two radios.

The radio tenders and I had to scramble in the next 20 minutes, trying to get him to the medics and to restore communications.

And now I was in temporary command of the whole heavy weapons company.

A day or two later, they made it official and I appointed Forster to be my exec. I recommended him for a battlefield commission and battalion said they'd think it over.

Now that the Krauts' attack into the bulge had been stopped. We entered a defensive pause and our mail finally caught up with us.

Dearest Allan –

It was wonderful hearing from you every day. Not just hearing, but knowing you were well and safe. I'm sorry events delayed my letters. I have written daily because doing so makes me feel as if I actually speak with you, and that you reply in my soul. Obviously, I miss you desperately. I miss your warmth next to me and I wish you were here to witness the changes that our Little Life is causing in me. As they say, I am beginning to show. The doctor reports I am doing well, and that our child is to be born in late March.

Lady Alice has twigged on to what was happening. She doesn't cry easily and, despite what you may think, I don't either. But we were crying and laughing together when Sir Alfred walked in. We broke the news to him. He started clearing his throat rather gruffly and became a bit misty.

He's as happy as Alice. He said it would be wonderful for the manor to have a son and heir.

I said you planned to stay in the army and he said, "Well, of course he does! But you two could still have this old place. Turn it into a museum for the bloody tourists."

I snorted. Somehow, I just couldn't picture me as the father of a child entitled to an English estate – or even as a tour guide.

On the other hand, I sure could see Katherine all dolled up as a princess or a duchess.

But then . . . *Crap! If my son grows up English, will he want to play baseball? Or American football?*

"Oh well," I muttered, "what the hell?"

"What?" Forster asked.

"I'll tell you later, Mike. We got things to do now."

Neither Forster nor I had time to re-read and savor our mail – or even talk about it -- because, after its blooding, the 84th now was being moved again and filled with replacements.

Supposedly we were getting a 10-day rest. But when you convoy the equivalent population of a small city over a distance of 25 miles, nobody rests. Even the troops who are only riding in truck relays can't really hope to relax.

Meanwhile, the officers and the NCOs must ensure that every damned bootlace, bullet, and baseplate goes along for the ride – plus rations, paperwork, and the other kind of paper work, toilet paper, plus spares, machine guns, radios, flare guns and on and on forever.

Our new home, a sector lying west of the Roer River, was no prize.

"I don't like it here," Halls groused. "There's no cover."

"Stop bitching," Timmer said. "At least we're not getting hit with any tree bursts either."

This area – where the borders of France, Belgium, the Netherlands and Germany come together like a mad jigsaw puzzle -- wasn't wooded country like Luxembourg or southern Belgium. You could see for fair distances over relatively flat land. And compared to the Christmas scenery where we had been, this place looked more like a slag heap.

And it made me nervous, just like Halls, because in unforested land, you can't hide. The bad guys can spot us as easily as we can spot them.

At least the Krauts didn't have spotter planes.

There was another reason we didn't like the new setting. We could feel in our bones that something big was coming. As we proceeded to the front, we passed long lines of trucks, tanks and guns plus block after block of bridging equipment and enormous stacks of artillery shells. I'd seen nothing like this since before the St. Lo break-out.

And the Army's post offices were closed, neither distributing nor accepting the troops' letters.

# # #

We began attacking and moving, digging in and defending, then attacking and moving – a constant drumming cycle of murderous fighting always with heavy bombardments.

It was somewhat different because Germans sometime surrendered now -- the kids and old men, anyway. I kept hearing a lot of wishful thinking about us being just about to break through a last crust of resistance which supposedly would end the war.

"Yeah, sure," Timmer said. "To the guy that gets hit, that so-called crust is hard as boiler plate. Seems to me the Wehrmacht is putting up a hell of a hard fight."

"You sure can tell we ain't welcome here," Halls said on our third day in action. "The Krauts are just *real* touchy about us getting this close to the Roer, you know?"

"Of course they're fighting," I said. "You would be, too, if this was the Ohio or the Mississippi. But even so I've kind of got the feeling that we're on the downhill side of this thing."

Timmer was visiting my HQ, now in a captured concrete bunker, and we were flinching in unison as medium artillery pounded the earth around us.

"I don't know, Dud," Timmer said. "The closer we get to the Third Reich, the tougher it seems to be."

The barrage quit. But when we stepped out into the open, we stopped dead. Right there at eye level a big shell – maybe 155 size -- was wedged halfway through the trunk of a thick oak. You could see the rifling cuts on the shell's bronze band. And as its steel cooled, it just sat there going *tink, tink, tink.*

We immediately ducked back to the bunker and I placed a call.

"Yo, this is Lt. Dudley at heavy weapons. Can you send somebody up here to disarm a 155 shell that's right outside our HQ? Yeah, it split a tree trunk at head level and it's just wedged there. Tomorrow? Ye Gods! So now I've got to move headquarters?"

# # #

We all had another fight, namely with the cold. It never stopped and you never got warm even sitting in front of a fire. And usually there was no fire.

Halls told me of two guys in his section waking up to find their feet trapped in the puddles that froze solid at the bottom of their foxholes. Their buddies had to free them by carefully chipping away the ice with bayonets.

Funny thing, though -- they didn't get frostbite.

I didn't have anything like that happen. But one of my radio tenders cried out at night when he tried to turn over in his sleep. His head was frozen to a clump of mud on the bunker floor and he'd torn out a wad of hair. We had to chip the rest away from the concrete and then he had to sit with his noggin next to a Coleman lantern until the mud thawed.

He wondered if all the yanked-out hair he qualified for a Purple Heart.

Another guy at B Company headquarters did something unbelievable. He wrapped his boots in some burlap-type sacking, and then trickled water on the burlap until it gradually froze in a boot-shaped block. It was noisy when he walked, but he claimed it kept his feet extra warm

My fingers always were numb, so it was very difficult to write next-of-kin letters. It even made me shrink from writing to Katherine.

We had to send eight men from Heavy Weapons to the hospital because they had pneumonia. All the rest of us just felt like we had pneumonia because the flu made us cough constantly.

The weather warmed a bit so we felt a bit better, but the mud robbed our mortar shells of some effectiveness.

The shells penetrated the soupy earth before detonating, so that the mud dampened the force of the blast. But then the same muffling effect protected us somewhat from Germans' return fire.

After a week, they pulled us back so that the surviving Mortar Forkers were able to meet again – Halls and Timmer both had scratches, but so far Forster and I were not in line for more purple hearts.

And the boys were bitter because the rum ration had stopped. The U.S. Ninth Army had asked Gen. Horrocks to return the division from the British XXX Corps.

Back under U.S. Army auspices, the troops occasionally got a couple of beers, but the U.S. military just didn't prioritize beer the way the British did their rum.

Chapter 75
Feb. 19, 1945 – The Roer River

"Now you men might be asking yourselves why you are being singled out for this mission."

Yeah, good question. Just how did we get so lucky?

The briefer, a staff major in spotless starched fatigues with knife-edge creases, went on, "Well, men, we have *not* being singled you out! This assault, Operation Grenade, is by the whole Ninth Army.

"It's an attack by four whole corps to cross the Roer River. We're assaulting with six divisions on a 30,000-yard front. All told, we're sending about 300,000 men against the Krauts."

Oh, brother! So in reality about 40,000 of us actually will fight, and the Krauts probably have 40 million bullets. They sure as shit know we're coming, too. No surprises.

"We're going to surprise them," the major droned on.

Yeah, right.

"The river still is at flood stage because the Germans opened the floodgates in the dams upstream.

The German command doesn't expect us to attack until the flooding subsides at least a week from now. But the engineers know how to get us across it."

In iron-clad canoes, maybe?

"Men, we're putting everything we have into this attack. It's a strategic operation. With us pushing north and east and the British Second Army attacking south from Holland, we're going to trap a hell of a lot of German troops before they can retreat across the Rhine River."

Now Timmer was whispering behind me. "Trap Germans? Bullllshit! That's like trapping rats. I say let 'em go into Germany and stay there. Then we just bomb them into oblivion."

I knew how Timmer felt. I felt the same doubts that overtook me when they briefed us for Operation Cobra to break out of Normandy.

As if on cue, the major said, "We'll also have tremendous artillery preparation. About 2,000 guns will fire a 45-minute barrage before we take off. And we'll have smoke screens. Really, this is all a rehearsal for the Rhine which we'll cross probably next month."

Halls, also behind me, whispered back to Timmer, "A fucking rehearsal? Shit, rehearsals always go badly."

"And as for the shelling," he said, "the bastards already are dug in. You know what all that shelling will do? It'll just wake them up before dawn and then they'll *really* be pissed off."

"Finally," the major announced with a bright smile, "Once it's light, we're going to have the full support of the entire 29th Tactical Air Command. The flyboys will be on call for us the whole time."

"Great," Timmer said. "Now I can fling myself into that meat grinder with a lighter heart."

I turned and hissed. "Will you bastards shut the fuck up?"

And that rattled me. I suddenly remembered Forster using almost the same words during the briefing for Operation Cobra . . . which turned out to be a two-day fuck-up that killed about half of us.

At least this time we wouldn't have to worry about off-target carpet bombing by a thousand B-29s.

Chapter 76
Feb. 23, 1945 – The Crossing

"My God," Forster screamed, "it's starting out just like Operation Cobra -- sheer SNAFU."

My heart sinking, I just nodded. Bowyer was with us looking grim, saying nothing.

The barrage almost was deafening – literally. It was as if several thousand bass drummers were pounding their instruments. When a mortar round exploded about 50 feet away, you couldn't distinguish the noise. The light from all the exploding ordnance didn't flicker – it was so constant you could read by it.

Yet nothing seemed to work.

A squad of engineers towing steel cables had managed to cross 350 yards of fast-flowing river. But because the light from artillery flashes was so bright, the Krauts could see and pin them down with mortars and MG fire

"Bastards are brave." Forster yelled again. He was pointing to a flat-bottomed pontoon boat tied on our bank of the river. Five dead engineers were sprawled around it and a sixth was inside it, fruitlessly yanking the starter cord on an outboard motor.

Other engineers were in the water, trying to secure small pontoons to the cables. The current was so strong that it pulled their bodies horizontally from their lifelines, water breaking over them as if they were boulders. They had to be freezing their nuts off. About every five minutes, other engineers would splash into the flood to relieve them. The men who emerged from the river were shuddering.

Other engineers sheltered with us behind a tank. Stacked next to the tank were piles of 10-foot walkway sections. The walkways would form a footbridge over the river if the engineers survived to assemble it. But it looked hopeless because the flooded Roer's current was so strong.

Forster and I were resting our binoculars on the tank's fender, scanning the tree line and small village beyond the far shore.

"There!" Forster said. "I think I've got him, Dud. See that 2-story house with half a roof? Right where the road bends out of sight?"

"Yeah," I said. "Got it."

"Well, keep watching. Something pops up in that window beneath the roof peak. It pops up and then disappears, and then eight or a dozen mortar rounds come down where we want our bridgehead to be. How 'bout having Halls and Timmer try a couple of Willie Petes." Halls was in charge of two guns a quarter mile north, upstream, and Timmer was an equal distance down-stream. The third section's two guns were sheltered behind the levee just at our backs.

"Let's not expose both sections, Mike. You get back with your boys up behind the levee. I'll alert Timmer that Halls is going to mark the target with Willie Pete. If that doesn't break things up, then I'll ask DivArty to hit it with 105s. For now, let's save the mortars for Kraut infantry." I got on the horn to Timmer and Halls.

In the next two minutes, three white phosphorous shells bloomed around the building, the fourth detonating on the roof. The resulting phosphorous shower seemed to discourage the Kraut observer, because mortar shelling stopped.

I was back to being the mortar platoon leader because now our heavy weapons company had a new commander, Capt. Billy Kenton. He was a no-nonsense West Pointer still limping from a Normandy leg wound and he was good to work with.

With the Kraut mortars stopping, several more engineers behind the tank raced down the bank to join their buddies in the water. Others began pulling the walkway sections to the water's edge.

A burst of green MG tracer raced toward us from across the river and rattled among the walkway sections. One engineer gasped and fell and another toppled into the current and was swept away. The others kept working.

Capt. Kenton glanced at me, but I was already on the horn, getting all three mortar sections sighted in where I thought the MG was.

Our five-minute barrage didn't seem to work. At 400 yards it was hard to tell the MG's exact location. I got on the tank's hull phone and asked the tank commander try a couple of shots where our rounds were falling.

Because it was one of the new Shermans with a high-velocity 75 mm gun, the blast about tore off our scalps. But the MG kept harassing and killing engineers. Capt. Kenton went gimping away and returned 15 minutes later towing the solution – a quad .50 antiaircraft gun.

Just about then, the prep barrage stopped so we could yawn to clear our ears and hear ourselves think again.

"By God," Kenton said, "this thing ought to get their number. Dud, please drop a couple more Willie Petes where you think that MG is."

So much for our ears.

One .50 caliber machine gun is loud, like a very big dog with a very loud, quick bark. Four of them firing together is shattering. The gunners swept their fire across the village like a hose gushing scarlet water. At 400 yards, you couldn't see a lot of detail, but the village seemed to crumble in clouds of dust.

We saw no more green tracers for at least an hour.

# # #

The engineers got the last walkway section installed about 0800. Two squads of infantry – trotting five yards apart with their M1s at high port – got across the footbridge with two of Kenton's machine gun squads crossing right behind them.

We were displacing forward to take our own crew across, when a DUKW, an amphibious assault craft, came downstream. You could hear the men in it trying to start the craft's motors, but they wouldn't catch. So the current was carrying it, out of control -- a floating battering ram.

An engineer major, veins standing out in his forehead and neck, screamed, "Oh, no! Goddam stupid bastards." He jumped up and down in the mud and in the next 30 seconds did some of the most inventive, vile swearing I've ever heard.

But it didn't stop the DUKW.

The men riding in it waved frantically for Halls' section to get off the footbridge and back to dry land. The craft struck the walkway, snapping it like a rotten twig. The current pulled both halves of the broken footbridge toward their respective banks. One hapless soldier clung to a piece of decking slowly spiraling downstream in the DUKW's wake. Halls and three of his boys made it to the far bank.

We stood staring at each other across the river in disbelief.

The engineer officer swore again.

But then it got hard to hear him because the Krauts began dropping mortar shells – big ones – on both banks.

Chapter 77
Feb. 25, 1945 – The Cologne Plain

Military radios distort voices, but even through the static I could tell Halls was rattled. "Dud, I think we have a situation over here."

"What's up?"

"Well, you remember seeing two knocked-out Tiger tanks outside the village? Well, I don't think they're knocked out."

"What do you mean?"

"Well, sir, they're showing signs of life and I don't want to be in this neighborhood if those big bastards go on a tear."

Five minutes later I braked my jeep beside Halls' half-track in front of the battered stone office building. As soon as he saw me, Halls beckoned and headed up the steps. The place looked something on the order of a county court house back home. It was stately even with documents strewn all over and chunks of concrete and shards of window glass crunching underfoot amid dusty black swastikas on walls and desks.

We climbed a broad staircase to the second floor and peeked east through an office, staying well back from the broken windows. Halls pointed and there they were -- two Tigers less than 300 yards away, visible through a tangle of leafless tree limbs. They were ugly and enormous -- massive sloped turrets, thick telescoping cannons, blocky hulls. They looked battered, as if they'd taken some hits. The earth around them was cratered from shell impacts. But they still looked sinister.

"Early this morning, Dud, all three hatches on both tanks were wide open. The turret hatches and driver hatches. Look at them now."

The turret hatches were closed.

"What's more, when we got here this morning, their guns were all cattywampus -- one elevated way high and pointed off to the west. The other was level and pointed straight ahead. Now both guns are aimed more or less this way.

"So what I think is maybe they can't move because their engines are conked out. Tigers have to crank up their diesels every four hours and they haven't been doing that. But they're sure as hell manned, and maybe someone's getting ready to use these 88 mm cannons."

I got out my binoculars and gave a quick scan of the fallow fields around the tanks. This area was cut by ditches and occasional windbreaks or hedgerows. From my limited view I saw no troops.

"You were right to call me," I said. "Let's see if anybody's out in the fields. Fire a few Willy Petes over along that tree line and see if they spook anybody. Meanwhile, be ready to drop some phosphorous on those tanks, too, just in case."

We didn't get the chance.

Halls and I were walking out the entrance when a sledge-hammer concussion knocked us flat in a big cloud of concrete dust. He and I still were looking cross-eyed at each other when a second 88 blasted another big hole in the building.

As we picked ourselves up, Halls glanced through the east wall's brand-new ventilation. "Holy crap! Infantry!" A glance showed me four squad-sized groups of German troops, weapons at high port, trotting straight toward us and a longer line of troops to their rear.

Chapter 78
Feb. 25, 1945 – Hitler Kommt

We half-ran and half-tripped down the steps. Halls got his boys firing and called for help from the other two mortar sections.

I got on the horn with the fire direction center. "Yo, this is Dud at Feature 17. We're looking at Kraut infantry -- 200 yards off coming straight at us. Two Tigers firing in support."

"Dud, it's only a spoiling attack. They just don't have that much."

"Spoiling attack, my ass. I'd say at least a battalion is coming at us."

"Okay. Back your boys out west of the village and link up with Able Company."

We pulled stakes, Halls relaying the instructions to the other Mortar Forker sections. We were racing west beneath showers of MG tracers. Between bursts we heard the Krauts yelling, "*Hitler kommt zürruck!*" Hitler's coming back.

We set up behind Able Company's fighting positions which lay along a haphazard series of drainage ditches and shell holes.

The German infantry poured out of and around that little town in spread-out squads, each with its own MG-42. Mortar shells started coming down on us. Between mortars, cracking machine gun fire and an occasional hair-raising blast from the tanks, they had us hugging the dirt.

We were just getting set to fire our mortars at the assault when Timmer yelled. "Visitors!" A big knot of Nazis was racing at us on our flank from the north. They were 50 yards away and if they overran us, they'd devastate Able Company from behind.

"No time for mortars," I yelled. "Carbines and grenades! Stop the bastards." *God help us, 18 of us to hold off maybe 50 Krauts.*

Everybody dropped everything and started shooting with carbines, M1s and the machine guns on the tracks. That caused the Krauts to hit the dirt, and start pouring fire at us.

Capt. Kenton showed up on *their* flank with a light .30. Shooting from the hip, he walked toward them. He fired a full belt into them before a potato-masher nailed him. At the same time, another Kraut grenade went off near me, knocking me flat and half-silly.

Timmer screamed bloody murder, getting six men to start throwing four grenades apiece in unison with him. The rolling explosions caused the Krauts to start pulling back.

"Okay," Timmer yelled, "now's the time to attack. Right Dud?"

"Right," I yelled, staggering upright and waved, "Come on! Kill the sons-a-bitches! All of 'em!"

I can't remember how many of us barrel-assed across that belt of writhing Krauts. I know Forster was right beside me and we were yelling at the top of our lungs and shooting from the hip. I don't know if we actually hit anybody, but when they saw us coming they turned and ran full speed. We stopped, took a knee and tried to aim carefully. It was hard for me because I was breathing so heavily, but I know we hit four of the bastards in the back.

Another one popped up right in front of me, looking terrified, a crying kid who should have been home smooching in the barn with Elke or Bertha. Maybe he wanted to surrender.

I got him right between the eyes.

We raced back to the guns and began firing Willie Petes at the main assault. The plumes of slowly descending flakes started breaking up the attack. Nobody racing across a field littered with dead buddies wants to run through a cloud of burning phosphorous.

The Krauts' mortar team got our range and for five minutes it was hell to pay. I saw Halls slammed sideways when one round landed near his section. Seconds later I noticed Timmer using his left hand to drop rounds down the tube. Blood was dripping from his dangling right arm.

Forster yelled. "More Krauts. Fuckers snuck in close!"

They were so close we had to meet them with pistols, fists and anything else handy. I backhanded a Squarehead edgewise with an entrenching tool, the blade biting through his nose to his ears.

I don't think they retreated. I think we exterminated them before having to duck when our own private shelling resumed. Somebody finally got DivArty to pitch in with airbursts both above the village and the assault. It cut them to pieces – literally, strewing bleeding bits of Kraut all over. Yet they kept coming maybe emboldened by occasional shots from the Tigers. Eventually, however, the Air Corps dispatched a pair of P-47s to drop napalm canisters on the Tigers.

When it was over, my legs were limp. I just wanted to practice my 1000-yard stare.

My watch told me the spoiling attack – a mere skirmish in the Ninth Army's day – had eaten up 45 minutes.

Duty could go to hell. I didn't want to think – not even about Katherine and our baby.

That's when a last Kraut mortar shell came down about 50 feet away and something hit my face.

It certainly messed up my vision. I heard Forster say, "Easy, Dud, I'll get a dressing . . . oh, my God!"

I glimpsed the shock on his face.

"What is it, Mike? They attacking again?"

"Shut up, Dud. I'm shooting you some morphine."

Chapter 79
Feb. 28, 1945 – Back To France

It was dark when I awakened. At least I thought it was dark. But when I put my hand to my head I felt a thick dressing that covered the upper half of my face, eyes included.

"Anybody there?"

A female voice answered, "Oh, lieutenant, you're back with us. How do you feel?"

"Well, my face and my nose are sore as hell and I can't see anything, so I'm a bit worried."

"Well, don't be. Shrapnel hit you, but the wound is actually relatively minor."

"Good. So where am I and how soon can I get these bandages off?"

"Relax, GI."

It was Forster's voice.

"Where are we, Mike?"

"Well, you and me and Halls . . . yep, and Timmer . . . are where Timmer has wanted to be ever since the breakout. We're in Paris. Actually, *near* Paris, place name of Garches. We're patients in the U.S. Army's 203rd General Hospital. I had a hell of a time keeping us all together. Cost me eight Lugers – plus a little help from Sgt. Bowyer."

"So, Mike, how is everybody?"

"Halls is worst off. He got hit by six mortar fragments, including one through the guts. So he might be going home, but they said he'll recover fine. They got some new medicine, a wonder drug called penna-something, that deals with infections from gut wounds, you know – peritonitis."

He explained he and Timmer both sustained assorted muscle-tearing wounds, none life-threating, but enough to keep them in official Army robes, pajamas and slippers for 10 days to two weeks.

"Okay, what about me? Did I lose my eyes?"

"Nope. Your chart here says, let's see, oh yeah . . . you suffered 'trauma-induced left maxillary exophthalmos.'"

"Oh, well, is that all? I thought it might be something serious. Now, damn you, Mike Forster, give me the straight poop! What the hell happened to me?"

"Okay, simmer down, Dud. You got hit in the face by a chunk of Kraut mortar and I about upchucked when I saw the wound. The left side of your face looked a piece of Mom's strawberry-rhubarb cobbler and your eye was lying right there in it just like the cherry on top. All it needed was some whipped cream."

"Goddamit, Sergeant!"

"Easy, Dud! Easy. "They popped your eye back in place and sewed up your mug. They say you'll have some heroic scars, but your optic nerve was undamaged so your sight should be okay. But they've had you bandaged to give both eyes a rest. In fact, the nurse said the bandages come off in two or three days."

"Whew!"

"'Whew' is right, Buddy. We came mighty close to redoing Custer's last stand. Got to hand it to those Kraut kids. Little bastards fought like tigers."

"Screw them. So did we. They outnumbered us. Had better weapons. But we kicked their asses. I remember Timmer with his grenade brigade."

Neither of us spoke for a minute.

Finally, I said. "I guess not much is left of us."

"Still four of us, Dud."

"Right. So we've had 200 per cent casualties and four survivors out of 12 men. I guess that's about par for an infantry outfit."

"Hey, don't forget Jacobs, Wilson and Manthei. They're probably all back stateside. I think we did a lot better than if they'd just dealt us out one-by-one to some repple-depple."

Chapter 80
March 4, 1945 – Back To The Manor

Reassurances from doctors, nurses, Forster and Timmer were all very nice. But I gave a great big whoosh of relief when the bandages came off and I could see clearly, even though they had the room darkened.

The docs ordered me to wear an eye patch for the next 10 days. They also said I couldn't return to duty for at least a month.

My first look at my face was reassuring -- two rows of stitches across my left cheek reaching to my ear. Another railroad track up the side of my nose. But so what? My mug was no prize to begin with.

I immediately applied for a transfer to the British naval hospital at Abbot Manor.

Personnel at the 203rd hemmed and hawed. It was, er, irregular. True, I had been in the care of that same hospital before, but . . . and, yes, somehow the very primitive Limey doctors had managed to keep me alive back then, but . . .

Bowyer, with all the behind-the-scenes finesse and leverage of a lifer NCO, somehow greased the skids for me. "Dud, you've just got to deal with their reality. They're under pressure to find room for all the fresh casualties. So I showed them the way."

"Well, I'm sorry to disappear on you guys."

Timmer, arm in an Army-issue sling, said "Dud, don't sweat it. The first shirt got us transferred too. We've just got to report daily to a satellite clinic."

"Yeah? Where's that?"

"Downtown Paris."

I asked a stupid question. "Where you guys gonna stay?"

Timmer grinned. "Where the company is soft and pretty and rent is some soap and three cartons of Chesterfields, Luckies or Pall Malls."

I just grinned back as I eased into the jeep taking me to the railway station. I actually wasn't sorry to leave the remaining Forkers. Their loved ones were an ocean and half a continent away. I was the luckiest bastard on the face of the earth because the manor was only 250 miles away as the crow flies.

Unfortunately, I couldn't travel by crow and the French railway passenger cars had seen better days. The one in which I rode was cold and drafty thanks to numerous holes which seemed to be .50 caliber or 20 MM strafing hits.

Beside me was an RAF flight lieutenant, Cecil Barrow, whose right arm and shoulder were in an elaborate horizontal cast jutting out like his own white wing.

He said the damage to the passenger car looked to him like 20 MM. But he explained he couldn't be certain because, being a Typhoon jockey, he'd never been on the receiving end of a strafing run.

Seated across from us was a heavily made-up rather meaty lady who was displaying unnecessary amounts of leg. In French-accented English, she told me that my eye patch made me look like a dashing pirate. Then she said it might be nice to have dinner together once we got to Le Havre, because some fine restaurants there now were back in business.

I had Katherine on my mind, so I was a little slow on the uptake. And it irked me that she excluded Lt. Barrow from the invitation. But in the next 30 minutes she slowly made it clear she wanted something more permanent than a dinner date with me. I assumed she meant something like the arrangements she probably had with Kraut officers during the occupation.

So I smiled, leaned forward and quietly asked, "*Wie viel?*"

She gave a coquettish lift to her shoulders and fluttered her mascara. "*Oh, wir sprechen das später.*" Then she blushed scarlet, snarled and stamped out of the car.

"What was that about, old boy?"

"Well, Leftenant, let's just say that she learned a bit of German during the occupation."

"Indeed?"

"Yes, sir. I asked her 'How much?' in German, and she automatically answered in German. She said, 'Oh, we'll talk about that later'."

He chuckled. "Pity. With Fritz gone now, the poor lass must fear she'll starve if she doesn't find a Yank to replace him."

"Why not one of you RAF fly boys."

"Oh, good Lord, our pay is terrible," Lt. Barrow said. "Unless we have independent wealth, we make very poor prospects for the Angels of the Night."

We yarned until he dropped off to sleep.

With my good eye, I enjoyed the sight of buds on the trees and early bursts of color from beds of what looked like the crocuses Mom used to plant. Meanwhile, I got the impression from a day-old *Stars and Stripes* that the allies were virtually romping into Germany.

The paper gave the most coverage to Patton's forces nearing Koblenz. But it also mentioned Ninth Army approaching Düsseldorf and Cologne, while the Canadian 1st and British 2nd Armies were pushing toward Wesel and Essen – all these cities lying along Germany's great military barrier, the Rhine River.

We got to LeHavre by dusk and by midnight Lt. Barrow and I were aboard an old military ferry leaving for Southhampton.

Chapter 81
March 5, 1945 – Domestic Life

Lady Alice's eyes widened next afternoon when she opened the door for me. "Oh, my God! Allan! You gave me such a start! And I see you have managed to be wounded again. You need to be more careful, sir."

"It's not a bad wound. Lady Alice. May I see Katherine?"

"Of course you may. Come in! Come in! But no, not just now. She's visiting the doctor."

"Is she okay?"

"Oh, she's doing wonderfully. And now with you here, she'll feel even better. I hope this wound keeps you out of the war for good."

"It's only good for a month, but I'll take all the time I can get here with Katherine and you and Sir Alfred."

"We'll start with tea," she said. She put on the kettle and we sipped tea and yarned until we heard the door open.

Katherine was wearing a black beret jeweled with rain drops when she came in. Her face lit like a flashbulb when she saw me. We hugged forever. "Oh, your poor face," she mumbled. I felt her tears first on my ear and then on my nose as we kissed.

"Don't worry, sweetheart. It's fine." Our embrace still didn't seem long enough.

Finally, Lady Alice interrupted. "Allan, for God's sake, do let the poor girl take off her coat and sit down. The doctors want her to stay off her feet."

I fell all over myself getting her to a chair and her feet on an ottoman. Before she could ask, I told her the patch was temporary. That my sight was unaffected.

When we went to bed that night, Katherine cried that it wasn't possible to make love because her pregnancy was so advanced.

"Now, darling, you are being just plain silly," I said as I cradled my head on her shoulder and rested my hand on her stomach. "We're making love right now."

# # #

We kept on making love the next day as Katherine brought out all the pictures and letters from Mom. Mom's letters were warm, welcoming Katherine to our family and gushing of her excitement, and Sis's, about becoming a grandmother and aunt.

The snapshots, taken in direct sunlight, were so overexposed you could see little more than dots for eyes and semicircles for smiles. But Mom also had commissioned a studio portrait. She looked good and I practically didn't recognize Sis, now suddenly looking like a grown woman.

Mom and Katherine were exchanging letters weekly. Katherine wanted a photo of the two us for Mom and Sis once my patch was off and the sutures removed. "Right now your face looks like a bit of a football."

"Now, dear, is that an American football or . . . ?"

"Yes, Allan, an American football with all its stitching. Goodness!"

I casually resurrected the subject of marriage. I didn't want to badger Katherine, but I suggested if the idea suited her, we had time for the banns to be published and to exchange vows before I went back.

She was quiet for a minute. "Allan, will you have the same duty?"

"Maybe. But I'm applying to be a fire direction center officer. Almost a headquarters job and somewhat further from the line. With me now having a Purple Heart with an oak leaf cluster . . ."

"What does that mean?" she asked.

"It means I've been wounded at least three times. Anyway, with the cluster I think they'll consider it favorably."

"So, Allan, do you think you'd be safer?"

"I guess my odds would be better than in running a mortar platoon. That's why I want the job and why I'd like to land my guys in an FDC, too."

She asked me to tell her about my friends, so I sketched Halls, Forster and Timmer for her. "What about the others? You mentioned 12 to begin with."

"Well, several were wounded and sent back to the states where they'll be discharged once they recover." Now I choked up a bit. "Let's just drop that subject, okay?"

When Sir Alfred returned, he told me he'd received a letter from Gen. Horrocks expressing both regrets and congratulations. It tickled him that I had related his comparison of Horrocks and Patton.

Katherine invited Sir Alfred and Lady Alice to discuss whether we should wed. At first I felt a stir of resentment, but then relaxed. After all, they were her only family.

Anyway, I don't know how – maybe Lady Alice waved a magic wand or just steered the conversation -- but suddenly we were making wedding plans. Katherine asked whether we couldn't somehow get permission to waive the banns. Since both of us were military, she said, maybe the hospital chaplain could perform the service immediately so that we'd be a legal family when the baby came.

Sir Alfred had a chat with the authorities. Early the next Saturday, the patch came off. And early that afternoon we exchanged vows and were wed in the manor's little chapel.

Three days later the sutures came out and we took pictures. Then, at dawn the 20th, Katherine went into labor. She was probably the only mommy in wartime England to give birth in a private hospital room. It had just been vacated by dried-out alcoholic admiral.

She named our daughter Elizabeth Anne after her mother and sister.

Having trained, you might say, with my sister when she was a baby, it amazed me how light a newborn feels. The baby looked vague -- tiny and pink, but I had the gumption to tell her mom and Lady Alice that she was a beauty.

Sir Alfred, Lady Alice and I went to Palm Sunday services together. The ceremony sobered me, and when we came back, merely holding my daughter brought tears to my eyes.

It suddenly hit me I no longer merely was in love with a great woman. Almost overnight I was a husband and father. My view of everything underwent a hell of a change. For the first time in my life I realized I had something critically important to lose.

Sir Alfred sobered me even more. I read on the 28th that the British and Canadian Armies and the Ninth U.S. Army at last had flooded across the Rhine. Nonetheless, he looked glum. I asked if things were going badly.

"Oh, no," he said. "Jerry's forces seem to be losing both cohesion and coordination. We're advancing swiftly in some places, and progressing rather well. Unfortunately, our losses are progressing rather well, too. Where they can, the Germans defend their ground tenaciously and counterattack ferociously. And, confidentially Allan, the British and Canadian armies no longer are able to make up their losses. The manpower pool is nearly exhausted.

"To be sure," he added, "new American formations arrive in theater daily," he said. "But in order to get them over here quickly, their training is greatly abbreviated. So they don't know what they're doing and they're dying like flies."

Roughly an hour later I received a call that my convalescent leave was ending a week early. So I packed, and kissed and cuddled the new Mrs. Dudley and held Little Liz briefly.

As I left, that old saw about "tearing yourself away" finally meant something.

I felt ripped from my life.

Chapter 82
March 30, 1945 – Crossing The Rhine

The battalion exec acted relieved when I reported in, but he seemed extremely nervous. Apparently my arrival only solved one of his problems, and he was talking non-stop.

"Glad you're here Dud. Damn glad. You're replacing Maj. Walsh at FDC. He's moving on to DivArty. You're going to have to be on your toes with maps and grid coordinates, Lieutenant. Otherwise you kill Americans instead of Krauts. Well, hell, you know all that. By the way, we finally got up-to-date maps. No more by guess and by God with those old World War I charts."

"That's great, sir," I said. "Now, did Maj. Walsh take The Broom with him?"

"No, we bumped Vanderboom to sergeant and kept him here. He's a good man."

We shook hands and I immediately went to look up the First Shirt. Over coffee I asked, "Sarge, what the hell is with the exec? He's nervous as a whore in church."

"You will be too, Dud." He said the CO and exec were terrified by the surge of rear echelon replacement officers coming into the 84th during its refit from the Roer River crossing.

"God help us, these guys are from Personnel, Signals, Supply, you name it, and day after tomorrow – Easter Sunday -- the 84th Infantry and Fifth Armored are going to convoy across the Rhine. We're headed about 15 miles further into Germany to join the rest of XVI Corps already in combat.

"The replacements are willing enough," Bowyer said. "At least most of them are. But we have to practically lead these people around by the nose. And it ain't their fault."

He explained that when, say, a captain or first lieutenant from Supply or Signals joins an infantry company, he usually becomes its commander.

"See, he ranks the second looie who has led that outfit since his own CO and XO got the hammer six weeks ago on the Siegfried line. So, the second looie knows his men and knows what he's doing. But the new CO don't know shit.

"Jesus Christ, a veteran Pfc. is better suited to lead! But that's the damned system. And a lot of the new guys feel bad about it."

I asked whether the replacement officers listen to their subordinates' advice.

Bowyer rubbed his bristly gray scalp. "You sure as hell hope so. The CO and the exec told them to draw on their subordinates' experience." He looked around to see that no new officers were listening. "But who's got time for meetings and discussions when you need action?

"And, lieutenant, you know as well as I do that for a new guy it's all fucking bewildering. He's got to know the ground; got to know platoon leaders and NCOs like they're his brothers. Got to keep HQ up to date and he's got to *be* up to date. On everything! Got to know whether you need artillery or air support or mortars or all three. He's got to coordinate with tank commanders. He's got to do liaison with the tank destroyers."

"Well, Sarge," I said, "they'll learn fast or die. Just like us. Say, are Timmer and Forster back?"

"Oh, yessir. And so is Halls. His wounds weren't near as bad as they thought. Right now Forster is running Heavy Weapons. His commander is a supply lieutenant who's got the brains to keep his trap shut and learn from his sergeant. Timmer's heading the mortar platoon."

"Great, I better go meet with them."

# # #

Thanks to The Broom, the FDC ran smoothly from the start. All I had to do was take a running jump to get on the wagon. And our battalion's first few days of combat went better than we had any right to hope. That's because it was becoming more and more an artillery battle. The infantry companies would make contact, probe with an armor platoon. If resistance was stiff, they'd call us for mortar and artillery.

And if the Krauts were stupid enough to counterattack, we'd feed them what we called our banana split – merciless mortaring while DivArty laid on aerial and ground bursts, shrapnel or Willie Pete, your choice, or – we aim to please and the customer's always right -- try a mix of both.

We could do it because those mountains of ammo stacked behind the Roer were coming forward to the guns about as slick as water through a firehose. The command "Fire for effect," used to worry us because we had to conserve on shells. Not any more.

Forster would call. "Hey, Dud, how about a little cherry on top of the banana split? Say another four rounds from all the guns"

"Nahh, not this time, Mike. The infantry is moving forward now with their brooms and shovels."

Chapter 83
April 4, 1945 – Crossing The Reich

And the Army was moving . . . flooding, actually . . . into Germany. Two days after crossing the Rhine, we overran Lembeck, a tiny place with a great castle on a lake and quite a collection of half-destroyed *Whermacht* barracks.

The FOs reported in, "We don't have to shell this burg. The Krauts pulled out as we came in. Not even a roadblock." Like Audyville in Normandy and Gourock in Scotland, it reeked with that same air raid stench of smoldering mattresses, burned clothes and rotting bodies.

Germany's equivalent to the Pennsylvania Turnpike, the Autobahn ran past the town but we couldn't use that section of it. A big viaduct over a local river was collapsed beside an enormous hole. For once it wasn't Kraut demolition. One of the British earthquake bombs had dropped the whole span, creating what looked like an open pit mine beside it.

As the engineers bridged the river, Timmer came back to us to get maps for Westphalia, the state we were starting to overrun. "You can't believe it, Dud," he said. "Every house has a white surrender sheet hanging from the windows. And not one soul in this town was a Nazi. Nosirree Bob! Nobody at all. They *hate* Hitler! Some of them even have written '*Hitler weg*' on the walls of their houses."

I snorted. "It's a little late to be telling the bastard to get out, eh?"

As we drove through Lembeck, we saw German civilians were fat – even flabby compared to British civilians. But they weren't the least bit sassy or happy. They just peeked from their windows until they learned we weren't going to slaughter them right and left. The kids became friendly when the troops threw candy to them. And, contrary to antifraternization rules from SHAEF, some of the troops tried to chat up the frauleins.

But when we liberated a nearby camp of French POWs we were shocked. The Frenchies were ill and -- compared to the local hausfraus and their bureaucrat husbands – they were rack-thin. The frogs told us they had spent four years as slave laborers.

It was much the same two days later at Bielefeld, a good-sized town that bombers had half leveled. We had to fight on the outskirts for a while, but facing our artillery and new tanks – the Pershing with a 90 mm gun that could take out even a King Tiger -- the main Kraut force backed out.

When we moved forward, however, we found that almost a platoon of *Landsers* had deserted and were patiently waiting to surrender. They were sitting on the ground next to a big pile of their Mausers, Schmeissers, MGs and potato-mashers. A few of the *soldats* looked about 13, but most of them were ordinary ground-pounders in their very ratty uniforms. It also hit me, not for the first time, how much they looked like ordinary guys . . . many of them like Americans, actually.

"I talked with some of them," Timmer told me. "They've had it. At lot of them are half-starved. You can see how far their belts are cinched in."

"Yeah," Forster said. "I gave one a box of C Ration and he and two other guys just wolfed it down. They can see the writing on the wall and they don't want to die now that it's about over."

"I don't either," Timmer said.

Forster nodded and went on. "Dud, one of the German corporals says he thinks their commander might be persuaded to surrender."

I talked with the corporal, a very depressed and tight-lipped guy. When he found out I spoke German, he clicked his heels and snapped to attention. He said he'd be willing to find his battalion CO and bring him to us to maybe talk surrender.

I called HQ about the idea, but soon heard back that the regimental CO could give a damn. Sgt. Bowyer told me the colonel said the Krauts were free to quit any time. "But we're not stopping for any bullshit. We're arrowing northeast up the Autobahn toward Hanover and then due east to Berlin."

We started pushing fighting patrols through the town. In the back of my mind, I wondered why the CO suddenly was being such a hard ass. Two days earlier he would have leaped at a surrender deal.

We soon found out why.

Word filtered down that in addition to freeing allied POWs, British and American units had started coming across places they were calling death camps. We didn't grasp what that meant until *Stars and Stripes* published unbelievable pictures of walking skeletons and stacks – *huge* stacks -- of naked stick-like bodies; people thrown away just like so much household trash tossed onto the town dump back home.

What the Krauts had done to the French POWs was bad enough, but systematic annihilation was beyond us.

The troops stopped tossing candy to kids and glared at the frauleins. Halls said he'd shoot the next German who called him "comrade." It was a long time before I could look at any German, military or civilian, without disgust.

# # #

Meanwhile, the campaign almost became a motor march.

We passed masses of unarmed Krauts sitting hunched in the fields or marching without helmets along the autobahn's shoulders. Groups of Kraut officers looked pretty arrogant with their high-peaked caps and haughty faces, but seeing endless American columns roaring along *their* autobahn stunned them.

I interviewed one captain at length. "Such power is overwhelming," he said. "Had we known . . . well, some of our officers are committing suicide."

We started crossing bridges that hadn't been blown. Our engineers – with tanks, MGs and mortars in overwatch -- would check the spans for explosives. Massive demolition charges often were in place, but there were no detonators or, if there were, nobody hung around to set them off.

So on we'd go, alert for the next roadblock. Some roadblocks often were little more than a few tree trunks and some construction trash.

Every now and then, though, a pocket of damned fools would cut loose with mortars or MGs and a *panzerfaust*. They'd take out a tank or half-track and kill five or six GIs. We'd retaliate furiously, using mortars, artillery and P-47s and turn that ambush into a smoking hole.

But we just didn't encounter any sustained defense until a beautiful spring day, April 9, when we got to the Weser River and we spotted the spires of Hanover . . . and the smoke from the air raids.

By this time, I was spending most of my time with the battalion S2 as an interrogator. He begged my help because my German was much better than his. The Broom, an expert FDC leader, could easily handle barrages of roadblocks.

Halls forwarded to us an eager prisoner who had the defense plans for Hanover. He described an elaborate set of bunkers and pillboxes northwest of the town. So, with our find, the regiment arranged for the engineers to bridge the Weser River southwest of town..

Instead of attacking from the north, we swooped in, taking the place from the rear. The Krauts had some tanks in the town, but our Pershings and upgunned Shermans handled them, and opened the town for the infantry.

Chapter 84
April 13, 1945 – Brought To Battle

This was the day we learned President Roosevelt had died. Even Timmer was subdued about it.

"I hated the bastard," he said. "But the SOB was the president. I wonder what the new guy will be like." At the time, none of us had even heard Harry Truman's name.

The only trouble we encountered – correction, that *I* encountered -- was a major from division who came in to take over the fire direction center.

I was just returning from the S2's desk when I heard the familiar rasp in his voice as he tried to lord it over Bowyer.

"Yes, I know you're the First Shirt, but I'm a major and I've done a fair amount of time with mortars and artillery. So just back off and introduce me to my men."

Unbelieving, I came in through the tent flap.

There he was, big as life, staring wide-eyed at me.

It was The Dick.

I recovered first and grinned. "I cannot believe you'd actually come this close to a combat zone again."

"What do you mean? What are *you* doing here?"

I reached down and raised the flap on my holster, pulled out the .45 and checked to see that a round was chambered. "Major, I run the fire direction center and I help out at S2. And what I'm doing now is arming myself with a loaded, cocked .45 whenever you're around. I'm not taking another chance on being murdered by you."

Maj. Dick sputtered. Both Sgt. Bowyer and Sgt. Broom stared open-mouthed at me.

I turned to them. "I'm serious, gentlemen," I said. "This officer deliberately shot me in the chest with a carbine. Tried to kill me. That was – let's see, Major -- was it five or six days after we landed at Utah Beach?"

"You're crazy," he said. "It was an accident!"

"No it wasn't. It was attempted murder and I have a copy of the court martial proceedings that convicted you. I'll show them to the First Shirt, the exec, the CO and go right up the line to Ike himself if need be. But I'm not going to be at a duty station with you. You're incompetent, a coward and an idiot.

"And by the way," I added. "this time you can't count on having one of the president's buddies going to bat for you. FDR, God bless him, is no longer the commander in chief."

Maj. Dick's hooded eyes widened as the implications struck him.

I turned to The Broom. "Anything coming in?"

He shook himself of kind of a daze. "Well, a Baker Company FO wanted to alert us to a possible target."

Meanwhile I heard Sgt. Bowyer say, "Major, I think you and I had better go see the exec."

"I think I'll come with you," I said.

It was a 50-yard walk, and Maj. Dick was blustering all the way about my insubordination and the pathetic state of the army.

At first the CO and the exec were furious. With me. They thought it was just a clear-cut case of sheer insubordination and were ready to turn me over to the MPs.

But that's when some Kraut idiot – bless him and damn him alike – decided to undertake a final futile gesture.

He fired a full barrage from his battery of Screaming Meemies in our direction. The howl of Nebelwerfers rockets was scary any time, but having 20 or 30 of those 350 mm monsters saturate the neighborhood was staggering – it sounded like one monster explosion that was 30 seconds long.

The HQ tents were shredded. So was my left leg. At that point it didn't hurt. Just a giant tingling. "Oh, Jesus," I said, looking down at the wounds which had the look of a platter of spaghetti with meat sauce..

Bowyer and the colonel got to their feet and were shaking their heads and yawning to recover their hearing. Seeing me, Bowyer yanked out my field dressing and began applying it to my leg. Then he had to get several more dressings. Suddenly the pain began. I didn't want to scream but my clamped mouth was mewing. Honest to God, I couldn't help it.

The exec appeared to be dead, but the colonel seemed focused on Maj. Dick who was lying, fists clenched against his mouth, screaming, "I can't take this! I can't! I can't!"

My interest rapidly faded because Sgt. Bowyer had administered a morphine syrette to me.

Chapter 85
May 13, 1945 – The Road Back

It was a quiet *thum-thum-thum*
But I noticed the noise always made the sweat bead up on Cox's face.
Cox was in the bed across the aisle from mine.
It was Cox that named it the Agony Cart.

Armed Forces radio told us today that the 84th Division had reached the Elbe River and was mopping up along its west banks. Nothing about Berlin. That was the first bit of news I'd heard about the 84th and I really wasn't terribly interested.

My main concern here at the 203rd General Hospital was whether the surgeons would amputate my left leg.

Every day it was the same damned drill. The surgeon and two nurses would go from bed to bed in this particular junior officers' ward.

One of the nurses pushed the Agony Cart, a steel table on hard rubber casters that produced the *thum-thum-thum* as it rolled along the linoleum strip down the center of the room between the lines of beds.

The cart was lined with layers of snowy towels, but on the towels lay the surgeon's torture instruments, probes, scalpels, scissors, things that looked like dental picks, great big tweezers and other sharp steel things with which he would peel back bandages and examine and probe our wounds.

The cart's lower shelf contained a small steel tub for the used torture instruments and another for old bandages.

As they moved from bed to bed, the younger nurse pulled the curtains – a distinctive *shhhsssssss* -- to screen the beds from each other. Then you'd hear the doc ask, "How are you, today?"

The answer always was something like, "Pretty good, Doc," or "Comin' along, Cap'n." I always wanted to answer, "I'm scared about how much you'll hurt me." But I always braced myself and said, "Not bad, sir."

Cox, whose lower legs were sliced with mortar shrapnel, usually just hissed, "Fine, sir.".

Each time they moved the cart, its hard rubber casters rumbled from the linoleum strip going with something of a bump when they turned it onto the pine flooring between the beds.

shhhhsssssss

Each time the cart went from one surface to the other, the torture instruments jiggled with a cheerful tinkling, like small bells – very scary tiny bells.

It was nice of the doc to ask how we felt, but how could he really care? His rounds involved maybe 50 patients . . . more or less . . . depending upon how many died since yesterday.

shhhhsssssss

He'd look through the chart and murmur with the patient for a minute. Then *shhhsssssss* again – twice – as one screen was pulled back and another one pulled into position

Like everybody else, I braced myself as the older nurse rolled the tinkling cart to the left side of my bed and the younger nurse pulled the screen between my bed and Kirby's bed to my right.

I don't know why she bothered.

Kirby was in a coma.

The nurse pulled back the sheet from my leg and, trying to be gentle, the doc peeled open the dressing. "Mmmm."

"Aren't you going to ask how I'm doing, Doc?"

He glanced at me and gave a polite grimace that, I guess, was supposed to be a smile.

"No. I think I can tell."

He stopped talking as he snipped at something. "I'm taking out some sutures this time," he said. "Doesn't hurt much. "But it looks to me like you'll get to keep that leg. The infection seems cleared up.

"Maybe you can start therapy sometime next week."

"Great news. Thanks Doc. I mean it. Thanks a hell of a lot."

The younger nurse smiled.

shhhsssssss

Chapter 86
May 14, 1945 – A Fork In The Road

I was looking at *Life* magazine's photos of occupied Europe when I got a gentle jab in my shoulder. It was First Sgt. Frank Bowyer in full dress uniform with about 20 rows of ribbons and his right arm in a sling.

"What the hell, Sarge? What happened? And how did you find me?"

"This outfit has a great locater system, Lieutenant. And I'm here because I got a little bit of shrapnel from those Screaming Meemies that hit us. I didn't pay attention to it because we had so many other people hurt. But the damned thing got infected so here I am."

"Is it healing?"

"Yeah, dammit. I dump the sling this afternoon and I'll have to start saluting again just as I get over feeling guilty about not being able to salute.. I head back to Division tomorrow."

He brought me up to date, telling me that when the 84th captured Hanover, it found two concentration camps packed with dying slave laborers.

And that led to Forster, Timmer and Halls being pulled away from combat to work with Division G2 as German linguists.

"Regiment snatched your sergeants from Battalion to hunt for the camps' officers. They caught three of those bastards before I had to leave for the hospital. And I want to talk to you about that."

Just then a tall figure loomed over his shoulder. Sir Alfred in full uniform.

Bowyer came to attention and said, "Damn, sir. Sorry. I can't salute."

"Nonsense Sergeant. I apologize for interrupting. I just wanted a word with my son-in-law. Do go on."

I broke in. "First off, Sarge, will the CO arrest me for insulting an officer?"

Bowyer laughed aloud. "Hell no! He just arranged a transfer for Maj. Shiltz to the CBI."

"To what?"

"Seems our commander has a buddy who's whose other buddy's cousin needs an American liaison officer to work with the British 14th Army."

"So?"

"Dud," he said, grinning hugely, "the 14th Army is in Burma!"

I laughed aloud. "Hoo, that's wonderful. I'd slap my knee if I could. Wonderful! The Dick should enjoy the jungle. I hope the British don't defeat the Japs too fast."

Bowyer turned serious. "Look, Lieutenant, I'm no medico, but I think your days with infantry and mortars are over. That leg don't look so great and I'd say you've used up all your luck."

Sir Alfred chimed in, "Precisely what I wanted to tell him. But please continue."

"Look, after the Krauts and the Japs have surrendered," Boyer said, "the Army will demobilize so fast it'll make your head spin. They'll RIF you."

"What?"

"'RIF' -- Reduction in Force. They'll cut you back to sergeant again. They might give you a reserve commission, but my money says you've got a good chance of getting a medical discharge."

"Damn it! I wanted an Army career."

"That's why I wanted to talk to you, sir. The Army will need a lot of German linguists for some time to come. I've already put in paperwork for Timmer, Forster and Halls to transfer to CIC -- the Counterintelligence Corps. I can do that for you, too. I don't think a bum leg would keep you out of Intelligence, especially a German linguist."

"An excellent thought, Sergeant," Sir Alfred said. "Allan, I think you should consider it."

"You'd probably keep your rank a bit longer," Bowyer said. "You're on convalescent leave so when they discharge you from the hospital, you can spend some time with your wife and little girl. But if you're in CIC, you'd be coming back to Germany to hunt Nazi criminals . . . like that major who murdered your wounded.

"Think about it, Dud," he said. "I'll come back tomorrow before I leave."

# # #

"Interesting chap," Sir Alfred said. "I have selfish reasons for hoping you take his advice."

"Selfish reasons?"

"Yes indeed. First, the longer you have duty in Europe, the longer Katherine and little Elizabeth stay with us. We know you'll spirit them away to the States one day, but we'd love to delay that day.

"Second, I told you I was in Planning with SHAEF. But actually – this is confidential, of course -- I'm with MI5, a bit like your Army's CIC. Been a part of it since things started looking sticky in '37.

"I wouldn't mention this to your people. They'd take a dim view of your having a relative with a foreign intelligence agency . . . even if he's an ally.

"Mmmmm. I see what you mean," I said.

"We'd both be in the family business together, so to speak," he added. "Of course," he twinkled, "we couldn't discuss it. Otherwise we'd have to shoot each other."

Epilogue

In early 1946, we all tried to hold back the tears as we shook hands and said goodbye. Because they had been in constant combat, Halls, Timmer and Forster had more than enough demobilization points to go home, be discharged and return to civilian life.

The Army allowed me to stay on as a counterintelligence special agent. But as it shrank, the Army also decided it had a surplus of company grade officers. So, just as Bowyer predicted, they reduced me to staff sergeant, but retained my commission in the reserves.

Funny, though.

The Army's hefty surplus of generals didn't seem to diminish one bit.

I had no time to bitch about it because we were so busy hunting war criminals. At first the task seemed impossible – like seeking a few thousand special needles in boxcars packed with ordinary needles.

I was lucky in being assigned to our field office in Oberammergau -- a beautiful little town that the war hadn't touched. It lay in the mountains south of Munich. I even got to see Katherine and Elizabeth regularly, because in those days it was easy to hitch Air Corps flights to and from England.

At first, our team worked out of a beautiful old *gasthaus* built the same year Tom Jefferson and the boys adopted the Declaration of Independence. Later, the brass moved us out, giving generals a place to flout their own regulations against fraternizing with beautiful frauleins.

Our initial problem in finding war criminals – such as the major who butchered our wounded -- was that no German in Bavaria would even admit ever being a Nazi even though Bavaria was where Hitler founded the Nazi party.

As for war crimes, they knew *nichts*.

So progress was slow because it basically meant sifting tons of Third Reich records. But then our luck began to turn.

See, as our troops streamed home, repatriated Germans flowed back to Germany from POW camps in the United States.

You could spot the returnees immediately. Unlike the haggard, half-starved *landsers* who fought to the last, the POW Germans were bronzed and beefy thanks to outdoors work and a solid American diet. Most of them felt somewhat well-disposed towards the United States. In fact, a hell of a lot of them wanted to immigrate back to the States and were willing to help us find Nazis if it would boost their chances.

The Krauts didn't like us running their lives, of course, but they knew they were damned lucky to be in the US occupation zone as opposed to the Russian sector. As for German POWs in Russia – they weren't coming home at all. They were starving and dying in Siberia as enemies of the State condemned to the hardest hard labor Joe Stalin could find.

Then a real break came one summer afternoon when I was limping to our quarters and almost bumped into a tan, fit German still in Wehrmacht uniform. He obviously was just off the boat from the States.

He snapped to attention, saluted and said, "Howdy, pardner."

My first impulse was to yank the .45 from my holster and shoot him. Death camp memories remained vivid and I still hated all Germans. He paled a bit when he saw the look in my eyes.

But then I recognized him and remembered how he saved our lives. I also remembered Col. Snaggletooth's pep talk at yesterday's briefing. "We need sources, dammit. Find the good Krauts. Cultivate the bastards. You don't have to like 'em, but we need to use 'em."

So I saluted back and thanked him for not butchering us. I asked for a private meeting where the colonel and I sought his assistance in locating that major.

He did help, and then some. It turned out that this particular *Leutnant* – a civilian teacher of English and American literature – was rather bitter about the Nazis and the ruin they had brought upon Germany. He not only helped us nail the major, but he also persuaded hundreds of other Germans to come forth and work with us.

Our meeting also sparked a friendship that lasted until five years ago when a heart attack took him to Valhalla.

We never caught all the war criminals, of course. In fact, one of our grandsons said he read recently that Angela Merkel's administration launched a final set of investigations to ferret out the last of those geriatric butchers.

Sometimes, I get the feeling that even though we celebrated VE Day and VJ Day, the war never actually ended. It just kept going in different parts of the world: the Balkans, then Greece, then Palestine then Korea, Indo-China, and Vietnam and then back to the Mid-East, downtown New York City, and so on until who knows what.

I'm far past fighting age now, but I keep my .45 handy in case some nasty little terrorist bastard decides to shoot up the neighborhood.

Katherine says I'm nuts, but she's still willing to hold hands with me as we rock on the porch and wait for the sun to set.

If You Enjoyed This Book . . .

Please be so kind as to give it a brief, honest review at its site in Amazon Books.

About The Author

J. Scott Payne began his career as a cub reporter with the Kansas City Star. He served with the Army in Korea, Vietnam and – worst of all – Washington, D.C. Subsequently, he worked as a reporter and editor for an assortment of Midwestern newspapers and magazines. He and Jane retired to a small college town in west Michigan where they enjoy the woods, the birds and the battles -- or perhaps the games, they can't tell – between Burt, their black cat, and Bailey, their white terrier.

Also From Argon Press –

Mateguas Island
A Novel of Terror and Suspense, by Linda Watkins

Return To Mateguas Island
A Tale of Supernatural Suspense, by Linda Watkins

Ghosts of Mateguas Island
A Mateguas Island Novel, by Linda Watkins

The Universe Builders
Bernie and The Putty, by Steve LeBel

The Universe Builders
Bernie and The Lost Girl, by Steve LeBel

The Short of It
Poetry and Short Stories by H. William Ruback

Bargain Paradise
A novella, by Darlene Blasing

Made in the USA
San Bernardino, CA
08 December 2016